PRAISE FOR BOO WALKER

An Unfinished Story

"Walker's attention-grabbing and surprising plot highlights the engaging characters in this tale of second chances. For fans of women's fiction such as Nicholas Sparks's and Kristin Hannah's work."

—*Library Journal*

"*An Unfinished Story* is an immersive tale about a quest to find something real and true after life turns upside down. Boo Walker has written a book with a tender heart, cast against the soft background of coastal Florida, a setting rendered with a hand for delicate detail. A great story of redemption that carted me away."

—Barbara O'Neal, bestselling author of
When We Believed in Mermaids

"*An Unfinished Story* is the perfect mix of character-driven, heartstring-pulling drama and sharp-witted humor. I was thoroughly entertained and found myself in awe of Walker's talent as a writer. I'm not even sure where to begin . . . His story line was poignant and meaningful. His prose was masterful and full of gorgeous imagery that made the setting come alive for me. His pacing was spot-on. The dialogue was brilliant—deep and soulful at times, witty and amusing at others. On top of all that, he has created a complex and marvelously memorable character in Whitaker Grant, who charmed and amused me at every turn. I could go on and on. At the end of the day, this was a wonderfully enjoyable book. Clearly, Boo Walker is an author whose time has come."

—Julianne MacLean, *USA Today* bestselling author

"I love books with breathing characters you can root for, a narrative of human life to which you can relate, a conclusion that can stop the heart, and an author who can bind them all together with passion and soul. Boo Walker proves he's that kind of writer with *An Unfinished Story*."

—Leila Meacham, bestselling author of *Roses* and *Titans*

"Grieving widow Claire Kite and frustrated writer Whitaker Grant cross paths in Boo Walker's moving novel, *An Unfinished Story*. Accurately conveying the complexity of human emotions, this story of love and healing kept me turning pages and tugged at my heart. Not to be missed."

—Karen McQuestion, bestselling author of *Hello Love*

"If Nicholas Sparks and Maeve Binchy had a baby, he might sound a lot like Boo Walker. *An Unfinished Story* strikes a perfect balance between humor, warmheartedness, and the daily pathos of being human."

—Jodi Daynard, bestselling author of *The Midwife's Revolt*

THE
SINGING
TREES

OTHER BOOKS BY THE AUTHOR

THE SINGING TREES

a novel

BOO WALKER

LAKE UNION
PUBLISHING

Published by Lake Union Publishing, Seattle

www.apub.com

Amazon, the Amazon logo, and Lake Union Publishing are trademarks of Amazon.com, Inc., or its affiliates.

ISBN-13: 9781542019125
ISBN-10: 1542019125

Cover design by Caroline Teagle Johnson

Printed in the United States of America

For Patty

Prologue

December 2019
Cape Elizabeth, Maine

At the top of the steps, with a gloved hand on the icy railing, sixty-seven-year-old Annalisa Mancuso gasped in awe at the hundreds of wind chimes that dangled from the many snow-dusted branches in what had become a forest of singing trees.

The set that she'd made almost fifty years earlier—the center-piece of her friend's collection—hung halfway up a red oak directly ahead. Vintage keys and silver cylinders circled a gold pendulum bob that had once driven the movements of an antique grandfather clock. Considering they had been here since the eighties, the parts had taken the weather well, as if each were frozen in time.

Annalisa had found each forgotten component in the clock shop where she'd started to make a life for herself, before the angry storm had parked itself overhead, revealing a world tarnished by hidden agendas, lies, and war. That ambitious eighteen-year-old girl had no idea what was to come, the dark of night always following the bright of day.

A swath of memories rose up—flashes of the countless hours she'd spent under her mother's tutelage on their side porch in Bangor, working their paintbrushes to the hypnotizing melodies of the wind chimes they'd made together when Annalisa was a toddler, a set crafted with antique spoons and silver bells. There, on the porch in front of their easels, was one of the few places they could escape her father's dark moods, and it was also where she first discovered the healing power of these wind-driven instruments.

The disturbance in the calm started as a rustle deep in the forest, a white whisper that rose in volume as it grew near. The wet dead leaves on the ground stirred and spun up into the air. Then a bitter winter wind came rushing through, sending the chimes into a mad dance.

A shiver came over Annalisa as she closed her eyes and listened to the symphony of sound that filled the air, and the past wrapped around her, both like a shawl and a snake.

When the wind calmed, Annalisa let go of the dangerous thoughts, the ones that had plagued her for so many years, and looked back at the chimes with another shiver. Growing up a Mainer, there was a time when she could have stood out here in this frigid cold all morning, but the years had shed the warming blanket of youth, so she knew she better get started. Hopefully, considering her objective, she could still scale a ladder.

Descending the steps and crossing the snow-patched yard, she entered the garden shed and found an extension ladder leaning against the wall, next to the leaf blower. "This seemed like such a good idea earlier," Annalisa said to herself, remembering her promise to her friend, who was knocking on death's door a few miles away. Reaching the point of calling Emma a friend had taken a lot of catharsis, but the designation rested comfortably now both on her tongue and in her heart.

And it had all started with these chimes.

"Are you sure you feel comfortable climbing?" Emma had asked, knowing her request came with a certain element of danger.

"Are you kidding me?" Annalisa had responded with a smirk. "You're looking at four years of overpriced barre classes. I could climb the steeple of the Cathedral of the Immaculate Conception."

Emma had let out a smile. "Always with the jokes."

Making her way toward the red oak, Annalisa wondered what barre classes had to do with plucking wind chimes out of tall trees. She extended the ladder and locked it into place, then leaned it up against the branch. After testing its security, she carefully made her way up, feeling the burden of her nearly seventy years on earth in her knees. Her legs shook as the distance between her and the ground grew. She forced herself to take a breath as she finally reached the hook of the wind chimes and attempted to pry it from the branch.

Though she should have been focused on her balance or her mission, in actuality, she was thinking that if someone was secretly filming this absurdity, she'd be the laughingstock of YouTube, might even break the internet. God, life used to be so much simpler before smartphones.

The chill of the ladder crept into her gloved hands as she took one more needed step up and pulled hard at the hook until it came free. The keys and clock parts pinged against the pendulum bob as she carefully lowered herself and her memories back down the ladder.

Thankful to still be intact after her daring stunt, Annalisa carried her prize through Emma's beautiful and well-kept house to the sunroom and gently set it in the box of tissue paper she'd prepared. After making sure the tabby cats had water, she carried the box out to her Subaru and climbed inside.

She drove along the wild and rocky, utterly miraculous shore of Cape Elizabeth, then worked her way through the quaint neighborhoods of South Portland and over the bascule bridge to Casco Hospice in Portland, where she'd spent the early morning. To save her back, she pushed a wheelchair with the rather heavy box of chimes in its seat through the lobby and down the hall.

"Mission accomplished," Annalisa said as she wheeled the chimes into the room.

Emma, wan and obviously hurting, cracked a smile with her chapped lips and muttered a thanks. She wheezed as she drew oxygen from the cannula resting against her nose. "Did you have much trouble?" Each word seemed painful to discharge. She had aged tremendously in the last year, and the skin of her face hung loose and pale. Annalisa thought it overwhelmingly sad and strange to watch a woman four years younger than she deteriorate in such rapid fashion.

Glancing through the two neighboring windows into the December morning, Annalisa wished there were a way to open them—despite the cold. A little fresh air might do wonders for this place. "I don't know if the chimes will make much noise once they're up, but at least they'll put some good energy into the air." Both women knew well the power of the chimes resting inside the box.

Annalisa looked at the desk with the white phone and box of Kleenex on it, and to the cheap print of a bunch of lemons with their bright-green leaves, framed above the bed. The tropical image was wrong in so many ways, so un-Maine. It was a lifeless room that no amount of color could resuscitate. Not the white walls or the light-blue bedspread or the many flowers springing from vases, sent from the veterans Emma had helped over the years as a counselor.

After disappearing to the West Coast, Emma had spent two years in Marrakech as a Peace Corps volunteer. Upon her return, she'd become a certified counselor. For more than thirty years, up until she'd become sick, she'd worked with veterans (mostly Vietnam vets) to help them escape their nightmares. Knowing she couldn't help her brother, she'd chosen to help other warriors like him. If the amount of flowers sent to this room by her former clients was any indication, Emma had saved many lives.

Still, this room, this hospice, was nothing more than a holding room for the end, and it could provide only a trace of comfort as the cancer ate away at Emma's body.

"Don't you want to get out of here?" Annalisa asked. "Don't you want to go out on a lounge chair somewhere tropical, sipping piña coladas while a suntanned, bronze-skinned lover rubs lotion all over you? You say the word, and I'll grab the wheelchair. We'll be on the next flight to Aruba."

"If only I had the energy," Emma said, speaking as if she were tasting the idea in her mind like a touch of sugar on a strawberry margarita glass.

Twisting around and looking to the tile ceiling, Annalisa said, "Where shall we hang these?" She glanced at the swivel chair tucked under the desk. Considering her climb earlier, she thought this daring feat might just kill her. Maybe she should enlist some help.

"Annalisa?" Nothing more than a whisper.

"Yeah?"

Emma put her hand on her own heart. "Thank you. You truly are a saint."

"Oh, *stop* it." Imitating her late grandmother's stilted Neapolitan cadence, Annalisa said with wild hand gestures swatting the air, "Annalisa a *saint*? *Tu sei pazza!* Are we talking about the same girl who gave me the calluses on my arthritic fingers as I worked my way through the rosary praying for her soul?" Just as her grandmother had done, Annalisa blew out a blast of air as if she were extinguishing Mount Vesuvius.

The woman chuckled weakly, a flash of teeth and a slow and mild shake of her shoulders.

Annalisa sat on the edge of the bed and gathered her long white hair into a ponytail, thinking of her *nonna*, who'd taken her in when she was fifteen. "God, I miss her."

"I can only imagine," Emma said, licking her lips. She seemed to be waking up now, her speech flowing easier. "Joking aside, she'd be proud of you for so many reasons. I know you hate talking about the past, but after what I did to you . . . and what you did for me . . ."

Annalisa brushed a hand through the air. "The past is the past. The way my memory has faded, I can barely remember the Our Father, so you're off the hook for anything that happened years ago."

Annalisa was lying: she could remember everything.

Every single day.

"If it were only that easy," Emma whispered.

Annalisa was sure that Emma's inability to separate from the past was why she'd turned down any sort of treatment, including chemotherapy. She was ready to say goodbye. After days of trying, Annalisa was through arguing with her on the topic and had come to accept the fateful decision.

Annalisa raised a finger. "Let me see if I can find someone to help." She pressed up from the bed, poked her head out of the room, and looked down the hallway. A nurse in teal scrubs, bearing an uncanny resemblance to James Dean—without the styled hair—walked toward her with a stack of bedsheets in his hand.

"Excuse me. Can I borrow you for a moment?"

"Sure." He sped up and followed her in.

"Would you mind hanging these chimes for us?" Annalisa pointed into the box.

The man shrugged. "That's a first in my ten years of rounds, but I don't see why not."

After discussing the best method, the nurse slid the squeaky swivel chair toward the end of the bed, and as the women urged him to be careful, he climbed up. With one arm steadying the chair, Annalisa handed him the chimes.

Nineteen seventy, she pondered. That was the year she'd made these chimes, and they'd sung to her for many years before she'd given them to Emma. It was funny how she thought in years now. That was something that she'd been doing since her fifties. Everything that had happened in her life had a time stamp to it. Nineteen sixty-nine: the year she met Thomas. Nineteen seventy: the year she escaped the small-town clutches of Payton Mills to move to the city. Nineteen seventy-three: the year she first went to Bar Harbor.

Nineteen seventy-seven: the year Annalisa almost saw Elvis perform. He, her favorite musician of all time, had died the day before the performance had been scheduled in Portland. Her unpunched ticket stub (section 122, row F, seat 6) hung in a frame in the studio of her house. Nineteen seventy-nine: the year she'd gifted Emma the chimes as a symbol of her forgiveness.

While the nurse was stretched tall, Annalisa couldn't help herself and took a moment to appreciate his very toned tush. She glanced at Emma, who happened to be enjoying the same view. They shared a knowing smile. Some things stick with you from your youth.

The man with the pleasing posterior slipped the hook over one of the metal brackets that supported the tiles and carefully climbed back down. "There you go."

Once he was gone, Annalisa went to Emma's side and gently took her arthritic hand. It felt like she'd just picked up a snowball without gloves. "I'm sorry I can't put *him* on a hook in here for you. Wouldn't that be a sight. I guess the chimes will have to do."

Emma snorted. "When are you going to start getting old like the rest of us?"

"Please. If you only knew what I looked like naked. I'm as ancient as Rome."

Annalisa patted her hand reassuringly, trying to make some sort of wordless case that everything would be okay, even if it wasn't true. They stared at each other for a long time, and Annalisa's heart burned in the silence.

Emma asked, "Would you help me write him one last letter?"

A tear escaped Annalisa as she nodded. She went to the desk and rummaged around until she found a notepad and pen in a drawer, then sat on the swivel chair and slid toward the head of the bed.

Emma wheezed again as she drew in oxygen. After a long pause—the seconds marked by the chirp of the machine—she finally spoke.

Dear Thomas,

What is there left to say? You know I'm sorry. You know I miss you. How many letters can a sister possibly write to her brother before he believes her? My heart breaks again and again. Did you ever truly find happiness, or did I steal it away forever? How I wish you could sit in this room—as awful as it is—and tell me the stories of your life.

You were such a wonderful brother, putting up with me during my teenage years. Can you believe the things I did? So desperate for attention. And you were the only one who ever gave it to me. You even gave up living in the dorms to stay home for me. What would I have done without you? I still laugh about the time you beat up Jim Harrison for calling me a skank.

How strange we never spoke of Vietnam. Or the fall of the Berlin Wall, the war in the Middle East. Can you believe we all have computers? Can you believe Tom Brady? That's right, I keep up a little. How about Portland's evolution? I thought the Maine Mall would ruin our city forever.

I hope you know that after hitting rock bottom, I've dedicated my life to making up for my sins and attempting to honor you. I suppose it's not much, but it's the most I can offer. I love you, Thomas.

Always your sister, I hope,

Emma

Part I

JULY 1969 TO JUNE 1970

Chapter 1

Not Like Other Girls

July 1969
Portland, Maine

Crammed into the back seat of her cousin's brown beater, the Who playing "Pinball Wizard" on the radio, a wide-eyed Annalisa peered through the window at the skyline of the city she'd loved since she was a little girl. When someone from small-town Maine said, "Let's go to the city," she wasn't referring to Boston or New York. She was speaking of Portland, a city that had been pulling at Annalisa long before she'd lost her parents and been forced to endure the rest of her high school years in Payton Mills, a town known for nothing but its football team and textile mill.

For Annalisa, Portland might as well be Paris, and Congress Street downtown resembled the Avenue des Champs-Élysées. The buzz of the city: the museums and art galleries, the clusters of protesters pumping their signs, the psychedelic shops oozing incense, the exciting restaurants bustling with conversation, the concert posters plastered on shop windows promising wild nights, the hippies with their long hair and colorful clothes brushing past the businessmen toting their briefcases, even the honking of the horns, called to her as if moving here were her destiny. Here in this bustling port city, she imagined she'd never run out of creative inspiration.

Her cousin Nino, her best friend and one of the only reasons keeping her from hating Payton Mills, slid to a stop by Monument Square and turned back to her. The son of Annalisa's paternal aunt, Nino was Annalisa's age, had a baby face, and his wavy, slicked-back chocolate hair featured a little curl above his forehead. He was six three, could out-dribble almost anyone on the basketball court, and had a smile that lit up a room. It was no wonder that one of the prettiest girls in town, a cheerleader named Sara, sat shotgun, smacking on a piece of gum. Yes, she was Italian. Dating someone other than an Italian was not acceptable in the Mancuso family.

"All right, *cugina*," he said, throwing an arm over the back of the seat, "we'll catch you later. Don't take no for an answer, all right?"

"When have I ever taken no for an answer?" Annalisa cracked open the door, and the sounds of the city—the car horns and police sirens, the hammering from a nearby construction site, the loud banter of the city dwellers, the arguing and laughter, the pure excitement—rushed over her. "Just don't get too blitzed to drive us home," she added.

"When would I ever?" Nino asked with a charming and devious grin. Annalisa wasn't sure exactly what he and his girlfriend planned for their day in the city, but she could only imagine it had to do with booze and fooling around.

They had to be back to Payton Mills by seven, or her grandmother, who was a million times stricter than her parents had been, would ground her for her entire senior year. Though she was no stranger to breaking the rules, this was the first time Annalisa had ever been allowed to go to Portland without the accompaniment of her aunt or another adult, and she didn't want it to be her last.

Annalisa stepped out of the car and immediately noticed Our Lady of Victories, the bronze statue of a woman holding a sword and shield, looking almost directly at her. *Yes, let today be my victory,* she thought.

Popping open the trunk, she grabbed her purse with her sketch pad and the orange portfolio tote that had once been her mother's.

After shutting the trunk and giving one last wave, Annalisa filled her lungs with the salty air blowing in from Casco Bay and crossed Congress Street, walking with determination toward the most well-known art gallery in town. Having been painting since she was two years old and selling her pieces since she was ten, she felt like she was finally ready to garner some attention here in the city.

The gallery was sandwiched between a boutique clothing store and a travel agency in a fancy brick building. Every Mainer knew about the great fire of 1886 and how Portland had been rebuilt with mostly brick and concrete.

Stalling, she wondered if she'd dressed too casually. She could have chosen one of the conservative and dull dresses that she wore to church, but that wasn't her at all. Inspired by a green dress she'd seen in *Vogue* a few months back, she'd created a Butterick-patterned peasant top with a yard of green cotton she'd found on sale at Grants. She wore it with a caramel sash, blue-jean bell-bottoms, and hand-me-down leather boots. She had her mother, aunts, and home ec class to thank for her skills with a sewing machine.

Just as she put her hand on the doorknob, she paused. Somehow she'd managed to brick wall any fear that had arisen in the car, but it was hitting her hard now, burning her insides. It was no exaggeration to say her entire life was on the line.

Since her grandmother didn't have a car, Annalisa rarely made it to the city and had been in this gallery only three times before, always taken aback by the curator's eye. Jackie Burton was a strong supporter of female artists. Annalisa knew she was good and could probably find another gallery owner to take her on, but she wanted to be on this woman's walls. A Jackie Burton stamp of approval was a ticket to the top of the artistic world in New England.

Before fear pushed her heart rate out of control, Annalisa pulled open the door and stepped inside, first noticing the polished sheen of the hardwood floors. Fighting a timidity that she rarely felt, she raised her head to the pieces adorning the bleach-white walls. She instantly recognized a very busy piece by Sharon Maxwell, a legend of the East Coast art scene.

Mrs. Burton herself was thumbing through a magazine on one of the modern fuchsia chairs that formed a circle in the center of the room. Her hair wasn't quite jet-black, maybe more blackberry, as if God had used just a touch of violet when He'd created her. She wore a tight-fitting black dress with black heels, but her bright pearl-and-turquoise necklace rose out of the black of her outfit in a tasteful joust between dark and bright.

Annalisa gripped the handle of her tote as the two women's gazes met. "Oh, hi."

Mrs. Burton set her magazine down on her lap. "Sharon's great, isn't she?" She'd clearly been watching Annalisa.

Annalisa turned back to Sharon's paintings. "As much as I don't love abstract expressionism, I can definitely feel the emotion in her work."

"Listen to you." Mrs. Burton popped up from her chair. "Impressive. Is there something in particular you're looking for?"

It didn't take knowing that Annalisa came from a poor mill town for the lady to know she was out of place. This gallery wasn't for teenagers, but she thought it was nice of Jackie to go along with the idea that Annalisa might be looking for something special to adorn one of the walls in her West End mansion.

Annalisa raised her tote, completely focused on making this woman love her. Not allowing any shake to be heard in her voice, she said, "I am a big fan of yours, Mrs. Burton. Of your eye and your gallery, and I wanted to see if you might be interested in taking a look at my work."

"Oh, you're a painter," she said enthusiastically, taking away some of Annalisa's fear. "Yes, I'd love to see what you're up to. Call me Jackie. What's your name?"

"I'm Annalisa." She felt a bright light of excitement. Could it be this easy?

"Why don't you come sit down with me, Annalisa? We'll take a look."

Annalisa thanked her and tried to temper her nerves with a deep breath as she took a seat next to Jackie in one of the stiff fuchsia chairs. All Jackie had to do was say she'd love to bring in her work, and the doors leading to Annalisa's future would open wide. She wouldn't have to worry about the fact that she couldn't afford college. She wouldn't have to worry about what she'd do to support herself for the rest of her life. All she'd have to do was capture the world with her brushes.

Like she'd done it a million times before (maybe she had), Jackie took the tote, unbuttoned the clasp, and reached inside. Annalisa had chosen ten of her favorite paintings from the past year of her work; some she'd done in art class, and a few at home.

The first piece was a scene of workers crossing the bridge over the Linden River to the textile mill in Payton Mills where her father had worked before he'd left for college in Bangor. Annalisa had waded through a tremendous amount of suffering in the days it had taken to finish this painting. When her father was her age, a brilliant young athlete with big dreams, he'd hurt his back in a forklift accident in the mill's warehouse, which had led to his drifting to the bottle to kill the pain, and then to ultimately driving himself and Annalisa's mother into a ravine—albeit unintentionally.

"Okay," Jackie said, holding the piece out in front of her. "I wasn't expecting this. You're quite good. What exceptional detail."

Annalisa muttered a barely audible "thanks." Was "quite good" enough to get a few paintings onto these walls?

Flipping to the next piece, Jackie scrutinized the scene of her parents' funeral. It was a bird's-eye view of their friends and enormous family standing around the bodies that would soon be lowered into the ground. It was the first time Annalisa had ever inserted herself into a painting, and she stood there with her hand on her mother's casket.

"You're a realist, aren't you?" Jackie asked, turning to Annalisa and ripping her from the memory. "Not afraid to paint the truth. These are quite . . . almost dreary. Is this you?"

Annalisa fidgeted with her hands before finally locking them down in a clasp on her lap. "I lost my parents two years ago."

Jackie put her hand on the armrest of Annalisa's chair and apologized.

"It's been a long time. I don't think about it much anymore," Annalisa lied, seeing her grandmother standing outside of her school in Bangor that day, waiting to break the news.

After a reverent pause, Jackie flipped to the next painting. "I can't get over your eye for detail. You've obviously been painting a long time."

"All my life," Annalisa said, hoping her experience made a difference.

Jackie glanced at her before continuing to the next piece. "You're like a budding da Vinci. Do you like his work?"

It was the kindest compliment anyone in the history of her life had given her, and she had a sudden urge to wrap her arms around Jackie's neck with thanks. "I'm Italian. Of course I love da Vinci."

The curator went back to studying Annalisa's pieces. Hopefully, she could see that Annalisa had put everything she had into them, the purging that she'd felt as she'd immortalized each subject with her acrylics. Jackie was right; many of them were on the sadder side, but how couldn't they be? Sunshine was rare in her world.

When Jackie finished, she carefully slipped each one back into the tote. "What to do with you?" she asked herself. As if the answer were on the ceiling, she looked up for a while. More than anything in the entire world, Annalisa wanted her to say, "I think you are an extraordinary artist, and I'd like to bring your work into my gallery. You belong here."

"I think you have a talent like I haven't seen in a long time," she said, finally lowering her head. "Art must be deep in your genes."

Was she finally about to get a break for once in her darn life? She could see herself strutting into this gallery a week from today, seeing some of her own pieces mounted in gorgeous frames on the walls next to New England's greatest. She could see herself collecting her first paycheck, knowing she'd finally made it after working her butt off for so many years.

Jackie bit her bottom lip. "You're not where you're supposed to be yet. I think you have what it takes to make it, but there's something missing, a consistency. I'm not seeing your voice . . . maybe that's what it is. Do you know what I mean?"

Unable to get a word from her constricted throat, Annalisa gathered her brown hair into a ponytail to busy herself. She could remember similar discussions with her mother, who urged her not only to try every medium but to experiment until something felt right. Well, the paintings in the tote in Jackie's hand right now did feel right to Annalisa. She was not new to art. She'd played with watercolor, oil, charcoal, and even pen and ink. Then, when she'd gotten her hands on acrylics, she'd known it was her medium. She'd started with still lifes like her mother had, then gone on to landscapes, ocean scenes, and animals. It was people she enjoyed most, though, and that was what she'd been doing for at least two years now, as if she was subconsciously trying to understand them.

So why wasn't Jackie seeing her transformation?

Jackie put her hand on the armrest again, making Annalisa feel slightly invaded. "The one with you at your parents' funeral; that one hits me hard and shows me you have what it takes. Believe me, your ability with detail is first-rate, and I don't mind the sort of realist, almost bleak outlook, but I don't see your voice breaking through. If you look at works on my wall for even a second, you know exactly who did them. How old are you, anyway?"

Annalisa forced herself to perk up. "Seventeen."

Jackie leaned in. "Seventeen? No wonder. You can't have a voice when you're seventeen. None of my artists did. You need to go to school, find some good teachers, and keep at it. Trust me, you're going to be great one day. You just need to find exactly what you're trying to say and then say it loud." She finally sat back in her own chair, giving Annalisa the space she needed.

"Where are you from?" Jackie asked. "What's your plan? Surely, you'll be attending the art school, right? You know Sharon Maxwell teaches there."

Annalisa straightened. "I wish. I'm from Payton Mills and live with my grandmother. We can't really afford college, but I'd like to move after I graduate." Truthfully, she wanted to grab her tote and run.

Jackie raised both hands, palms up, as if she were carrying a globe— the whole world balancing on her fingers. "You have to. What are you going to learn in Payton Mills? I mean, no offense to the place, but you need to be around other artists. You need teachers. You need inspiration that I'm not sure a small town can give you."

"I totally agree; believe me." Moving to the Mills, as many called it, had been a death sentence. Not that Bangor was this big metropolis, but she'd at least had some good friends and a wonderful high school art teacher.

The door swung open behind them, and they both turned to see a well-dressed older woman with fancy jewelry strolling in, carrying a large magenta purse.

Jackie called across the echo chamber of the gallery, "I'll be with you in just a minute. I'm wrapping up with this talented young lady." She scooted to the edge of the chair and faced Annalisa. "You just missed it, but Sharon Maxwell does a show every April in the Old Port.

Very cutting-edge stuff, some even risqué, but everybody who is any-body is there. Do you know of it?"

"Art news gets to Payton Mills about as fast as new releases make it to the drive-in."

"Trust me, you should check it out if you ever get the chance," Jackie said. "I think you'll find some of the answers you're looking for." She clasped the button on the orange tote and handed it back to Annalisa. "I want you to come back and see me. I'd be happy to help you along the way, finding a teacher or whatever it is. And please know that one day, if you keep working at it, I'd be honored to hang your paintings in here."

Annalisa offered her best closed-lip smile, knowing that she should take Jackie's words as a compliment, but the reality of the rejection was pulling her underwater, drowning her. "I really appreciate you taking the time to look through them."

"Oh, the pleasure is mine." Jackie set her hand on Annalisa's knee. "I cannot *wait* to see your development as an artist. What's your last name, by the way?"

Annalisa forced herself not to pull her leg back. "Mancuso."

"I'll remember your name, Annalisa Mancuso. Good luck to you." With a last goodbye, Jackie was off to help her customer.

Annalisa pressed up from the chair and left the gallery with her portfolio in her hand and purse on her shoulder. Couldn't she get a break? As if life were that easy. Even in the worst moments of her life, like when her father was drunk and attacking her mother, or when she'd moved in with her grandmother and had been hopeless, parentless, and afraid, painting had been the thing that had saved her. Not this time.

She rounded the corner and slipped down a quiet alley. Stopping near the back of a seafood restaurant that stank of used frying oil, she let her head fall and broke into a sob. Jackie was right. As confident as Annalisa could sometimes be with her talent, she still hadn't found her voice. What if she never found it? Or worse, what if she did and it wasn't anything extraordinary?

A man burst out of a door with a bag of trash in his hand. As he slung it up into the large dumpster, Annalisa scurried away. Just like her grandmother, she hated for people to see her cry.

Though there had been happy moments in Bangor, her father had never failed to stomp on them. She'd seen her father twirl his mother around the kitchen floor and not thirty minutes later scream at her with spit spraying out of his mouth. If he'd had enough to drink, he would hit her. Though he never hit Annalisa, he'd certainly lashed out at his daughter a thousand times with words that cut so deep she could still hear them when she closed her eyes at night. She was living in a town she hated, nearly broke and surrounded by her father's family, and all of it could have been fixed if Jackie had just said yes.

⁓

After taking a seat on a bench and spelunking through the dark caves of her mind for half an hour, repeatedly revisiting every single word Jackie had said, Annalisa found herself disgusted by her own thoughts.

What would Mary do? she wondered, thinking of Mary Cassatt, the American painter her mother had first introduced her to. Coming of age during the American Civil War, Mary left the closed-minded and male-dominated confines of Pennsylvania for France so that she could expand her mind, find independence, and home in on her creative voice. *Yes!* Annalisa had always thought when pondering Cassatt's story. *That's me!*

She stood and started along Congress Street to the Portland Museum of Art, which was a bit dated but displayed a few inspiring pieces that Annalisa visited on occasion. If she was to ever become great, it wouldn't be from that bench, nor wallowing in grief. She had to keep fighting. Art was in her DNA, as Jackie had suggested, and a life without a brush in her hand seemed like a life not worth living.

Deep within the museum, in the center of a quiet room adorned with masterpieces, she sat on a black leather-cushioned bench, sketching an ocean scene by Winslow Homer, who had traveled all over the world but in his later years had lived on the coast of Maine, where he'd explored the power of nature over man.

As part of her lessons on the side porch in Bangor, Annalisa's mother had urged her to emulate the work of the greats. It was a practice Annalisa did often back in the Mills with the art books she'd check out from the library, and she'd done it a few times here, when she'd been lucky enough to get a ride.

Though she was partial to female artists—anyone from the great Artemisia Gentileschi of the baroque period to the ultimate modernist, Georgia O'Keeffe—Annalisa had taken a fondness to Winslow Homer, in particular his intimate takes on solitude. Often feeling alone herself, she empathized with his subjects, the men who warred with the ocean in their wooden boats, like Santiago in *The Old Man and the Sea*.

As she shaded the waves with her charcoal pencil, someone sat beside her. Slightly agitated, considering there was another bench next to this one, she scooted toward the left edge without looking up.

She put her pencil back to work, noticing Homer's impressive use of value in summoning movement out of the waves. She thought she might try painting an old woman in a boat, paddling through an angry sea. Why did it have to be a man?

"It's interesting," the person next to her said, invading her space. "The juxtaposition of this composition conflicts with the atmosphere that he's trying to create."

What in God's name is he talking about? Annalisa wondered.

Apparently, he wasn't done. "But the precarious nature of his brushwork is too impressionist to allow for any real ethereal motives."

Cracking a slight grin, Annalisa twisted her head at the ridiculousness. "Let's hope you're not studying to be an art critic."

It was a guy about her age with shaggy blond hair and eyes the color of blue topaz, perhaps a shade lighter. His long-sleeved cotton shirt was unbuttoned enough to reveal blond chest hairs. A couple of wooden beads dangled from a leather necklace. He was coastal Maine preppie, with maybe a little edge, almost like the guy from *Barefoot in the Park*. What was his name? Robert Redford. If she'd been forced to admit it, the guy was a hunk.

"Maybe not impressionism but certainly pointillism," he said, crossing his arms and studying the Homer painting with intense interest. "He's left no impression on me. The abstract nature goes exactly against what watercolor is trying to be."

Annalisa set her pencil down and looked at his attempt to bury his smile. "Oil," she corrected him. "Not watercolor."

"Ahhhh," he said. "I'm a sculptor myself, so I'm not as familiar with these mediums."

She tried her best not to reward his absurdness with her own smile, but her lips apparently had a mind of their own, turning up just enough to urge him on. "A sculptor, huh?" Annalisa asked with a dipped chin. "Somehow I doubt that."

He gave a smirk. "Nothing gets past you, does it? I'm Thomas."

She wondered what color blue she might start with if she attempted to paint his eyes. "Good to meet you, Thomas. I'm going to get back to work now."

He peeked at her sketch pad before she could flip it over. "You're good. Are you a student in town? I'd love to see more of your work."

"I bet you would." She sounded much colder than she'd intended to as the nature of his intentions showed itself. "Thanks for the laugh. Now I gotta go."

As if he hadn't heard her, he asked, "What's your name?"

She closed her pad and ran the pencil through the spiral binding. "I appreciate what you're trying to do, but I'm not interested." Sometimes honesty saved agony. Dropping the pad into her purse, she collected her tote and stood. "Take care."

He held out a hand to stop her. "What if we were meant to have met right now?"

She would have rolled her eyes if he hadn't been so serious.

"I don't know about you," he continued, "but one day, hopefully sooner than later, I'm going to meet the love of my life. I want to remember that moment forever. What if that is us? Right here, right now. What if you're walking away from your best chance at love?"

Annalisa looked down at him, seeing through his confidence a gentle sincerity. For a second, she thought he might actually be a good guy. But that thought didn't last. She knew better than anyone how destructive men—and love—could be.

"I'll take my chances," she said, backing away.

The game seemed to end as his smile straightened into defeat. "Take care," he said with honest disappointment.

When she finally broke eye contact and turned away, she smacked right into the wall, shoulder first, knocking the tote out of her hand.

He rushed her way to help. "You okay?" he asked, as he leaned down to retrieve her tote.

Her face flushed hot as she snatched it from him. "Yeah, I'm fine."

"Please tell me your name," he said, as if he now deserved a treat for helping her. "At least I could think about you if we never see each other again."

Annalisa noticed his eyes had turned green. "My name's Alice," she lied.

"Alice," he said. "I'll be thinking about you, Alice."

"Take care, Thomas." She pivoted and raced out of the museum, refusing to allow herself to make the same mistakes her mother made.

Chapter 2

NONNA'S HOUSE

They reached the Linden River Bridge leading into Payton Mills just in time, a testament to how seriously even Nino took Nonna's rules. She was not the kind of grandmother you messed with. Nino and Sara had spent the day shopping and eating—and probably fooling around in one of the more wooded parks.

The tall smokestacks of the redbrick textile mill defined the unimpressive skyline of the Mills. Constructed in 1827, the mill had been set on the river to make use of the running water as the main energy source. Even her earliest memories of visiting her grandmother had provided barely a glimpse of a thriving town. One didn't have to listen long to find disgruntled mill workers talking about losing textile production to countries overseas.

In her neighborhood on the other side of town, trees hovered like giants over the tiny homes that had been housing mill employees like her father's family and other working-class Mainers for more than a century. Fishermen and lobstermen who couldn't afford to be closer to the coast formed part of the population too. To Annalisa, Payton Mills was a town whose inhabitants dreamed of taller buildings they'd seen only in the movies. Heck, half the people in her church had never even been to Portland, that long hour-and-a-half drive too daunting a journey. Portland was full of trouble, anyway, many of them thought, no one more so than her grandmother.

Annalisa said goodbye to Nino and Sara and stepped out into the night. It was barely seven and eerily quiet. With the exception of Friday nights during football season, when Payton Mills played their home games, the town rolled up the sidewalks with the falling sun.

She crossed their tiny dooryard, which Annalisa dutifully mowed each Saturday morning per Nonna's command. Up the three steps to the front porch was Annalisa's outdoor studio, complete with a chair, easel, and her trunk of paints. A set of wind chimes that she and her mother had made with antique spoons and silver bells hung from the center of the ceiling. It was a windless night, and the chimes were silent. Still, Annalisa could feel their power as she thought back to those countless hours on their side porch in Bangor, when the tinkling of the chimes had been the soundtrack to her time with her mother.

Finding strength from her renewed commitment to her dream, she dashed through the door, calling for her grandmother. Nonna was where she always was: the kitchen. Though the floors in most of their tiny home were in good shape, the linoleum in the kitchen was worn down and showed the scuff marks of Nonna's black orthopedic shoes. The salty and herbal smells of a simmering chicken soup on the stove reminded Annalisa that she hadn't eaten dinner yet.

"How'd it go?" Nonna asked, standing in front of the sink, where hot water steamed up behind her. Her entire English lexicon was drenched in her native tongue's bounce.

Annalisa stood right behind her, towering over her. "Jackie says I'm good—she loved the one of me at the funeral—but that I haven't found my voice yet."

Nonna shut off the water and turned, drying her hands on the apron wrapped around her little waist. "I see." Her short white curly hair sometimes looked to be a pale shade of lavender in the right light, and a mole above her right eyebrow called attention to her receding hairline. She wore thick-framed black glasses that were decades out of fashion.

"But you'd be proud of me," Annalisa said. "I'm not letting it get me down. She really was excited, says I'm very talented." She hoped Nonna was in a good enough mood to hear what was coming next.

"Of course you'll be a big deal," Nonna agreed, always one of her biggest fans. Long before Annalisa had lost her parents and moved to the Mills, Nonna had started the single largest collection of Annalisa art in the world. Now nearly every wall was covered. "How many times do I have to tell you that you're good before you'll believe me?"

Here goes nothing, Annalisa thought. "She said something else too."

Nonna's eyes narrowed. "What now?"

"She says I need to move to Portland. That's the only way I can get any better."

Nonna reached up and grabbed a handful of her own hair. "Jesus, Mary, and Joseph, this again."

"Yes, this again." Her grandmother should have gone to Hollywood with her drama skills. To give her credit, though, she had a long list of reasons she'd always discouraged the idea, but it came down to the fact Annalisa's father had picked up his drinking habit in Portland.

"Jackie's right," Annalisa pressed, hoping this time to convince Nonna. "How else am I going to get better?"

"It's not your location that makes you a better painter. It's hard work."

"And enriching experiences," Annalisa argued. "Great teachers. New scenery."

Nonna brushed her hand through the air. "There are plenty of teachers here. You just don't like any of them."

"Oh, you're right. Mr. O'Ryan is amazing." She rolled her eyes at the thought of her high school art teacher, tapping into her own dramatic potential.

"If you want a new teacher," Nonna said, "maybe we can find someone in Davenport. Nino can take you to lessons."

Davenport was no doubt beautiful—and certainly ritzier—but just like the Mills, it was a long way from the real world. "So I can paint rocky cliffs and lobsters and lighthouses in between my bridge group and spa session? No thank you. I want to be in Portland, where the action is. I need some grit, some reality. I'm tired of living in a bubble."

Nonna reached for a hand towel and began to dry the dishes on the side of the sink. "So you mean where the derelicts are? Is that it?"

Annalisa's whole body drooped. "Oh my God. Says every Mainer north of Portland. You all think the rest of the world is crazy." This is exactly what made her unglued about small-town Maine. It was always *us* versus *them*.

"It is," Nonna assured her, stacking one dry plate atop another. "The world is a dangerous place. Believe me. And Payton Mills isn't as bad as you make it out to be."

"I'm not going to end up like my father, Nonna. I'm not going down there to party. And as far as Payton Mills . . . to me it's hell on earth." As quickly as she'd said it, she regretted her words.

Smacking down the wooden spoon she'd just dried, Nonna said through gritted teeth, "Watch your mouth. This place is your roots. Never forget that."

"Trust me," Annalisa said, trying not to react, "I won't. And I'm sorry I said that. It's just that everyone is in everyone's business. I can't sneeze without the whole family discussing it. The whole town, even. And no one wants to admit there's a whole world out there with people that have different views . . . views that aren't all wrong."

Nonna's forehead wrinkled as she set down the towel and turned. "One day you'll realize that nothing is more important than family, and you'll regret hating the Mills like you do." Then she poked Annalisa's head. "Sometimes it's what's in here that's causing the problem."

Annalisa sighed; Nonna was the *only* one on earth who could get away with poking her in such a way. "It always comes back to family, doesn't it? Our family is great, but I need some space every once in a while. You might not understand it, but I have to go. I'm going to keep saving every dime I can, and I'm going to paint every darn minute, and when I graduate next year, I am moving to Portland."

"I don't know about that," Nonna said.

"It won't be your decision. I'll be eighteen." Annalisa softened. "But I can't bear leaving without your blessing. Maybe I'll come back, but I know I have to go."

Nonna crossed her arms and glared at her. More than once Annalisa had joked that Nixon should send Nonna to Vietnam if he really wanted to rid the world of communism. This was exactly why. It was a good thing Annalisa never brought boys home, because they couldn't have gotten through the door before scurrying away in fear.

With the glare frozen on her face, Nonna asked, "So you're going to move to Portland with your ice-cream savings?"

For more than a year now, Annalisa had been working at Harry's General Store, scooping ice cream and weighing candy. "And from selling everything I paint between now and then to anyone who will give me a couple of dollars. I'll shack up in a deserted warehouse in the Old Port if I have to."

"I forbid it!" Nonna snapped, coming alive like a soldier snapping to attention.

Annalisa stood her ground. "You can't. I'm not letting anyone hold me back. That's exactly what my father did to my mother."

Nonna struck the counter. "Hold you back? You're the one holding yourself back with all this . . ."

"With all this what?" Though the soup was at a simmer, she felt like the top of the pot if she'd turned the knob to boiling.

"With all this anger," Nonna finished. "You have to start moving on. It's been more than two years, Annalisa. I'm tired of putting up with your rebellion."

Even Annalisa would admit her disagreeable nature had a lot to do with losing both parents, but she'd been a wild child long before she was parentless. Maybe it was the Taurean in her—the stars having something to do with it. Whatever it was, probably an amalgam of her Italian blood, her April birthday, *and* her jaded and often furious father, who'd essentially murdered her loving mother, she was not making it easy on her grandmother.

Perhaps she and Nonna butted heads because they were so similar. Annalisa stood a foot taller, but there was no denying their resemblance. Whenever a guest of the house saw the black-and-white photograph of Nonna in Naples, Italy, as a young teenager, they'd never fail to compare her to Annalisa, mentioning the same big brown eyes (*Enough with the big eyes!* Annalisa always thought) and that thick, wavy hair. More to the point, the two women were as stubborn as anyone in Maine.

Annalisa backed away from the counter, as if in retreat. "I'm trying to move on. By getting out of here."

Nonna leaned back against the sink. "Moving on from your grief doesn't mean driving away. You don't need to move to Portland to find yourself. You just need to find peace."

"Peace?" Annalisa let out a cackle from the center of the kitchen. "What kind of peace is there anywhere in this world? You mean in Vietnam?" She felt so frustrated and sad, thinking that she'd actually found some excitement today, only to be knocked down once again. "Peace doesn't exist," she continued. "Happiness doesn't exist. Sometimes, I don't even know if God exists."

Nonna pounded the counter so hard the dirty dishes in the sink shook. "Don't you ever say that."

Annalisa snapped her hands to her waist. "It's true."

Mimicking her, Nonna said, "Then you need God more than ever."

"He's welcome to pop down for a visit," Annalisa said. "He knows where I live." She'd been going to church and praying to God all her life, but after losing her parents, God had a lot of making up to do as far as she was concerned.

Nonna took the wooden spoon she'd dried and stuck it into the pot of soup. "You're not the only one who lost someone."

"I'm the only one I know who lost both parents."

"He was my son," Nonna said, stirring the soup. "I lost him too. And then I lost my husband of forty-four years. Don't pretend you're the only one in this family who is suffering."

"He was my father!" Annalisa yelled to her grandmother's back.

"He was my son." Nonna whipped around and slapped her hand against her own chest. "My son!"

Seeing and hearing Nonna's pain cut to Annalisa's core, and she got the point. Everyone in the family had lost her father. He was a father, a son, a brother, a cousin. They'd all lost him to alcoholism and then to that car wreck.

And they'd lost Annalisa's mother, Celia, as well. From the first day her parents had met, the entire Mancuso clan had hoped that the talented, beautiful, and smart Celia Russo could rescue Tony Mancuso from continuing down his path of trouble. She'd done a pretty good job for a while, but eventually the whiskey had won.

Annalisa couldn't take it anymore and turned away. With tears sliding down her cheeks, she stomped out of the kitchen. After slamming her bedroom door in frustration, Annalisa reached for her heavy Michelangelo book on the dresser and slung it across the room. The book crashed into her easel in the corner and knocked it, and her work in progress, to the floor. She collapsed onto the bed.

Through the thin walls, she could hear the crashes of her grandmother finishing the dishes, as if every collision further drove home her point.

Curling up, Annalisa lost herself in the lava lamp on the bedside table, letting the neon-green blobs absorb her anger. The drama of which her tiny grandmother was capable was extraordinary. She was the poster woman for fiery Italian *nonne*, and no woman could deliver a rant with such Oscar-worthy passion or issue a guilt trip with such sniper-like precision.

Even though they fought on occasion, she admired Nonna for being so strong and for being the cornerstone of the family. That being said, Annalisa certainly didn't want to grow up to be like her grandmother.

She didn't want to be barefoot and pregnant, confined to the kitchen and shut out from the world. That life didn't interest Annalisa at all. She could never stand for the way things were arranged, almost as if their lives were predetermined for the females in their family.

As much as Annalisa hated her father, she did like that he'd broken out of the Mills himself and actually chased his dreams. Even after hurting his back and discovering alcohol, he'd cleaned himself up and gone to college and landed a well-paying job at a bank in Bangor. By the time he'd met Annalisa's mother, he was back on top. For a while, at least.

Like her father, Annalisa craved independence. She didn't want to be told what to do, where to live, whom to marry, or what to believe. No wonder he'd gotten the hell out of this town. Nonna was probably drowning him.

She didn't like spending much time comparing herself to him, though—or even thinking about him—but she could feel his presence here. She was living in his old bedroom, for God's sake, where he and two of his brothers had been crammed in all the way through high school. Her indoor studio was in the very space where her art-hating father had slept! In addition, almost every face in the Mancuso family, with the exception of Nino and a couple of others, bore a strong resemblance to the man. Talk about holding her back. The bottom line was that she could never be the artist she wanted to be here, and nothing Nonna or anyone else said or did would change that fact.

When she finally calmed down twenty minutes later, Annalisa decided she'd better apologize. Though Nonna couldn't care less, her mother had never let Annalisa go to bed angry, and it was a practice she'd held on to. Stepping into the hallway, she saw amber light shining through the crack in Nonna's closed bedroom door. She walked down the hall decorated with family photos and some of Annalisa's earlier works and stopped at the door.

She raised her hand to knock but stopped at the last second, putting her ear closer. Her grandmother always prayed for a long time before going to bed, and sometimes Annalisa had heard her talking to someone, probably her late husband or even Annalisa's father.

Tonight, it sounded like she was crying.

Annalisa felt terrible. What kind of awful person had she become, being so nasty to the woman who had taken her in? Nonna was right anyway. Why did Annalisa always have to make it about her?

"Nonna?" she said, rapping lightly on the door. "Can I come in?"

After a moment, Nonna cracked open the door, dressed in her nightgown. "Yes, *nipotina*?"

Annalisa lowered her head. "I'm sorry."

Nonna's bottom lip jutted out as she pulled open the door and opened up her arms. "I know you are."

Annalisa bent down and hugged Nonna's shoulders. "I'm so confused." She noticed fresh prints in the kneeling pillow by the bed.

Nonna patted her lower back. "It's okay to be confused. I am too sometimes." She let go of Annalisa and took her hands, looking up into her eyes. "You might not believe it, but I love having you here. It's not easy being alone."

"You're not alone," Annalisa assured her, pulling her grandmother back into one more hug.

After a long, loving embrace that Annalisa needed so badly, the two bid each other good night. Returning to her room, Annalisa knelt by her bed and prayed, asking God to forgive her for being such a mess and to give her some guidance, and maybe a little help. Leaving Nonna would be incredibly hard, but how could she deny herself the opportunity rolling out ahead of her? She wasn't sure if He existed, but she thought she'd at least give Him a chance to prove Himself.

Chapter 3

ALICE AND THE WHITE RABBIT

Annalisa worked her tail off over the summer and into the fall as the temperatures fell. She pulled double shifts at Harry's General Store, and even when school started, she worked any time he'd let her. What she didn't spend on art supplies went straight to her savings to move to Portland.

Promising herself she'd do at least three pieces a week, she painted with every spare minute. To find new ideas, she caught rides with Nino or her aunts whenever they left town—sometimes to Freeport or Brunswick or Davenport—and, using her photographic memory, cataloged her experiences. Even when she was stuck in the Mills, the newspaper and television showed how extremely turbulent the world had become, and Annalisa could see its influence in her work. How could it not? Even Nonna had admitted these years might be the strangest of her long lifetime.

All in the span of a few months, so many crazy things were happening. Senator Kennedy had driven that woman off the bridge. Neil and Buzz had walked on the moon. Nixon continued to ship more soldiers to Vietnam, backing away from his pledge to end the war. The heartbreaking Manson murders happened less than a week before Woodstock. Talk about a juxtaposition to explain the times.

She had desperately wanted to go to Woodstock (it was only a few hours away) with a group of her friends from Bangor, but she knew that getting caught would doom her entire senior year and earn her a one-way ticket to becoming a Sister of Mercy. Still, she wanted to join this movement of young people desperate for the truth.

Annalisa would listen to her often-drunk and closed-minded uncles as they talked war and politics after weekend suppers. In her family, there seemed to be only one way, and that was strict conservatism and Catholicism. Any other opinions were wrong. The women in the family typically agreed, and that was why Nonna was still discouraging Annalisa from moving to Portland, the epicenter for sin. But like so many people her age, Annalisa didn't want to mindlessly accept what she was told to believe. She wanted to get out into the world and form opinions of her own.

The only thing the country seemed to be in agreement on was the war. She'd never heard anyone argue for it. Sure, the US wanted to rid the world of communism—who didn't?—but how was attacking soldiers and their families in a jungle thousands of miles away doing that exactly?

All these questions came out in her most recent works, where Annalisa explored themes of uprising. She painted protesters picketing against Nixon and the war. She painted scenes of women attempting to break through the infinite and impenetrable glass ceilings—and hippies and musicians and poets and artists expressing themselves through an endless array of mediums. Of course, many of these works weren't popular in her family, so she kept them hidden under her bed.

On the fourth Friday in October, three months after being rejected by Jackie in Portland, Nino talked Annalisa into attending one of their high school football games. She wasn't much of a sports fan at all. Quite the opposite, actually. Her father used to drag her to watch his alma mater's team, the University of Maine Black Bears, play their home games, and revisiting those memories was never easy.

Still, even those rare Payton Mills residents who didn't follow their team knew tonight was the biggest rivalry of the year: the Spartans versus the Davenport Eagles. When it came to great restaurants or golf courses, Davenport won. Prestige and money, it wasn't even close. Beautiful scenery, Davenport excelled. But when it came to football, Payton Mills wore the crown.

In the sprawling grounds behind the very fancy Davenport High, Annalisa sat with Nino and their other friends in a sea of Spartan blue on the visitors' bleachers. It was cold out, just over forty degrees, and many of the spectators had blankets draped over their legs.

Under the powerful bright lights, the Spartans' star running back broke through the line. He ran to glory, and everyone in the visitors' stands sprang to their feet.

Everyone except Annalisa, who stayed seated in both protest and shock, wondering how so many people could obsess over such a silly sport—especially with everything else going on in the world. It was a distraction, rooting for a victory in a conflict more controllable than war.

When Nino sat back down, she continued the conversation they were having about her departure after graduation. "You see," she said, surveying the field. "This is exactly why I don't belong here. I'm not sure a girl can live in Payton Mills and not care about these brutes running around tossing their weird-shaped ball. It's not that I hate Payton Mills. Not exactly. It's just not for me, you know? This is my father's town. It was his school. I want nothing to do with it."

Nino adjusted the crucifix dangling from his neck. "I get it, *cugina mia*. You're not hurting my feelings. All I care about is having a couch to sleep on in Portland. Or maybe an extra bedroom so I can take a city girl home."

She hit him in the arm. "Ew. You are definitely not bringing any girls back to my place in Portland. Besides, with the kind of money I'll have, there won't even be room for you to stretch your gangly self out on the floor."

"Ha," he said, keeping an eye on the kicker lining up behind the line. "Like I keep telling you, you're so pretty; just marry a rich guy. All your problems will go away . . . and I'll have a place to stay. Find a guy who has one of those big houses in the West End or a place on the water in the Cape."

She shook her head in disappointment. "You would think my cousin would know me by now."

"You wait and see," he said. "A month in the city and you'll be showing off your diamond and telling us all about your tennis lessons."

She hit him on the shoulder. "You're such an idiot, Nino. If I do that, please come kill me in my sleep. A relationship is the last thing I need. You might recall it was my father who destroyed my mother's chances to make something of herself." While the Spartans' cheerleaders did a post-touchdown routine on the side of the field, Annalisa stood. "I'm gonna grab a Moxie. You want one?"

"No one ever wants a Moxie except you," he said with repulsion. "I'll take a Crush, though."

Annalisa worked her way down the stands, past the cheerleaders, and around the end zone toward the concession stands on the home-team side. She noticed a younger girl sitting alone on one of the picnic tables lined up under a cluster of trees near the corner of the field. Her elbows were propped on her thighs, her hands clasped together, and she seemed to be staring at the ground, ignoring the game.

Annalisa had spent many hours since moving to the Mills with that same sad posture and lonely stare. She looked at the concession stands ahead, long lines of teenagers laughing as they waited to get their red snapper hot dogs and sodas. Surprising even herself, Annalisa cut toward the girl.

"Hey, are you okay over there?" she asked from ten feet away.

The girl looked up like a tortoise poking its head out of the shell, so timid she might retreat at any moment. Her brown hair looked ironed and was parted in the center. She wore a brand-new Bean jacket, revealing that she most definitely lived in Davenport and not Payton Mills.

"Yeah, I'm fine," she said, her breath turning to fog. She looked back down, as if a weight were tied to her chin. She was extremely skinny, too, as Annalisa had been right after the funeral, when she'd stopped eating. It was obvious the girl didn't want to talk, but seeing her younger self in her made Annalisa not quite want to give up.

Hearing the crowd cheering behind her, she took a step closer. "I like your jacket."

The girl's eyes flitted up. "Thanks."

Annalisa wasn't sure what to do. She didn't want to pester her but didn't want to leave her alone, either, thinking the girl might need someone to listen. Guessing she was probably thirteen or fourteen, Annalisa remembered how hard life had been for her back then.

"Listen," she said, "I'm sorry to bother you, but you don't seem fine. Unless there's a riveting movie showing on the ground there that only you can see. What's your name?"

She attempted to smile at Annalisa's joke. "Emma."

Another step forward, approaching like a hostage negotiator. "Is everything okay, Emma?"

The girl finally raised her head and kept it up. She put her hands where her elbows had been. "Everything's just great," she said sarcastically. "I'm so happy to be here."

"What? You don't like football?" Annalisa asked. Another step.

Emma looked left. "I hate football."

Annalisa seized the opportunity to take a seat next to her up on the table. "You're not the only one. Seriously, look at them." As they both looked at the field, where the teams lined up near midfield, she said, "They're a bunch of sweaty grunts running into each other. And then the fans. They're even worse. You might be an Eagle, so I don't know if it's the same, but the Spartan fans, they live and die by this sport. As if anyone on that field is doing anything that actually mattered."

A series of grunts on the field was followed by clashing helmets and more cheers.

The girl let out a small smile, which served to spur Annalisa on. "Seriously, what are they doing that matters? Oh, far out. They just threw a ball in the air, and another guy caught it. Then he ran over a line. Oh God, let's give him the Medal of Honor."

The girl laughed, and Annalisa decided she would tell Father Laduca during confession Sunday that she'd made a sad person laugh. He might give her absolution for being nasty to Nonna.

"You're funny," the girl said, glancing over.

"Well, thanks, but football's an easy target." Annalisa put out her gloved hand. "I'm Annalisa." After shaking, Annalisa asked, "So why are you even here then? If you don't like it."

A shrug as Emma found a spot to look at on the ground again. "Because being here is better than being at home."

Annalisa hurt for her but wasn't sure how much she should pry. "Can I . . . help?"

Emma shook her head. "My brother's here, but thanks."

Annalisa looked toward the concession stands, smelling hot dogs and popcorn. "Where is he?"

Emma crossed her arms and shivered. "He's up in the stands with all his friends. He's always nice to invite me, but I just didn't feel like being with them anymore. They're all older."

"And they're all football fans," Annalisa added, "which doesn't give them much hope for being great conversationalists."

Emma let out another smile, and Annalisa thought she could get used to this, dragging girls out of their misery. She wished someone had done that for her. Or *would* do that for her now.

"So what are you into?" Annalisa asked, deciding she'd much rather talk to this girl than return to the stands. "You don't like football. What is it you *do* like? I'm an artist. That's all I do and what I *should* be doing right now."

Emma leaned back on her hands. "I guess I'm into music."

"Oh yeah, like who?" At that moment, something like a leaf dropped on Annalisa's head. She tried to find it and wipe it away but gave up after a few seconds.

"The Beatles," Emma answered. The crowd cheered again, another pointless play on the field.

"Yeah? Me too."

"Really? Have you heard *Abbey Road*?" Emma asked, coming more alive with each word.

"No, I haven't," Annalisa admitted. "I'm typically a little late to new releases. This'll crack you up, but I still love Elvis." Another something hit Annalisa's head, and she looked up. They were under a tree, but it had shed all its leaves.

"I'm sneaking out to go hear Cold River at Fairhaven next Friday night," Annalisa said. "Do you know them?"

"I think I've heard of them."

"They're worth checking out. Kind of Creedence-like, I guess."

Something hit her head again and then fell into her lap. It was a piece of popcorn. "What the . . . somebody's throwing popcorn at me." She turned to see where it had come from, saying, "Cut it out!"

Up came a head from behind one of the other tables. He carried a bag of popcorn in one hand and waved with the other. It took her only a second to recognize him once the lights above caught his face. It was the guy from the museum: Thomas.

He let loose the grin she remembered so well as he approached them. "Are you stalking me?" he asked.

"I should ask you the same thing," Annalisa said, seriously considering that possibility.

He pointed to Emma. "That's my sister you're talking to."

Emma shrugged. "Yep."

Looking back at Thomas, Annalisa noticed his red sweater for the first time. "You're an Eagle?"

"For the rest of my days," he said, stopping directly between her and the field. "I graduated last year, go to Weston now," he said, referring to the little Ivy League college a few miles away. "I was with my art class when we first met."

"That's right; you're a sculptor," Annalisa joked.

"A sculptor?" Emma said, as if he'd claimed that he was an astronaut. "He couldn't sculpt a snowman."

Thomas shot his sister a glance. "Don't call me out. I thought you had my back, sis."

Annalisa laughed loudly, both to poke fun at Thomas and to lift Emma up. Emma joined her and then finally Thomas.

"So you're a Spartan, I'm assuming," he said to Annalisa, wiping away his smile.

"For seven more months."

"How about that," he said. "What are the chances?"

He took a seat next to Emma's feet and rested an arm on her thigh. "So you disappear for a minute and I find you talking with the enemy?" Then, more lovingly, he asked, "Everything okay? We've been looking for you."

Emma shyly glanced over at Annalisa and then back at her brother. "Everything's fine. I just don't care about the game."

Thomas patted his sister's leg. "It's all groovy, just making sure." In an apparent effort to save his sister from further embarrassment, he said to both of them, "This isn't allowed, you know, you two talking. Emma, this is the girl I was telling you about. From the museum in Portland. Can you believe that?"

"No way," Emma said skeptically.

Annalisa instantly thought: *Why was he talking about me to his sister?*

"I hoped I'd run into you again." He looked entirely too excited for this coincidence. "To think you've been living right down the road."

Annalisa decided things were getting a little too mushy and that it was time to go. She turned to Emma. "It was good to meet you."

"Good to meet you, Annalisa," Emma said.

Oh crap, Annalisa thought. She was busted.

"Annalisa?" Thomas said. "I thought your name was Alice."

Emma nearly snorted with laughter. "Ha ha. Looks like you must have made a great first impression." She turned back to Annalisa. "He's not used to being turned down."

Annalisa jumped to the ground. "I guess there's a first for everything."

Waving from a few feet away, she said, "Emma, good to meet you. So how can I convince your brother that he's not my type?"

"Why not?" Thomas asked, standing and going her way. "Give me that, and I'll let you go."

She'd better end this for good, or he might show up at her doorstep one day. "For one, I'm not allowed to fraternize with non-Italian men. My grandmother would kill me. And she'd kill you too."

He inched toward her. "How do you know I'm not Italian?"

"I bet you're not even Catholic."

His voice shot up an octave. "You can bet your sweet bippy I am."

Annalisa turned back to Emma, who was finding all this very funny. "Is he telling the truth?"

"I can't say." His sister grinned ear to ear, a complete transformation from the girl earlier.

Back to Thomas, she said, "Say a Hail Mary."

"Right now?" He was suddenly standing a foot from her.

Annalisa gave an if-you-think-I'm-worth-it shrug.

"Hail Mary," he started, "full of mace, the gourd is in me . . ." He trailed off. "Okay, I'm not Catholic. I might not be Italian, either, but I love pasta." He said the last part as if it was a question.

A laugh—nearly a cackle—escaped without her permission, and she started backing away.

Just as she opened her mouth to say goodbye, a burly guy about Thomas's age, with a shaved head, approached. He said in a gravelly voice, "There you are, Emma. I went all the way out to the parking lot looking for you. You all right?" He assumed the same seat Annalisa had taken on the picnic table and put his arm around the young girl. "We not cool enough for you?"

"Alice, this is Mitch Gaskins," Thomas said. She wasn't sure if he meant to introduce her with the wrong name, and it niggled at her. "Despite being a pretty good mechanic," he said, "Mitch is the dumbest guy you'll ever meet. As you can see by his ugly scalp, he enlisted and just got back from basic training. He can't get to Vietnam fast enough."

Mitch shrugged. "It's in my blood. What do I do? Good to meet you, Alice."

"It's actually Annalisa," she corrected, feeling the weight of the war as she imagined this Mitch on his way to fight for his country. And he'd enlisted, so by choice.

Thomas slapped his head with gusto. "That's right. *Annalisa.*" Then he gave her a grin, showing that he was messing with her.

She made a face back at him. He was too sly for his own good.

Turning to the visitors' stands, where Nino was probably wondering where she'd gone, she said, "I need to go find my friends. Goodbye, Emma. Goodbye, Mitch."

"What about me?" Thomas asked with a charming puppy-faced grin.

"Bye-bye, boy who loves pasta," she said.

Boys could be so tempting at times, and Thomas was charming—but slick. The perfect example of how a girl could get reeled in and then hurt.

Chapter 4

COLD RIVER

On Halloween night a week later, Annalisa slipped out of bed already dressed. She picked up her boots and purse, wrapped her red scarf around her neck, and slipped out of the room. As much as she wanted to rush, she took her time passing through the hallway, tiptoeing with such exaggeration as to feel like a cartoon character. Entering the living room, she breathed a sigh of relief. Part of her was surprised her grandmother hadn't been waiting with a wooden spoon, with which she would have smacked Annalisa on the rump—or more harshly on the shoulder—and spat: *You think you can fool me,* ragazza*!* If Nonna had noticed that Annalisa wasn't wearing a bra, being in trouble for sneaking out would be the least of her worries. Annalisa didn't care, though. No one wore bras anymore.

Crossing the bare living room floor, the volume of creaking pine planks nearly unbearable, Annalisa trudged on, one stockinged foot after the other. She glanced at images of the three men who stood guard over the entryway. For as long as Annalisa could remember, a framed glossy of Frank Sinatra and a printed portrait of Pope Paul VI had hung to the right of the door. Shortly after John F. Kennedy had been shot, a twelve-year-old Annalisa had delighted Nonna with a charcoal portrait of him on newsprint paper. Having always loved the man, Nonna had framed and hung Annalisa's drawing directly below Mr. Sinatra, completing the trifecta.

Dipping two fingers into the holy water font hanging to the right of the pope, she crossed herself and asked for forgiveness (from all three), then stepped out into the night. She wasn't only asking for forgiveness for sneaking out tonight. She was looking for absolution for all the sins she was about to commit, because Nonna had just laid into her again about her desire to move to Portland.

Teased by a brisk breeze, the wind chimes sang, and she wondered if her mother was up there watching her, shaking her head. If so, surely Celia Mancuso could understand that she'd left her daughter alone to deal with all these situations that no seventeen-year-old girl should have to navigate alone. All her mother had had to do was find the courage to leave her husband, and then she'd be alive and able to help Annalisa deal with life's confusions, such as boys like Thomas and decisions like leaving the Mills. Surely her mother would have supported her decision to move to Portland. But time and time again, her mother had taken Annalisa's father back, and it had turned out to be one time too many, leaving Annalisa to fend for herself.

When she turned left at the sidewalk and walked through the neighborhood, carved pumpkins with jagged teeth smiling at her from many of the front stoops, the sound of the chimes faded and gave way to a barred owl hooting from somewhere up high. Glancing back, she searched for lights on inside her grandmother's house. Looked like she'd gotten away clean, thank God. As much as she needed to let loose some steam tonight, the last thing she wanted was to get in another fight with Nonna. For both of their sakes.

"Hey, hitchhiker, you looking for a ride?" Nino asked, sticking his head out the window of his beater, which was coming to a stop a few feet away from her. Annalisa couldn't have said what the make and model of the car were, but it seemed a miracle the old thing was still clunking along.

Seeing Nino's flavor of the month sitting shotgun, Annalisa climbed into the back seat next to their friend Christina, who handed her a can of Old Milwaukee. "Here you go, babe." If Annalisa was a dragon and Nonna was a tiger, Christina was somewhere between a lynx and a kitty cat. She still had claws but was far from intimidating. She was probably Annalisa's closest girlfriend in the Mills, but that wasn't saying much. Outside of Nino, her true friends were back in Bangor, slowly losing touch.

As always, Roger was next to her. He was nice enough, but Annalisa found the guy borderline barbaric and couldn't remember ever sharing an interesting conversation with him. He and Christina had been dating since ninth grade, and Annalisa knew way more than she wanted to about their sexual escapades. To put it bluntly, it wasn't his brains Christina liked.

"It's about time you joined us," Christina said. "We were making bets. Nino thought you would back out."

"Oh yeah?" Annalisa said, smelling the pineapple scent of the air freshener dangling from the rearview mirror. "That's because he's more afraid of our grandmother than I am."

"What's not to be afraid of?" he asked.

With the cool air rushing through the windows, they listened to rock 'n' roll and sped through the night. Still reeling from her argument with Nonna and missing her mother like crazy, Annalisa drained her first beer—perhaps a little too quickly—and reached for another from the box on the floorboard. Aside from her terrible day, it was nice to take a break from working so hard.

"There you go," Roger said. "Get after it."

Though he couldn't see it, she rolled her eyes.

On the hour-long drive north, she took down four more beers, more than she'd drunk in as long as she could remember. The others seemed to be keeping up, though, and they stopped twice to relieve themselves in the woods off the road.

The alcohol dulled her frustration with Nonna, and she settled into the good music from the radio: Led Zeppelin, Three Dog Night, the Who. Letting her troubles go, she was suddenly having fun, though slightly annoyed by Christina and Roger making out. Couldn't they wait until they parked? And what was with the sounds?

Following the long line of cars packed with eager music lovers, Nino eased his beater along a gravel road through a thick forest of lumber trees. After a quarter mile, they broke through the forest, and Annalisa saw the weathered brown barn she'd heard so much about, glowing by spotlight high up on the hill. Some of the best bands in the Northeast played inside those walls. She felt a rush of excitement. If she was going to take the night off from painting, she'd much rather hear music than attend a sports game.

Men with flashlights directed the cars toward the large grassy area being used as the parking lot. When the five of them rolled into their spot, they all piled out into the raw energy of the night. Bluegrass, rock, folk, and who knew what else played from many of the cars at the same time, competing over each other. Tobacco and marijuana smoke and waves of incense spun through the air.

She watched Roger cut a slit in his beer with a key and then shotgun it. Apparently eating Christina's face had made him thirsty. Was there any wonder Annalisa wasn't dating anyone? Between men like Roger and her own father, men weren't high up in her book. No wonder she wasn't letting Thomas in, no matter how hard he tried.

As her friends gathered around the trunk and drew others to their party, Annalisa leaned against the front hood and watched the cars line up and the people walk by. The hippie strumming an acoustic guitar three cars down sounded just like Paul Simon. Or maybe it was the beers that made him sound good.

She spied a couple sitting on a truck bed across the way, passing a joint back and forth. Stepping their way, she asked, "Mind if I get a toke?"

The guy replied through a cloud of smoke, "Yeah, sure, man. All yours."

She took a long pull from the half-smoked joint and let it settle in her lungs. Nino had introduced her to marijuana over the summer, and she'd partaken with him every couple of weeks since then. Everything back in Payton Mills—the cage in which she was trapped, Nonna's warnings about leaving her family and the Mills, even her grief—faded even further away.

The guitarist sang "All Along the Watchtower," and she lost herself in the words. Music was the only thing outside of painting that could take her away from the grief that clawed at her daily. Well, that wasn't exactly true. Alcohol and Mary Jane had delivered the same effect tonight.

"Hey, daydreamer," Nino said. She'd found her way back to leaning against the hood of the car, staring up at the stars. "You coming? The band's about to start."

She joined her friends as they wove through the parked cars and made their way up the hill to the barn. She tripped once but found her balance before falling. Maybe that joint wasn't the best idea.

Several hundred young people piled in through the large doors. Once she was comfortably inside, she realized she'd lost her friends. Winding her way toward the right, she found a spot of fresh air along the wall of the barn and looked for Nino's head bobbing above the sea of people. When the crowd cheered, though, she gave up and faced the stage.

The four young men who made up the band Cold River appeared, and Annalisa joined everyone in another round of cheers. Whereas the bands she'd seen on television over the years might be in matching blue pants and white shirts with neatly trimmed haircuts, these guys were disheveled, long-haired mavericks. She stood on her toes to watch as they took to their instruments in front of a giant gold curtain that lined the back wall.

The overhead lights went dark, leaving only the stage lights brightly shining at the band. They broke into a tune, and the large amplifiers punched through the chatter. The crowd burst into a swarming, chaotic dance. Though her buzz was a little stronger than she liked, she did enjoy the numbness of it, and she let the beat start to move her body.

Dressed in an army jacket and jeans, the singer had swagger and let out an easy smile, acknowledging the crowd. She let her body experiment to the groove, exploring feelings of freedom, feeling like she was floating in space. Her thoughts disappeared into the night with the volume of the music, the thump of the bass, the stinging guitar solos, the soul of the singer, and the band's harmonies.

These men, this band, had found their voice, and they couldn't be much older than her. Surely she wasn't far away from the same discovery.

The next song was a slow one. Couples paired up and slipped their arms around each other. She closed her eyes and lost herself in the music. Her buzz was even stronger now, and she wished she could turn it down a few degrees.

She was flying when she heard a voice behind her.

"Want to dance?"

She turned to see the person who dared to invade her space.

The coastal preppie with an edge stood there with his familiar smile. "Annalisa in Wonderland. Or was it Alice?"

"You have got to be kidding me," she said, wondering if she were seeing things that didn't actually exist. Her words had certainly come out slurred, proving that her grasp on reality had slipped away.

He moved closer and said loudly over the music, "Three strikes and we have to go out, right? I think Fate has deemed us one dance." He held out an arm.

She looked at it like a loaded gun pointed at her stomach and took a step backward. "No thanks." What a cruel joke. No matter how charming he was or how drunk and stoned she was, Annalisa knew he was nothing more than a sharp-and-deadly fishing hook dressed up with enticing bait.

Thomas lowered his arm and stopped his approach. "All right, well . . . I tried, Annalisa." His piercing hazel eyes were almost too much to take. She had the urge to both hit him and kiss him.

"What else do I have to do to show you I'm not interested?" she said, hearing herself slurring more. A cloud of marijuana smoke floated by, making her feel even more stoned.

He took another step forward. "What was that? I couldn't hear you." He pointed to the band and leaned in, coming within inches of her face.

"I said . . ." She lost her thought, noticing an attraction to him, as if she'd let down her guard. After a long breath, she said forcefully, "I said you have to stop this. No matter how charming you might be, I'm not interested."

He lit up, acting like a beacon of light in her own haze. "So you think I'm charming? Does that mean I'm wearing on you?"

"I think it's just the . . . the alcohol talking," she said, stumbling backward, bumping into people, the room spinning.

"Hey, are you okay?" he asked, sticking his hand back out.

She slapped it away angrily but then realized she'd turned her ankle the wrong way. As she fell, she saw him reaching for her. Her butt hit the hard dirt, and her head dropped back.

She saw three or four of him as he knelt beside her, saying things she couldn't interpret. Strobe lights flashed above, and she saw the legs of dancers moving to the loud music, and then it became blurrier, turning into a wash of color.

Chapter 5

A Ride Home

Annalisa's head spun, and she felt like she might throw up at any minute. She was conscious enough to know that Thomas had helped her off the floor and was carrying her out of the barn. With one arm under her back and another under her legs, he pushed through the crowd of people, who were all dancing to a fast-paced song that combined with the flashing lights to make Annalisa feel all the worse.

She noticed people turn to see what was wrong with her and heard Thomas speaking with someone, but she was beyond blitzed. When the cool night air hit her, though, she felt a wave of clarity. Thank God she was out of there. She wanted nothing more than to be home in bed.

"Where are you taking me?" she mumbled, wondering if she'd made sense.

Thomas was still talking to someone, something about getting her home. "It's okay," he told her. "I'm just getting you some fresh air."

The sky looked like a swirling black hole, and she could feel her eyes rolling back. This had to be the worst she'd ever felt, and she just wanted it to go away.

He set her down on a patch of grass, and she saw that there were two of them. Or three, maybe.

"I need to go home," she mumbled.

Thomas knelt beside her and asked a few questions, and none of it made any sense. She heard herself saying something about coming with her cousin Nino. He replied with more questions, none of them registering. She tried to speak but wasn't sure anything was coming out at all.

He seemed to be asking the same questions repeatedly. Something about who she came with, what he looked like, what he drove. She felt her mouth moving to attempt an answer, but she was so close to throwing up that she closed her eyes and wished it all away.

She heard, ". . . get you outta here before you get into trouble for drinking underage."

That sounded like a good idea, so she said, "I just wanna go home."

He said more gibberish, and she tried hard to make sense of it. Something about her cousin's car. Leaving a note.

"A big ugly brown car near the back," she said. "With a pineapple air freshener."

More gibberish.

"Home, please," she muttered. "I want to go home."

Thomas took her hand. "I'm taking you back to the Mills. You remember Mitch from the game? He'll make sure your cousin knows what's going on."

She heard his words, but they made little sense, as if he were saying things at random. Either way, his voice was comforting and reassuring, and he seemed to have a much better grasp of the situation than she did, so she nodded.

A moment later, he picked her up again and carried her down the hill, telling her everything would be okay. For some reason, she trusted him and let her eyes close. The next few minutes were doors opening and closing, a car engine coming alive, Annalisa finally able to sit back into a chair, some sharp movements until things were smooth—and then the darkness of her eyelids consumed her.

Annalisa peeled open her eyes and saw with foggy vision the highway lines lit up with headlights. She looked around, assessing her surroundings. She was in a car. The windows were cracked, letting in a welcome stream of cold air. Looking left, she saw Thomas, one hand on the wheel and the other resting against the door.

"There you are," he said. "How ya feeling?"

Some of what had happened came to her like a movie playing in slow motion. She could see him in the barn, approaching her under the strobe lights. She remembered talking to him before falling backward. Then he was carrying her out.

"Where are we going?" she asked, her mouth feeling like she'd been sucking on cotton. She sat up in the yellow-and-white-striped seat. Was this a VW? She pulled off her scarf and let it fall to the floorboard. "How long have I been sleeping?"

"I'm taking you home," he said. "We're about halfway back to Payton Mills."

"What about my cousin?" Nino would kill her for disappearing.

"My friend Mitch went to find him. Tall Italian guy with a crucifix, beat-up brown car. If he can't, he'll find the car and leave a note. Don't worry; Mitch is good like that."

"But the concert. Why did you leave? I . . ." She was still out of it, feeling overwhelmingly nauseated.

"It's no big deal," he assured her. "I didn't want you to get in trouble, and you kept asking me to take you home."

Was she out of her mind? Why would she have asked him to take her home? Had she led him on? Her memory was hazy; even putting thoughts together was a task. God, she never wanted to drink or smoke again.

He pointed at a pack of Clark's Teaberry gum on the mesh parcel shelf hanging under the dashboard. "You want a piece?"

Her nausea worsened. "I think I'm going to throw up."

"Serious? You want me to pull over?" He let his foot off the gas.

Annalisa nodded, feeling embarrassment coat her stomach.

He came to a stop on the shoulder of the road. It was probably close to midnight, and there were no other cars. If he wanted to take advantage of her, he could have easily done so. Thinking about the Zodiac killer, who was back in the news, she felt the thought clawing at her as she opened up the door and tumbled out.

Running a few feet into the grass, she bent over. It took a few seconds, but then it all came up, her dinner and beers.

When she was done, she wiped her mouth and eyes and turned back. He stepped out of his banana-yellow VW Beetle and asked her if she was okay. Of course she wasn't okay. This sucked. Considering he'd left the concert for her, though, and that he looked far from threatening, she thanked him and said she was fine.

Back on the road, she took him up on that piece of gum. She was feeling better, and as a wave of clarity returned, shame overwhelmed her. This is exactly how her father might have acted, and her mother would be disgusted. She wondered what Jackie Burton would think of her now.

Thomas left her alone and sang along quietly to "Tell All the People" by the Doors. A Texaco gas station came up on the right, and he pulled in. "I'll go grab you a soda and something to eat. Any preference?"

"No, thank you," she said, still trying to process what an idiot she'd been. She was such a mess. And here she was being prickly to a guy who was trying to take care of her.

He returned to the car with two brown bags. Once he sat, he dug into one and said, "You pick. I have ginger ale or Coke."

She reached for the ginger ale and took a big, long sip, feeling more grateful by the minute.

"As far as food," he said, digging back in, "not sure what's good for your stomach, but I got two red snappers, one with ketchup, one with mustard and relish. If that doesn't work, I've got saltines, Ring Dings, pretzels, and a Twinkie. Have whatever you'd like."

Her sudden smile turned into a laugh. "This is ridiculous."

He smiled too. "Hey, it's first-class delivery, all the way home to Payton Mills. So what's your preference?"

"Some saltines for now would be great, thanks." Maybe Nino wasn't the *only* nice guy out there.

He opened the package for her and handed it over.

Once they'd gotten back on the road and she'd eaten a few crackers, she started coming around even more. She took the last swig of ginger ale and set it near her feet.

"How's your sister?" she asked. She'd thought about the lonely-looking girl more than once since that night at Davenport High.

He glanced at her. "She's okay, thanks. Actually, I have to admit something to you. She's the reason I was there tonight."

She looked at him. "What?"

"We were already planning on going," he said, "but when Emma told me you'd mentioned it, I had extra incentive."

"She ratted me out?" Annalisa asked jokingly, wishing the fogginess in her head would go away. "Wow, I thought we'd bonded."

He sipped his Coke. "Uh, yeah, I'd say so. My sister really liked you, which is saying a lot. She doesn't like many people at all. That's why she told me where to find you. Then she said I'd be lucky if you ever gave me the time of day."

She was right about that, but considering Annalisa was currently tasting the acidity of her stomach in her mouth after a debauched display of teenage angst, she thought Emma's comment might have missed the mark.

Annalisa watched the trees go by. "Tell her she's in trouble with me." Despite the haziness, she could feel herself having fun talking to him and didn't know what to make of it. This was exactly the kind of thing her mother would have helped her with; Nonna was great in a lot of ways, but not when it came to girl talk.

"I'll do that," he said with an unshakable grin. She wondered if he'd ever had his heart broken. It didn't seem like it. She wouldn't be surprised if his friends called him Mr. Sunshine.

He hummed a snatch of song as the highway blurred under their wheels. "So what do you listen to? Who's your all-time favorite? Hold on, let me guess. I see you as like a . . . a Motown girl. There's something kind of old soul about you." Then he corrected himself. "No, Emma told me. You like Elvis, don't you?"

She crossed her arms and twisted toward him. "Your sister's like your spy or something. I thought she was on my side. And what's wrong with Elvis?"

He found her eyes before looking back to the road. "He's . . . fine, but he's so yesterday."

She sat back in her seat. "I am an old soul; what can I say? My mother got me into him, so maybe it's nostalgia." Annalisa fell back in time to the days when her father was at work, and she and her mother would clean the house listening to *His Hand in Mine* and *G.I. Blues*. Not all of her childhood was bad. She cherished memories like that.

Thomas asked more questions, and she talked about her family and then told him about her aspirations of getting out of Payton Mills and her desire to be an artist. At this point, he'd totally bailed on the concert and pretty much rescued her, so she owed him some kindness and conversation. And she had to admit that he was enjoyable to talk to and appeared genuinely interested in her life.

"All I've ever wanted to do is be a professional artist," she said. "The same dream as my mother, but she ended up letting it go to be a wife and mom." She didn't mention that it was really her father who had dampened her mother's desire to be an artist for a living. He'd demanded that she stop working and stay home.

Thomas passed a slow truck in the other lane, working the clutch and gearshift with grace. "Was your mother as good as you?"

"Definitely better," she said, looking at him, noticing his rounded profile. He really was a hunk. "She was like Jackie O; anything she touched turned beautiful. She'd study fashion magazines and then make it all herself. Her friends begged her to make them clothes. And the way she painted was . . ." Annalisa stopped to revisit her mother's work in her mind.

Thomas looked over to urge her on.

"She had a certain style with her still lifes. Her arrangements, the shadows and colors." Thinking of what Jackie Burton had said about finding her voice, she said, "She had a very specific style that you could pick out in a heartbeat. That's not easy to do."

"I can't imagine it is," he replied. "I'd love to see her work."

"There are only a couple left in the family," Annalisa admitted, suddenly aching for her mother while at the same time wondering why she was sharing so much with this almost stranger.

She reached for the pack of gum at the same time that he grabbed the gearshift, and their hands collided. A spark of excitement came racing up her arm, and when she looked at him, they shared a smile. In the intimacy of this car, there was no denying their connection.

Not ready for it, she looked out the window to her right, noticing a sign pointing toward Payton Mills.

"Do you paint still lifes too?"

She shook her head, knowing she'd better stop getting emotional. "Not at all. To be honest, I'm not into them that much. I love my mother's, for obvious reasons, but it's not a genre I mess with anymore."

"What's your thing then?"

"Isn't that the question? I'm still trying to figure it out."

"Not that I'm as studied or into art as you," Thomas admitted, "but I don't get still lifes either." In a geeky and nasally voice, he said, "Here's a painting of a bowl of fruit. Enjoy!"

They laughed together. "Yeah, I know. They can be boring. My mom did have a way with them, though."

He looked over until she met his eyes. "So you're a seeker, then, as far as art goes? Trying to find what Annalisa Mancuso is meant to paint."

How astute of him. "That's why I want to get out of here, to get a taste of . . . I don't know, a wider world."

He switched lanes to pass another car. "I admire that about you," he confessed, looking at her a little longer this time. "I don't know that I've ever known an artist before, like one who actually takes it seriously. You're going to be a big deal one day. I could see your dedication at the museum, and I can hear it in your words now. I dig it."

As they drew closer to the Mills, she steered the conversation toward him. He told her about hoping to attend the NYU College of Dentistry after Weston, despite his father wanting him to join the family law firm.

"The last thing I want to do is sit in a courtroom all day," he said, glancing over so much now that she wondered if he might drive off the road. "Or work with my father and grandfather, two of the most difficult men on earth. All they do is argue; I'm sure that's half the reason my dad comes home being an asshole. Representing criminals all your life starts to consume your morals."

Unable to resist, she kept sneaking peeks at him, wondering if he was really this good of a guy. "So your sister doesn't want to join the firm?"

Thomas shook his head so quickly she thought he might hurt himself. "For reasons I don't want to get into, my father and sister don't get along, so she wouldn't join his firm for anything in the world, not that he'd let *any* woman join his firm, for that matter. It's an all-boys club at Barnes and Barnes."

Annalisa found herself worried about the girl. "What's going on with her?"

Thomas slowed to a stop at an intersection. Only a few more miles to go. "Ever since she was ten or eleven she's been pretty down, but some family stuff made it all worse. And the kids at school are mean to her, which doesn't help. She can't seem to get a break."

"Why are the kids like that?" Annalisa asked. What was it with people? Had it not been for Nino always sticking up for her and including her, she might have been in a similar situation when she'd first moved to the Mills.

He turned left and shifted into a higher gear. "She doesn't have the whole social interaction thing down and never fails to say the wrong thing. Like, I don't know. She's that person that makes a joke and no one laughs. She's honest to a fault, so no one wants to be friends with her. She literally sits by herself at lunch—not like she eats anyway."

"That's so sad," Annalisa said, knowing exactly what that was like, the not eating, the wanting to be alone. "Being a girl at fourteen isn't easy."

"Yeah, I guess it all starts at home with my parents. My dad can be the biggest jerk in Davenport. Can be. Is. One of the two. Depending on the time of day and the quantity of pills or martinis flowing through her veins, my mom bounces somewhere between being his cheerleader and his punching bag—not literally, but you know what I mean."

Yes, she did know what he meant.

"Anyway, that's way more than you want to know."

"We have a lot in common," she admitted, "especially when it comes to fathers." Her mother never abused alcohol or drugs—in fact, she would have killed Annalisa for tonight—but Celia Mancuso had certainly played her role as a punching bag for the last part of her life. Clearly Annalisa wasn't the only one who had it rough.

He was driving much slower than he had been, and she wondered if he was taking his time on purpose. In fact, she didn't recognize a couple of the roads and wondered if he was extending the drive. She wasn't exactly bothered.

"Emma's just always been so up and down," he said. "Sometimes I think she's strong enough to take on the world, but then she'll turn on a dime. My parents don't know how to handle her, so it's been up to me lately. That's why I haven't moved out yet. She needs me."

"She's lucky to have you." Annalisa couldn't imagine what she would have done if Nonna hadn't been there to scoop her up.

"I don't mean it like that, like I'm some sort of saint. I've had no choice, really. We had some things go down in our family, and I'm trying to help her work through it before I move on. I probably should stop there, though. As a lawyer's son, I've just laid out a pretty good case why you should steer clear of me."

She noticed they were finally back in civilization as they passed another gas station and hardware store. "No judgment here. Who doesn't have family issues?" More and more, he reminded her of Nino, a man with a kind heart and, perhaps, even good intentions.

When they crossed the bridge into Payton Mills, Annalisa glanced over at the mill, thinking that her father had been a charming guy just like Thomas—but he'd changed.

Sure, Thomas might be nice and handsome and potentially genuine, but she could guess what would happen if she let it go any further. They might date for a minute, even have some fun. Who knows how long they might last? By the end, though, their relationship would end up in a ravine, literally or figuratively, and she'd be holding an empty orange tote with a nonexistent portfolio, wondering how she'd let her dream melt away.

They drove along Main Street through the quaint and quiet downtown. They passed Harry's General Store, which was wedged between a salon and a casual restaurant called the River Place, with the best fried fish and clams in town. She didn't mention that she worked at Harry's. He'd probably show up for a scoop the next day.

Once through town, Annalisa directed him through the neighborhoods toward her house. When they were two houses down, she asked him to stop. "I can get out here. That's me down there."

"You don't want me to walk you in?"

"No. God no." Hearing the abruptness of her tone, she pulled back. "My grandmother would put you in her garlic chopper. She doesn't know I left."

He held up the two brown bags in the back seat. "Want all your snacks?"

"No, thank you," she said with a nervous smile. She put her hand on the door. "I really appreciate the lift and you taking care of me." To her surprise, she found that she meant it.

Before he could ask to see her again, she said goodbye and slipped out of the car. When an urge to turn back and wave hit her, she fought it off and started walking home. If she was intent on going to Portland and figuring out a way to make it in the art world, the last thing she needed was him tugging at her.

Chapter 6

The Mancuso Inquisition

The next day, the first of November, twenty-plus Mancusos filled Nonna's house. Annalisa stood in the kitchen with Nonna and two of her aunts, making Saturday supper. If Nonna wasn't making her cook right now, she would be hiding in her bedroom and trying to sleep last night off. Her family could be a little much at times, and with a hangover they were like a tenor singing an opera through a megaphone into her ear.

In a kitchen thick with the scents of Italian spices, Annalisa was chopping lettuce into a giant wooden bowl when Aunt Julia, the gossip of the family, said, "Who is the young man walking up with flowers in his hand?"

A lump caught in Annalisa's throat; a young man with flowers certainly wasn't there to see Nonna. Rushing to the window, she craned her neck around Julia's big hair and saw Thomas coming from his VW. Sure enough, he carried a bouquet of flowers, and an ambush of pleasure hit her before she could hide from it.

She raced out of the kitchen and, without a word, passed her family members drinking wine at the dining-room table. She ignored the others chatting in the living room as she ran to the front door, hoping she could get Thomas out of there before everyone saw him.

As Annalisa pulled open the door, she heard Aunt Julia running behind her, shouting, "Annalisa has a caller! Annalisa has a caller!"

The queasiness from the night before returned as Annalisa's family, like a swarm of bees, moved to the window. A mix of Italian and English phrases rose up into the air.

"What are you doing here?" Annalisa asked, almost attacking Thomas as she descended the porch steps.

He stopped his approach and raised her scarf in his left hand. "You left this in my car, so I thought I'd come by and check on you. And I brought your grandmother flowers—if you'll introduce me, that is."

He looked admittedly handsome in a sharp khaki suit with a blue plaid tie, and he seemed so out of place here in the Mills. His shaggy blond hair was combed back with a part on the left side. A bouquet of daisies was cradled in his right arm. His endearing smile showed that he'd brought his confidence with him too.

"You can't be here," Annalisa said, looking back at her family members with their faces pressed to the glass. "My whole family's inside."

He followed her gaze. "I can see that; sorry. I wanted to see if you were feeling all right. That was quite a night." As much as she didn't want to admit it to herself, she was happy to see him. She was less eager for him to meet her family. "Can I come say hi?"

A voice from behind said, "Yes, you can."

Annalisa turned to see Aunt Julia poking her head out from the cracked door. Her aunt rushed out of the house and nearly flew down the steps. She stuck out her hand to Thomas. "I'm Annalisa's aunt Julia. Your name?" To go with her big hair, Aunt Julia had big something elses that had been drawing stares since her prom queen days.

He took her hand and introduced himself. "Wonderful to meet you."

"You've come at the perfect time," she said, completely oblivious to Annalisa standing there. "I know you *begli uomini* are always hungry. We're just about to have dinner."

Oh my God. "No, no," Annalisa said desperately, "he was just dropping something off."

Aunt Julia peacocked her chest. "Well, unless he has other plans, I think he should join us. Would you like that, Thomas? We make some of the best food in the Mills."

"I'd adore it. Thank you." He looked at Annalisa for permission. "If that's okay with you?"

She was at a loss for words, trying to think of some excuse but finding herself reluctant to seem rude or hurt his feelings.

And then it was too late.

"Of course it's okay with her," Aunt Julia said, literally circling Thomas and pushing his back as if she were a shepherd herding him up the steps and into the house.

"Look at this *bell'uomo* I found out in the yard," Aunt Julia announced as she pushed him into the house.

Thomas turned back to Annalisa, who stood cross armed in the yard. He mouthed a quick apology and then flashed a smile before the family consumed him.

With a shake of the head, Annalisa followed them in, her face probably as red as the pope's velvet mozzetta. This couldn't be happening.

"Wait a minute," Thomas said, commanding the circle of Mancusos in the living room. "So you're Tony, and you're Tony, and then there's another Tony?"

"Don't forget both Rosemarys over there," her bald uncle Fredo called out, pointing to both Annalisa's aunt Rosemary and her cousin Rosemary.

"Well, this makes it easy," Thomas said. "I'll just call everyone Tony and Rosemary, and the odds will be in my favor."

Fredo smacked his hands together. "Bada bing!"

Everyone broke into laughter.

The Mancusos did not understand the concept of personal space. They swallowed Thomas, kissing him on the cheek, shaking his hand, showering him with questions tickled with an Italian lilt. *How do you know Annalisa? Why hasn't she told us about you? Where are you from? Where did you two meet? How many brothers and sisters do you have?* They wouldn't let him answer before hitting him with more. *What year is your Volkswagen? What does your father do? Are you Catholic?*

She wanted to scream.

When he finally worked his way through the family, shaking hands and kissing cheeks, he found Annalisa. "According to Aunt Julia, it's a kiss on each cheek. I don't want to be rude." Without hesitation, he leaned in, vanquishing her hangover as his lips touched her cheeks.

A flush of warmth rushed over her. Pulling away, she noticed her family watching them, and she slapped a hand through the air. "Enough."

As her family at least pretended to go on about their own business, he said, "You're never going to forgive me for this, are you?" How dare him for being so easygoing.

"Hey, I'm the last of your worries now," she said, determined to take the upper hand. "You just committed to a three-hour dinner with my family."

He looked over his shoulder at them. "What could be so bad about that?"

With a grin of victory, she said, "You just wait." Fate might have forced them together a few times, and Annalisa might have failed in keeping him away, but surely a night with her family would do the trick. Not that she wasn't flattered by his pursuit.

He held up the bouquet of flowers. "Shall we go find your grandmother?"

"Suit yourself." With a grin of warning, she gestured through the dining room to the kitchen. "She's in there." Annalisa's aunts still talked about how terrifying Nonna had been to their suitors growing up. She would eat Thomas alive.

He didn't seem to be as nervous as he should have been as he walked that way—a soldier heading toward enemy fire. After quietly shooing off the rest of her rubbernecking family members, Annalisa followed him into the kitchen to see the fireworks but found herself delighting in the pleasant scent of his cologne as it trailed behind him.

Nonna stood at the stove, stirring a red sauce made with tomatoes that they'd grown in the backyard and frozen for the cold months.

"Mrs. Mancuso?"

She twisted her head in slow motion. "Yes?"

"I'm Thomas Barnes."

Nonna lifted the wooden spoon and knocked it against the rim, splattering a few drops of red onto her apron. Holding the spoon like a sword, she said, "Thomas Barnes." Then she tsk-tsked, looking him up and down. "You're here to call on my granddaughter?"

"Well, I'm here to visit with her, so yes." If he was nervous, he hid it well.

"I see," she said, then mumbled something in Italian to herself.

He stood tall. "I'm honored to meet you. Annalisa has told me wonderful things."

Nonna cut her eyes to Annalisa. "I'm sure she has."

Annalisa wanted to say that she'd never encouraged Thomas and that she hadn't been hiding a relationship, but she didn't want to embarrass or hurt him.

He held out the flowers and stepped toward Nonna. "These are for you."

To Annalisa, she said, "He's a charmer, isn't he?"

Dangerously so, Annalisa thought, but she gave an I-wouldn't-know shrug.

Nonna set the spoon on the utensil rest and reached for the flowers. Thomas and Annalisa watched silently as she moved about the kitchen, arranging the gift in a vase and giving the flowers water. Once she'd set them on the windowsill above the sink, she asked, "Are you Catholic?"

Oh, here we go. Let the fun begin.

"I'm Presbyterian."

"Presbyterian?" she spat. "That's not a religion."

Somehow, Mr. Sunshine managed a smile. "It was the way I was brought up. I guess there's not much I can do to change that. At least for now."

Annalisa raised a hand. "He's not my . . . we're not . . . dating, Nonna."

Nonna didn't break her stare, and Annalisa almost felt bad for Thomas. "Do you have a big family?" Nonna asked, completely ignoring Annalisa's statement.

He laughed at that. "No, not like this."

Nonna crossed her arms and nodded, as if she'd proved her point. After another long and silent stare, she asked, "Are you staying for dinner?"

Annalisa's mouth fell open. She was supposed to run him off, and here she was encouraging him to stay.

Thomas didn't dare look away. "If I'm allowed, I'd be honored."

Nonna clapped her hands. *"Va bene. Mangiamo."*

Yes, let's eat, Annalisa thought, *and get this over with.* Because she sensed unfamiliar and dangerous feelings slithering into her heart.

Chapter 7

A Determined Young Man

When the family came over, which was often, they'd set up card tables and chairs across the house, as the dining-room table would only seat eight. Annalisa and Thomas sat on one end of the main table with Nino and his cheerleader girlfriend. Per the usual, the great tenor Mario Lanza sang from the record player in the living room. If there were ever room for one more person to join the trifecta of Sinatra, JFK, and the pope on the wall by the front door, it would be Lanza.

As usual, Nonna never sat and would appear from the kitchen with another dish, set it down on the already full table, and then march up and down the line like a general addressing her troops as they shoveled food into their mouths.

Despite the evil eyes Annalisa shot her grandmother's way, Nonna wouldn't leave Thomas alone. She kept demanding his attention and saying, *"Mangia, mangia."*

He already looked white faced when Nino scooped two more baseball-size meatballs onto his plate. "Let's go, Davenport Eagle," Nino said. "Show us how Presbyterians eat."

"No, really," Thomas said, waving him off. "I can't eat any more."

"What? You don't like my food?" Nonna called out, marching toward him as if he'd broken rank. The entire dining room went silent.

Annalisa grinned at him as he shook his head back at her, as if to say, *What have I gotten myself into?*

"Nino," her grandmother called out, "give him more sauce. That will make it go down easier."

Waving the idea off, he said, "No, it's not that at all. It's the best meal I've ever had in my life. I'm just . . . so full."

"Nonsense," Nonna demanded. "You want to take my granddaughter out, you eat until we clear the plates. I spent all day cooking."

"He doesn't want to take me out," Annalisa insisted, realizing that Nonna might see Thomas as a way to keep her in town. Was that why she'd been so welcoming?

"I really do," Thomas said, his words coming out like he was tasting a Calabrian chili pepper, curious about the heat level.

Well, guess what, Thomas, Annalisa thought to herself. *It's hot. Burn-your-mouth hot. I'm not who you think I am, and you don't want to take me out.*

A round of laughter rose up from the table. Nonna, on the other hand, stood stone-faced, waiting for Thomas to continue.

"Enough," Nonna said to everyone, and the room went silent. "Thomas, you eat until we clear the plates."

As more laughter followed, Thomas glanced at Annalisa pleadingly.

"Don't look at me," she said, unable to wipe away her smile. "You asked for it." *You asked for all of this,* she thought.

Like a boxer pushing up after a near knockout, Thomas picked up his fork. The color left his face. He cut the giant meatball and stuck a bite into his mouth. Everyone watched.

Thomas swallowed and then made a show of closing his eyes and enjoying the flavor. "Yummm . . . so good," he said.

Of course it was good. No one cooked better than her *nonna*.

"Nino, give him more *sugo*," Nonna ordered.

Nino chuckled as he spooned even more marinara on top of the meatballs and spaghetti.

"More, more," Nonna said, flapping her hands. "You like the garlic, right, Thomas?"

"I love garlic," Thomas muttered, flashing a look at Annalisa. "Matter of fact," he said, "will you please pass the bread?" He crammed another bite into his mouth.

Even Annalisa giggled this time. She had to admit he was a pretty good sport.

Thomas wiped the sauce off his plate with his bread. "I don't know if I'll be able to fit inside my car, but it's worth it just to see your smile." He was brazen enough to say it so that the whole table could hear.

"What a smooth talker," Aunt Julia said. "I think you're adorable. Annalisa, green light! Green light!"

Annalisa cut her eyes to her aunt, promising a word or two later.

Nonna stood behind Thomas. "Make sure you save room for *il dolce.*"

Thomas swallowed and queried Annalisa. *"Il dolce?"*

"Dessert," Annalisa whispered. This was too much fun, but she was starting to feel bad for him.

"Yes, dessert," Nonna said, finally letting out her own smile.

Thomas looked like he was going to vomit just as badly as she had the night before, and that was when she realized she needed to stand up for him. "Okay, everyone. Can we not watch him eat? You're embarrassing him."

Everyone in both rooms raised their voices, telling her to relax in two languages.

Thomas made it through another meatball and two slices of bread before he raised his napkin in the air. "I surrender. Please don't think any less of me. It was really wonderful. I'm just not used to eating so well. My mother likes to make chowder, but not this much of it."

"Well, that explains why you're so skinny!" Uncle Michael said.

Thomas looked directly at Annalisa and said almost heroically, "I did save room for dessert, though."

She refused to look away from him. It was almost competitive, the way he persevered.

"That a boy," Nonna said, uncrossing her arms. She clapped her hands, and half the people at the table, including Annalisa, stood and cleared the dishes.

When Annalisa returned, she put a tray of cannoli and a jar of cherries on the table. Someone had turned the volume up on the record player to mark the arrival of dessert, and Mario Lanza belted out "Night and Day."

Annalisa put two cannoli onto a plate and scooped the delectable cherries over them. "Nonna cans these in whiskey every season." She lowered her voice. "If you eat enough, you might catch a buzz."

Thomas rubbed his forehead. "Don't tell me this kind of eating is normal."

"This is every weekend. Want to come back tomorrow for leftovers?" As soon as the words left her mouth, she wanted to bite them back.

"Sign me up," he said.

Was he ever going to give up this chase?

She took pity on him: "Next time, start out with small bites; take your time."

"I see that now," he said with raised eyebrows. "Wait, are you saying there might be a next time?"

Annalisa shook her head and made a face at him. "I don't know what I'm saying." She really didn't. Never had she been more confused. A small part of her—a minuscule voice in her head—was telling her that he was someone special and that she'd be crazy not to give him a chance. Another voice, much louder, screamed, "Remember what your father did to your mother!"

Nonna hovered over Thomas while he tore through two cannoli. His face turned even paler than the vanilla crème inside. What Annalisa noticed was the pride and perhaps approval that her family showed.

Nino would have been shot dead had he brought home anyone other than a Catholic Italian girl.

When they all rushed to Thomas to say goodbye in the living room, Annalisa was reminded how lucky she was to have such a large family. It was a fact she so easily forgot, but in this moment, she felt their love and support and knew that she might not have made it if it weren't for them surrounding her with love after her parents had died. She thought of what Nonna had said back in July.

He was my son! My son!

Similar to when he'd arrived, the entire family pressed their faces against the window as Annalisa walked him to his car through the cold night.

"I had such a good time," Thomas said. "Really. Your family is incredible."

"That's one word for them." But he was right.

"Seriously, you're so lucky."

An itchy awkwardness filled the space between them, and it felt like the end of a date—not that she'd ever been on one. "Yeah, I guess I am."

He stopped near his car and waved at everyone in the house. To endure the Mancusos, he must be different from every other guy out there.

Returning his attention to her, he said, "I'd love to see you again."

Instead of a joke or turning to hide her blush, she found his hazel eyes, which were as green as shamrocks, and said, "I'd like that."

That he looked pleased would be an understatement.

They held eye contact for a long time. Would it be so bad if she let her heart lead? He might even be good for her painting, give her new feelings to explore.

Annalisa finally said, "Okay, can we stop giving them a show now? No hug—it's time for you to go."

He looked so purely happy, as if all he'd ever wanted was for her to throw him a scrap of attention. She liked the look on him, this sense of satisfaction. It was a good thing her family was watching, because otherwise she might have kissed him on the cheek.

"Could I have your number?" he asked, hitting her while she was weak.

No matter how strong she could be, there was no way she could reject him. Finally giving in, she asked, "Do you have a pen in your car?"

"I do indeed," he said, lighting up. He produced a pen faster than she'd ever seen a human move in her life. As she wrote her number on the top of his hand, she felt that same surge of energy as she had when they'd touched in the car.

As he cracked open his door, he said, "Call you soon, okay? Have a good night."

"Yeah, you too." Her body tingled as they shared one last connection. Watching him pull away, she wondered if this was the feeling that girls always talked about when they fell in love.

⁓

A while after everyone left, Nonna entered Annalisa's bedroom in her long nightgown. "How long has he been—"

"I haven't been seeing him," Annalisa assured her grandmother. "We keep running into each other; that's all."

Nonna nodded as if she believed her. "He's a nice young man."

Annalisa sat up, surprised. "He is, isn't he?"

Holding up her pointer finger, Nonna said, "But he's not for you."

Annalisa rested her back on the wall in defeat. "He showed up. What do I do? Julia is the one who invited him in. You invited him to dinner."

"I was being nice." Nonna touched her own chest and said with exhaustion, "I have a bad feeling about this. Makes my chest heavy. He's not like you. He's from Davenport."

Annalisa bit her lip, unexpected tears heating her eyes. In a whisper, she said, "I know, but . . . I think I actually like him."

Nonna moved toward her and said softly, "It's a wonderful feeling, isn't it? One day, Anna. One day you'll find a man who is perfect. Like Nonno was for me." She sat on the edge of the bed and put her hand on Annalisa's foot. "I know it's hard to hear, but I am truthful because I love you. It's nice to meet people that are different from us, but when it comes to settling down, it's always best to choose someone with strong similarities."

If you have to choose anyone at all, Annalisa thought. "You're probably right." She felt herself deflating, like a bike tire that ran over a nail. Her feelings for Thomas were dangerous and could upend everything—only to prove Nonna right down the line.

"I'm happy to see you smile," Nonna said, "but I don't want you to get hurt. Now, please get ready for bed. No skipping church again."

Annalisa nodded, thinking her graduation in May couldn't come soon enough. It wasn't Nonna she needed to get away from at all. It wasn't even the Mills.

It was Thomas. If she wasn't careful, her feelings could brick wall her career. It wasn't hard to figure out how it could happen.

Annalisa lets herself fall for Thomas. She loses her creative edge, maybe stops working as hard. Starts painting butterflies swarming in fields of lavender. Graduation comes and goes, and she decides to stick around, maybe until Thomas graduates. She paints some, but has lost her fire. The next thing she knows, she's trapped in his blue picket fence—or whatever color he'd painted it—with a stack of empty canvases and unfulfilled aspirations.

She couldn't let her mother's dead-ended path become her own.

Chapter 8

The Drive-In

After the school bus dropped her back home Monday, she found Nonna sitting at the small two-top table in the kitchen. If her grandmother ever took a minute to get off her feet, it was either here or her recliner in the living room. Above the table hung a calendar with a portrait of the Virgin Mary. Aside from the occasional doctor's appointment, the calendar was mostly filled with Nonna's obligations to the church, such as feeding a new widow, or providing flowers for the altar, or contributing to a bake sale.

"What's going on with you?" Annalisa questioned, studying the jagged lines on her grandmother's forehead.

Nonna shook her head, ignoring the question. "How much homework do you have?"

Annalisa couldn't stand it when her grandmother got into these moods, so she tried to lighten her up. "Seniors don't have homework. Something about spreading us too thin."

Nonna removed her glasses and set them on the table. Playing along, she said, "*Bene.* I have a long list of chores. What would you like to start with? The toilets and sinks need scrubbing. You know where the Clorox and gloves are."

"Actually," Annalisa said, continuing their joust, "I have more homework this year than ever before. I don't even know if I'll have time to paint this afternoon."

"Oh, is that so?" Her grandmother let out a smirk that might have required a magnifying glass to detect.

"You wouldn't believe it," Annalisa said sarcastically, "algebra, biology, reading. I have to finish *The Great Gatsby* tonight."

"*Tonight?* Didn't you just start it?"

"I know! And I don't even like it, what with Jay's absurd obsession with Daisy. I'd honestly rather scrub toilets."

Nonna rolled her eyes. "I bet you would."

Annalisa put her arm on Nonna's shoulder. "I'm just kidding. Can I paint for a little while, and then I'll happily do chores all the way to dinner?"

The phone rang.

Nonna pointed to the living room. "Yes, you can paint for an hour, but answer the call first."

The phone rested next to a starched doily on a wooden table between her grandmother's recliner and the couch. Lifting the receiver to her ear, Annalisa said dutifully, "Mancuso residence."

"Annalisa, is that you?"

She instantly turned into a statue, as frozen as the statue of the Virgin Mary staring back at her from the cabinet by the television.

Thomas.

Nerves shot off like fireworks, sparks working their way up her legs like fuses. She eyed Mother Mary and mouthed, "Stop looking at me." Then to Thomas, "May I ask who's calling?"

He announced himself as if she didn't know.

She sank down on the couch covered in plastic, her grandmother's way to ensure the furniture would always be brand new. Whenever Annalisa made fun of it, Nonna would say, "Italian men put too much grease in their hair."

"Oh, hi," she replied. Casual, not a care in the world, as if he were the fourth boy to call this afternoon.

"I was hoping you'd like to go to a movie tomorrow."

A flash of excitement straightened her spine. "Um . . . uh." She looked toward the kitchen to make sure Nonna hadn't poked her nosy head around the corner. There was no evidence of eavesdropping, but Annalisa couldn't be too careful.

Filling the silence, he said, "They're showing *Alice's Restaurant* at seven at the Davenport Drive-In. It seemed fitting for some reason."

Alice. He was funny. She could almost hear Mr. Sunshine's smile, enjoying his own joke. "You'll never let that one go, will you?"

"I couldn't resist. So have you seen it?"

"Not yet . . . the one with . . . ?" She bought time in an attempt to wrangle her racing thoughts. Her conversation with Nonna the previous night was still fresh in her mind, but she had a strong urge to accept his invitation.

"With Arlo Guthrie. What do you say? We'll have fun."

The voices in her head went to war. *Do it. Don't do it. What's wrong with a little date? Everything is wrong with it!* She liked him, though; she really did.

Remembering the napkin he'd waved in surrender at the dinner table, she smiled. A boy so committed at least deserved a date. "Yes, I'd love . . . I mean, I'd like to."

As they made arrangements, Annalisa debated whether to tell Nonna. A little fib might be best. After ending the call, she returned to the living room. "That was Christina, asking if I could go to a movie tomorrow after work."

Nonna turned, one eye squinted in skepticism. "Christina, huh?"

"Please, Nonna. They're showing *Alice's Restaurant*, a comedy." Nonna knew next to nothing about movies, so Annalisa didn't expand further. She certainly wasn't going to mention the movie starred Arlo Guthrie, who'd performed at Woodstock a couple of months earlier.

"How stupid do you think I am?" Nonna asked. "I hear when my granddaughter sneaks out, and I know when a boy calls."

Annalisa's eyes turned to silver dollars. Nonna knew she'd sneaked out?

"That's right," Nonna said. "You think I'm hard on you, but I let you get away with a lot. You can go to the movies with him, but no more lies. Promise me."

Annalisa almost denied the allegations, but then she realized what a gift her grandmother had given her. That little bit of slack was the biggest hug in the world. She found it hard to do anything but love her grandmother in that moment.

"Thank you. I promise, no more lies. And I promise I'll be careful with him."

Nonna pointed at her. "Don't say I didn't warn you."

⌒

Annalisa fondly remembered watching *Easy Come, Easy Go* and *Paradise, Hawaiian Style* and a long list of other Elvis movies at the Bangor Drive-In with her mother. Her father couldn't stand the King, so going to the movies was an unspoken escape. She remembered cuddling with her mother under a gray wool blanket, a texture she could still feel, the Yves Saint Laurent perfume her mother wore still lingering. Annalisa could still hear both their gasps when Elvis first appeared.

As the sun fell over the Davenport Drive-In and the previews lit up the giant screen, Annalisa and Thomas laughed hysterically at the people scrambling out of the trunks of cars. They'd do anything to avoid the two-dollar admission. Annalisa recalled it all from Bangor: the swath of light shooting from the projector to the screen up front, the fogged-up cars with kids making out in the back seat, the savory smell of buttery popcorn wafting through the air.

With a bag of popcorn between them and drinks in their hands, they chatted away as they waited for the feature. "What makes you want to be a dentist?" she asked. "Don't they have a high suicide rate?"

He finished chewing his popcorn. "Yeah, I heard that, too, but I'm not sure it's true. I caddy for a dentist at the club. A really good guy, a good dad. Only works four days a week, home by five, always has time for his two boys. All I want is to give my kids a good home life; it's the one thing I've always craved. I must sound so vanilla to an artist."

"I think it's sweet." Had she just said that out loud? It *was* true, though; he was sweet. What if she'd been wrong about love?

When they looked at each other, she saw a genuineness in his eyes that felt like a warm pair of socks for her heart. He said, "I don't need our big house and our Hinckley and our cabin up north to be happy. All I've ever wanted is a normal life. A wife and kids, a nice neighborhood. Maybe a sailboat, but it doesn't have to be the biggest on the water. And—"

"If you say a white picket fence," she interrupted, "I'll hurl . . . again." She wasn't exactly joking.

"No, I don't want a white picket fence. What about a . . ." He paused to think. "What about a nice blue picket fence?"

She reached for a handful of popcorn. "You are so in the car with the wrong girl."

"Why is that?" he asked, sliding his eyes toward her with his Mr. Sunshine grin. "If you don't like blue, I'll let you pick the color. You're the artist."

Popping a couple of salty kernels into her mouth, she thought that this notion was *exactly* him. He seemed so flexible, like he'd do whatever it took to include her in his life, even if that meant changing his plans—or the color of his fence.

A few minutes into the movie, Thomas turned to her and rested his arm over the back of the seat. When he leaned toward her, completely abandoning the story on the screen, she thought she saw her heart leap out of her chest, break the window, and go scrambling out into the night.

"If I haven't made it clear yet," he said, "I want you to know that I like you a lot."

Annalisa held her nervous hands up to the portable heater plugged into the ashtray. "Is that right?"

"You make me laugh," he said. "Even when you're not trying to. Even when I'm back in Davenport thinking about you."

How was she to respond? If only her mother were here to see Annalisa acting all squirmy and girlish. Celia Mancuso wouldn't know what to do, her daughter always the one shooing boys away. Studying the warmth that seemed to coat Thomas's face, she thought her mother would be delighted at the news.

"You're the one girl in all of Maine I can't wrap my head around, and I love that about you. All the girls at Weston are so . . . into themselves and so shallow. You are . . ." His sincerity couldn't have been more evident as he paused to find the right words. "You are so complicated, in a good way, I mean. I feel like you don't stop questioning things while so many around here are so quick to accept what they're told."

She raised her eyebrows. "You can say that again."

"So where does your curiosity come from? Is it the artist in you? And your drive and passion . . . I wish I had something I wanted as badly. Seriously, I don't mean to blow smoke. I look up to you, Annalisa."

Realizing she was smoothing her hands in front of the heater with such speed that they might spontaneously burst into flame, she pulled them back and rested them on her lap. "I don't know where it all comes from," she finally admitted. "Maybe because I feel like I have something to prove."

Thomas studied her eyes, as if he were searching for answers. He finally whispered, "I think you've proved it."

She knew it was coming. The way he was looking at her, taking a quick peek at her lips, zeroing in on them, his head inching her way. It was the moment before jumping off Braden Rock into the lake back in Bangor, standing there looking down at the cold water, the exhilaration surging through her body like electricity, taking her breath away.

"You're one of a kind, Annalisa," he said softly. "One of a kind."

His other hand went to her waist as he leaned in, and she almost jumped at his touch. Then their lips met in what was her first real kiss, and her worry inside washed away like it had never existed.

—

For the first time in a while, Annalisa peered through the windshield of Thomas's VW at the movie screen. They were about ten rows back.

"Is this still the same movie?" she joked.

Thomas cracked a grin as he looked up. "Arlo's still up there, so I think so."

Having not stopped talking—except to meet lips—they'd missed most of the feature. Annalisa looked toward his door and at the speaker, which he'd turned down almost all the way. "Let's just hope my grandmother doesn't quiz me when I get home." Annalisa wagged her finger. "Or I'm sending her after you."

He ran a hand through his hair. "I don't get the feeling she keeps up with the latest releases, so I think we're safe. That being said, if she comes after me, I will run very, very quickly."

She conceded his point with her own smile. "If it's not *General Hospital* or *Days of Our Lives*, then she's clueless." He was so easy to talk to, Annalisa thought, like she'd known him forever.

At the same time, she felt like she'd just hopped off a motorcycle after racing down the highway, her hair blown back, her legs quivering. What had she done? Was this okay? She almost felt guilty, wondering if she should be back home in front of her easel.

"Tell me more about this dream of yours to go to Portland," Thomas said, twisting her way and putting his arm back over the seat.

"It's not a dream," she assured him. "It's happening. The end of May."

"Ah." He slumped, as if she'd just broken his heart.

"What? You don't believe me?" She heard herself take the offensive, like a tiger who'd just been challenged in the wild.

"Are you kidding me? I wouldn't dare doubt you. I just hate the idea of adding more miles between us. What is it about Portland exactly, though? I'm just wondering."

Annalisa told him how it had always been on her mind, but Jackie's urging had given her the final push. "That was the day you stalked me in the museum. I'd just left her gallery."

He looked at her the way she stared at a captivating painting.

"Are you even listening to me?" she asked, laughing. "Will you quit with the eyes?"

"I can't help it." He pushed a strand of hair away from her face. "I'm just wondering why you made me work so hard. You and I . . . we're good together. I could talk to you forever. Why did you do everything you could to keep it from happening?"

Annalisa looked at the screen. Arlo Guthrie was behind bars, talking to a cop. She had no idea why he'd been arrested. "I guess I don't believe in happily ever after. Or maybe even true love at all. How's that for a reason?"

"It does present a challenge, doesn't it?" He didn't look discouraged, though, more curious than anything else.

A puzzling thought came to her. Admitting she didn't believe in love felt like saying she didn't believe in gravity after an apple dropped onto her head.

With his right arm still over the back of the seat, Thomas reached his left hand toward hers. "You shouldn't be afraid of finding love."

She turned more toward him, enjoying the tingle of his touch. "Says Mr. Sunshine and Picket Fences. Of course you believe in love."

He pulled her hand up and kissed the tops of her knuckles. "All I'm asking is . . . quit resisting."

She looked at her hand in his. "This doesn't feel very resistant."

"No, I guess it doesn't." Then, in a whisper, he said, "I'm not going to hurt you, Anna. I promise."

If he wasn't the real thing, then he was the sneakiest guy she'd ever come across. As her doubt fell away like bricks tumbling from a wall, she felt a need to explain herself. She pulled her hand away and sat back. "One of the last memories of my father and mother together was when he stumbled in drunk after being gone for a few days. He liked to take these weeklong sabbaticals from being a part of the family. I was sitting in a chair, talking to my mom while she painted, when he burst in and started yelling."

Annalisa could so clearly see her father's face, his thick mustache, his raging dark eyes. "He grabbed the painting she'd been working on from her easel and cracked it on his knee. I can still hear the wood of the frame splintering. And then he held the canvas in front of her face and tore it, so slowly and deliberately. I ran at him and he flung me to the ground. My mom rushed to me on the floor. Then we watched him rip another painting off the wall. He tore that one up, too, and then another, and another . . ."

"I can't imagine," he said, giving her hand a light squeeze. "You deserve nothing but to be loved."

Why was this memory still so fresh and painful? But even so, she felt comfortable telling him, like he was the only one in the world who could understand. He said he couldn't imagine, but he could. His father wasn't that different.

After a long breath, she said, "He was always so opposed to her doing anything other than raising me and cleaning the house and cooking. She would have been a great artist if he hadn't killed her dreams."

"For what it's worth," Thomas said, "I'll never kill your dreams, Anna. I wouldn't dare."

She offered a close-lipped smile. "Well . . . now you know what you're up against."

He pressed his forehead against hers, and she smelled his popcorn breath as he said, "We can't let our fathers affect us for the rest of our lives, you know? What about all the great love stories out there? Don't you want to feel what that's like?"

She pulled her hand away. "Oh, you mean like Romeo and Juliet? That ended well."

"We're different," Thomas insisted, not letting her make light of the conversation.

"We barely know each other," she replied, seeing that imaginary apple on the ground. "We aren't even a *we*."

He straightened. "I want to be."

She had no doubt about that, and as her heart kicked, she knew she wanted the same thing. It wasn't that easy, though. There was her mother, who'd been burned so badly by love. And Nonna, who not only was opposed to this relationship but was still suffering herself from losing her husband.

And yet . . . Annalisa knew she couldn't walk away from this guy, because she'd regret it for the rest of her life. So if she wasn't going to walk away now, then she better jump right into the fire.

"Okay, then," she said, leaning in. Tapping into her own confidence, in both herself and in her decision, she grazed her lips over his cheek and whispered into his ear, "Let's be a *we*."

Time seemed to slip away after that, and then a light flashed inside the car. "Okay, girls and boys," a voice said. "Time to go home."

They both looked up to see the credits rolling on the screen.

"Not yet," Thomas complained as he fished the keys out of his pocket. "I'd kill for a double feature right now." He went in for one last kiss, and she felt how excited he was that she was giving them a real chance. She was excited too. Annalisa Mancuso had her first boyfriend.

He started the VW and pulled away, following the car ahead of him. They didn't get far before hearing a snap and pop.

"Oh shit!" Thomas yelled. "I forgot to take the speaker off."

They laughed like crazy as he backed up, and she thought that even if they didn't work out, tonight had been worth it.

Chapter 9

DODGING BULLETS

After the night at the drive-in, her paintings took on a lightness that she used to avoid, almost lovey-dovey with butterflies and pastel colors and big silly hearts, all the result of the flighty feeling dancing in her stomach. Annalisa didn't think Jackie would think much of this phase as her voice, but for the moment she didn't care. The lighter colors and mood were a welcome change from the somber paintings she'd done since her parents' deaths.

They saw each other four more times in the following two weeks, twice including his sister. Though her fear—of potential heartache, of not heeding Nonna's warnings, of letting him get in the way of her art—seemed to follow her growing attraction to him like a black sedan in the rearview mirror, she committed to giving in to their relationship. She kept thinking about how happy Nonna's life had been with Nonno. Not all couples ended up like Annalisa's parents.

Surely there were great artists out there who had made their best works while bathing in these same feelings of love. She'd been painting nude women lately, mostly conjuring them up from her imagination after emulating a few Goyas she'd discovered. It was obvious she was wrestling with her own sexuality, knowing that with each time they were together, she and Thomas were moving closer to going all the way.

Not long after parking in a secluded spot on Sebago Lake on the Sunday before Thanksgiving, she let Thomas take off her shirt and continue where they'd left off at the beach a week before. A cold wind blew through the cracked windows, but the heat between them kept her warm as he encroached on her side of the car. Sly and the Family Stone played on the radio. She was not passive and matched his cravings as she pulled him into her, letting out moans that she couldn't control. It felt like it was only a matter of time before she'd take the next step with him.

When he slipped two fingers into her waistband, though, she felt her entire body turn to steel.

She grabbed his hand. "Stop. I . . . no."

"What's wrong?" he asked.

She couldn't have said exactly what caused this sudden rigidity. Was it her grandmother's warnings? Could it really have been a result of witnessing her parents' marriage fall apart? Or did it have more to do with their deaths? Was this a symptom of grief?

Thomas's hand felt like an impostor down there, and she was uncomfortably vulnerable. She was well aware that the unwieldy traffic lights in her head—the red and green randomly changing at any given moment—were as confusing to him as they were to her.

Collecting her thoughts, she said, "I'm not ready, okay?"

"No rush here; don't worry." He showed no frustration as he respectfully kissed her on the cheek and reached for her hand, assuring her he would stand by her no matter what.

She didn't want him to think she didn't like him. That wasn't the case at all. Trying to turn her mood around, she pulled two beers from the bag behind them. "Let's go explore."

They put on their clothes, pulling on jackets and gloves to fight the cold, and walked hand in hand along the trail wrapping around the lake. The sun dropped down behind the mostly leafless trees and painted the water the color of tangerines.

He talked about his family, saying that his parents had asked to meet her soon. "They want me to bring you to the country club," he said, "but I keep putting it off. I hope you don't feel like I am trying to keep you a secret. It's the other way around. I'm trying to keep *them* a secret."

"I know that. Don't worry." She almost said, "Don't feel like you need to force it," but let the thought go. She did want to meet them—eventually, but the idea rattled her nerves. The last thing she needed was more people like her father in her life.

"So, Emma," she started, feeling comfortable probing deeper into his family's life. "What's going on with her? You said she's been down for a long time."

He picked up a stick and tossed it into the water. As the splash shot out a ring of ripples, he said, "She almost killed herself."

"Oh, gosh, I'm sorry, Thomas." Annalisa hadn't actually tried to hurt herself, but she'd certainly thought about it after her parents had died.

He faced her. "Mitch saved her."

She'd originally met Mitch at the game, and he was the one who had found Nino in the crowd to report Thomas was taking her home. He was in advanced infantry training at Fort Polk in Louisiana, so she had yet to see him again.

Thomas kicked a pine cone, and it rolled farther down the trail, settling at the base of a tall fir. "At least we think she was about to. The three of us were at my family's cabin up north. I'd talked her into coming, just to get her out of the house. We woke up after that first night, and she was gone. Mitch and I split up and searched everywhere. He found her standing on the edge of a cliff—like a deadly one-hundred-foot drop—and she looked like she was going to jump. He brought her back."

Annalisa slipped her arm around Thomas's waist. "That's so sad. I hate that she'd ever feel that way." Emma's and Thomas's pain filled her heart. "Did you tell your parents? She might need some help."

He sighed as he gazed over the tangerine water at a flock of wood ducks landing near a fallen tree. A violet hue shaded the edges of orange sky. "That's not the way my family works. No daughter of Bill and Elizabeth Barnes needs to seek help. We're the perfect family." A humorless smile lifted his lips. "Absolutely perfect."

On December 1, Annalisa sat shoulder to shoulder with Emma and Thomas in a booth that offered a view of the small television resting on top of the Coke machine at the restaurant next to her work. The River Place was a small joint, mostly takeout. Three girls in matching red T-shirts stood behind the counter, taking orders. Behind them a giant menu offered all types of fried seafood in various combinations.

The other diners who had filled the six tables were glued to the CBS broadcast of the first draft lottery since 1942. On the far right of the screen, a large whiteboard displayed rows of numbers that would soon be populated with birth dates drawn from the bucket of blue capsules waiting in the center of the stage. The men in suits looked somber as they waited to begin.

Annalisa pushed her basket of fried clams and french fries away. The savory smell was tempting, but she was too unsettled to eat. It wasn't just Thomas's birth date being drawn tonight. Three of her cousins were eligible as well. Thomas promised her he was safe because of his 2-S student deferment, but his assurance wasn't enough to ease her mind. The idea of losing him to the war was terrifying.

She'd heard talk of some deferments going away because of both the Selective Service's attempt at making the draft more equitable and also the dropping number of enlistees due to the explosive antiwar sentiment. Though Thomas didn't agree with Annalisa's worry, the government could pull his deferment at any minute.

When Alexander Pirnie, a congressman from New York, drew out the first capsule, Annalisa wrapped her arm around Emma. Thomas wasn't the only one whose life was on the line—and that was what it was. She had been hearing horror stories for years, long before she was even old enough to understand them, about men dying or being wounded in the war.

To her left, by her soda, was a piece of paper with all her cousins' birth dates on them. Unlike Thomas, though, her cousins had no way to get a deferment. A low number for them was pretty much a death sentence. Thankfully, Nino was still too young.

Mr. Pirnie handed the blue capsule to another man in a black suit, probably someone from the Selective Service. The man cracked open the capsule and spoke into the microphone, "September 14."

Emma glanced over, and Annalisa squeezed her shoulder tighter. Not unlike Annalisa, she wasn't eating. Annalisa suspected her excuse that she'd snacked before they'd left the house to be a lie. You can't fool someone who'd walked in the same shoes.

The cashiers and the patrons in line and every diner in the booths went quiet, a silence that screamed of all that they'd been going through since the war had begun. Everyone in that restaurant—heck, everyone in Maine and even the entire country—was trying to go on about their lives like things were normal, but they weren't. Nothing was normal. This war was a shadow no one could ignore.

Annalisa glanced at the piece of paper. Everyone she loved was safe for now, but then she thought of all the men who'd been born on September 14, who had just been clipped at the knees, all the men who would be sent off to fight a war that more than half the country didn't believe in. She could feel all of them, their hearts either frozen or roaring.

"I don't know if I can watch this," Thomas admitted, stirring a fry in ketchup. He looked like he had a stomach bug. "Three hundred and sixty-four more capsules . . . Jesus. Maybe we should get out of here."

Annalisa shook her head. "No, this is important. We can't walk away and pretend it's not happening. What do you think, Emma?"

As Annalisa had noticed previously, Emma had an uncanny ability to completely check out from a situation and was startled when she realized they were staring at her. "What?"

Annalisa caught her up. "I think we need to stay; don't you?"

Emma clasped her hands under the table and rocked back and forth. "You're probably right."

It was a long, agonizing event, this draft, and Annalisa listened to each date as if they were playing Russian roulette, the muzzle of a gun pressed to each young man's temple. The three of them quieted, caught up in the action on the screen, only the occasional glance at customers coming and going.

Thomas was born on November 6. When they selected a date close to his, Annalisa felt like someone had struck her in the back. Tears welled up in her eyes, showing her just how much she cared for him. Emma looked equally worried.

Thomas turned to both of them. "Close one, huh? Don't worry, guys. They've never taken anyone out of Weston."

Though he may well have been right, as Weston was one of the best schools in New England, it didn't make Annalisa feel much better. She closed her eyes and said a prayer, promising God she'd never miss church again if He would keep Thomas and her cousins out of this war.

During a commercial, after sixty capsules had been drawn, Thomas excused himself to the restroom. Annalisa was still uneasy, but at least he and her cousins weren't in that first group. From what the talking head had said, maybe only half the numbers would be called in the following year.

Emma stayed close to Annalisa, their shoulders touching. She said, "You seem like you've come a long way toward liking my brother after not being into him at the game."

"Yeah, well . . . I wasn't. I mean, I'm . . ." Annalisa took the opportunity to be honest. "My home life was pretty tough before my parents died, so I don't have much belief in happily ever afters. Would you believe he's the first guy I've ever kissed?"

Emma's eyebrows pinched together. "Really? But you're so pretty. Don't guys ask you out all the time?"

"That's very nice of you, but I make it pretty clear I'm not interested." She raised her hand as if she were giving an oath. "I'm not the dating type and never thought I'd have a boyfriend."

Emma scratched the table. "Me either. But he's persistent, isn't he?"

"The most persistent," Annalisa said. "And you know what? Unless you know something I don't, he seems like a good guy."

Without a moment's hesitation, Emma said, "Every girl in Davenport is jealous of you right now; that's for sure. As far as a brother, he's the best." Out of the blue, she looked sheepishly toward the restroom door and said, "Can I ask you something? Don't tell Thomas I said anything, okay?"

Annalisa touched Emma's arm. "Of course."

"How are you so confident and happy? You and my brother seem like nothing ever gets you down. I'm . . ." She stopped and shook her head.

Annalisa took her hand this time. "I am flattered that you think that, but . . ." She pointed to her own head. "There's a lot going on in here. I'm still very much torn up over how my father treated my mother, and how she let him walk all over her. As far as the crash, I think about it all the time. Every day."

Emma's eyes, like little moons, begged for a better answer. "How do you do it then? It's like you just bounced back from all that."

"I guess I'm good at hiding it." She wanted to offer Emma some advice but wasn't sure what to say. Then it hit her, and she chose to be completely transparent. "No, that's not exactly true. If it weren't for my painting, I'm not sure I would be here. To be honest, your brother's had something to do with it too."

She could see Emma's wheels spinning and asked, "What's going on with you?" She saw a younger Annalisa in Emma, the one who'd put her hand on the casket of her mother's grave and wished that she'd been in the car with them when it crashed.

"I don't know," Emma admitted. "I'm having a hard time. I feel so trapped at home, but I have nowhere to go."

Having been in this spot, Annalisa thought maybe she could help. "What are you passionate about?"

"I don't have any passions." Her voice was monotone.

Annalisa wasn't sure that was true. "You like music, right?"

"I like listening. I don't play."

Annalisa saw Thomas come out of the restroom. "Your brother's coming back. Why don't you come over sometime? We could paint, if that interests you, or listen to music, or whatever."

"Really?" Emma looked like Annalisa had just handed her a bag of cash.

"Yeah, totally." She patted Emma's arm. "How else am I going to get the dirt on your brother? We'll get him to drop you off."

As the two girls attempted to hide their smiles, Thomas appeared at the end of the table. "What are you girls talking about?"

As Emma got up to let him in, Annalisa said, "Girl stuff. I think Emma might come over sometime."

"What?" He turned to his sister and with a big smile said, "She's my girlfriend. You can't hang out with her without me."

"Says who?" Emma replied, showing a flash of the confidence that she needed so badly.

They turned to the television as the commercials ended and the next capsule was drawn. Annalisa glanced at the American flag drooping in the background behind the men and women conducting the draft. She wondered if America would ever be the same again. Would it ever return to the days she'd heard about from her family, the easy fifties after the Great War, when everyone was happy to be alive?

Another man drew the capsules now. He handed one over to the guy from the Selective Service calling out the dates. He peeled open the small sheet of paper and read it like he might read the fortune from a cookie.

"November 6."

Annalisa lost her breath. She turned to Thomas, looking for his reaction as she studied his frozen profile. He was number *76*, a number that nearly guaranteed that he'd be called.

Before she could say anything, he took both Emma's and Annalisa's hands. "I told you guys. It's not a big deal. Don't worry. I'm not going to be the first student at Weston to be drafted."

Emma's eyes swelled with tears as she said, "I hate this fucking war."

"Me too," Annalisa and Thomas agreed at the same time, awkwardly chuckling at her bad language.

Annalisa asked, "What if they stop deferments? They wouldn't take away those who already have them, right? They'd just stop offering new ones?"

"Yeah, exactly," Thomas agreed, sounding almost certain. "If you want something to worry about, Anna, think about meeting our parents." He tapped Emma's arm. "Right, Sis?"

Emma whispered, "Yeah," as she reached for her Coke. Annalisa could see how badly the idea of losing her brother to the draft had bothered Emma, which was understandable. He'd stayed at home as opposed to enjoying dorm life just to protect her. It was quite possible that Emma loved her brother more than Annalisa ever could.

Looking past Emma, Thomas and Annalisa locked eyes. Worry colored his face, and it had nothing to do with the draft. It had to do with the love he felt for his sister. Eventually, he would have to leave her, and she'd have to learn how to fend for herself.

Breaking the silence, he said, "Actually, my mom asked about meeting you again yesterday, so I promised her next week. Is that okay with you?"

Annalisa slid her hand to Emma's. "You'll be there, right? From what Thomas has said, I'll need some support."

Emma looked at her. "I'll do the best I can."

Tenderness seeped into Annalisa as they put their eyes back on the television. Seven numbers later, her cousin Michael's birth date was drawn.

Chapter 10

THE COUNTRY CLUB

A few miles past the quaint downtown of Davenport with its art galleries and seafood restaurants, and another five miles past the pristine grounds and hallowed halls of Weston College, stood the Davenport Country Club.

As Thomas found a spot in a parking lot full of fancy cars, Annalisa looked out over the snow-covered fairways dotted with tall firs and wondered if she might bump into a Kennedy or a Rockefeller here. When they climbed out of the VW, even the bitter cold couldn't zap her nerves. Couldn't they have met for a simple lobster roll in town? She worried her red holiday dress might not be fancy enough or her one-inch heels tall enough.

The main building was a white monstrosity with a seemingly never-ending porch lined with rocking chairs that made Annalisa think of words like *tradition* and *exclusivity*. She wondered how many deals had been made in those chairs. Upper-crust Boston and Manhattan accents rang in her ears.

"How long have you worked here?" Annalisa asked Thomas as they climbed the steps to the grand entrance, which was flanked by two bronze statues of golfers holding the finish of their swing. As a gift to the Barnes family, she carried a white box with a red ribbon holding a panettone that Nonna had baked.

"I've been dragging bags since I was fourteen," Thomas said. "Maybe thirteen, actually. This is my second home."

She heard a tremor in his voice and stopped him by grabbing his arm. "I'm the one who is supposed to be anxious here."

"What?" he said, looking at her like she was crazy. "You have nothing to worry about. You're the best thing that's ever walked through these doors. I just hope my parents behave."

"If they don't, I won't hold it against you, okay?" She kissed him. "Not too much, at least."

Thomas ushered her through the doors to the lobby, and Annalisa's eyes went straight to the Christmas tree, which might have rivaled Rockefeller Center's in size, though she'd never been to New York, to be sure. A sparkly gold star rested at the top. Her nerves turned to excitement. She was a sucker for Christmas.

Thomas seemed to know everyone, and they spent the first few minutes after having their coats checked making small talk with other members. Then he guided her into the dining room.

A man in a tux played "God Rest Ye Merry, Gentlemen" on a shiny black grand piano. A well-dressed and talkative crowd sucking down fancy cocktails with stirrers poking out of them packed the bar. In the dining area, candles twinkled in the center of each table, which were covered in bleached-white tablecloths. Beautiful garlands with bells and red ornaments hung from the walls. Pots spilling over with poinsettias rested under the windows that overlooked their own private cove. She saw one lone light out there on the water and wondered who would be crazy enough to go out in this cold.

"There she is," a woman said, appearing from the crowd near the bar. She balanced a martini with two olives in her hand, and Annalisa saw an abundance of Thomas's features in her. "After all this time. Where has Thomas been hiding you?"

"Hello, Mrs. Barnes, it's so nice to meet you." His mother seemed nice enough, a far cry from intimidating. Maybe this wasn't going to be too bad after all. Annalisa offered the gift. "I brought a panettone from my grandmother. It's an Italian tradition during Christmastime."

Mrs. Barnes took the box. "Please thank your grandmother for me. That's very sweet."

"Not too sweet, though," Annalisa said. "My *nonna* doesn't put a lot of sugar in hers." She let out a nervous laugh.

Emma stood beside Mrs. Barnes in a long blue dress and said hello. Annalisa offered her best smile. "You look beautiful," Annalisa said. "I hope you're still up for coming over soon?" Then Annalisa shielded her mouth from Thomas and said for only Emma's and Mrs. Barnes's ears, "And to tell me all of Thomas's secrets."

Emma rewarded her with a grin. "That might take a few hours."

Annalisa winked at her. "Then we'd better get started. How about right after Christmas, before school starts back up?"

"Sounds good."

Mrs. Barnes smiled at their little tête-à-tête. "I'm so glad you two get along. Thomas isn't always so lucky with his girlfriends."

Emma turned to her mother. "That's because they're mostly ditzes."

Bill Barnes was still wiping off a smile from an apparent joke with buddies when he left the bar and thrust out a hand to introduce himself. "Great to meet you. Welcome to the club."

This is going to be easy, Annalisa thought, as she met his eyes and shook his hand.

He was dressed in nice slacks and a sweater with the logo of their country club. His thinning hair was combed creatively to cover up a bald spot. Thomas had told her his father could be charming, and he was right. Bill wasn't as good looking as Thomas, but they shared the same confident smile, and he was comfortable making eye contact. Annalisa thanked him for having her, and he said it was his honor.

The early conversation was a breeze, and she and Thomas told the story of meeting each other at the museum and then reconnecting at the football game.

"Oh, I didn't quite realize you were from Payton Mills," Mrs. Barnes admitted. "For some reason, I thought you might be attending Weston."

Annalisa side-eyed Thomas. He hadn't told them?

"I thought I mentioned it," Thomas said.

Mr. Barnes cleared his throat in apparent disappointment. "Not to us."

As the pianist began to tease "White Christmas," Annalisa pulled at the tablecloth dangling over her lap. "I'm a senior at Payton Mills."

"Ah." Elizabeth dabbed her lips with a napkin.

"The good ol' Mills," Mr. Barnes said sarcastically.

Saving the conversation from going downhill, Elizabeth—between giant gulps of her martini—told the story of how she had met Bill (to Annalisa it sounded more like a formal arrangement, but she laughed with the rest of them). Then Emma opened up (or, more accurately, poked her head out) and talked about the Stooges, whom she'd been listening to lately.

Annalisa felt wealthy—and slightly guilty, considering what her family might think of her in this moment—as she followed everyone at the table in ordering an appetizer and then a main course. She went for the seafood bisque and the haddock with asparagus.

Just as Annalisa wanted to whisper in Thomas's ear that this wasn't so bad, the conversation took a turn for the worse. It was as if they'd dispensed with the pleasantries, and now that food had been ordered, it was time to swipe the charade off the table.

"Annalisa," Bill said, "into which colleges have you been accepted?"

She heard an agenda in his tone. "Not any, actually. I . . ." She didn't want to admit that there was no money for college. Her father had amassed severe debt by the time he'd died, so she had no inheritance, and the rest of the family certainly didn't have the money. That was none of Mr. Barnes's business, though. "I'm an artist, a painter, so I didn't think college would be necessary."

"I see." Making his own assumptions, he said, "I hear they toss scholarships around like candy to you Payton Mills kids. I'm surprised to hear you wouldn't take advantage. Surely you have more to learn as far as art goes."

"I'll always have more to learn; that's for sure." She wondered how the other guests would feel if she sprang across the table and stabbed Bill with the crab fork, or whatever they called that stupid shiny silver fork in the lineup to the left of her plate. How quickly the energy of the table had changed.

"She's moving to Portland," Emma said, saving her.

"That's right," Annalisa admitted. "I'm finally breaking out of Payton Mills and moving to the city."

"To do what?" Bill asked. "What does one do without a degree?"

She deflected his jab. "I'm not convinced an artist needs a degree."

"Oh my," Mrs. Barnes chimed in. "How brave of you. What kind of things do you paint?"

Annalisa flashed a smile, thankful to talk about what she loved. "I moved to acrylics a while ago but learned with oils from my mother. I'm hoping a move to Portland will help me home in on my voice."

"She's very talented," Thomas said, giving Annalisa a boost.

She gave Thomas a smile of thanks and then continued. "I'm looking forward to city life. Exploring, you know. Being independent." As if he were listening in on the conversation, the pianist started an extra-lively version of "Jingle Bells."

"Without a degree," Bill mused, "but with a brush she goes. That's what the world needs: more artists." He followed his words with a subtly mean chortle that doused out the joy of the melody springing from the piano.

Annalisa stiffened, thinking Mr. Barnes was no different from her own father, who'd said similar things. She heard the patrons at the bar laughing at something, which made her even more uncomfortable.

"Oh, Bill," Mrs. Barnes said. "Leave her alone. I'm sure she's perfectly capable of finding work."

He raised defensive hands. "I was just asking."

"Well, you're living up to your reputation of being a jackass, Dad," Thomas said.

"Thomas," Elizabeth whispered sharply, casting an eye toward the closest table to them, where an older couple sat in silence, probably pretending not to listen in on this escalating fiasco. Then again, Annalisa thought these types of conversations were as abundant as hard dinner rolls in this dining room.

Under the table, Annalisa dug her fingernails into her thigh. "It's fine. They're good questions." She reminded herself that no good would come of going to war with Mr. Barnes.

"Do you intend on marrying and having children?" Mr. Barnes asked. "That's what Italians do, right? Breed and eat and breed. What aspirations does a girl from the Mills have? You want to be the next . . . what? Michelangelo? He was Italian, right?"

"I'm not sure that we Italians all share the exact aspirations," Annalisa said with a bit of attitude, "and I'm trying not to make big decisions like that right now. I don't know. I feel like I've been cooped up all my life. I want to get out and fly, to see the things I've only read about. Maine seems so small to me sometimes. I want to see other cultures, meet other artists." She reached for Thomas's hand, the first time they'd shown any affection in front of Elizabeth and Bill. "But who knows?"

"I see." Mr. Barnes straightened his collar, as if he was ready to return to the bar.

By the time their first course came, Annalisa was miserable and felt herself sweating under her dress. She'd been burned at the stake by questions designed to belittle her. If Mr. Barnes wasn't careful, he was about to see the wrath of Annalisa Mancuso, and if it wasn't for Thomas and her hope for a future with him, she would have already Frisbee'd a plate into his jugular.

Emma was off in space, staring through the Christmas tree into a world far away. Thomas had been doing his best to defend Annalisa, but Mr. Barnes was relentless.

As Annalisa blew at a hot spoonful of bisque, and the nutty aroma of sherry rose into the air, he wiped his mouth. "May I ask about your parents? When did you move in with your grandmother?" She'd mentioned her living situation a few moments earlier.

Oh, here we go, Annalisa thought. If only the rest of her family could see her now. The Mancusos had nothing on the Barneses when it came to interrogations.

Through gritted teeth, Thomas demanded, "Dad, can we give Annalisa a break? This is ridiculous."

"It's fine," Annalisa said, dropping her spoonful of bisque back into the bowl with a ping. "We're just getting to know each other."

"That's exactly right," Mr. Barnes said. "We've worked hard to put Thomas in a position to be successful. It's too early into his studies to be seriously dating. Your age, you fall in love and think you have it *aaalllll* figured out." He carried his "all" so long the soup had probably cooled before he'd moved on to the next word. "Next thing you know you're walking down the aisle without a damn clue, ruining everything you've worked for." He locked eyes with Annalisa. "Do you understand what I'm saying?"

She didn't dare look away.

"I do have to agree with Bill," Elizabeth said, saving the moment once again. "Especially someone with whom you share so little in common."

Mr. Barnes continued to eye her as he stirred his drink, and Annalisa was impressed that he'd been able to keep his mouth shut long enough to let his wife finish a thought.

"Yes, Mr. Barnes, I do understand what you're saying," Annalisa said, her anger flaring. "I know that I'm not the ideal girl for your son, me being from the Mills and all." Finally breaking her glare, she glanced at Thomas. "But I do like him a lot."

"Well, isn't that nice," Mr. Barnes said harshly.

Silence stung the air until Emma began to butter a roll, the knife scraping the porcelain ramekin. Annalisa took a long breath and wished herself away. No wonder Emma excelled at disappearing.

Annalisa felt eyes shooting at her like laser beams. She was no stranger to racism and classism, but staring both traits in the face right now made her realize she'd never been this close to them.

"Feel better, Dad?" Thomas said. "Being an asshole really does suit you, doesn't it?"

"Thomas," Elizabeth snapped. "Your sister."

Annalisa looked at Emma, who didn't seem to realize she'd been mentioned.

"I do feel better, actually," Bill said to Thomas. Then, "I appreciate your candor, Annalisa. As much as I like it *and* your strength, your mother and I do not approve of a serious relationship. It's fine if you want to have a little winter fling, but you two youngsters need to make sure it goes no further."

"Are you kidding me?" Thomas asked, slapping his napkin down and pushing away from the table. He looked at his mother. "Are you really going to let him talk like this? I can't think of two people more unqualified to offer relationship advice."

Mrs. Barnes pointed to his chair with a barely audible "Sit down." She darted her gaze around the room, clearly terrified that they'd made a scene.

"Don't you talk to us that way," Mr. Barnes said.

Thomas put his hand on Annalisa's shoulder and urged her to stand and join him. "Talk to you this way?" he said, the volume of his voice escalating with every word. "Do you hear yourself? You think you can decide who I want to be with? Oh, how *wrong* you are."

Mr. Barnes sat back in disgust, as if the rest of them at the table had lost their minds. "A strong Davenport family breeds well. Trust me; you two will end up destroying each other. I've seen it all my life. Sure, a crush is fine, but once you get to know each other, you'll see you have nothing in common. I'm sorry to burst your little daydreaming bubbles." He pounded the rest of his drink.

Annalisa wondered if maybe her grandmother was right, after all. Choosing not to engage further with Bill Barnes, she looked at Thomas's mother, who stared at her soup like she was trying to part it as Moses had the Red Sea. "Thank you for dinner, Mrs. Barnes."

Moving on to Emma, Annalisa said, "See you soon."

Emma shook her head. "I'm sorry."

Annalisa managed a wink.

Standing, she followed Thomas across the dining room. By now, people had stopped what they were doing and watched the couple take their leave.

Thomas and Annalisa grabbed their coats in silence and spoke only once they were out in the cold under the stars. He turned and took her hand as he marched to the car. Shaking his head in disgust, he said, "I can't believe him."

Annalisa squeezed his hand. "They don't change how I feel about you. It's okay."

"No it's not!" he spat, turning away from her. "Is it really possible to hate your own father? Because that's exactly how I feel. And my mother just lets it all go down. She's so weak. No wonder Emma is losing her mind."

As they drove by the long powdery fairways and the country club faded in the side mirror, Annalisa worried that they both might be into more than they could handle, and it was a long and quiet drive back to the Mills.

When they arrived home, Thomas escorted her in. Nonna sat in the recliner in the living room, watching the news. Nonna's hearing wasn't the best, so she'd cranked the volume, something about Fred Hampton.

"Hi, Mrs. Mancuso," Thomas said over the broadcast, stepping into the living room. "I just wanted to come in and say hello."

"That's very kind of you," Nonna said. A small glass of brandy rested on the table next to her.

As Annalisa went to lower the volume, she heard the newscaster talk about the aftermath of Hampton's death in Chicago a few days earlier. The Black Panther Party leader's controversial death had ignited even more uproar from around the country, the Panthers claiming the FBI had raided Hampton's home and shot him in cold blood as he lay in his bed asleep.

When she turned back to listen to Thomas attempt to charm Nonna, Annalisa was reminded how badly she wanted to leave small-town Maine and all the narrow-mindedness, as had been exquisitely illustrated by Mr. Barnes earlier. How could she keep hiding in this bubble? She wanted to know the truth about what was happening in the world, and the only way to do that was to get out in it.

"My father was a jerk to your granddaughter tonight," Thomas told her. "Quite frankly, I'm embarrassed."

Nonna's shoulders fell. "I'm sorry to hear that."

"I keep telling Annalisa how lucky she is to have family like you." He smiled with closed lips. "Anyway, you guys have a good night. I need to make sure my sister's okay."

Annalisa followed him out and took his hand on the porch. "It's okay," she assured him, noticing the soft sound of the wind chimes.

He turned to face her, his breath fogging up. "I just wish things were different."

"Hey," she said, mustering the courage to take a stance, "nothing your father says affects us. I'm certainly not judging you because of your family."

104

"I appreciate that." He leaned in and kissed her lips. "I'll call you tomorrow, okay? At least we got it over with."

After he'd left, she sat on the couch next to Nonna. The television showed people paying their respects to Fred Hampton as they walked by his open casket in a packed church.

"His dad is a complete jerk," Annalisa said. "And please don't go into an I-told-you-so rant. I don't need to hear it."

"I didn't say a word," Nonna replied, crossing her ankles.

Annalisa told her about the dinner and how they'd stormed out.

Nonna looked her way. "I'm not saying *I told you so*, Annalisa. It's just the way it is. We, meaning our family, our people, have different values from others. That's why I want you to find someone more similar. Maybe someone from the church."

Annalisa rolled her eyes and pointed to the television. "I can't hide in Payton Mills while all this is going on."

Nonna raised her voice. "So you want to be in the thick of it? What good will that do? You might get yourself killed."

Annalisa imagined Nonna had said the same thing to her father when he was her age. "I might find the truth. Or at least hear some other opinions on life." She was still reeling from watching the draft, thinking that it shouldn't be right that men should have to go to fight a war with which they disagreed. And if you happened to disagree in some way, like Fred Hampton, the government would kill you.

"It's a terrible time," Nonna admitted, crossing her arms. "All I can say is that I pity your children, who will have to grow up in this mess."

Annalisa sat up, hearing the plastic crackle underneath her. "My children? Let's hope you're not counting on me for children." She was still trying to work her way through the first relationship of her life.

"I want you to be happy," Nonna said. "That's all."

"Then you have to let me be me. I'm not like the other girls at our church or at school. I want different things."

"Don't you think I know that?" Nonna unfolded her arms. "Why do you think I give you so much slack?"

"If that's true, then support me. Quit jabbing me about wanting to go to Portland. And let me enjoy dating a guy for the first time in my life, without you shaking your head." Annalisa pointed at the door. "He's a nice guy."

Nonna followed her finger. "It appears that way."

"Thomas is different," Annalisa insisted, wanting so badly to believe it. "He's not like his father. Or mine," she added.

Nonna looked over with wise eyes. "I hope not."

Chapter 11

THE BROKEN ONES

Thomas brought Emma over three days after Christmas. Following a quick exchange among the three of them about the nightmare that was the country club dinner, he left the two girls and took his skates to a local pond for a workout. Annalisa couldn't deny that his willingness to drive so much out of his way for his sister was terribly attractive. If he wasn't careful, she might actually fall hard.

Though Emma was growing more comfortable around Annalisa, she was very shy around Nonna when they were introduced. "It's good to meet you, Mrs. Mancuso." Her words fell out of her mouth like stones as she pulled at her green sweater.

Nonna surprised Annalisa by warmly approaching Emma, who was a few inches taller, and looking up at her. "And you, too, Emma. I hope you're hungry." They were in the kitchen, and for the occasion Nonna had made a batch of Italian pastries called *sfogliatelle*, which had filled the house with a delicious candied aroma.

"My brother told me to bring my appetite," Emma said, looking toward the oven.

Nonna smiled at her and patted the girl's cheek. "Always when you come here."

Emma's body instantly relaxed, and Annalisa's heart soared. Her grandmother could be so incredibly sweet when she wanted to be.

Annalisa took her around the house, pointing out her favorites of the pieces she'd done over the years. Either Emma was extremely impressed and interested or putting on a great act. The pieces featured most prominently in the living room were typically from the happier stages of her life. Though she'd never admit to it, Nonna tended to hang the more depressing paintings in less conspicuous spots, like above the toilet. Still, she did hang all of them, which meant something.

Once in Annalisa's bedroom, she said to Emma, "This is my room and my studio. I like to paint outside when it's warm, but this is where I am all winter."

They both looked from right to left: the bed pushed as close as it could be to the closet and then her messy work space with an easel, chair, and a desk splattered with acrylic and cluttered with paint tubes, brushes, palette knives, and color studies.

Emma studied the pieces hanging on the wall, where Annalisa kept her latest works, including two nudes that were still drying. She quickly realized it might have been a good idea to take them down before having a fourteen-year-old enter the room. "Sorry, they might be a bit much for you."

Emma blushed. "My mom would never let me paint these. Nonna doesn't care?" The girl looked at the painting of a nude brunette stretched out on a yellow couch like it was an image of the Loch Ness Monster.

"I'm a little bit older," Annalisa said. "This is part of learning. In fact, every art school has classes with live models who sit nude while you paint them. How about that?"

"No . . . ," Emma said, with equal amounts of shock and excitement.

"Yes!" Annalisa loved this. Emma could be beautiful when she opened up.

Still staring at the brunette, she asked, "Have you had a class like that?"

"Not yet," Annalisa admitted, thinking that the Mills would never offer such a class, even for adults. "But I'm sure I will one day. All these paintings are from books and my imagination. Do you want to paint something? Not a nude but anything you'd like."

Emma finally pulled her eyes away. "Are you sure?"

"Why not?" Annalisa asked. "It's the only thing I'm good at. If you're interested, I'd be happy to teach you."

"What would we paint?" Emma glanced over at the table of paints and brushes.

Annalisa crossed the room and waved Emma over. "I think abstracts might be the best way to start. The less thinking the better for now. Sometimes it's fun just to see what comes out."

Though Annalisa preferred painting on stretched canvas, their financial situation had steered her to heavyweight paper. As Emma sat, Annalisa handed her a smock and took a sheet of paper she'd already primed with gesso and clipped it to the easel. Very often, Annalisa sketched her paintings on a separate pad before mixing paints, but in this case she wanted to keep it simple.

For the next hour, she showed Emma the basics, starting with choosing a brush, applying a color wash, then mixing the paints to obtain the perfect color.

"Let go of any kind of rules for this one," Annalisa coached her. "Just have fun. Nothing matters but finding colors you love and putting them on the page."

"So anything?" Emma looked like she'd been set free for the first time in her life.

Annalisa handed her the brush. "There are absolutely no rules. Well, there is one today. Whatever you do, put your heart into it. But don't worry about what comes out. Just enjoy the motions and fall into the spell."

Emma shed the rest of her nervousness and started to find the meditative beauty of brushing colors across the paper. As the painting came alive in a blast of abstract shapes, the two fell into conversation.

Annalisa knew Emma had some heavy things to get off her chest, so she prodded her enough with her own story until the girl felt very comfortable speaking to her. Emma talked about her childhood first, and all her memories seemed to revolve around Thomas.

"I'm just glad he stuck around," Emma said a few minutes later. "He wouldn't ever admit it, but I know he stayed home for me." Annalisa knew that to be true and was still impressed by his devotion to his sister. Using a fan brush, Emma dragged a streak of turquoise across the top corner of the page.

"Try a little lighter touch with that one," Annalisa said, kneeling next to her. "Can I show you?" She took the brush and used a much more tender motion, the bristles mere feathers. Annalisa noticed Emma gravitated toward circular movements but wasn't sure what to make of it.

Emma copied Annalisa's technique as she let loose more of her inner world. "I don't know what I would have done if he'd left me. Probably run away. My dad doesn't like me, and my mom isn't even awake half the time. You saw firsthand. Ever since she found out my dad was cheating, she's been like that. I'm sure Thomas told you about it."

"What? He didn't, actually." Annalisa was surprised, considering how much they'd shared with each other. Not that Mr. Barnes being a cheater shocked her.

"Yeah, a few years ago," Emma said. "I came home sick one day, while my mom was out of town visiting her parents in New Hampshire. My dad walked out of his bedroom with another woman."

Annalisa touched her arm. "That's horrible."

Emma kept painting, as if the act were as comforting to her as it was to Annalisa. "He tried to keep me from telling her, and I didn't until about two years ago. I just couldn't take it anymore."

Annalisa's mouth had fallen open in disgust. "And that's why you say your dad doesn't like you, because he didn't have the guts to tell your mom himself?"

Emma pulled the brush from the page. "Welcome to the Barnes family. We're like the Cleavers on the outside, but once you crack us open, there's a whole world of crazy to explore. He was the nicest guy in the world for a little while, trying to keep me on his team, until I broke his trust. Then he flipped. On all of us."

Was that why Emma was on the cliff that day? Annalisa wondered. "So when did Thomas find out?"

"I told Thomas first, and then we told my mom together." Emma showed her hurt as if it had happened yesterday. "That was the day our family fell apart. Thomas started hating our dad and started sticking up for me. That's why he didn't move out, to protect me. And I guess to be with me . . ."

"What a good brother he is," Annalisa said. "God, I bet you want out of Davenport as badly as I want to get out of here. Maybe you should come with me."

Emma glanced over. "Oh God, I'd love that more than anything."

Realizing Emma had taken her too seriously, Annalisa backtracked, "As soon as you graduate, Portland and I will be waiting."

Emma deflated. "Yeah, I know. Three more years. Then I'm definitely leaving. I mean, I think so. I hate to leave my mom with my dad alone, but I can't take it."

Annalisa tried to lift Emma back up. "So where would you go? If you could go anywhere in the world after you graduate."

Emma dabbed her brush into the paint and took it to the paper. "If my brother goes to NYU, then that's where I'd like to go. I just have to keep my grades up."

Thinking Emma had to let go of Thomas at some point, she said, "Let's switch brushes." Taking the fan brush from Emma's hand, she dropped it into the water and handed her a small round one. "This is what I use most. If you're steady, you can paint some wonderful detail with this brush."

While Emma tested out an even lighter shade of blue, Annalisa said, "Before New York then, you just need to find something you love to do. I'd be happy to keep teaching you to paint, or you might find something else. Maybe buy a guitar. If you're like Thomas, you can start watching hockey, though I think we both feel the same way about sports." They shared a knowing smile.

There was a knock on the door, and Thomas poked his head in. "Hi, guys. Having fun yet?" He was like a ray of light entering the room.

"You're already back?" Emma said with disappointment. "We're not done yet."

He took a step back. "No rush, sis. I can hang out with Nonna for a little while." He looked at Annalisa for approval.

"Give us a few more minutes," Annalisa said, smiling at her boy-friend. *That's right, her boyfriend!*

After he closed the door, they finished their conversation. Then Emma dropped her brush into the can. "Maybe I could come back and finish it one day?"

Annalisa studied what Emma had done. There was a beauty in the circular motion of the painting and in the colors Emma had come up with. Emma had certainly followed her one lesson: to put her heart into it. "I think there's an artist in you just begging to get out."

Emma loved that comment. "I had a lot of fun."

The two girls hugged, and Annalisa said, "We'll do it again soon."

When the girls left the room, they found Thomas sitting on the couch, talking to Nonna in her recliner. Annalisa wondered if he was slowly chipping away at her grandmother, or if she was holding strong. Either way, he was very sweet to make an attempt.

"Thank you for having me," Emma said to Nonna.

"You're welcome," Nonna replied happily. "Come back anytime."

After walking them out, Annalisa returned to the house, wondering what Nonna was thinking about all this, these two Davenporters in her home. Apropos Annalisa's own opinion, she thought that she had a lot in common with Thomas and Emma, and she enjoyed having them in her life. Both of them gave her a sense of purpose outside of her art.

Back inside, she settled onto the couch. "So? I know you have something to say."

Nonna pointed to the door. "I'd be careful with that one."

"Who?" Annalisa asked. "Thomas? I think you've warned me enough."

Nonna sat up and started to stand. "No. Emma. She likes you a lot. You'll break her heart if something happens between you and Thomas."

"As if I can control that."

Nonna pressed up. "I think it's very nice of you what you're doing, but she's troubled, Annalisa. Maybe more than you ever were." With that, her grandmother disappeared down the hall.

⌒

Thomas returned every few days through the winter, and Annalisa craved time with him. He brought Emma over twice more, and the two girls spent an hour or two painting and chatting while he killed time in the Mills or hung out with Nonna. He always made it a point to tell Annalisa how grateful he was for her help with Emma and that Emma had been in such a better mood lately.

Annalisa painted more than ever, wishing she could leap forward in time to her graduation. She'd been so caught up in the news lately, and in attempting to understand it, that most of her newer ideas came from real life. She captured a group of protesters going up against the police in Boston. Still wrestling with her feelings about the draft, she painted Nixon having his head shaved. She'd seen enough images of soldiers in Vietnam that she painted them, too, imagining their daily lives in a far-off land.

Wishing she had more access to the outside world of art, Annalisa counted the days leading up to the art show in April that Jackie had mentioned, the one run by Sharon Maxwell, the abstract expressionist and teacher at the Portland School of Fine and Applied Art. More than anything, she needed to see and experience some great pieces firsthand. Enough with all the books.

On the third Saturday in February, Annalisa agreed to take the day off so that Thomas could take her skiing. Though she didn't want to lose the money from skipping a shift, the idea of skiing for the first time won out. Besides, between painting, schoolwork, and afternoon and weekend shifts at Harry's General Store, she needed a break.

Wearing her heavy jacket, she slipped out the door and shook her head when she saw that the snow had already covered up the walkway that she'd shoveled an hour earlier. What was the point? At least they didn't have a car, or Nonna would have made her shovel the entire driveway.

Two sets of skis were strapped to the top of his Beetle, and he wore a ski hat and white wool sweater. Jumping inside, she gave him a quick kiss, hoping Nonna wasn't staring out the window. Her grandmother seemed to be coming around as far as Thomas was concerned—at least she hadn't said anything discouraging lately—but Annalisa didn't want to get a lesson about the birds and the bees when she returned that night.

As they left the neighborhood, she said, "I forgot to tell you, my cousin Michael, the one with the low draft number? He enlisted in the navy today." Men with Thomas's birthday had been called up three days earlier, so this was a hot topic between them. Thank God, as Thomas had promised her, his deferment had kept him safe.

"I don't blame him," Thomas said flatly. "Why wait until his number's called?"

Everyone knew that enlisting, as opposed to waiting for a draft notice, gave young men a better chance at surviving the war. Drafted men most often went straight to the front lines in the army, whereas the enlisted men could pick and choose their trajectory, and very often secure a safer path.

"Exactly," Annalisa agreed, wondering if she detected something off in his tone. She noticed he was driving slower than usual too. "So what's going on with you? You know, you're terrible at hiding it when something's wrong."

Thomas cast a serious glance her way. "You won't believe this."

Her excitement about learning to ski hit the floorboard. "These days, I'll believe just about anything."

He didn't speak until he'd reached a stop sign. "My dad says he's cutting me off and that I have to be out of the house by the end of the semester if you and I keep seeing each other. He even threatened taking away my inheritance."

Annalisa's jaw instantly tightened. "What? Are you kidding me?"

He nodded, not moving on from their position. "He says I have to end it by summer, says if I keep supporting this relationship and choose distraction, then he isn't going to support me."

Annalisa threw her hands up into the air as a bitter taste hit her tongue. "How does he even know we're still together? Has he hired a private investigator?"

"No," he said with disgust, watching a car pass by them in the other lane. "I told him. I'm tired of keeping us a secret. And you know what? If he doesn't want to support me, I don't need it."

Was she truly such a bad person, a bad match for Thomas, that his father would attempt to destroy his son's life over it? Screw Mr. Barnes for such judgment. What a small-minded jerk. Could he not see how wonderful a man Thomas was? Couldn't he trust his son's decisions?

"I'm so sorry," Annalisa finally said, wishing life didn't have to be so cruel.

He side-eyed her and nearly hissed out, "What's there to be sorry for? That my dad's an asshole? You have nothing to do with that."

Annalisa kept quiet and ended up staring at the dashboard until he pulled away, driving them away from town. As much as she was giving to this relationship, doing everything she could to let her walls down, it was moments like this that felt like a huge step backward.

The energy in the car tightened with Thomas's anger. Was this how it all began? Were they getting in each other's way?

"What if I transferred to UMPG?" he asked, knocking the wind right out of her. UMPG was the public university in Portland.

"You can't drop out of Weston," Annalisa said, thinking about his deferment.

His forearms tensed as he gripped the steering wheel hard. "I absolutely can. Matter of fact, I couldn't afford it without my parents' help anyway."

Trying to soften him, she placed a hand on his leg and asked quietly, "What about a scholarship?"

He calmed down some. "They won't give me one at Weston, but I can easily get one at UMPG. That's what I'm saying."

Her heart sank at the idea that she might be the reason he lost his dream of dental school or of an inheritance. What if they broke up after moving there? He couldn't change his life because of her. The pressure alone could be like an iceberg poking at the hull of their relationship.

"You'd be foolish to leave one of the best schools in New England— maybe even the country—to move to Portland. And what about your sister?" The trees were getting taller and the buildings sparser.

He pressed down the gas pedal, suddenly racing toward Sugarloaf. "My father thinks I'd be stupid, but from where I'm standing, stupid would be choosing my education and inheritance over you."

She didn't know what to say, flattered but afraid at the same time.

"As far as my sister, she'll support me. She knows I can't live at home forever."

"I'm not so sure." Annalisa felt very strongly that Emma was in no position to lose her brother.

He reached for her hand, and she could see that he was trying to relax. "I love you, Anna, and I want to marry you. I don't care about a degree from Weston."

The L-word and the M-word scared her. She had strong feelings for him, too, no question. He'd shown at every turn that he'd be there for her, but every single day created more vulnerability—with her heart, her career, *his* heart and career, and even Emma's.

Unsure how to chip away at the conflict between her head and heart, she attacked the more obvious point. "What about dental school?"

"I can still get into dental school from UMPG." He let go of her hand to change gears. "Think about it, Anna. You graduate in a few months. I could wrap up the semester and transfer. My deferment wouldn't change. And we could move down to Portland together, get our own place."

It was a good thing he couldn't see her face. She felt like he'd just intentionally swung off the road for a bumpy race through the trees.

He said, "Imagine that. You and I in the city, finally free of all this bullshit."

In theory, the idea was nice, even wonderful, but . . . "I'm not ready to get married, Thomas. I'm not even ready to talk about marriage—not that I don't have strong feelings for you. It's just . . . a few months ago I wasn't even interested in a relationship."

"Things have changed, haven't they?" he said, glancing over. "For both of us. I didn't know I'd find you. The day before I met you, I thought I'd have to leave the state to find my soul mate."

"You weren't *supposed* to find me," she said with frustration. He was right; they were soul mates, but they'd met too soon. "I had everything under control. I had my life worked out."

Thomas shifted down to make a turn. "Well, I'm sorry. What am I supposed to say? It's happened. We've happened. And there's no going back. Not for me, at least. I love you, and my whole life changed the second I saw you in that museum. Sure, we don't come from the same places, and we have a few obstacles to deal with, but I don't care. Nothing is going to stop me. Nothing can stop us."

She gripped her jeans, desperately wanting to tell him how she felt. "I . . . I . . ." She couldn't do it.

"What?" he asked.

Was it this hard to tell a guy that she loved him? The problem was it felt more like an admission out of guilt than it did a gesture of attraction. It was way too heavy a conversation. Annalisa had climbed into his car to go skiing, not to map out the rest of her life. Her mind and heart were in overload. Yes, she loved him, but was that enough? Admitting it could make things worse.

She gave up trying. "I don't know what to say, Thomas. You're the thing I didn't plan for in life, and I do care about you. But we're young. What if we're too young to make such big decisions? What if choosing *us* is the one thing we end up regretting?"

He bit his lip. "I'm not asking you to put me before your career. Is that what this is about? I never would ask that of you. I want to join you in whatever it is you have planned. I get that you're an artist, and that's what gets you out of bed in the morning. I love that about you. That might be my favorite thing about you, but you don't have to choose; that's what I'm trying to say. Let's chase our dreams together. The deal is . . . *you* are what gets me out of bed in the morning."

The love pouring over her was almost more than she could handle, and part of her could have opened the door and jumped out, her body rolling off the shoulder into the safety of a ditch. "I'm afraid."

He put a hand on her thigh again. "I know you are. Me too. But I'm more afraid of what happens if we say goodbye. I don't need my parents' approval. All I need is you. The rest will fall into place."

Would it fall into place? she wondered. He couldn't know that. They could just as easily run off the road into a fiery explosion.

Chapter 12

A U-Turn

A few warm days in mid-March melted what was left of the snow from the blizzard a week earlier. Though that meant mud season was upon them, it also meant Annalisa could start painting outside again.

In preparation for another visit from Emma, she'd rolled out the giant sheet of paint-splattered canvas that she used to protect the brick floor of the front porch. While setting up a second chair to face the easel, she saw the yellow Beetle pulling up.

They exchanged waves as the siblings approached the porch. Setting eyes on Thomas in his Bruins sweatshirt, she thought that she was melting for him just like the last of the snow melted for spring. Forget for a moment the near cosmic physical attraction she felt. The thing getting her was his devotion to their relationship. Undeterred by his father's warnings, Thomas had continued to see Annalisa and kept showing her in so many ways how much he loved her. Sure, his dropping the L-word and suggesting he move to Portland had scared her, but why? What was so bad about him following her? She had to admit that having a partner in crime to join her on her adventure did sound wonderful.

The other tug of her heartstrings was the genuine care he showed for other people, despite his troubles at home. Here he was sacrificing his day, even his time with Annalisa, so that his sister could continue to break out of her shell. You didn't find men like that every day.

He jumped two steps at a time to steal a kiss from Annalisa. "Look at this," he said, seeing her outdoor studio for the first time. "This is where it all goes down, huh?"

"Days like this, for sure," she said, looking up to the sun, feeling its warmth on her skin. She hugged Emma at the top of the steps. "What a nice day to hang out. I'm so glad you're here."

"Me too," Emma responded, and Annalisa could tell she really meant it. In a way, they were each the sister the other never had. As if proving Emma's newfound confidence, she said, "I'm gonna say hi to Nonna, let you two talk for a sec. Be right back."

"Yeah, right on," Thomas said, acting casual. Annalisa could tell by the lightness in his demeanor, though, that his sister's uplifted spirit was a miracle to him.

Once Emma had closed the door behind her, Thomas took Annalisa's hand. "She's coming around, isn't she?"

"Must be the weather," Annalisa said, tracing a shape on his chest.

Thomas brushed her hair away and kissed her forehead. "I think it's you. She really looks up to you, you know. And loves coming over here. You've awakened her."

"I like having her here," she said, thinking she didn't deserve that much praise. "Who else do I have that will paint *and* make fun of sports with me?"

He shook his head at the dig.

"So . . ." Annalisa started, changing the subject, "I have something that's kind of a big deal to ask you."

He cocked his head. "Yeah?"

Pulling her hand away, she crossed her arms and stared into his eyes. "How would you feel about going with me to Sharon Maxwell's art show in April?"

His eyes widened. "I never thought you would ask."

Annalisa hadn't been sure, either, but now she was. It wasn't exactly like committing to moving in together, but it was a big step for her.

She was letting him into her art world. Joking, she said, "Well, I do need a ride."

"Ah," he said, not taking offense. "And here I was thinking you were desperate to hear more of my art critiques."

A laugh leaped out of her. "That too." She kissed him, feeling the sun spraying down on them as if they were in the spotlight of love. "I'm really excited to go with you, seriously."

Just then, Emma came back out to join them. "All right, Thomas," she said. "Time to go. Girls only for a while."

Thomas grinned as he looked to his sister, then to Annalisa and back. "So that's how it is . . . I see. Just let me know if you girls want to talk hockey sometime. I can always hang around."

Annalisa put her arm around Emma. "Bye-bye, Thomas."

The two girls waved at him in sync.

Annalisa could feel how happy he was to see his sister in this way, and he met her eyes one last time before he drove away. Just then, a gust of wind came through and tickled the chimes, and Annalisa's first thought was that she wished her mother could have met Thomas. She definitely would have approved.

As she let go of Emma, Annalisa noticed—and not for the first time—how hard it was for Emma to be apart from her brother, even for a couple of hours. The girl watched her brother's car all the way until the Beetle disappeared. This nearly unhealthy connection—or maybe reliance was a better word?—was a big part of what had worried her when Thomas had suggested he follow Annalisa to Portland. Not that it was Annalisa's business exactly, but Emma would not take it well. Gosh, at this point, Annalisa worried that Emma wouldn't take it well when Annalisa left for Portland. What could she do now, though? Stop inviting her over?

"Ready to get started?" Annalisa asked. She reached for a tube of brown paint and squeezed a blob onto the palette. "I thought we'd practice trees today . . . what with the leaves finally coming back."

"Have these always been here?" Emma asked, clearly not listening.

Annalisa turned to find her mesmerized by the wind chimes. The breeze was still tickling them, and the antique spoons danced around the silver bells. "My mother and I made those a long time ago."

Emma was glued to them. "The sound is . . . so pretty. I love them."

Annalisa took a moment to appreciate them, too, falling back through the years. "That's my mother's spirit you hear."

The girl smiled. After listening for a little longer, she said, "I could sit back and close my eyes and listen to them all day."

"That's kind of what I do," Annalisa admitted, going back to getting the paints ready. "My cousin sucked on a blanket—his *coperta*, he called it—until he was like five or six. That's what the sound is for me, I guess. It puts me right back in my mother's arms. She and I used to listen to them as we painted."

"Imagine what it would be like if there were thousands of them together," Emma pondered out loud. "I bet it would be magical."

Annalisa stopped. She had never really thought about it and loved the idea. The vision came alive in her imagination.

"One day I'm going to do just that," Emma said with a rare and strong determination. "One day I'm going to have an entire choir of them, like a big forest of singing trees, and I'm going to sit out there for hours and listen and let the world go."

The idea nearly made Annalisa cry. She turned back to Emma, who'd closed her eyes to bask in the song. "What an amazing thought."

Emma whispered, "I can hear them now."

Annalisa could too. She put down the paints and approached her, taking her hand. "You're such a beautiful person. And I think that artist inside of you is coming out, isn't she?"

A smile played on Emma's mouth.

She proved to be very talkative over the next two hours, seemingly more interested in chatting than in a painting lesson. That was fine, though.

While layering an imperfect circle with shades of brown, Emma whispered, "What's wrong with Nonna today? She seems kind of sad. Or quiet."

"Nothing to do with you, *or* Thomas," Annalisa assured her. "My grandfather passed away six years ago tomorrow, so she's struggling. She's been wearing black for a week."

Still working the brush around the circle, Emma said, "This is exactly why I'm never getting married. Who wants to go through that?"

"You sound like me," Annalisa said.

"Seriously. All I need is my brother. He's the only one who cares . . . and you, I guess."

"Yes, me. *And* your mom," Annalisa added, uncomfortable with the responsibility Emma had put on her.

"Yeah, I guess that's true. Outside of them, though . . . there is only you. I don't have any other friends."

As Emma kept talking, Annalisa could vividly remember the agony of being so alone. She didn't want that for Emma . . . but was she ready to let the girl count on her so completely?

The wind chimes rang louder in a strong gust of spring air that came rushing up the steps. Was Celia Mancuso up there listening to her thoughts? If so, was she urging her daughter to quit worrying so much?

When Thomas returned, he did as he always did and sat with Nonna as Emma and Annalisa finished up. To Annalisa's surprise and delight, Nonna invited both of them to dinner, which felt like a positive vote for Thomas and Annalisa to stick together—even if it was oh so subtle.

Though Nonna rarely sat for a meal, she did take time to enjoy the company of Thomas and Emma over a giant dish of manicotti. Nonna even laughed when Emma and Annalisa lightly poked fun at Thomas for his love of hockey and his blue-picket-fence dreams. He took it all so well, and Annalisa wondered if Nonna was seeing how wonderful he truly was, a guy who was simply happy to be alive. What better person to have in your life?

When the siblings had gone, Annalisa helped Nonna clean the dishes.

"Nonna," she said, covering the pasta dish with plastic. They'd eat the rest for days. "I think I'd like it if he came to Portland."

Her grandmother gave a brief chuckle as she started on the dishes. "I never could have guessed."

Annalisa put the dish in the fridge and then leaned against the counter to face her grandmother. "I know you think he's a bad idea, but I'm falling in love, and I can't imagine leaving him. Is this how you felt when you met Nonno?"

Nonna looked like she had a lot to say but conceded with, "It was a long time ago, but I'm sure."

Annalisa reached for a rag to wipe the counters. They were a team that had cleaned this kitchen together nearly every day for two years. "I feel so torn," she said, gathering crumbs into her hand, "like something isn't letting me fall for him all the way, but I know he's supposed to be in my life. I'm just afraid. What if we go to Portland together and it doesn't work out? He would have given up everything for me. What if he gets in the way of my career? I can't have that. And I can't bear to think of how Emma would take the news."

Nonna scrubbed a plate. "They are valid questions. And this is why I've been hesitant."

"He's a good man, though."

Nonna acquiesced. "You could certainly do worse, but what will loving him cost you? And what will it cost him and Emma?"

"So you don't think it's a good idea?" She desperately wished Nonna would urge her on, to let go of her worries and chase this love coming alive in her heart.

Nonna set down a plate and stared out the window toward the sky. "I can't know God's plan, and I'm afraid this choice is up to you, *nipotina.*" She frowned and gave a quick shake of the head. "Yes, I worry—just as you do. But I won't be the one who breaks you two apart or tells you that it's a bad idea to let him follow you to Portland."

Annalisa didn't like her grandmother's answer. "What would you do if you were in my shoes? Just end it and move on?"

Nonna resumed her chore, cleaning the next dish. Finally, she said, "No. This is a decision between you, your heart, and God. And this is a part of growing up. I can't tell you what to do, but I will support your decision."

Annalisa stopped. "You will?"

Nonna gave a firm nod. "Your parents and I have raised you to the best of our abilities, and I'm very proud of the woman you're becoming. Whatever you decide will be the right decision."

Annalisa set down her rag and hugged her grandmother from the side. "That means so much to me. Thank you."

Nonna patted her back, but Annalisa could tell she wanted to get back to cleaning. Losing her granddaughter to Portland would not be easy.

But that wasn't enough reason to stay, Annalisa knew. Either choice would have consequences. As she closed her eyes to find the quiet inside, she knew there was no decision to be made at all. Her love for Thomas was stronger than any feeling she'd ever known, and she'd hate herself forever if she didn't fully leap into his arms.

If he was willing to risk it all, then she was too.

Chapter 13

SHARON MAXWELL'S SILVER EYES

When Annalisa first looked at Sharon Maxwell, she felt like she was laying eyes on someone from out of this world. The antithesis of Payton Mills in every way, she wasn't only an artist; she was art itself. Her flamboyant dress made Annalisa want to throw away her own entire wardrobe.

Sharon's long white hair had a streak of purple dye running through it and was held back by a purple headband. She wore giant turquoise earrings that matched the color of her dress, which was more like a layer of fabrics elegantly draped over her generous body. Her large loop scarf was designed with bright peacock feather patterns that didn't quite match the turquoise but worked in the most dazzling of ways.

And her silver eyes and confident smile . . . so soothing. Annalisa had never seen a woman so comfortable in her body and with whom she was as a woman. Her magnetism pulled at Annalisa, literally forcing her to stare as Sharon entertained the people circled around her. She was by no means beautiful but certainly striking, and even Thomas was drawn to her.

It was a few minutes past one in the afternoon, and Annalisa and Thomas had been walking through Sharon's warehouse space off Exchange Street, staring at exorbitantly priced and miraculous pieces—many of them very counterculture and risqué—from all over New England. Annalisa would graduate in six weeks, and then this art life would be her life, and she could barely stand the wait.

They were in the Old Port, which was the sketchier part of Portland, mostly made up of old shipping warehouses that had long stood empty. Annalisa had once joked to Nonna that she would slum it in one of these if she couldn't afford a proper place to live after her move. Sharon made the whole block hip, though, and had transformed the giant first floor into a gallery and studio, making Annalisa both inspired and jealous.

Never had she considered the idea of owning a gallery, despite her mother wanting to open one, but being here now showed the appeal. Sharon had it all: her own abstract works (which Annalisa had decided were absolutely brilliant) hung on one of the brick walls of the enormous room, but on the other walls hung the pieces she'd curated throughout the year. The woman's eye was beyond reproach, and Annalisa thought that maybe the skills of being a great curator could almost match the skills of a great artist. Or perhaps you had to be a great artist before you could be a great curator.

Sharon's studio, which was open for perusing, was an artist's dream. Annalisa began to see for the first time the beauty of abstract expressionism, perhaps because she caught a glimpse of Sharon's less abstract works as well. Annalisa had read so many times that you had to learn the rules before you could break them. It could be said that Sharon had earned her right to chase the abstract after mastering the basics.

"Go talk to her," Thomas said, poking her in the side.

"I don't want to bug her," Annalisa said, feeling butterflies flutter in her stomach as she looked past one of the brick columns that served to break up the vastness of the space.

"What are you talking about?" he asked. "She should be nervous to talk to you."

She slipped her arm around his waist and kissed his cheek and thanked him. "I just want her to ask me to be a part of this show. That's what I want more than anything."

With eyes she hoped to wake next to one day soon, he said, "Then that's what you'll get."

Her mind spun as she saw the prices written on cards under each painting. She imagined such a wonderfully fulfilling life ahead of her, one where she could do exactly what she was meant to do while making enough money to remove the worry about her financial situation. She wasn't ashamed of being poor, but she did crave a world where her decisions were not always based on money in the bank.

In this moment she felt so incredibly fulfilled, both as an artist and as a woman. She hadn't yet told Thomas that she wanted him to come to Portland, but as they'd stridden through the city before the show, and now, as they shared their thoughts on each piece, she was beyond sure she wanted him there. This moment was so much bigger because he was with her.

"Annalisa," said a voice from around another brick column. "So easy to remember, sounds like Mona Lisa." Jackie Burton, the curator with the blackberry hair who'd first told her about this show, approached.

"It's so nice to see you," Annalisa said. "Thank you for telling me about this show. I'm so jazzed."

"Isn't it wonderful?" Jackie dragged her finger through the air, pointing at some of the pieces. "Maybe one day your pieces will be on this wall."

Annalisa touched her own chest, thinking that would be a lottery ticket win for her heart. She introduced Jackie to Thomas, and the three of them moved away from the traffic to speak.

Jackie told them of a few pieces they couldn't miss and then asked, "Have you spoken with Sharon yet?"

"I haven't gotten a chance," Annalisa said, not wanting to confess that she was too intimidated.

Jackie opened up her arms. "You know she's going to start teaching some classes in here? That are *not* affiliated with the college."

"What?" Annalisa felt like someone had just handed her the final piece to the puzzle of her life.

"Yeah, you should sign up. Like right now. I don't know if she has any spaces open, but she's a great teacher."

Forget the intimidation; she was about to bulldoze her way across the room. "Would you mind introducing me?"

"Let's do it." Jackie started directly toward Sharon. Annalisa whispered to Thomas that she'd be right back and then raced after her, thinking that if the classes were full, she'd simply have one of the students murdered. Not in a mean way, a gentle murder without any pain. No way she would miss out on this opportunity.

Jackie pulled Sharon away from the five people peppering her with questions about her work. She looked to be Annalisa's mother's age—if she were still alive—probably early fifties. It wasn't exactly intimidation she felt at all, Annalisa realized. Being close to Sharon was more like being around someone who'd been blessed with superpowers. Annalisa was in awe.

Jackie clasped her hands together and introduced them. "Annalisa has real talent, Sharon, and she's moving to Portland this summer. Are you still doing those classes? And more importantly, are they full?"

Annalisa held her breath as she watched for a tell on Sharon's face, any hint that she had a chance, a ticket to the rest of her life.

Sharon put her hands on her waist and looked into Annalisa's eyes as though she were interviewing Annalisa's soul. She looked at Jackie and then back at Annalisa. "I just so happen to have one more spot available." Even the way she spoke was magical, her voice like the sound of an angel. "If Jackie says you're good, that's all I need to hear."

Annalisa froze. No more jokes about what she'd do to get into this class. This was a very serious moment. A wave of chills ran up her arms.

She couldn't believe what was happening as she swallowed a flood of emotions rushing up her throat.

Unsure how much time had passed, Annalisa came to her senses as Jackie waved a hand in her face. "You in there? She has a spot available."

Coming to, Annalisa nodded like a woodpecker going after a spruce tree. Finding Sharon's silver eyes, she said, "I want that spot."

⸻

"I'd love for you to come with me," Annalisa said, finally taking the leap into love.

They'd stopped on the way back to Payton Mills at a secluded beach Thomas knew about on the shore of Maquoit Bay. Pulling on jackets to fight the wind, they'd left his car along the road and hiked with two beers through a patch of woods until it opened up to the still water. Other than their talking, the only other sound was the birds calling to each other from their hiding spots in the trees.

He sat cross-legged, facing her. "Wait, really?"

Annalisa lay on her side a few feet away, sketching him. She was still high from the show, thinking she'd just met one of the most interesting people on planet Earth and that she had the chance to take lessons from her and that she'd one day show her pieces on that wall, no matter what it took.

There was something else too. She was high on Thomas.

"If you're still interested," she said, thinking he was the only man she'd ever want to walk through an art show with, the only man she'd ever love. She'd be crazy not to give him her all.

He pushed his beer can into the sand. With severe seriousness, he said, "Actually, no. I've decided to stay at Weston. Sorry to bust your bubble, but I love living with my parents, and my dad sure has come around."

Catching his tone, she inclined an eyebrow. "Oh yeah?"

"You betcha. He and I played a round of golf yesterday. Said he was proud of me and profusely apologized for threatening to cut me off. In fact, he asked about you. Wants you to come by for tennis and dinner soon. Says he wants to commission one of your works."

No one could make her smile like him. Even when his jokes were corny, his smile was as sweet as the candy at Harry's General Store.

With her pencil, she shaded in his eyes on the page, wondering if the two of them could go the distance, if those eyes might be hers forever. "Then I guess I'll find some other guy to go to Portland with. I was never into sculptors anyway."

He crossed his arms. "You wouldn't dare."

"I guess we'll see." She shrugged as she worked on the rest of his face. He was easy to look at and even easier to draw.

Jumping right ahead, he said, "So you really want me to join you?"

Her walls crumbled as her subject in this drawing she might call life waited for her to show that she was serious. He didn't have to wait long. "I'm in if you're in."

"Hmm, let me weigh my options." He lifted his hands like they were a scale. Jiggling his right hand, he said, "More years with my pain-in-the-ass, closed-minded father here." He jiggled his left hand. "Or an adventure with you, my dreamy, brilliant, creative, funny, Elvis-loving girlfriend. Who do you think's winning that one?"

Her heart suddenly sprang geysers of pure joy, rising out of her in a smile that melted all her doubt. This was the splash into the water after the leap, and it was everything she'd imagined and more. Forget all the reasons they couldn't be together; forget all the worries she'd had about holding one another back. This was it, the reason for living.

He looked at her with a Buddha-like smile as she said, "You know what it is about you, Thomas Barnes? I can't remember what it was like to be sad anymore. It's like you came in and wiped it all away, and I feel very grateful and lucky to have met you. Why in the world wouldn't I want this to continue?"

He looked genuinely touched by her words. "That's the nicest thing you've ever said to me. That anyone's ever said to me," he added.

"You'd better bottle it," she suggested, "because it doesn't come easy."

He started to push up and go to her, but she held up a hand. "Nope, I'm not done. Don't move." Using her finger, she shaded in his shadow cast by the setting sun, locking in this moment forever.

Her only reservation suddenly goaded her. "We'll have to make it easy on your sister, make sure we include her. You know this will break her heart."

"Yeah . . . ," he said, "but I can't always be there for her. I have to live my life too. And you're right; we'll make sure she knows we still care about her. She can come down whenever she wants. I'm happy to pick her up."

Annalisa sighed, wanting to make sure, as though her doubts had one last stand in them and they needed to be slayed. "I'm all in, Thomas, but I don't want to be responsible for messing up your family."

"Then you know what?" he said, shifting in his seated position. "You shouldn't have been at that museum. You shouldn't have gone to the Eagles game that night. You shouldn't be so . . . you. Because I'm in it now, and I'm not going anywhere. Forget my dad and forget my prestigious education. Right after this semester, you and I are driving down to Portland and not looking back."

There it was, her feeble last stand slayed by his love for her. Nothing was going to get in their way. Except for this piece that she was determined to finish before he moved.

After telling him so, she picked back up her pencil and said as she worked, "But we can't get a place together. Nonna would kill us both. And *stop* moving; you're messing with my light." Of course she was joking, and he went along with it, letting her, like always, put her art first.

He spoke without moving his mouth, like a ventriloquist. "How would Nonna know? And besides, I think she's starting to like me."

Bouncing her eyes back and forth from the page to him, she said, "You can move your lips, dummy. Just stop flapping your arms; I'm almost done. She might like you, but she'd never approve of us sharing a place." Annalisa almost said, "Not until we're married," but she didn't quite let that out. It was okay, though. One thing at a time.

He grinned. "So, seriously, how would she know?"

"How would she know?" Annalisa asked, feigning mild shock from the question. "Have you not met Nonna? We're not talking New York here. Portland isn't that far away. For one, she'll send the family down to scout things out, and I'm sure she'll drop by herself too. No way we're getting a place together." She raced to finish the drawing because she wanted to be closer to him, to let him come her way.

"Okay, fine, we'll get two separate places." He crossed his arms again in obvious defiance. "With adjoining doors. Until we make it legal."

She pointed the pencil at him. "What did I say about moving your arms?"

He pushed up to his knees and started her way. "I'm having a hard time hearing you from over here."

"You're in so much trouble," she said, tossing her pad and pencil to the sand. Who cared about a silly drawing when the real thing was right in front of her?

He crawled toward her, making a big deal of it, almost prowling like a lion. She felt playful, too, and laughed as she played the part of a tigress being circled by her mate. When he reached her, he lifted a leg over her waist and straddled her.

She lay back against the sand, his eyes like slivers of stardust staring down at her. A wolf howled from deep within the forest. Or was it deep within her?

He slowly lowered his head down, stopping an inch from her face. "I love you, Anna. More than you could ever know."

She ran her fingers through his hair and stared into his irises, losing herself in the galaxy of his love. Without a doubt in the world, she said, "I love you too."

Chapter 14

EMMA, THE EXTRAORDINARY

Thomas broke the news to his family that weekend, and it went much like they'd thought it would. As Thomas had relayed to her on the phone, Mr. Barnes had stormed out after a shouting match, assuring Thomas he'd never give him another dime. Mrs. Barnes had finished her drink and poured another. Emma had gone to her room.

Over the course of the next week, Emma refused to take Annalisa's phone calls, and Annalisa had to work hard not to let the Barnes family's lack of support knock her down. She and Thomas had made their choice, though, and as Nonna said, it was theirs and theirs alone to make.

Toward the end of April, after the snow was gone, Annalisa invited herself over to their house for the first time. Try as he might, Thomas was having very little success prying Emma from her gloom, so Annalisa hoped she might have better luck. She'd been there, feeling all alone, and she didn't want Emma to think she'd abandoned her.

It was just a matter of finding a time when Mr. Barnes wasn't home. Thomas suggested that coming Saturday. His father, desperate to get out on the course after the long winter, planned to play thirty-six holes at the club and then would have dinner with his buddies.

Thomas picked her up early in the morning, and as they'd done several times lately, he stopped at an exit to let Annalisa test her driving skills on a quiet country road. She practiced parallel parking between two logs that Thomas had rolled out onto the road. It took her quite a few tries before she finally pulled it off. She rewarded her driving instructor with a kiss and a little bit more before they continued on to see if they could team up to help Emma.

When they arrived, Annalisa found the Barneses' house to be even more intimidating than Annalisa had anticipated. "This isn't really yours, is it?" Annalisa asked as they crunched gravel down the long driveway leading to a big white colonial revival house with tall columns.

"I know. It's almost ridiculous."

Almost? she thought.

Thomas parked on the left side and pointed through the windshield toward the water. "That's Wilby Island out there past the cove."

This was the first time she'd truly grasped what Thomas was losing. He'd told her they were wealthy, which was no surprise considering his father was a lawyer and they lived in Davenport, but seriously. "I can't believe you grew up in this house. Are you sure you want to say goodbye to all this . . . for me?"

He took her hand and pecked her cheek. "If I were an emperor, I'd say goodbye to my entire kingdom for you. What's all this if you don't have the person you love to enjoy it with?" She would have rolled her eyes had he not said it so sincerely. As much as a sports guy as he was, she thought he, like his sister, had art in his soul.

Fair enough, she thought. He won. Again. And she loved it, the idea that he would never waver from his love or their decision. To give this all up for her. What a display of his affection. No, not affection. What a display of his devotion to her.

Leaving the car, they rounded the monstrosity to take in the full view of the cove. A wide expanse of grass turning green after winter looked to have been rolled down like carpet from the house to the water. Annalisa imagined it would take her six hours to mow all of it, but surely they had a team of landscapers. It was a splendid cloudless day, windy but magnificent. Whitecaps collided on the surface of the water. She wondered what it would be like to live here, to never have to worry about money, to wake up with a view of the water. Was it jealousy she felt? Perhaps more craving than jealousy.

Atop a tall pole near the shore, the Maine flag and a yellow-and-blue windsock gently whipped in the wind. Thomas pointed to the sailboat that danced with the current at the end of the dock. "That's our new Hinckley, my dad's pride and joy." She followed his finger to the smaller boat tied to the opposite side of the dock. "And that Boston Whaler Montauk is mine. Well, at least it was. I'm sure my dad will be reacquiring it."

He led her through the side door into the kitchen, where Mrs. Barnes waited with a tray of cookies. "I'm delighted you're here, Annalisa, truly." Her bright-green apron looked like it had never been worn before.

Annalisa took one of the chocolate chip peace offerings from the tray and took a bite. "They're delicious," she lied, thinking that if you dated outside of Italian, you were lowering the bar as far as food was concerned. She tried not to gape as she looked at all the fancy appliances peppering the elaborate kitchen. Nonna would have flipped.

Mrs. Barnes set down the tray. "I'd like to say something to both of you, if you don't mind."

Annalisa glanced at Thomas, who looked as caught off guard as she was.

"I'm . . ." Her eyes reddened. "I'm happy for you both, and I'm sorry for the way Bill is handling the situation. I've tried to talk to him, but he's as hardheaded as they come. Thomas, as I've told you a million times, he only wants the best for you—"

"And he's the best at showing it," Thomas interrupted.

"Let me finish," Mrs. Barnes said sternly. "I'm afraid he doesn't know what the 'best' is. His parents were the same way. They essentially forced him into law school and tied him to a desk at the firm. I'm glad you're going your own way, and I suppose choosing the woman you love is a part of that freedom." She turned to Annalisa, who was happy to hear such sincerity.

"From what Thomas and Emma have told me," she said, "he's lucky to have you, and . . . he cares so much about you. No matter what Bill has to say, I don't want to miss out on my son's future. On both of your futures. I support the two of you in your move, and I'm happy to see that you're so in love. Believe it or not, Bill and I felt that way for a long time . . ." Pain suddenly painted her face.

"Thank you, Mrs. Barnes," Annalisa said, truly touched by her words.

Thomas stepped toward his mother. "That means a lot, Mom. Thank you." They hugged awkwardly, and Annalisa thought that Mrs. Barnes looked terribly lonely, just like Nonna.

After they broke apart, she brushed off her hands on her apron like she was dusting away the past. "Anyway, you two go enjoy yourselves. I just wanted to say my piece."

"Where's Emma?" Annalisa asked. Maybe Mrs. Barnes and Emma were both coming around. "I'd like to say hi."

Thomas started to leave the kitchen and gestured for her to follow. "She's upstairs."

Mrs. Barnes untied her apron, as if her work were done. "She'll come down in a little while."

Annalisa followed Thomas down a hallway, took a left, then a right, then went down another hallway before entering the living room. She almost said that she could fit her whole house in this room, but she didn't want to show how uncomfortable she felt. It wasn't only the house. No matter how many cookies Mrs. Barnes made—or how many confessions she gave—this place still didn't feel warm. Neither the moose head above the mantel nor the watercolors of golf courses helped.

"I've never seen so many pillows in my life," she whispered, studying the fancy furniture that was arranged to look through the large, polished bay windows out over the water. She gawked at the massive oil painting above the couch, wrapped in a gold-gilded frame. It captured a typical Maine day in the fall: sailboats and fishing boats bobbing on the water, seagulls nose-diving into the water, lobstermen dumping their catches onto the deck, the wind snapping the mast lines and rippling the water.

This was exactly what she never wanted to paint: classic Davenport. Impressive but not disruptive. She sat on a couch, noticing its stiffness. She put her hands behind her head and stared out over the water. "So this is what it's like to be Thomas Barnes. What a life."

Thomas sat next to her. "Trade you."

He had a point there. "Maybe for an afternoon, but I can't paint this view."

"And it won't be mine to trade anyway," he added with an uncharacteristic coldness.

Feeling like she was on a mission and hoping she might melt some of the cold in this house, she asked, "Do you mind if I go see Emma? It's really been bothering me. Which one of the fifty bedrooms is hers?"

Armed with his directions, she climbed the stairs and enjoyed a look at Thomas's family photos as she walked down the long hallway that echoed with each step of her boots. When she reached Emma's door, she gave a quick knock. A Beatles record played on the other side.

"Hi, Emma, can I come in? It's Annalisa." Putting her ear to the door, all she could hear was Paul McCartney's voice offering to sing a lullaby.

After a second knock, she said much louder, "Emma?"

"What do you want?" came her angry voice from the other side. "I have nothing to say to you."

It had been more than a week since Thomas had broken the news, and it was clearly still an open wound. "Please, I just want to talk."

When no answer came, she tested the knob and pushed the door open. A sallow-faced Emma sat in a puffy chair in the back of the room next to her record player. Her arms were wrapped around her shins, and she was barefoot.

"I didn't say you could come in," Emma snapped.

"I want to explain myself," Annalisa said softly, stepping farther into the room uninvited. The walls were a mustard yellow, and other than the records scattered across the floor, the room was clean and orderly. She could see the sailboat through the window behind Emma.

"I get that you're hurting," she said, "but I don't want you to think we're leaving you. The first thing we talked about was how excited we were to get you down to Portland . . . as often as you'd like."

Without even a glance Annalisa's way, Emma said, "You're taking him from me."

Not surprised by the accusation, Annalisa took another step, noticing Emma seemed off in some way. Was her anger causing her glazed eyes and slurred speech? "You're seeing it wrong. I'm not taking him from you at all. We're good together, the three of us. Our moving doesn't change that. We'll still see each other all the time. I love your brother, Emma. Surely you can understand that."

"Oh, I understand it all right."

The Beatles song ended, leaving only the crackle of the record. Emma unfolded and put her bare feet onto the rug. "He doesn't even see me anymore since you showed up," she snarled. "He's leaving me and it's your fault!"

"That's not true," Annalisa said, unable to believe this was the same girl who'd painted with her on the front porch, the one who'd spoken of a forest of singing trees. "I've never seen a brother love a sister like he does you, and nothing will ever stop that. There's room for both of us, you know?" Still a few feet away, Annalisa knelt down so as not to be intimidating. Though she was trying to act calm, she was burning inside. "Are you okay?"

Emma turned her glazed eyes her way. "I can't stand you, and I hated painting with you. You're not even that good."

"I know you don't mean that." The girl's words hurt.

The music started up again, the Fab Four singing "Carry That Weight." Emma sloppily pushed up from the seat. Annalisa wondered if Emma was about to attack her. Instead, the young girl wobbled and dropped to the floor.

Instantly terrified, Annalisa rushed to her. "What's going on with you?" The music was so loud suddenly, making the situation even more tense.

Back on the chair she saw a pill bottle, and a tremendous fear seemed to wrap its fingers around her throat. She grabbed the bottle and read the typed print. Under Elizabeth Barnes's name, Annalisa found the prescription: Valium.

Running on adrenaline, she pulled Emma up onto her lap and steadied her face, patting her cheek to wake her. Her eyes were open, but she was long gone. Out of pure instinct, she pushed her fingers into Emma's mouth, feeling and searching for pills.

"How many pills did you take?" she asked.

"What does it matter?" Emma slurred. "I'm not living here alone. Why do you care?" Her glazed eyes rolled into the back of her head. "I'm making it easier on everyone . . ."

Emma seemed to be losing consciousness, and her eyes closed.

"Thomas!" Annalisa screamed, trying not to completely lose it. "I need help!"

She wasn't sure what to do but needed to act quickly. After screaming for help again, knowing this house was too damn big for her voice to carry across it, she decided maybe she could get the girl to throw up. Not that she had any training, but it was worth a try before she left her to find help. Emma rolled over without any resistance, and Annalisa thrust two fingers down her throat.

"Emma," she said desperately, "you have to help me here. You need to throw up."

The girl mumbled incoherence.

"Thomas!" Annalisa yelled, hearing the fright in her voice.

Emma heaved, as if she were choking, and Annalisa pushed her fingers deeper down her throat. Then up it came, Emma's vomit spilling out onto the rug. Annalisa saw melted orange pills and syrupy orange liquid amid the muck.

Knowing there was nothing else she could do, Annalisa pushed up to a stand. "I'm getting help, Emma. Be right back." She raced out of the room.

━

Straight off the golf course, Mr. Barnes came running into the waiting room of the Davenport Medical Center. "Where is she?" Fear and anger gripped his words. A grass stain striped the cuff of his right pant leg, and his golf glove poked out of his back pocket.

Thomas and Annalisa had been at the hospital for an hour and sat in one of the chairs that lined the wall, half of which were occupied by people anxiously awaiting more news about their loved ones. The room reeked of bleach, sickness, and sadness.

Upon hearing Mr. Barnes's voice, they both looked up. Thomas pointed down the hallway to their right. "Room 301. With Mom. She's okay, Dad. Annalisa saved her life."

Mr. Barnes gave a viciously angry shake of the head and ran past the front desk and pushed through the swinging doors.

Thomas slumped over, and Annalisa put her hand on his back. She didn't have much left to say, but she hated that he felt responsible. It was almost all he'd talked about since they'd arrived at the hospital. Thank God, Emma was stable. The doctors had pumped her stomach and given her fluids. She was now talking.

Annalisa felt responsible too. How couldn't she? No, she hadn't given Emma the pills, but Annalisa had known all along Emma wouldn't take the news of their moving to Portland well. She should have been there when Thomas broke the news to Emma. Or maybe she should never have asked Thomas to go in the first place. She felt so incredibly torn apart inside, and her heart hurt for Emma, knowing that she'd taken such a horrific step to end her life. It was an action that would be hard to ever leave in the past.

As they sat there in silence, doubt filled her mind. That morning she was all in, but she couldn't shake seeing Emma's face as she lost consciousness, her vomit spilling out of her mouth.

All Annalisa had to do was to listen to those around her, and none of this would have happened. Nonna, who had no hidden agendas, had warned her. Even Mr. Barnes, who was proving to be right in this circumstance, had told Thomas and her that they should end things.

But no, Annalisa had let her heart steer the way. She'd ignored Nonna and Thomas's parents, and most important, her own rationality, deciding that her feelings for Thomas had to be explored. A lot of good that decision had done. She was effectively breaking this family apart.

She attempted to tell herself, *No, this has nothing to do with me.* If it wasn't for Thomas deciding to leave Davenport, Emma might still have eventually ended up in this hospital. She was fragile . . . and she'd tried to hurt herself once before. That line of thought carried only so much weight.

Pressing her eyes closed, she wished it all away, wondering where Emma might be if Annalisa had chosen not to go to the Cold River concert, or if she'd at least been sensible enough not to drink and smoke herself into a stupor. Even the next day, she could have told Thomas to leave before her aunt had forced him into the house for Saturday supper. Or all she had to do was restrain herself and her little schoolgirl heart from writing her number on his hand. That was what had done it. That was the moment that had switched the tracks of poor Emma's train, eventually bringing her to this hospital while Annalisa had her hand on the back of a guy whose life she was ruining.

No doubt she loved Thomas—and Emma, too, and she knew it because her heart broke for both of them. Seeing Thomas slouched over, his hands covering his face, she knew he was blaming himself, and she wanted to pull him out of it. As if she could. She'd told him it wasn't his fault, that he'd been Emma's only light. Her guilt choked her as she thought about what she was doing to this family, wedging between all of them.

Annalisa wondered if he was thinking the same thoughts, wishing he'd never pursued Annalisa. Or maybe not. Maybe he wasn't questioning their relationship, but he was surely questioning his decision to move to Portland.

She questioned his moving too. As much as she loved him and wanted to be with him every minute going forward, life wasn't that simple, was it? As they'd both anticipated, his going to Portland would have consequences not only for his life but for Emma's too. Her throat tightened, and her stomach ached with guilt as she rubbed his back.

Mr. Barnes burst through the double doors. Without regard for the others who were living similar fates, he screamed, "You see, Thomas. Now you see!"

Every head in the waiting room twisted to him, his angry words piercing the silence. Annalisa felt her body constrict as Thomas looked up with defensive eyes.

Mr. Barnes marched toward them, stopping three feet in front of his son. Pointing at Thomas much like Emma had pointed at Annalisa, he said, "You proud of yourself? Do you finally understand the consequences of your stupid decisions? They're like pushing the first of a long line of dominoes, aren't they?"

Breathing with such fury that he might have a heart attack, he pointed with that same finger back toward the swinging doors. "This is both of your faults."

Annalisa couldn't disagree. Thomas slouched lower.

Mr. Barnes stepped toward them. "All that I care about is that you and your sister succeed. You had everything: Weston, an open door to the firm, but you blow it all for this girl that's *no* good for this family. Look at me, son."

Annalisa was too terrified to stand up for Thomas as he looked at his father with tightened jaws. She felt herself cowering like she'd done a thousand times when her own father had unleashed his fury.

"All you had to do was listen to me," he continued. "I might be a hard-ass, but I've been around the block." He thrust up a finger and spat, "I *know* what I'm talking about."

Annalisa was shaking with fear when she noticed a nurse rushing toward them.

"Excuse me," the short-haired woman said. "I can't have this in here."

Mr. Barnes took a long breath, finally running out of steam. Or so Annalisa thought. He kept going. "You're damn lucky your sister is okay."

Thomas had finally had enough. "How in the fucking world is this our fault, you clueless sack of shit? You are the waste of oxygen that has poisoned this family. How in God's name could Emma grow up normal with a father like you?"

"Gentlemen," the nurse interrupted, "I am going to call security if you don't tone it down and leave my waiting room."

Mr. Barnes's face turned so red Annalisa thought the vessels in his forehead might explode. She put her shaky arm on Thomas, trying to be strong. "Let's go, Thomas."

"No, Anna, it needs to be done." Thomas popped up and got in his father's face, inches from it. His spit sprayed onto his father as he said, "You are the reason my sister tried to kill herself. You and your fucking affair poisoned her."

"I'm calling security," the nurse said loudly, racing back to her desk.

With the last of her energy, her head a spinning blender of fear and anger, Annalisa sprang to her feet. "Thomas, stop it. Let's go." All she wanted to do was run away from all of it, but she had to protect him.

Mr. Barnes whipped his head toward Annalisa, his red and angry eyes burning into her. "You stay the hell out of it, country girl. Had you not showed up, none of this would have happened." His attack was a punch in the face.

As she saw her father in those eyes, she lifted up her hands to protect herself. Just as she did, Thomas took a swing at Mr. Barnes. She saw Thomas's fist meet his father's cheek with a crack that sent the man stumbling backward and dropping to the floor.

Thomas lunged for him, and Annalisa watched in frozen shock as the man she loved jumped on top of his father. Mr. Barnes fought back like a bull until two security guards dragged them off each other.

Trembling, Annalisa watched the guards escort the two men, still shouting at each other, out of the waiting room. When they rounded the corner to the exit, Thomas looked back at her with swollen, defeated eyes.

They stared at each other for a long few seconds—and it felt like a daylong conversation was had between them—not a word uttered, just a stare so dense with emotion that Annalisa lost what was left of her breath.

When the guard finally tugged Thomas out of view, she very much felt like she was the reason his life was caving in.

Chapter 15

A Straitjacket

How do you leave someone who might need you now more than ever? And how do you leave someone that you love so much that it hurts? Those were the questions that plagued Annalisa in the days following Emma's suicide attempt. Nino was the one who ended up giving Annalisa a ride back to Payton Mills that day. She was so shaken up that she barely spoke to him or to Nonna before rushing to her bedroom and climbing under the covers.

For days she cried, feeling like any progress she'd made in the two years since losing her parents was lost. It was as if all the pain she'd felt watching her father scream at her mother and all the sadness she'd felt at her parents' funeral had been dug up and dangled in her face. To think that all she'd done was love someone, and that she'd even tried to help a girl who was going through similar circumstances.

As she went yet another day without eating, without painting, her love for Thomas scraped her hollow insides. Nonna was so kind to her, bringing her food, letting her skip school, knowing she was in tremendous pain.

Other than going to the bathroom, the only time she left her room was to watch the coverage of the Kent State shootings, which seemed to prove how devastatingly awful life could be. Nixon was still breaking his promises, sending more men to die, now even pushing into Cambodia.

Kids Annalisa's age had tried to stand up for what they believed in, which was a right of every American—or at least so they thought. The National Guard had shot them down in cold blood, just like the FBI had shot the Black Panther Fred Hampton.

Why should Annalisa ever get out of bed?

Annalisa had spoken by phone with Thomas a few times. Emma was okay now, safely back at home. Thomas wanted to come see her, but Annalisa told him she wasn't ready yet. She knew he needed her, but she couldn't be there for him.

At night, she could still see Mr. Barnes's eyes glaring at her, his tongue spitting angry words, thrashing her. When she'd finally told Nonna what had happened, her grandmother rolled out a long string of Italian curses, praying that God would deliver vengeance.

After a week of missed school, Nonna gave her a stern talking to, telling her that she had to get back to her life. "All you've talked about is graduating, and here you are, weeks away, and you're hiding. You can't keep lying in bed all day."

"Why not, Nonna? What's the point?" When she said that, she remembered Emma saying the same thing. Oh God, was she on the same path, one of hopelessness and despair? She thought about the poisonous bite of love. Who could blame Emma for shutting down and choosing the easy way out?

When she asked Nonna that question, she responded, "The point is that God will help lift you up, but you have to take the first step."

Annalisa pulled the covers up higher. "And what would that be?"

"You have to get out of bed." As if it were that easy.

It took a few hours for Nonna's advice to settle in, but Annalisa knew she was right. She'd spent so many days staring at her work space, the paints and brushes, wondering what it would feel like to get a brush into her hands, wondering if painting could be the salvation she needed.

Annalisa finally climbed out of bed and knelt. With steepled hands, she said a long prayer, asking God for direction. Nonna was right; she couldn't keep lying in bed. As she pressed up, she turned back to her easel. She had no idea what she would paint, but she knew she had to do something. It was the only way. Though she'd been painting outside all of April, she wasn't ready to be sprayed down by sunshine—or hear the song of her and her mother's wind chimes.

With what felt like great courage, she sat and faced the blank paper clipped to the easel. She stared inside, wishing she could jump into it, wishing she could start over. Finally finding the urge, she chose a forest green and a jet-black and squeezed them onto her palette. Taking her large flat brush, she dipped the bristles into her colors, working them into a deep dark green that felt like greed.

Satisfied with her color, she gathered a generous portion and took it to the canvas. She had no idea what she would paint, but that was okay. Like getting out of bed, she had to take the step of putting paint on paper. Not having done a color wash, she put a long stroke of this dark green across the white. She wished that had been a moment of awakening, but it didn't feel that way. It felt like a waste of paint, a mindless swipe at the enemy.

She painted another stroke and then another, feeling like a ship with plenty of wind in her sails but no compass on the deck. A pang of sadness hit her so hard that she swung her brush at it, spraying dark paint across the paper and rug. Her throat tightened as if she were being strangled, and she swung the brush again and again, a mad Jackson Pollock splattering her entire room.

A primal urge came over her, and she screamed like a wild animal, letting everything bottled up inside rush out of her, both through her mouth and off her brush. This wasn't art, though, and she wasn't making some kind of breakthrough. She wasn't finding her voice with abstraction. What she was doing was losing her mind.

She threw the brush, and it spun like a knife across the room, splattering the covers of the bed and ceiling. With bright-red rage burning her skin, she reached for the easel and flung it to the ground. Then she swatted at the items on her desk, sending her palette with that putrid green and the other paints and the jars of brushes to the ground, all one big crash that signified exactly how she felt inside.

Nonna burst into the room. "What in God's name?"

Annalisa looked at her like she'd just broken out of a straitjacket. Annalisa had no reply, but she knew she'd found her answer. Without any shadow of a doubt, art and love could not coexist.

<hr/>

"You're breaking up with me?" Thomas asked, caught off guard. They were walking along the sidewalk in her neighborhood the next day. He'd tried to hold her hand, but she'd sheathed hers in the pocket of her red gauchos.

Having escaped mud season, they'd welcomed spring. The grass of each tiny lawn had sprung up in brilliant green. Gardens showed sprouts of life. Though her heart was ripped out, a part of Annalisa Mancuso was right there with them, a flower finally coming to bloom, perhaps a flower growing out of ashes.

"Yes," she replied, looking at him like he was a casualty of war. Not the war of Vietnam, no. He was a casualty of the war of love, as so many young couples were. And he was a casualty of the war of art, because she'd been forced to make a decision. Whenever she doubted herself, she thought of Sharon Maxwell. Sharon was in her position today because of an unwavering devotion to her craft.

There was that word: *devotion*. Thomas was no doubt devoted to her, and in almost all ways, Annalisa to him. In fact, she was so devoted to him that she was setting him free because of it, saving his life from getting worse. A few weeks or months later, he'd move on and be glad they'd parted.

Seeing him hurt, though, was agony defined. What did he think Annalisa was going to say when she'd finally called? *Oh, what have I been up to? Just painting and studying, and . . . you know, hanging out . . . the thing with Emma and then your dad screaming at me? No biggie. You and your dad slugging each other? Hadn't thought another second about it. Everything's great. You about ready to leave for Portland?*

It had been two weeks since Emma's suicide attempt, and she was as sure as ever that she loved Thomas—and Emma—enough to put them first. Ending her relationship with Thomas was excruciating, but it was the right choice, the best move for all three of them. She kept telling herself that if you love someone, you must set them free.

From a selfish point of view, Annalisa hadn't painted one single stroke since having her breakdown. So not only was she getting in the way of Thomas's family, but her love for him had stifled her art.

But! And there was a but . . .

As she'd come to the decision to leave him, she could feel the need building back up inside like a volcano rumbling. The paper clipped to her easel with dark-green smears was no longer taunting her. It was pulling her in. She was ready. The only thing stopping her now was ending this relationship and moving on. This breakup hurt, more than she was letting on, but she also felt a sense of pride rising up. She was making the hard choice, but the right one. The Sharon Maxwell choice—the choice Annalisa's mother should have made. No more being vulnerable, setting herself up for further pain.

She had a job to do, a commitment: to herself and to her destiny. She was to go, brush in hand, to Portland and realize her calling. She was to do whatever it took to get onto the walls of Sharon Maxwell's warehouse for an April show.

"Don't tell me you think this is working," Annalisa finally said, crossing her arms, knowing nothing he could say would change her mind.

He was so frustrated that he balled his hands into fists. "Of course I think it's working. None of what happened has changed how I feel about you. And I've thought long and hard about leaving, and I'm still in. I've spent my whole life—or a lot of it, anyway—trying to find you. No way I'm letting you go. Emma will be okay, and she'll find her way—we'll help her. But I want to go to Portland with you. I want us to start our life."

They crossed the street together. "Thomas, you want a normal life with a wife and kids and a dental practice and a picket fence. I can't give you that. Don't you get it?" Maybe that wasn't exactly true, but she needed to put up a wall that he couldn't break down.

"Oh, I get it, and I've already told you . . . I can let all of that go."

Telling him that she couldn't paint wasn't enough, nor was assuring him she wasn't worth the cost of letting go of his family and education—her point proven by his last statement.

When they reached the other side, they swung a left to circle back to her house. "That's what you think now, but trust me, one day you will grow to resent me for it. When we're fighting for having gotten in each other's way, and when you've lost your family for good—and your inheritance—you will resent me." She quieted as they passed a shirtless man putting up a new mailbox. When they'd gotten far enough away, she whispered, "And I would resent you and hate myself."

"Don't you see?" he asked. "You'll never be a great artist until you open yourself up to—"

She stopped and turned to him. "To what? To love?" As brilliant as he was, he was still naive.

"Yes, to love," he said with certainty, nothing short of stabbing her heart with a dagger.

She looked up into his eyes, trying to show him. "Don't you see that I do love you? I love you so much that I'm doing what's best for you and your sister—even if you don't know it." Making the decision earlier had been much easier than telling him now, and so much of her wanted to leap into his arms. But she pushed it all away with the reminder that love required sacrifice.

"It's not your job to decide my life," he argued. "Or to protect Emma's."

She sliced a hand through the air, forcing herself to be strong. "Trust me; one day we'll know that ending us now was the right thing, and I'll always look back on these days, remembering how much I loved you."

He ran a hand through his hair, pulling at it. "I'd never look back at us with regret; that's for sure."

Desperately hoping she was making the right decision, she started walking again. The problem was so much easier to wrap her head around when he wasn't by her side.

As he started to follow, she said, "I'm worried that I would regret us if we didn't end it. Look, I'm making the responsible decision. For both of us. I am going to Portland by myself, and you are going to finish Weston and go on to dental school in New York, and then you're going to find a woman a million times better than . . ."

She stumbled through the last of her words, choking on them. Her heart bled as she said, "Better than me." The idea of Thomas being with another girl was hell, pure hell, and she batted away the thought.

His agony collected between his eyebrows, and his cheeks quivered. "You don't believe any of this, Anna, and I don't know whether it's because of your parents or because of mine—or because you're just afraid—but you *don't* break up with someone you love."

She stopped again and faced him. "You do, Thomas." She took his hand, his touch like that dagger twisting in her heart. "That's exactly what you have to do sometimes."

Shaking his head, he said, "And who makes you the expert?"

"Oh, I'm no expert. But I'm not an idiot either. All you have to do is look at what's happening. Your sister is suicidal and needs you. Your mom probably does too. And you're talking about abandoning them and your education and your inheritance for a girl who can't promise you the things you want. I have to keep painting; that's all that I know right now."

Thomas pressed his eyes and lips closed and let his head fall. She'd crushed him. Who was she kidding? She'd crushed herself too.

After a long breath, he said, "To break up with someone you love is nothing but the wrong decision. In every case. It's never going to be easy. Jesus, Anna. If it wasn't your parents and mine, or my sister, or me leaving Weston, it would be something else."

"Maybe." He should have gone to law school because he sure could lay out a case with emotion, and she was dying inside.

"The thing is," he continued, "when you love someone, then you have each other, and you can face all these things together. That answer isn't in ending us; it's in finding a way through it together."

A tear slid down her cheek. "I don't see it that way. Things change. What if we fall out of love? Then all the destruction we've left in our path will be for nothing. I'm not ready to give up painting, and if we stayed together, I'll lose my drive, and I will grow to resent myself for not being strong right now, and I'll certainly come to resent you. I love you too much to ever let that happen."

His eyes were blue today, and it was the saddest blue in the world.

"Let me go," she whispered, letting his hand fall from hers.

"How could I ever let you go?" He looked like he'd just lost everything.

She couldn't bear to see him this way for much longer. "By loving me that much. I know you do. So let me go . . ." It was the hardest thing she'd ever said.

Her words drifted into the air and lingered like the last notes of a lone piano reverberating at the end of a piece. It was sad as all hell, as painful as losing her parents, but she had to be strong. Dammit, she had to.

By the time they returned to Nonna's house, she was utterly depleted and defeated, a girl so let down by the world and by God.

Standing by his car, he drew in a long breath and let it out audibly, as if he was trying to let out all the pain. Standing only a few feet away, she couldn't look at him and wished he'd just go. Before her legs gave out on her.

"Take care, Anna," he finally said, swinging the ax down on the last of their relationship. He'd finally conceded, and it was over.

She forced herself to look at him one more time. Words wouldn't come, though, as she opened her mouth to speak. It had all been said, and he had to go before she took them all back. She loved him. That was what she wanted to say . . . but she couldn't do that. It wouldn't be fair. Wasn't that ironic? She loved him so much that she couldn't tell him that in this moment.

Finally, tasting the ashes of their love on her tongue, she said, "Goodbye, Thomas."

He turned and climbed into his car, and her tears spilled even before he'd pulled away. She hid herself from him, though, and walked away, using the last of her strength to climb the stairs.

And then he was gone.

She collapsed into a chair on the porch and cried—cried like she'd cried after losing her parents—cried tears that seemed to pull all the life out of her, like a mortician draining the blood from a body. Her lips shuddered with loss, and she hoped to God she'd made the right decision.

The wind chimes pinged lightly above her head. Was her mother affirming her decision, telling her to get up and keep fighting?

Chapter 16

A Goodbye to Remember

The bouts of sadness and loneliness over the next few weeks as she prepared for her move to Portland sent her into a tailspin at times, but she slammed shut the many doors, shielding her gut-wrenching feelings about losing Thomas and Emma from stabbing her.

Staying focused, she painted the image she'd seen of Mary Ann Vecchio kneeling over Jeffrey Miller at Kent State, among others from that awful day. She painted what she'd seen of the Hard Hat Riot and the shootings at Jackson State. Trying to understand both sides of each conflict, she painted the police officers and construction workers too. As hard as she tried, though, she couldn't get into their heads. How could she possibly understand what they, or anyone else, for that matter, was thinking or feeling? Did she really think she could paint from television images?

Nonna would point at the coverage of these terrible events on the television and say, "This is why you should stay here."

Annalisa cataloged each image, desperate to paint them, as she replied, "This is exactly why I have to leave, so I can paint things that matter."

A day after that, Annalisa had slapped her uncle Tony for telling her she better get in the kitchen where she belonged.

How could Annalisa ignore such comments or these horrendous events by staying in the bubble that was the Mills? She didn't claim to understand politics or have all the facts, but at least she could paint them and attempt to feel what it was like to live in their skin.

On the Friday after the Jackson State shootings, while the family was together, Annalisa asked Nino if he would help her hunt for jobs and apartments in Portland.

"So you finally want to hang out again?" he asked, shoving a forkful of orecchiette into his mouth.

"Hey, you're the one who kept pushing me to date someone," she said. "I'm back, though." As much as she did look forward to reconnecting with Nino, whom she'd ignored for the last few months, it would have been nice to make that drive down to Portland with Thomas, to start their life together. As forcefully as Nino had shoved his pasta into his mouth, Annalisa suppressed the thought. There was no good in wondering what could have been.

"I'm sorry," she said to Nino. "It's been a wild few months."

The next day, he took her down to Portland to hunt for apartments and jobs, and it felt almost surreal that she was finally making this happen. *What a long and winding road it has been,* she thought. None of the places she could afford with the money she'd saved excited her. The best of the six they'd looked at was owned by a very questionable character who'd made Annalisa feel sick inside. The other apartments were dirty and rat-infested or located a long way from the action. Considering she didn't own a car, she wanted to be near Congress Street, where she could find constant inspiration.

As far as jobs were concerned, she had no luck finding anything available other than restaurant work. If it came down to it, she would settle for being a server, but she hoped to find something that paid better—or offered some sort of upward trajectory. That way she could afford her art supplies and Sharon Maxwell's art classes, while starting to save at the same time.

Annalisa thought working at a gallery would be the most perfect opportunity, as she could meet other artists and maybe talk a gallery owner into selling her work, but there weren't as many galleries in Portland as she'd built up in her head while in the Mills.

She tried Jackie Burton first, because that was whose walls Annalisa wanted her art to adorn. The curator was thrilled to see that she was following through with moving, but she couldn't offer her a job. Neither could the other galleries Annalisa visited. She didn't even bother showing them her portfolio because she certainly had not found her voice yet. If anything, her relationship with Thomas had sidetracked her.

After a long and unsuccessful day, Nino drove her back home. Feeling discouraged, she wondered if she could make it in Portland. What if she had to repeat this same drive in a few months, a retreat back to the Mills with her tail between her legs? As the challenges of moving to the city presented themselves, she let doubt fill her soul. It was so easy to have dreams, but to actually make them happen wasn't always possible. Though she hated to admit it, some of the dream had lost its luster without Thomas. If he'd been there with her, the challenges would have been more fun to navigate. *Stay strong,* she told herself. Her wound would heal, and he'd fade away, just as she must be drifting from his heart.

By the next morning, she'd pushed her thoughts of Thomas back down into one of the manholes of her mind, and she'd burned all her doubt and was back on track in front of the easel. Nothing ever came easy. If she gave up now, what was the point of any of it?

Two days before her graduation, Annalisa was lost in her world of painting on the front porch, Elvis singing to her through the windows, when she heard the familiar purr of Thomas's Beetle. The sound made her heart stumble like a horse who had clipped a hurdle with her hoof.

She expected Thomas to put up a fight and had been surprised she hadn't seen him since their breakup weeks before. At times, she'd even been sad that he hadn't fought for her. When she'd reminded herself of the determination in Sharon Maxwell's silver eyes, though, she found renewed faith in her decision to move on and was grateful that he was letting her go as she'd asked.

Until now. What was he doing here?

She went to the top of the steps and watched him climb out of the car, suddenly feeling like a rope in a deadly contest of tug of war: love on one side, their separate dreams and opportunities on the other.

A taxi appeared and parked behind Thomas's car, making Annalisa's brow furrow in confusion. Thomas waved to her and then went to say something to the driver. When he finally came her way, she was perplexed.

"What's going on?" she asked, looking past him to the taxi. Late May had brought warmer weather, and she was in short sleeves for the first time that year.

He didn't respond until he was standing right below her, looking at her. "Hi."

All the emptiness she'd felt lately went away as a smile rose on her face. "Hi." It was like he'd just plugged into her and charged her soul.

He bit his lip, then: "I wanted to see if you'd take care of my car. I'm going away for a while."

"What? Where are you . . . ?" Even though she'd ended it, she couldn't imagine him leaving.

He pinched his chin, not breaking eye contact. Whatever it was, it was hard for him to tell her. "I'm shipping off to basic training in the morning."

She felt her chest caving in as she shook her head. "What are you talking about?"

He shuffled his feet, his arms dangling at his sides. "I got drafted, Anna."

She couldn't believe it and waited for a smile to show that he was telling a terrible joke. No smile came.

"What happened to the deferment?" she asked, descending the steps to meet him. He was drafted? He was going to Vietnam? He looked like he hadn't eaten in days, as if he had been stranded at sea and needed vitamins.

"My grades slipped a little lately," he said, avoiding her gaze. "Listen, I didn't come here for any sympathy, just to see your face and to ask if you'd take care of my car. It's not going to do me any good for the next two years."

A pit grew in her stomach. She was right back in the diner when they'd drawn his number, sharing a booth with Emma and him. "Is that how long it is?"

He nodded.

"Why didn't you tell me?" She felt incredibly selfish to have abandoned him when he'd needed her most. "I would have been there for you."

"I know you would have," he said, excusing her with the brush of his hand. "But I didn't want to make you worry. Besides, I thought I could appeal or that my dad could get me out of it. He knows one of the guys on the board. Turns out even a case of Johnnie Walker Blue Label can't get you out of a two-year stint once you've gotten your notice."

She crossed her arms, wishing she could hug him but feeling like she didn't have the right. "What happened to your grades?"

He shook off her question.

Ah, she got it. The answer showed in his eyes. He'd let them slide because of the whole thing with Emma—and, of course, between Annalisa and him. Fresh waves of guilt hit her hard.

"It's been a long month, and I missed a few tests."

Seeing him this way wrecked her heart, and she was sure that all of this was her damn fault. Had she not let the two of them happen in the first place, he wouldn't be standing here with his sights on Vietnam.

"You've done everything?" she asked, feeling his fate like it was her own.

"I'm shipping off to Fort Dix in the morning. It's done." He had a certain resolve about him, as if he'd accepted his path with the same grace he seemed to do everything.

"Will you definitely go to Vietnam?" She'd seen the countless body bags being carried off planes, and her heart burned at the idea of his body being among them.

He shrugged. "No way to know. It took Mitch nine months to get there. After boot camp, I'll have advanced training and then who knows. Maybe the war will be over by then. Or I could get lucky and get shipped to a base in Germany or somewhere safer."

"Oh God, Thomas," she said, her eyes letting loose agonizing tears. She opened her arms to him, and they embraced. She'd hoped their connection had waned some, but touching him, feeling his protective arms wrap around her, was like returning home after years gone.

The English Leather he wore drew her in, reminding her how intimate they'd once been, and now here he was saying a much more severe goodbye than the one they'd shared not so long ago. She cried into his chest, thinking that the love of her entire life might not come home. *What-ifs* blasted through her mind. What if she hadn't broken up with him? What if she'd never said yes to their first date? What if she hadn't invited Emma over?

Eventually letting go, she wiped her eyes. "What about Canada?"

A quick shake of the head. "I'm not running. It's all right. I'm good with it now."

She looked up at the sky, where a cloud slowly passed by. Her mind went to darker places, to the news reports she'd been watching and reading about for years, all the men who never came home. Or the ones who had, but without all their limbs. Or others who'd made it home intact physically but so broken emotionally that they hadn't been able to reintegrate into normal life.

The truth was if he came home, he would come back a different man. They all did.

It was Vietnam.

"Anna, I'm serious. It won't be much different than my war at home. Maybe a few more guns. I'm ready. Mitch is still there; maybe I'll get to see him. I wanted to say goodbye and . . ." She watched a tear slip down his cheek. ". . . and ask if you'd write me," he finished. "I respect that you don't want a relationship, but I'm hoping we can be friends. If you don't—"

The floodgates opened, and she wept for him again. "Yes, I'll write you. Of course I will."

He pulled her back in for another hug.

When they broke away this time, she asked, "How's Emma taking the news?" She mopped her face, realizing that she herself wasn't the only one losing him.

"As you can imagine, she's pretty torn up. I hate leaving her, but I have no choice . . ." He started to say more but stopped. Did anyone love their sister like he did?

Feeling like all bets were off, Annalisa reached for his hand, not wanting to let go, not wanting to lose him. "I can only imagine what she's going through. Life's just not fair, is it? Such a childish thing to say, but it isn't. Just when you think it can't get any worse."

He looked at their interlocked hands. "Tell me about it." Did he feel that same connection? Or was he already off at war, with no more time for love?

"I'll check in on her from Portland," Annalisa promised. "I know she's gonna need someone. Please tell her I'm here for her . . . if she ever wants to see me again."

He offered a smile. "That's very kind of you. I'll definitely tell her. So would ya take care of my car, Anna? You'll need it down there, so you can come back up and visit Nonna."

"I'm not taking your car, stupid," she said, laughing through her tears.

He looked back at the taxi driver. "I've already paid him to follow me all the way here. I'm leaving the car, Anna. Let me do this for you. As a friend."

As much as she didn't want to—as much as she knew that driving his car would crush her—she thought that maybe he needed her to take it. Perhaps it would serve to keep their connection and give him a reason to stay alive and figure out his way back home.

"I'd be honored."

He let go of her hand so that he could dig the keys out of his pocket. Was that the last time they'd ever touch? *Oh God, please take care of him,* she prayed.

Annalisa took the keys and thanked him. She wanted more of him. She wanted to grab his hand again and take him away, to Canada or anywhere. *Please God, don't take him from me.*

"Bye, Anna," he said, attempting to be strong.

"Goodbye, Thomas," she whispered, crying again.

He rubbed his eyes. "I love you," he said, and without forcing her to respond, he turned and walked toward the taxi with his head held high.

"I love you too," she whispered back, not loud enough for him to hear.

Part II

JUNE 1970 TO JANUARY 1972

Chapter 17

BREAKING OUT OF THE CAGE

It took longer than Annalisa had anticipated to find an apartment in Portland, and she was starting to worry that she wouldn't have a place by the time the art classes started on June 30. Nino had taken her to the city four times in May, chasing down leads. She wasn't excited about anything, and she refused to move until it was the perfect place. She had to feel inspired, or what was the point? Of course, even the finest apartment in all of Portland might not give her the inspiration she needed.

Thomas was gone, and he was on his way to war, and she was to blame.

Three weeks after Thomas left her his car, Annalisa got lucky—if anything could be called lucky, considering the circumstances. She'd been scouring the Portland newspaper every day and found a new listing for a small place a block off Congress Street. She called the slightly grumpy landlord and told him she could meet that day. After a little begging (a lot, actually), he reluctantly assured her he wouldn't show it to anyone else.

She could feel Thomas's presence in his car, and she wished that he was with her. Time and distance and even the brighter and warmer days of summer had done nothing to soften her love for him—if anything, it was growing stronger—and she found it so incredibly hard to shake the idea that he was supposed to be here. What if she'd never broken up with him, despite Emma and his father and her fears? Then maybe his grades would be okay, and he wouldn't have lost his deferment. They'd be together and he'd be safe.

Having had her license for only a few weeks, she wasn't the savviest behind the wheel, and a few angry drivers honked at her as she entered Portland. She waved her apologies and kept driving toward the center of town. She had gotten to know her way around, but she still had to pull over a couple of times to consult the *Maine Gazetteer* splayed open on the passenger seat.

She rode past Pride's Department Store, where she'd dropped off an application for an open position drawing fashion ads. Satisfied women dolled up with the latest fashions sashayed out of the revolving doors with giant bags swinging at their hips. Once she was close to the address, she eyed an available parking spot between an armored truck and a vintage car painted a sky blue.

The only problem was that she had to parallel park, a skill she had yet to master despite Thomas's worthy efforts in teaching her. She could still hear him reeling in laughter as she'd attempted to parallel park in Davenport for the first time, and had she shut out the memory with any more delay, she might have fallen apart.

The first try was beyond embarrassing; someone could have fit a motorcycle between her and the curb. Her nerves fired at the possibility of finally finding a place, and this parking challenge didn't help matters at all. The second try was a little better but still way off the mark. Maybe you could squeeze a moped in the space between. She pulled ahead and attempted, as Thomas had taught her, to line up her tires with those of the armored car. A line of cars piled up behind her, forcing her heart into overdrive.

On the third attempt, as the particularly angry driver in the sedan pressed on his horn while simultaneously yelling out the window something that sounded like, "Take the bus!" Annalisa committed to doing it right. She matched up the tires, swung the steering wheel all the way right, then eased backward. She tasted a bit of confidence as she watched through the rearview mirror and saw that she'd finally done it. Thomas would have been proud, and for an instant she heard his voice from the passenger seat, urging her on. *There you go, Anna. Take your time.*

His voice echoed into the emptiness in her chest, making her long for him. If only he could be here.

The driver behind her slammed on his brakes and held the horn down, turning her memory of Thomas into a ball of flames. Love was so damn messy! Burning with frustration, she decided to stop the car to collect herself. Forget the obnoxious jerk and his stupid horn!

With too much force, she pressed down the wrong pedal, reversing directly into the fancy blue car. Her head slammed into the back of the seat as the sound of metal on metal tore at her ears.

"Oh, no, no, no," she said, quickly moving out of reverse and pulling away from the car. With the Beetle sticking out into the middle of the street, she pulled the brake and stepped out of the car.

Without a lick of compassion, the asshole driver behind her sped past with an ugly shake of the head. Annalisa couldn't stop from giving him back a five-fingered flick off the chin, followed by a string of Italian that could have come straight from Nonna.

As the other cars passed by, she inspected the damage. The blue car's hood read PLYMOUTH in big silver letters. Showing only a long scratch in the bumper, the car had fared much better than Thomas's Beetle, which had a huge indentation to the right of the shattered rear taillight.

Annalisa knew next to nothing about cars and absolutely zilch about getting them fixed, but the first thing that came to mind as she picked up the pieces of her scattered thoughts was that this accident was an omen, telling her that she'd screwed up everything, that maybe she shouldn't even be here—certainly not after betraying him. And then the money it would cost—there went her savings.

She glanced down the street, searching for her destination. Part of her wanted to get back in the car and return home. Who was she kidding, an eighteen-year-old from the Mills trying to make something of herself? Was it a sign from up high for her to go back to where she belonged? And why in the world had she taken Thomas's car in the first place? What a fool she was.

Glancing at her Timex, Annalisa decided she still needed to make her meeting with her potential landlord. First, though, she had to figure out what to do about the damage. Considering the Plymouth was only scratched, she decided it would be best to avoid the police and an insurance claim. Jumping back into the driver's seat, she finished parking. It turned out she was much less nervous after the damage had been done. She wrote a quick note with Nonna's phone number on it to the owner of the Plymouth and then placed it on the windshield. She cringed at what Nonna might think, but what could she do now?

Trying to forget what had happened, she wandered along Congress Street and followed the addresses until she found her destination. On a small brown awning above a large display of fancy watches and clocks read: WALT BURZINSKI'S WATCH AND CLOCK REPAIR. The three-story brick building seemed out of place, like it was left standing from a forgotten era, more modern efforts towering over it. She raised her eyes past the awning to the small balconies on the second and third floors. Two apartments per floor. She wondered if one of those would be hers.

The bell above chimed as Annalisa pushed the glass door open. She'd never seen so many clocks in one place in her life. They covered every wall and almost all the available floor space. They collectively ticked and tocked, this wonderful and mesmerizing army of metronomic movement coming from every direction, a sound that momentarily drowned out her frustration about Thomas's car. As she bounced her eyes from one clock to the next, she recognized the smell of Murphy Oil Soap, which was what her grandmother and she used to clean the floors.

A man called out, "I'm back here. Better not be selling anything. I've no time for such things."

Following the throaty and obviously cranky voice, she wound her way past two tall grandfather clocks and past a long glass display of shiny gold and silver watches. Though the glass had been polished, she fought off a sneeze as the heavy dust in the shop crept up her nose.

Behind a glass counter with an antique cash register, Annalisa found a man who looked to be in his seventies. She saw his side profile, and he was hunched over a busy work desk, tinkering with the insides of a watch under the light of a lamp. Keys and watches, both with white tags attached to them, dangled from hooks behind him on the corkboard wall. The surface of the desk was covered with tiny screwdrivers and what looked like an oil dropper and dozens of other tools she didn't recognize.

The old man wore a tattered cardigan over a dingy white shirt and tie. He had a big nose and big ears, and what was left of his gray hair formed the shape of a horseshoe across his scalp. Stray hairs sprung out in random directions. His eyebrows were thick, gray, and unkempt too. He wore circular glasses with a magnifying glass extending from the right lens.

"I'm not interested in buying your things," he muttered, never breaking his focus from the watch. He had knobby and gangly fingers, and they shook slightly as he worked.

"Are you Mr. Burzinski?" Annalisa asked, stopping in front of the cash register.

He side-eyed her and then went back to work. "Either you're selling something that I'm not interested in or your name's Annalisa."

She gave her best smile. "Yes to the second one, inquiring about the third-floor apartment. You can call me Anna if you like."

Mr. Burzinski lifted the watch and used the lamplight to analyze it. "What brings you to Portland?"

Wasn't that a loaded question? "I'm an artist, a painter, to be exact, hoping to break into the art world. There's a teacher I'm coming to study with."

"The art world, huh?" He chuckled to himself. "I didn't know there was much of one here."

"Compared to back home in Payton Mills, there is. I just graduated and have been planning this move for a long time." *Ever since my parents died and I left Bangor,* she thought.

"You're young. I don't want parties up there. If you're looking to bring home a big swath of your loony tune friends and make a bunch of racket, it's not the right place for you. I live on the second floor right below, and I won't have it."

Annalisa told him that she was laser focused on honing her craft and wasn't interested in late nights or partying.

"Fair enough," Mr. Burzinski said, finally looking at her for more than a second. "I think I've priced the place fairly. I won't put up with late rent. Where will you be working?"

"I'm not exactly sure yet, but I'll have a job soon." She listed some of the places she'd applied (Bernie's, Benoit's, Rines Bros. . . .), and he looked at her skeptically. In that moment she recognized something wildly familiar in this man. He was cold, but he was warm, too, just like his shop was covered in a layer of dust but charming at the same time. Nonna was the same way. She could be intimidating but had a heart of gold. Annalisa did well with these kinds of people and decided to push him.

"I'll be a great tenant, Mr. Burzinski."

He didn't respond, only kept working. She wondered how long he would continue this game. Little did he know, Nonna had practiced these same intimidation tactics, so Annalisa could wait in the uncomfortable silence all day long if she had to.

Just as she dug for her confidence, the shop came alive in a cacophony of sounds. The clocks had struck noon, and cuckoo birds poked out of their holes to chirp, and the grandfather and grandmother clocks clanged, and the other clocks on the walls chimed and pinged and dinged. Annalisa spun her head around, drinking in the magic of this place. Mr. Burzinski was a grumpy old watchmaker from a fairy tale, and he had a shop that sang at noon.

When his clocks had quieted, she said, "I've never even imagined such a thing. That was . . . wonderful."

Ignoring her, he said, "Rent's seventy dollars a month. I'll need first and last month's, a security deposit, and a one-year commitment."

There went all her money for art classes, Annalisa thought. An hour in the city and she was already broke. She knew what he was charging for rent but hadn't anticipated the additional asks. She wondered if she should mention the car she'd hit. God, she didn't want to lose this place. The location was dreamy. "Mr. Burzinski, here's the thing. I just got in a wreck."

He looked at her. "A wreck?"

Talking with her hands, she said, "Well, I backed into an expensive-looking car and messed up the back end. Not that it's anything you need to worry about, but I have to get it fixed. My . . . my friend who loaned it to me loves that car. So would you please allow me to only pay the first month's rent for now?"

He gave a look like she'd just asked him if she could live for free.

"I am incredibly hardworking," she assured him. "I don't know how much getting his car fixed will cost, but I need to do that before he comes home from Fort Dix. If you'll give me a little leeway, I'll find a job as quickly as humanly possible and give you every dime I can until we're square. This is the perfect location and price." The truth was it was the *only* place she'd found that was affordable near Congress Street.

"I don't even need to see it," she said desperately. "I just need a break right now. Please. I'm quiet, respectful—"

He held up a hand to stop her. "And verbose, no doubt. Take a deep breath, young lady." As she followed his suggestion, he continued,

"Why the desperate need to get out of Payton Mills? Can't you paint there?"

She thought about her response carefully as she set a hand on the counter by the register. "Because this is where it all happens. For a girl who grew up in Bangor and Payton Mills, Portland is the big city. This is where the artists are, the galleries, the teachers. The museum. I can't become the artist I want to be in Payton Mills. It doesn't inspire me."

He gave a closemouthed chuckle. "Well, you sure make it hard to say no. You'd be a good saleswoman."

Annalisa said a quick prayer, hoping he would give her a chance.

Mr. Burzinski put down the watch and reached for one of the keys on the wall behind him. "The place is yours if you want it, but I'll expect you to make good on your word."

"Yes, I will," Annalisa said, wishing her mother were there to see her now.

He led her out of the shop, and they walked toward the side of the building. "I hope the driver of that Plymouth doesn't kill me," Annalisa said. "I left a note and—"

Mr. Burzinski froze. "You hit a Plymouth?"

"A very nice and polished one too. I put a big scratch on the bumper. Oh God, I was nervous and people were honking and—"

"A blue Belvedere? On Congress?"

"Yes, Mr. Burzinski."

The realization struck her a second before he spat, "That's my car you hit."

"No." Her throat tightened. She wanted to run away, to disappear.

Without another word, he marched toward the accident. She ran to catch up with him. "This can't be happening."

He mumbled something under his breath and stomped around the corner and up Congress Street, moving so quickly that he lost his breath and broke into a cough. That didn't slow him down, though.

When they reached the two cars, he went straight to the front bumper of his Plymouth and shook his head. He raised his hand to his forehead and lifted his eyes to the sky, saying either a prayer or a string of curses—she wasn't sure.

After quite possibly the most uncomfortable minute of her life, Walt lowered his head. "I've had this car for eighteen years," he finally said with abundant frustration, his Polish accent becoming stronger with each word. "It has barely any miles on it. I just so happened to take it out of the garage for a spin this morning. Never once has this had so much as a scratch and now this. Now you come along."

"I don't know what to say, Mr. Burzinski, but I'll pay for it—one way or another. They can fix that pretty easily, right? It's just a—"

"Who in the world issued you a driver's license? You kids these days. Don't even know how to park a car."

She stared at the damage she'd done, wondering if she was ready to handle the city. Even in between the beeping horns and loud chatters of those passing by, there was a constant noise here. A hammering over there, a screeching tire there, a machine kicking on down the street. "I've been learning for a while now. The parallel parking thing gets me, though."

"Clearly," he said, bending down and running his hand along the scratch.

She apologized again, thinking this accident had cost her not only a good bit of her money but also her chance for a place to live. Had it also been a sign that she'd made a mistake leaving Thomas? Or was this punishment for dragging him along in the first place? She didn't want to cry, but the tears and apologies came all at once.

"Oh, don't do that." He took her note off the windshield and crumpled it.

She wiped her cheeks. "I can write you a check right now."

"How am I to know how much it will cost? Did you see a crystal ball in my shop?"

"Do you have a mechanic?" she asked, thinking Mary Cassatt would find a way through this. So would Sharon Maxwell.

"Oh, I'll take it from here, and yes, I'll get my car to him straightaway."

She dared to ask through her tears, "Does this mean you won't rent me the place?"

He let out a loud cackle and then a big sigh. "You aren't one of those people that breaks everything they touch, are you? Do I need to worry about you burning my building down?"

"Not at all. I was nervous coming here. Moving to Portland has been my dream for as long as I can remember, and I . . . ugh."

"Oh please. Really, you must stop that. I'll still rent you the place, but I'll expect you to find a job posthaste. You owe me quite a lot of money."

"Absolutely. Thank you so much." A thread of hope worked its way into Annalisa's frustration and sadness.

"I'm just glad to find someone who won't annoy me with noise. You artist types are always so quiet." He glanced at the bumper of his car one more time and then looked at the Beetle. "My guy will be able to make your friend's car look good as new. It'll cost you, but such is life. Now let's go take a look at the place."

She put her hands together in prayer. "Thank you so much. I love your car, by the way."

He moved his head ever so slowly until he was looking at her. No words were needed. He read right through her compliment.

Chapter 18

Onward and Upward

Walt opened up a door that led into the stairwell and ushered Annalisa inside. A set of mailboxes hung on one of the white concrete walls that could have used a touch-up.

He moved slowly, and it took them a long time to wind their way up the steps. "A woman by the name of Eleby lives in the other one on the third floor. She keeps to herself. A little scattered, I think." His voice echoed.

"Scattered?"

He fell into a coughing fit and paused on the steps.

"Are you okay, Mr. Burzinski?"

He waved her off and started up again. "Yes, yes, yes, I'm fine." A few steps later, he said, "Scattered . . . I think that's a good word for her."

Annalisa smiled as they went down the hall to the apartment. He swung open the door and invited her in. To her delight, the small one-bedroom apartment was clean. As she breathed in the space, she felt like she was walking into the rest of her life. The walls were white and refreshing. The old furniture—the cracked leather sofa, the dated fabric chairs, and the wobbly table—would do.

The kitchen made up one corner of the main room. It was small but clean. Opposite the couch was a small television with rabbit ears stretching toward the ceiling. She peeked into the bedroom and saw the double bed, a mild upgrade from her twin back in the Mills. There was enough space by the window that it could be her studio in the colder months.

Mr. Burzinski stood in the kitchen and watched her as she poked around, eventually making her way to the little balcony, which couldn't have been more than three feet by six feet. Sliding open the door, she stepped out into the gorgeous day and put her hands on the railing. She felt like she was Cleopatra looking out over her city.

Across the street, there was a candy shop, a law office, and a bakery. Next to a fir tree that leaned heavily to the left was a phone booth with a person pushing in coins. She was a block off Congress Street, away from the madness, but it was lively enough here—enough subjects to keep her painting for years. She could already see her easel set up there against the railing, her trunk of paints just below. She looked up and saw a fern with brown leaves swinging on a hook, and she thought that her mother's chimes would hang wonderfully there. Another hook hung on the opposite side, and Annalisa thought making another set wouldn't be such a bad idea. This little balcony was an artist's dream.

"What do you think, young lady?" Mr. Burzinski asked as she walked back inside.

"I think that plant out there needs some water. I hope you've got a pitcher. As far as the apartment, I'll take it. And I won't let you down; I swear to you." A rush of happiness came over her and no doubt showed itself on her face as she rifled through a cabinet looking for a pitcher.

"When would you like to move in?"

She turned to him, pitcher in hand. "Tomorrow morning?"

Mr. Burzinski chuckled, this time more warmly. There was something so wonderful about seeing and hearing a person who typically held their cards close to their chest open up, and she hoped she'd hear him laugh again. It was like that with Nonna, too, the joy of putting the first bit of color on a white canvas. Even Emma was that way, a part of this small group of guarded people who had a wonderful heart desperate to get some air. Not for the first time, Annalisa saw a flash of Emma's singing forest, and she hoped so deeply that Emma would one day realize that vision in reality.

Mr. Burzinski extracted a fine silver watch attached to a chain from his pants pocket, and it caught her eye. She imagined a watchmaker keeps only the finest watches for himself. He shoved it back into his pocket. "I need to see to an appointment, but you can come by anytime tomorrow. I'm always in the shop."

Despite all it had cost her, Annalisa had taken a big step toward her dream.

⌐

When she returned home that night, she could barely hide her excitement. Even the earlier accident wasn't holding her down. "He's just like you," Annalisa told her grandmother.

"What does that mean?" Nonna had her eyes on the evening news.

Annalisa tried to ignore the anchor, who said something about soldiers in Cambodia. She sat on the couch next to her. "He's grumpy, but when he laughs, it's the most wonderful thing in the world."

Nonna scowled and waved a fist, but a smile tickled the corner of her mouth as she said, "Who says I'm grumpy?"

"The whole world, Nonna."

Annalisa went to her room to finish packing. She didn't have much to take—her clothes, her trunk of art supplies, her best paintings, her sewing machine, the wind chimes she'd made with her mother, and her records and record player. Nonna had put together a box of old kitchen things, too, including a garlic chopper and one of her wooden spoons, which was like a samurai bestowing her sword upon an apprentice. The gesture had filled Annalisa with incredible appreciation.

As Annalisa finished folding her clothes and cramming them into her suitcase, Nonna came in and tossed a white envelope onto the bed.

Annalisa opened it to find two twenties. The gesture of kindness nearly buckled her. "You don't have to do this."

"I want to."

Annalisa closed the envelope and held it out to Nonna. "I can't take it."

"You most certainly will."

After a battle of wills that Annalisa knew she had no chance of winning, she pressed the envelope against her own chest and thought of the things she needed for her new apartment: silverware and dishes. Sheets and blankets. A broom and dustpan.

"Thank you," she said, shedding a silent tear. This woman had done everything for her, picking back up her mother hat in her late sixties. As ardently as she'd wanted to leave Payton Mills, at times thrashing like a tiger in a cage, the realization that Nonna wouldn't be there when she woke or when she came home from school hit her hard.

All this wanting to leave and now that the day was finally upon her, she was slightly afraid. What if she couldn't get a job? What if she ran out of money? What if she never made it as an artist? Even if she did, would leaving Nonna now have been worth it?

She wrapped her arms around her grandmother. "I'm going to miss you."

Nonna did what she always did and sort of half hugged with a light pat on the back. "Oh, don't give me that bologna. You'll be glad to get rid of me."

"Not at all," Annalisa said. Sure, she couldn't wait to make her decisions, watch her own shows on the television, do something other than chores on Saturdays. But this woman meant the world to her.

"Promise you'll come see me," Annalisa said.

"You're the one with the car. You know where to find me."

"I'll come pick you up or Nino will bring you down. We can go shopping and get lost in the city. I'll even take you to church. They say Mass in Latin at Saint Peter's from what I've heard."

Nonna lifted a hand to her face and turned away.

"Wait," Annalisa said. "Are you crying? Nonna doesn't cry."

In that moment, Annalisa felt like she was abandoning her grandmother. She'd been so caught up in her own dream of getting out of the Mills that she hadn't considered what she was doing to Nonna, leaving her alone. As much as Annalisa had been a pain in the butt, maybe Nonna did like having her around.

Guilt caught her like a spiderweb as she considered Nonna's life going forward. She'd have family over as always, but she'd lost her son, her husband, whom she'd lived with for more than forty years. Now she was losing Annalisa.

With her back to her granddaughter, Nonna said, "You behave and go to Mass every Sunday. *Every* Sunday. And say your prayers."

Annalisa went to her and touched her arm. "I will."

Still hiding her moist eyes, Nonna shook her head. "And on holy days." She turned, and they hugged like they never had before. Both women choked up, knowing they'd fought the odds and were still standing.

Letting go of her grandmother, Annalisa asked, "Why don't you come with me to Portland? Sell the house and move with me. Into your own place, of course. But close by. Not too close but close enough."

Nonna blew out a blast of air. "*Pazza!* This is my home." How unfair that she had loved her husband her whole life, only to be forced to live the last of her years alone. Love seemed quite awful, if Annalisa was being honest. Still, she wished Nonna could find someone. As dogged as she was, she might easily live twenty more years.

"I'm gonna keep working on you. Could be a fresh start for both of us."

Nonna crossed her arms. "I'll never move from this house."

Annalisa smiled at her grandmother's defiance as if she were looking in the mirror. "I'm going to get you out of here one day, whether you like it or not."

Nonna shook her head, and Annalisa thought she heard a growl.

"Though I haven't always shown it, I'm so grateful for all that you've done for me," Annalisa said. "So incredibly grateful."

Nonna pinched Annalisa's cheek. "Your mother would be proud. Just like I am."

God, Annalisa was going to miss this woman.

Chapter 19

ONE NEEDS MONEY TO EAT

Before Annalisa had even bought groceries for her new place, she rang Sharon Maxwell to announce her arrival to Portland and make sure classes were on for that coming Tuesday, the last day of June. When Sharon mentioned the cost of the classes (almost as much as her rent per month), Annalisa nearly choked, but this was why she was here: to excel. She'd rather take classes than eat.

As she'd done back in the Mills, she put one easel in the corner of her bedroom and the other outside. Then, after apologizing to the plant for stealing its hook, she hung her mother's wind chimes. They instantly broke into their first Portland song.

Overcome with a need to start a new piece—her first in the city—she decided to put off her other errands until the next day and carried her trunk out to the balcony. Thank God she was young, she thought. Dragging it up the stairs had not been easy.

With Van Morrison singing to her from the record player inside, she sat with her canvas pad in one of the two chairs. Knowing her most inspired ideas came in moments of silence, she sat back and breathed in her view. This was her city now. She could see so much more than her little block with the people and the cars rushing by. She could see her dreams coming alive.

Even the dark clouds that had marched in to swallow the blue above didn't hamper her enthusiasm. In fact, she relished the abutment of colors, those gray shades seeping into the June sky. As she readied her pencil and framed her scene, the sky opened up with water. Protected from the rain by the overhang above, she looked down to the street and saw a businessman dashing past the left-leaning tree and into the phone booth. There was something so incredibly urgent in his movements, and Annalisa reached for her sketch pad and pencil.

"That's it," she said to herself. What captured city life better than the urgency that Payton Mills lacked? Once she was satisfied with her sketch, she reached into her trunk for the rest of her supplies and went to work.

Annalisa plugged into the city as much as she could over the next few days, searching for inspiration. She went on long walks to take in all the new sights and sounds. She checked out her first stack of art books from the library. Needless to say, the options in the Portland Library were much more abundant than those back in the Mills. She dipped into all the galleries to get an idea of her competition, and she went back to the museum a few times to remind herself of what she wanted. Of course it never failed that the museum reminded her of Thomas—and even Emma—and she had to almost ruthlessly push away thoughts of them.

Portland, however, lived up to her assertion that the city buzzed with a current of urgency. The quote to fix Walt's and Thomas's cars was much more than she'd anticipated, which meant she needed a job immediately. No more walking dizzily through the city without a care in the world. As if her meager bowls of homemade chicken soup for each meal weren't a constant reminder. Nonna had taught her all about repurposing bones and carcasses and fat in every way she could.

Not having a car, she marched all over the city, looking for jobs. She even revisited the places she'd already dropped résumés. Her initial hope that she might find something in the art world melted away quickly, and by the third day, she was desperate.

On Monday, she decided to spend one more day trying to find something more enjoyable than taking people's orders and delivering food. Not that she was above being a waiter, it was just that she would have preferred something more in line with her skills as an artist. But as she'd been reminded by the wall of rejections she kept collecting, a lack of a degree meant a lack of choices.

Walking by Pride's on Congress Street, she decided to try one more time. Pride's was the fanciest department store in all of Maine—at least of any that she'd seen. She'd first dropped off an application for the fashion illustrator position when she'd come with Nino. Then she'd followed up with several phone calls and a visit the second day after moving in. Fashion illustrators used pen and ink, which was a medium Annalisa felt very comfortable with after first learning in Bangor.

Annalisa strolled with dazzled senses through the cosmetic counters, where girls offered to show her the latest lipsticks and blush and let her take sniffs of the most popular perfumes. How nice to be one of the women in the dressing rooms, trying on the latest styles or having her hair done in the salon.

Fantasies aside, she wasn't afraid of doing the hard work to get there. Reaching the center of the store, she looked at the escalators teeming with people either riding down to the Bargain Bin in the basement or up to the second floor where they had Men's Fashions and the Personnel Department.

Feeling like she was starting to wear out the floor of this place, she approached the secretary sitting at a tiny desk at the beginning of a long hallway. Jazz piano music played quietly in the background.

"Hi there, Betty," Annalisa said. She'd been here so often the two were on a first-name basis. "Is Patty available by chance? I still haven't heard from her." As Annalisa had learned, Patty was the manager in charge of the Advertising Department, and also one of the only women who'd climbed to a position of power at Pride's. People spoke of her like she was a myth.

Betty looked around as if she were in trouble. "Sorry, I specifically gave Patty your résumé, telling her I really liked you, but she said the position's filled."

Annalisa felt so let down, instantly thinking that she was beyond qualified. If only she'd worked harder for a scholarship to college—she'd just been so messed up by losing her parents.

"You know what, though," Betty said, lowering her voice again, as if she was passing on the secrets of the universe, "I hear Mr. Miller is hiring for the Bargain Bin."

"Oh." Annalisa thought about it. The Bargain Bin certainly wasn't the Advertising Department, but it might be better than waiting tables. "Is he around? I'd love to talk to him about it."

"Let me go see," she said as she swung out from her desk and disappeared down the hall.

Soon, a man came waltzing Annalisa's way with a wide duckfooted canter. He combed his thin mustache with his fingers. As awkward as he was, he had the kind of confidence the owner of the building might have. Annalisa thought his yellow-dotted bow tie was absolutely fitting and showed his desperation to find his individuality.

"Hello, Annalisa," he said, taking her hand. His palm was clammy, and she pulled away as quickly and politely as possible.

"Betty tells me you're looking to fill the Bargain Bin position," he said.

"Yes, Mr. Miller." Annalisa had almost corrected him, saying she wanted a job in the Advertising Department, but she chose to be grateful for any opportunity. These first few days in Portland had sent a strong message to the small-town girl from the Mills: *You're not in Kansas anymore.*

"You're a cute little thing, aren't you?" he asked and then made an effort to extract something stuck from his teeth.

Right then and there, Annalisa decided she didn't like him. How dared he say such a thing? If this hadn't been her chance to land a real job, she might have punched him in the nose.

Taming the urge, she kept her clenched fist holstered by her side and said kindly, "I don't have any experience in retail, but I'm a fast learner." She subtly wiped off his hand sweat on the back of her dress.

"Oh, I bet you are." He looked at her like he was undressing her with his eyes, all the while aggressively going after the piece of food in his teeth. Though she wasn't opposed to using her looks to her advantage in getting a job, he made her want to throw up.

"Why don't you come back and sit down with me?" he asked.

Annalisa almost pivoted and dashed away before even finding out what the available job might entail. Reminding herself of how desperately she needed money, she thanked Mr. Miller and followed him back.

His office smelled of burned coffee, and she eventually noticed the half pot waiting for his consumption on a small table near the window. She put on her best smile and started answering his questions.

Finally, he said, "Yeah, one of my girls quit on me a few weeks back, and we could use you. It's hard work, you know. A lot of folding and making sure the pricing's right and taking care of the customers—Pride's most challenging customers—as you can imagine. Something about good bargains brings out the worst in women. Do you think you can handle it?"

She suspected he had spoken snidely but let it go. "Yes, I think I could." She slowly patted the air with her hand. "Pardon me if I'm overstepping my bounds, but I thought I might mention that I'm also interested in a job in the Advertising Department. I know the fashion illustrator position was filled, but if there's anything else—"

"An artist, huh?" He seemed overly interested, possibly being sarcastic. "What kind of art do you make?"

"I'm a painter mostly, but I studied pen and ink in school, so I could draw ads. I'm a hard worker, Mr. Miller. I could bring in some examples to give you—or Patty—an idea of what I can do. I'm creative in general and might be of use to the team."

His jaw flopped up and down as he faked a laugh. "Aren't you cute? This isn't home ec class, sweetie. What are you? Eighteen? No offense, but you'll fit right in down there in the basement. You'll get along great with the girls."

She was a minute away from peeling the skin off his face, but she bit her lip and muttered, "I'd love anything you have available."

He clapped his clammy hands together. "The Bargain Basement it is."

Not letting the demeanor of her new boss get her down, Annalisa nearly flew down the escalator. A step in the right direction was always worth celebrating.

Chapter 20

THE CONTOURS OF A NAKED MAN

On the same day her art lessons with Sharon Maxwell began, Annalisa started her new job. She was nervous when she rode the escalator down to the basement. Though it wasn't as glitzy as upstairs, and it smelled like mothballs, the Bargain Bin was lined with racks of incredible clothes that she could buy at a very nice discount—once she was more financially stable, of course. The order of priorities might be art classes and supplies, a few bargain outfits at work, and then eating. Most of the clothes were a season or more out of style, but just like her mom, she could always pull out her Singer for some alterations to make something current.

Greta, Barbara, and Catherine welcomed her to the team, and they spent a few minutes prodding her with questions before returning to their tasks. Greta was the manager and showed her how to work the cash register and fold clothes to company standards and all the other details of her new gig. Between instructions, Greta mentioned that her husband had enlisted and was currently in Vietnam. Considering both Annalisa's cousin and Thomas were on a similar path, Annalisa could empathize, and the two instantly hit it off. Annalisa caught herself asking Greta what she knew about the training process for a soldier on the way to Vietnam, as she often wondered what Thomas's (and her cousin Michael's) life was like now.

After her shift, she decided to swing back upstairs to see if she could get a moment with the manager of the Advertising Department. Before she even passed through men's shoes, Ted Miller came duck-footing from out of nowhere. "What are you doing here?"

She wondered if he was constantly on patrol. "I'm sorry, Mr. Miller. I was on my way home and hoped to speak with Patty." Annalisa felt like a cat burglar who'd been busted creeping toward a diamond.

He shoved his hands into the pockets of his khaki pants. "What would this be in regards to?"

"I want her to know I'm interested should a job become available."

"Oh God," Mr. Miller said, extracting his hands from his pockets. He punched a fist into his palm. "Let's not start daydreaming. Frankly, I'd prefer you stay in the basement, where you belong."

Annalisa wanted to snap at him but couldn't possibly risk losing her job. "Yes, sir, Mr. Miller." She turned and felt so damn small as she went back down the escalator and out the revolving doors.

⌐

Nearly a year after she sat to show her portfolio to Jackie Burton at her gallery, Annalisa found herself sitting across from Sharon Maxwell with the exact same feelings of excitement and fear, as if the keys to the universe hid in the woman's pocket.

Sharon had asked her to arrive a few minutes early so that she could take a look through Annalisa's portfolio. They were in Sharon's studio in the back of the warehouse where the two had first met, both facing a long wooden table covered with Annalisa's favorite pieces. On the walls and multiple easels were the many works Sharon had in progress, and the aftermath of her work was splattered in a rainbow of colors on the concrete floor. She had enough art supplies in that room to equip a small army of painters, and Annalisa thought she could only dream of such a studio.

Annalisa had included a couple of the pieces that she'd shown Jackie, including the one of Annalisa standing over her mother's casket, but she'd mostly included works she'd done during her senior year.

Incense burned and the Grateful Dead played in the background, filling the studio with a very easy vibe. Sharon was Annalisa's first true hippie experience, and Annalisa was intrigued in the way one might follow a butterfly through a field. Sharon was dressed as wildly as she'd been at her show, bright fabric with rings on almost every finger and large, dangly earrings. She'd been so kind in receiving Annalisa a moment ago, her silver eyes incredibly inviting, but now she—and the moment—were about as intimidating as any experience Annalisa had ever known.

Annalisa studied the paintings along with Sharon, all of people dealing with the struggles of the modern day. Never had she worked so hard as this past year, and she was sure she'd gotten better, but Annalisa's opinion didn't matter now. Sharon was the critic, and her opinion was gold. The more Annalisa had heard and read about Sharon Maxwell, the more impressed Annalisa was of the woman's talent, and the more sure Annalisa was that she'd found the right teacher.

As a man with a gruff, bluesy voice sang, "Turn On Your Love Light," Sharon finally took a step back to formulate her words. "You have an incredible gift."

Her words hit Annalisa's ears like the breath of God. By now, enough people had told her that she was good to know it was true, but to hear Sharon tell her that she had a gift was validation she could trust. She was in the big city now, and Sharon was the real thing. All she had to do was agree to let Annalisa show some of her pieces at next April's art show, and Annalisa would skyrocket to stardom.

Annalisa held her breath as her new teacher meandered down the line of ten paintings, touching the edges, breathing them in. "There's something missing, though."

Wham, there it was. Annalisa could already hear the rest, that she was gifted but not quite there yet. Still searching. As much as she'd gotten used to rejection during her job search, her heart sank.

"Now, now, don't get down," Sharon said, reading Annalisa's mind. "You really are good, but I'm not feeling you in these paintings. I'm not seeing a connection between you and your subjects."

So much for getting into the show in April. Couldn't it have been that easy? Wasn't there such a thing as a break? It's not like she hadn't worked her tail off to get to this moment. How many paintings had she done since she was two years old? Hundreds, thousands!

Not connecting with her subjects? That had been her main focus in the last year, diving into the feelings of everyone living through these wild times. She looked at her ten pieces: a soldier in the jungle, a protester pumping an antiwar sign in the air, Nixon getting his head shaved, a nude woman looking in the mirror. How could she ever connect if she hadn't done it by now? How could Sharon see it anyway? Was she some sort of mystic?

Sharon pointed at the one of Annalisa placing her hand on her mother's casket. "Except for this one. This is you, isn't it?"

Annalisa remembered Jackie pointing out that painting, saying close to the same thing. "How'd you know?" Annalisa asked.

Sharon jabbed her finger down hard onto the table next to the painting, her bracelets jiggling like musical beads. "Because this painting is incredibly rich with life. I can feel this young girl." Sharon wiped her eyes. "You're putting tears in my eyes with your brush. This is who you need to find with the rest of your paintings."

Annalisa felt so frustrated. "But she's easy to connect with. She's me."

Sharon faced her. "Let me ask you this. Why do you think Sophia Loren is so wonderful on screen?"

A shrug. "I don't know."

"Because she becomes her character. That's all you have to do, Annalisa. Become your subject. Understand exactly what it's like to be

192

in their skin. Look at this protester. Have you really thought about his life? Sure, he's angry at the war; that's easy. What's he going home to after the protest? Who does he love? Or does he love at all?"

"I hadn't quite gone that far."

"You're eighteen, Annalisa. Don't beat yourself up." She paused. "I want you to do something with me." Sharon stretched her arms out in a star shape and drew in a long breath. The Grateful Dead still played in the background, and they were into a musical jam that Sharon's movements seemed tuned in to. "Let's go."

Annalisa looked at her like she was crazy.

"What's wrong?" Sharon dropped her hands and put them on her waist.

"I feel silly."

"Who cares?" She looked across the giant space of the warehouse. "No one is even here yet. What are you worried about? Now, c'mon."

Sharon closed her eyes and opened up into a star, as if nothing could hold her back. "Turn on your love light," she said, repeating the singer from the record filling the room with sound.

With a burning face, Annalisa mimicked her. She couldn't believe she was doing this.

"Now, breathe," Sharon said. "Take it all in. Take in the atoms that make up all of us. Connect with me and with this music and with all the other souls out there fighting their own battles. Don't open your eyes; just let go. Let your love light shine."

Annalisa felt like a fool as she sucked in air. Her eyes were closed, and she was thinking that Sharon might be a bit too much when she felt the woman's hands touch her elbows, urging her to raise her arms higher.

The touch startled her so badly that she gasped, and she jerked her arms back down as her entire body tightened. The music turned to noise and made her even more uneasy. She was so ashamed as she looked Sharon's way, but the teacher wore a smile, as if nothing were wrong.

"Come here," she whispered. "Take my hands."

Annalisa felt afraid, but that was absurd. This woman holding her hands out was so utterly warm and kind.

Sharon gestured again with her fingers until Annalisa finally took Sharon's hands. They stood three feet apart, but Annalisa felt like they were inches away. She wanted to recoil or turn or . . . she had to close her eyes.

"Look at me," Sharon said.

Annalisa opened her eyes as if there were an openmouthed snake with fangs waiting. It wasn't a snake, though. It was Sharon's silver eyes.

"Annalisa, you can't connect with your subjects on canvas without connecting with people in the real world."

As if someone had just ripped off her dress, exposing who she really was, Annalisa's eyes watered. "I . . . I . . ." She'd asked for this in moving to the city, but she wasn't sure she could handle it. She dropped her head without getting out a word.

Then Sharon took her into a hug, and all Annalisa's troubles went away. She had never felt so safe and secure.

~

Annalisa felt like she'd crossed the finish line of a marathon as she took her seat on the opposite side of the warehouse, where Sharon had set up twenty chairs and easels in a horseshoe around a stage. A man in a robe sat in a chair in the center of the stage, speaking with Sharon.

Knowing the man was nude underneath that robe, Annalisa was nearly frozen with nerves. After what she'd just been through, she now had to paint her first naked man? Had she not already committed with so much money, she might have run out of there. It was too much after what Sharon had done to her. She was all about becoming better, but this was not what she'd expected on her first day with Sharon Maxwell. What happened to learning to clean your brushes or a lesson on how to thin acrylics with water?

The man looked like a Roman god, and Annalisa could only imagine what he held under his green robe. Judging by what she could see, his broad shoulders and muscular legs, he was in superb shape and well toned. The artist in her was eager to study his contours, but the girl inside wrestled with a mild form of shock. He would be the first man she'd ever seen completely bare. Oh my God, why was she so embarrassed? She was young, yes, as Sharon had said, but not *that* young. She'd painted plenty of nude men from paintings. Still, the real thing before her was enough to make her squirm.

She looked to the other students in her class, a mix of all ages. Some chatted, some doodled on their sketch pads, and others looked toward the stage as if they couldn't wait for the big reveal. Annalisa felt like she was certainly the most nervous of all of them.

Sharon eventually clapped her hands and commanded instant attention. Her voice echoed off the brick walls as she spoke. "My job in the coming weeks and months is to make you better painters, whatever that means to you. We're all different, and we all have our obstacles. My hope is that we're going to break down every one of your walls. Some of you will quit, and that's the way the world works. I am going to tell you all how it is, and I'm going to push, and it won't be easy. You are all wonderful artists—that's why you're here—but you can all be better. Even I can be better. My promise to you is that I'll give you my all, and I want the same of you."

After talking details about what to expect, she turned to the model and asked him to disrobe. Annalisa couldn't believe this was happening, and by the time he'd dropped his robe off the stage and taken his pose, her jaw had hit China—or whatever was on the other side of the globe. The model was much more well endowed than the statue of David she'd painted at some point last year. He was lean with hardened ab muscles and tufts of brown hair about his . . . above his . . . below his belly button and across his chest.

Like a baby clawing for her pacifier, she reached for her charcoal pencil and opened up her sketchbook. She noticed some people reached straight for their paints. Sharon had suggested they follow whatever routine made them comfortable.

The model almost directly faced Annalisa, who now wished she'd chosen a position on the periphery of the horseshoe. *Wouldn't Emma get a kick out of this?* she thought, remembering the first day Emma had come to the Mills.

She avoided his midsection like the plague as she first outlined his body and then went to work on the curvature of his lower legs, shading in the darker tones and imagining the colors she might use once she took to the paper on the easel.

Thirty minutes must have passed as everyone silently worked. Annalisa had relaxed some, having gotten used to the naked man standing before her. She'd convinced herself he was simply flesh like herself. She'd moved to the easel now and was toying with skin-tone colors when Sharon, who'd been visiting with each of them, peeking at their work, interrupted the class.

"Annalisa and I were speaking about connecting with our subjects, and I think it's a common obstacle among you. So I'd like to do something I've not done before."

Annalisa couldn't imagine what this wild woman might suggest, and she felt her shoulders turn back to stones.

Sharon smiled, as if this were all a game. "I want you to paint the model."

The students looked around at each other in confusion. One of the older ladies said, "We *are* painting him."

"No," Sharon said, clearly enjoying herself, "I want you to take your paints up to the stage and paint him. Physically touch him with your brushes."

A collection of gasps rose up in the warehouse air.

"Wait, what?" that same woman said.

Annalisa's heart raced as she glanced at the model. He wore a smirk, clearly privy to this surprising turn of the lesson plan.

"Let's go," Sharon said again with a clap that seemed to be her calling card.

"Are you suggesting we paint all of him?" a guy Annalisa's age asked.

Sharon looked at him and then at the model. "I expect you all to work together to make Damon into a masterpiece. And we're not done till every last bit of skin is covered with acrylic. Now, let's go." Then she added, "Annalisa, no big flat brushes for you. I want you to use your smallest round tip."

Annalisa looked around as if someone were playing a joke and an audience was about to come running through the doors charged with laughter.

"Let's go," Sharon demanded. "I'm sure we all have parts we'd like to put our bristles on. We don't have all night."

What in the hell had she gotten herself into? Payton Mills felt a million miles away from this warehouse and this woman.

⁓

A few things were for sure: Annalisa had never had a teacher like Sharon Maxwell, and even if she hadn't learned anything as far as art was concerned during her first class, she could certainly say she'd never laughed so much in her entire life. The model had played his role with dignity, and by the end of the lesson, everyone in the class had come together, as if there were no strangers in the room.

When Annalisa returned home that night, she made a simple pasta with butter and parmesan and sat on the couch to call Emma Barnes. Because of her breakup with Thomas, she'd chosen to distance herself from his sister, despite wishing she could help. It had taken a while, but Annalisa finally dared to reach out, and with the story of the nude model, she had a good reason.

When Mrs. Barnes picked up, the two caught up with some forced surface chatter before Annalisa asked for Emma. Mrs. Barnes stalled with several long *um*s and *oh*s before finally saying, "I don't think she's ready yet."

Annalisa shook her head in frustration. "I understand. Well . . . please tell her that I'd love to talk sometime if she feels like it."

"That's very nice of you, and I will. You're getting along fine, Annalisa?"

"Yes, I am, thank you. How's Thomas, by the way?" They'd been avoiding the subject. "Any word?"

Mrs. Barnes said, "He's written once to say that he doesn't like push-ups and that the army makes even me a great cook."

Annalisa cracked a grin, thinking only Thomas would say such a thing to his mother and get away with it. "I never got his address at Fort Dix. Do you have it handy by chance?"

A long pause.

She shouldn't have asked. Mrs. Barnes was no more a fan of Annalisa than Mr. Barnes, apparently, especially now that Annalisa was no longer a part of his future.

"I promised him I'd write," Annalisa said.

Another pause. "One minute, let me see if I can find it."

Once Mrs. Barnes gave the address and details to reach him, Annalisa hurried off the phone. She reached for a pencil and paper and wrote Thomas the note she'd promised him. She didn't have much to say, so she simply told him in brief about finally finding an apartment and that it was above a clock shop that sang at noon and midnight. Then she asked him if he was having fun at summer camp and if he'd gotten to build a fort and shoot things with his little camp buddies. At the last minute, before she folded the piece of paper, she considered mentioning that she'd wrecked his car. Then again, she decided, some things were better left unsaid.

Chapter 21

A PHOTOGRAPH OF PAINFUL MEMORIES

Annalisa found meaning and peace in painting the city. Though she spent a little time with her new friends from work, she held fast to her dream, typically only breaking away from her brushes and paints for her shifts at the Bargain Bin or to hang out with some of her fellow classmates from Sharon's class. After nearly three years in Payton Mills, she was starved to talk with other artists. Having sent a clear message to the three guys her age in the class (none of whom compared to Thomas), they were no longer hitting on her, which made their group feel quite safe.

Behind her easel, Annalisa came to know her view from the balcony in ways she never could have imagined. With Sharon's urging to connect more with her subjects, Annalisa gave names to the tenants of the buildings across the street. She sneaked peeks of their daily lives when they left their blinds open, and then would give them life—or at least try to—on the paper. With each brushstroke, she would attempt to wedge her way into her subject's skin. She named and gave a story to the old lady across the way who was not ashamed to dry her underwear on the balcony, and to the younger family who always sat to dinner the moment the man came home from work.

To Annalisa, the phone booth across the street became a window to the world for all the people who lifted that receiver, and she dived into their skin too. There was a pigeon that hung around the phone booth, pecking at crumbs before disappearing into the leaning fir tree or into the elm tree protruding from a square of dirt outside of a real estate office on the corner, and Annalisa would often include the bird in these paintings.

In attempting to get into her subjects' heads, she let her imagination run wild with whom these callers might be speaking with. One woman might be calling her father for the first time in twenty years after learning he was dying. A man in a suit, whom Annalisa had named Philip, was making dinner reservations for himself and his wife, whose birthday he'd forgotten the day before. Perhaps this was what Sharon meant by connecting with her subjects. Maybe this was what Sophia Loren would do when stepping into a character's skin. If she understood their motivations, then she might finally paint them true.

She continued her lessons with Sharon Maxwell, and Annalisa learned so much about a side of painting she'd not explored enough. She'd been focused on the technical aspect, but no one had ever taught her about the emotional necessity in painting great pieces. In a way, Sharon's class wasn't about painting at all, more about self-expression than technique. They had even had a class where they could paint with only one color.

Of course, Annalisa knew painting was cathartic—that was exactly why she did it—but she didn't quite know that there was a philosophy behind giving everything you have to your art. How could she have, only knowing the hobbyist painters in the Mills? Sharon did a live piece in the end of July, painting for two hours as her students watched with mesmerized eyes. Annalisa thought it one of the most beautiful visions she'd ever seen, a true master who might have well cut herself and brushed her blood onto the canvas.

Sharon didn't offer much commentary on Annalisa's latest works other than quick tips or words of very mild encouragement over her shoulder. "What's behind those eyes, Annalisa?" Or, "What's going on inside your body right now? Paint it."

All Annalisa wanted was for Sharon to say, "Yes! Yes! You've got it. And would you do me the great honor of exhibiting your work on my walls in the spring?"

Getting tougher every moment, though, Annalisa gave each exercise her all and continued to fill her apartment with new works, so much so that she had to shift her budget around to afford the supplies. As much as she wanted to indulge in the deals she found at the Bargain Bin, she rarely allowed herself even one treat. Her diet suffered as well, and soup with a small chunk of bread, maybe a piece of fruit, became her routine. Though she'd grown up with food at the center of her life, it became little more than a means for sustenance, the fuel she needed to make art.

Annalisa didn't just paint on her balcony or in the studio in her bedroom either. Listening to Sharon's advice in one class, she set up her easel in places like Monument Square or Longfellow Square or even along the sidewalk on Commercial Street, where it stank like dead fish from the markets.

In late September, on a Saturday morning, Annalisa had a breakthrough. She was setting up her easel in Longfellow Square when a stunning woman strutted by. She was striking; the way she carried herself, the way her outfit popped, she looked almost like Brigitte Bardot but with darker hair.

As the woman disappeared down the sidewalk, Annalisa held fast to her image. She could still see the details of the woman's white-and-brown leather purse, the way it hung just past the hem of her plaid silk shirt. The woman was all color, from the velvet beret to the green handkerchief around her neck down to her stark white culottes.

Annalisa had always considered herself fashionable, a passion she'd carried over from her mother, but she'd learned so much more at Pride's, where she caught constant glimpses of some of the most fashionable women in New England. The woman who'd just walked by had the magic, and Annalisa felt a desperate need to put her on the page.

She gave the woman a name and a story and then reached for her pencil. Under Sharon's tutelage, Annalisa had become much more liberal in her art, stretching boundaries any way she could. She gave the beret on the woman's head flowers that rose up like fireworks to the top of the canvas. A trail of money spilled out of the purse.

After a satisfactory sketch, she reached for her paints. With the rest of the world on hold, she fell into her creation. She'd never worked so fast in her life, and after a couple of hours, she was mostly done. She stood back and examined her work. Something was clicking.

Deciding to do the finishing touches at home, she headed back to her place for a sandwich. She spent the stroll thinking about her subject and this particular piece. Was this the voice that Jackie had brought up so long ago? Was Annalisa finally breaking through? What if she was supposed to paint women?

Stylish, fashionable, powerful, and hardheaded women.

Something felt divinely right about it. She'd painted three pieces from the Women's Strike for Equality in August, and maybe that had been the seed. Her calling might be to give voices to these strong women. There was no doubt Annalisa wanted to be one of them herself. It wasn't necessarily about the money that these women possessed, but that was part of it. More so, it was their confidence and strength and fearlessness. That was what Annalisa liked the most about city women. Even seventy-year-old women weren't afraid to hop on a bus alone.

Passing by Walt's shop, she decided to pop in and share her revelation. After waiting impatiently as he helped a customer with a broken pocket watch, Annalisa met him at the counter by the cash register. "I think I've found my voice. Only a few months here and I've found it!"

Though he didn't share her elation, she told him about her idea of giving voices to all the women out there by putting the strongest of them on the page. Nearly shaking with glee, she drew the painting out of her tote and showed it to him.

"Oh my." Suddenly engaged, he pointed at it from the opposite side of the counter. "This is what you should be doing for a living."

She laughed. "That's the idea, Mr. Burzinski." Her heart raced with a youthful feeling of having discovered her true calling.

"Please call me Walt, young lady."

"*Walt*, I just need to find a gallery willing to take a chance on me." She'd been turned down by two other galleries in the last month. Then something occurred to her.

"Would you be interested in selling some of my work? For a cut, of course." She didn't mention that he could use a little color anyway. He had every shade of black and brown covered. Even her most lugubrious pieces might lighten up the place.

"I've got stacks of good stuff upstairs that needs a home," she continued. At least she thought they were good, even if the galleries weren't yet interested. Sharon still pushed her to connect. If Annalisa heard Sharon say, "Annalisa Mancuso, let go and dive into their skin!" one more time, she was going to throw someone through the warehouse window. Sometimes she'd even snap back, "I am letting go!" Then Sharon would give a silver-eyed wink and walk away. Maybe this new avenue of strong women would pique Sharon's interest.

Walt scratched his two-day-old beard. "You are a determined person, aren't you?"

Determined and thick skinned, she thought, as she decided to push the idea. "It might bring you some new customers. I imagine anyone looking for a fine watch or clock is in the market for a nice painting." She eyed him like he'd be crazy to say no.

"How sly you are," he finally said. "Well, I don't see why not."

Five hundred noes and two yeses, she thought. She could play those odds.

While discussing the terms, she eyed the back wall, where several metal shelves held boxes overflowing with mechanical parts and who knew what else. Feeling connected to her muse more than she could ever remember, she decided she'd love to make a new set of wind chimes that afternoon, a gift to herself for accomplishing so much in these first few months in Portland.

She leaned in. "Can I ask you one more thing?"

He chuckled in his very Walt way, almost as subtle as Nonna's. "I have a feeling you're going to ask anyway."

"I want to make a set of wind chimes to keep the others company. It looks like you have all sorts of goodies back there, and there's a hook that needs a purpose upstairs. Would you let me poke around and see if I can find something that might work?"

As grumpy as he could be, he might have said something about how the wind chimes hanging on her balcony now were nothing but a racket, but she'd told him about making them with her mother a few days prior, so that argument would have been rude.

As if realizing he couldn't say no for fear of feeling guilty, he said, "If you must. It's forty years of parts doing nothing but collecting dust." What wasn't collecting dust?

He went back to work, and she fought off sneezes as she rummaged around. For an artist, these shelves were a treasure trove of possibilities. A dusty one but special nonetheless, full of wonderfully alien parts.

After five minutes, she raised a beautiful brass piece. "What's this?"

He looked up from his desk, where he worked on a cuckoo clock. "That's a pendulum bob that used to swing in an old grandfather clock damaged when a roof caved in from the rain back in the . . . fifties, I think."

"Do you mind if I use it? It could be the perfect striker to put in the center."

He gave her a look like she'd asked for one of his kidneys but then acquiesced. "Yes, go ahead."

At that moment, the bells of noon rang and Annalisa smiled. It was funny how her life had come to beat to the sound of the noon and midnight bells.

She returned to the shelves and searched through the boxes. She found a spool of old black nylon cord and then a few old keys and some other parts that belonged to different timepieces. She grabbed a few tiny brass pieces that she thought might be fun to include in one of her newer paintings. That wouldn't be very "old soul" of her, but maybe some new tricks might lead her even closer to her voice.

In the next box, she came across an old photograph in a fragile frame. It was a picture of Walt from maybe twenty years earlier. He looked so much livelier back then. He rested his arm around a woman Annalisa could only assume was his wife. She had long curly locks of red hair. They stood on a beach with the ocean behind them. She flipped the photograph over. In a faded cursive, it read: *Graystone, 1951.*

Annalisa entered the shop from the back room, waving the photo. "Was this your wife?" She set the photo down in front of him.

She saw a slight change in his body, a slump of the shoulders, almost a deflation as Walt slowly pulled his attention away from a watch to inspect her find. "Please return that instantly."

"Oh, I'm sorry." Had she done something wrong?

"It's fine," he said, handing the photo back to her. "Just put it back where you found it, and that'll be enough snooping for the day."

"Where's Graystone?" she asked, too curious to let it go. "I want to go there."

"Please," he almost barked.

She tightened up, feeling how his past haunted him.

More calmly but no less deliberately, he said, "I'd like for you to put the photo back where you found it." With that, he returned his attention to the watch.

Annalisa glanced at the photo one last time. She could see in the younger Walt's expression how much he'd loved the redhead in his arm.

No wonder he was still in pain. That was the way Nonno used to look at Nonna. For a quick flash of a second, she wished Walt and Nonna could connect; they were both in the same spot. When they'd met, though, the first time Nonna had—albeit reluctantly—come down to visit Annalisa, the two had barely spoken a word to one another. *Eh, probably better that way,* Annalisa decided. Then they wouldn't be forced to endure even more loss down the line.

She collected her finds, feeling responsible for cutting open his wound. "I'm sorry for the photo."

"It's fine, it's fine," he said, waving her off.

"What was your wife like?" Annalisa asked, thinking she was playing with fire.

Looking to be at his wit's end, he plonked the watch onto his desk and removed his glasses. "I'll not ask about the boy you broke up with if you don't ask about my wife. Seems fair enough, yeah?"

She looked down at the ground hard.

"Good," he said, "now bring me down some paintings tomorrow, and we'll see what we can do about mounting them and finding some wall space."

She thanked him and uttered not another word as she slipped out of his shop. On the way up, she stopped to check her mailbox and found a letter from Thomas. Her heart leaped every time she'd found one of his letters, as if nothing else could bring her so much joy. She'd been corresponding since she'd sent that first letter to Fort Dix, mentioning the nude model. He'd written her back with lighthearted humor, much like what he sent to his mother. Perhaps humor was his way of coping. He'd joked about push-ups and running and more push-ups and said he spent Zero Week washing dirty jungle fatigues. The worst part was the inoculations delivered with an air gun. *Makes a measles shot feel like a kiss on the cheek.*

In the previous letter, he'd told her he would be moving to Fort Polk, also known as Tigerland, in Louisiana for advanced infantry training. She knew nothing about army speak, but he was slowly teaching her. It was all about acronyms. His MOS code was 11B. She still didn't know the meaning of MOS, but he'd explained that 11B meant he would be an infantryman and most likely ship to Vietnam and see frontline action. Reading that part had struck her harshly, and she could imagine only in her worst nightmares seeing Thomas as one of the battle-weary soldiers stationed in Vietnam, as shown on the news.

Not only was his MOS an indication of his trajectory, but he wrote that most everyone in Tigerland went to RVN. She did know what RVN meant from the news. Republic of Vietnam. Fort Polk shared similar weather with Southeast Asia, so soldiers were often acclimated there on their way. Knowing that she was in no small part culpable for his situation was enough to shatter any progress she was making if she let herself mull it over for too long.

Wishing he had written to say that he was coming home and that he'd heard word of the end of the war, she raced up the steps, sprawled out on the couch, and relished every word.

Louisiana is a hell hole, he started out in what was three pages of barely legible chicken scratch. *The only good thing down here is the craw-dads. They're like little lobsters and remind me of home. It turns out I love Maine. And you know what I really miss? Snow. It's so darn hot down here.*

She appreciated his humor but could feel his unhappiness. He wasn't built for war, and she could only imagine how Mr. Sunshine was losing his sparkle. All because of her.

He asked if she'd drawn any more naked men and wondered if Portland was getting cold. He also asked her if she'd sold any paintings yet and if she was still loving Portland. Instead of offering some weak apology for getting him into this devilish mess, she wrote him about her breakthrough and asked if he'd heard about Jimi Hendrix's death. She also mentioned that she'd tried Emma again with no luck. As she signed her name, an idea popped into her head. She went out to the balcony with her sketch pad and drew him a picture of the view. Then, to please him, she made it snow.

Chapter 22

A Speed Sketch

Annalisa found Thomas's response on her way back from work two weeks later, and she dashed up the stairs with Christmas glee, eager to read the letter. It was a Wednesday just after three, and she'd been thinking about her most recent class with Sharon on the walk home. She'd decided she wasn't quite ready to tell her teacher about her breakthrough with regard to painting these powerful women and wanted to play with the idea more.

Kicking off her shoes, Annalisa settled into the couch to read.

If you knew only how happy it made me to open your letter and find your drawing. Can we call that tree by the phone booth the Leaning Tower of Treeza? How clever he could be, she thought, as she read the rest of his letter. *Yes,* he said, *we heard about Jimi. Terrible. And Janis Joplin too. I'm sure you saw the Wichita State U plane went down. Tell me some good news, Anna.* He said that it should be a crime for Louisiana to be so hot in October, that he felt like he already had one foot in the jungles of Asia. Then he asked her for a drawing of one of these women she had written about, wanting to see the style she was going after. He always asked her about her art and was unwavering with his support, which filled her up but also made her question her decision to leave him.

Thinking of Emma, she wondered if she was doing any better, if maybe she'd found some happy moments in the sunshine of summer.

Annalisa wished there were something she could do, but Emma had shown she had no interest in continuing their relationship.

She sketched an idea of what she'd been doing and then accompanied it with her response. *The good news is that Nixon is finally pulling soldiers out.* She'd become an avid watcher of the news since she had such a vested interest now in the outcome. The day before, Nixon had promised to pull forty thousand troops out of Vietnam by Christmas. She felt so hopeful for Michael and for Thomas and for the other soldiers. *Is there talk of the war coming to an end? When do you think you'd have to ship out? I pray every day that you won't have to.* She asked him about Emma and if he was still able to keep up with sports and if he was happy at all. She wanted to cheer him up and make more jokes about summer camp and building forts with his pals, but the closer he came to his tour, the less humor she could find.

She'd done this to him. What was funny about that?

As she licked the glue of the envelope, she thought of their last kiss, during one of his driving lessons, and that led her to thinking about backing into Walt's car. She ultimately decided not to tell him about the accident, as she didn't want to give him anything else to worry about. His car was as good as new now, so maybe it was a forgivable white lie.

About five o'clock, Annalisa went down the stairs and around the corner to the shop to see if she'd had any success today. "Did we sell any, Walt?" she called out as she entered.

He was on one knee polishing the glass of his watch counter. "About an hour ago," he said. "That one with the money spilling out of the purse."

"Really?" Her heart fluttered. That made six paintings at a total of five dollars each. She went to the wall he was letting her use and proudly saw that only five were left.

He grimaced as he stood, then cleared his throat. "Keep this up and your efforts will pay the rent."

"Wouldn't that be something?" she called out. Returning to his side of the shop, she reached for the rag. "Let me help. You're gonna hurt yourself."

"Oh heavens," he said, as if she'd insulted him. "I've been cleaning glass around here for forty years. I think I can manage on my own."

"Nonsense." She snatched the rag from his hands and retrieved the glass cleaner from the counter. "So can I bring down more paintings?"

"Might as well." He watched her with his hands on his waist, as if he were skeptical of her ability. She'd show him. You didn't spend three years with her grandmother without coming away knowing how to polish glass.

She moved to the next section. "Tell me something, Walt. Why don't you ever talk about yourself? We've known each other since June, and I still don't know the first thing."

"What's there to know?"

She wanted to ask about his wife but didn't want to get into more trouble. "Where are you from? What brought you to Portland, Maine? How does one get into repairing timepieces?"

He pointed to a spot she missed—or at least he thought she did. "You must be terribly bored to want to polish glass and ask me questions."

"I'm curious; that's all."

As she polished the case that featured an incredibly stunning collection of wrist and pocket watches, he opened up. "I was always taking things apart—often to my parents' dismay. The watchmaker next door to my father's butcher shop in Manhattan took me in and encouraged my curiosity. I worked for him into my thirties, long after my parents passed."

She glanced back and saw Walt relishing in these memories, even as he coughed into his white handkerchief.

"Then a woman named Gertrude walked through the door," he continued, "and I was smitten immediately. I suppose we both were, and it was the Roaring Twenties, you see. Oh, you missed those years, Annalisa. The war was over, and New York was the place to be. I pranced her around like I was the king of Manhattan . . ."

Walt stopped and paused, and Annalisa knew he could see through the years back to one of those moments with Gertrude. "Then the Depression came and I lost my job. Gertrude's father owned a shipping company in Portland and offered help if we moved north, so that's what we—"

The bell above the door rang, and they turned.

"Oh good, you're still open," a lady said, searching the room, finally setting her gaze on Annalisa. "I'm looking for a gift for my husband. He's turning sixty tomorrow, and I've put it off to the last minute."

Annalisa had fallen into Walt's story with him but was ripped right out of the dream when she saw that it was Patty Garner, the manager of the Advertising Department at Pride's, the woman for whom she'd originally wanted to work. Patty was the hero of every woman in that store, a female who'd somehow shown enough force to climb her way to the top. She was Portland's own Dorothy Shaver, who had risen to the top of Lord & Taylor, arguably the finest department store chain in the country. Annalisa had painted Shaver a week earlier, so she was heavy on her mind.

Patty must have been in her fifties and had thick, wavy hair. Her gray-and-white checkered wool dress was conservative but stylish. Annalisa imagined she took long baths in her claw-foot tub after work and then drank dirty martinis with her obedient husband. No doubt she wore the pants in her marriage. A substantial diamond that was even bigger than that of Thomas's mother weighed down Patty's finger.

"I actually don't work here," Annalisa said, pulling her eyes away from the diamond.

Walt stepped forward. "Oh, I have just the thing for your husband. Are you thinking a watch or a clock? What would he enjoy? I've some new Omegas and IWCs."

Annalisa stepped aside, thinking she had to say something to Patty before the woman left. With Mr. Miller always lurking around, she'd never get a chance at work. She went to the other side of the shop and looked at the paintings left on the wall. Only one of them was recent, since her breakthrough. Deciding the time was now, she raced out of the shop and ran up the steps.

Finding her favorite pieces of late, including the one of Dorothy Shaver, she crammed them into her orange tote and dashed back down the stairs. Walt had put several watches on the counter that Annalisa had just polished, and Patty was inspecting them, one at a time.

Annalisa wanted so badly to interrupt, but she didn't want to get in the way of a sale for Walt. He'd been letting Annalisa use his workshop to mount her pieces onto wood, so she stepped back behind the cash register and pretended to be busy. She was anything but busy, though. Her mind exploded with excitement at the chance of finally asking for a job.

Once Walt had made his sale and flung the cash register drawer closed, Annalisa came from the back and said to Patty, "Excuse me, Mrs. Garner? I have to say something. My name's Annalisa, and I work in the Bargain Bin. We've never met, but I know exactly who you are. Actually, I applied for the fashion illustrator job that was open this summer."

"Oh, I see," Patty said, holding the bag with her husband's new Patek Philippe watch. "So you're an artist? And call me Patty, please."

"I paint mostly but have been drawing all my life. I'm very comfortable with pen and ink." She knew the fashion illustrators all used pen and ink.

Annalisa feared Patty was a second away from asking her age and then inquiring about a degree. Instead, she said, "Interesting."

Reaching for her tote, Annalisa said, "I just so happen to have some of my work." She unclasped the button and pulled out the three top pieces and set them on the counter. Each one featured one of Annalisa's signature women, and she felt like Patty could have easily been one of them.

Patty looked them over. "I love these ladies," she finally said. When she reached the one of Dorothy Shaver, a copy of an old photograph with Dorothy resting her chin on her knuckles, she said, "Look at her. You know she's my idol, right?"

"Isn't she everyone's?" Annalisa asked.

Patty looked at Dorothy and then back to Annalisa. "My kind of girl. Why don't you come by the office in the morning, say, eight on the nose? We can discuss."

Annalisa had to keep from thrusting her right arm into the air as she said, "Yes, that would be wonderful."

—

"I would be so proud to work up here," Annalisa told Patty at 8:00 a.m. sharp the next morning. "No one will work harder."

"I'm starting to believe that about you," Patty said from the chair behind her desk. "Tell you what. Why don't you sketch out one of those dresses for me?"

Annalisa turned to the three dresses with busy patterns hanging by the wall. "Right now?"

"Why not?" Patty slid a legal pad and pen her way. "I'll be back in five minutes, and I want to see one of the women from your paintings adorned with your favorite of the dresses."

Before Annalisa could say another word, Patty was gone. In the quiet, she spun her chair around and went to work. Though her nerves tried to hold her back, she pushed through them and settled into her art. When Patty returned, Annalisa handed her the pad. Feeling like she'd been in this situation before, Annalisa crossed her legs and awaited her fate.

"Okay, you're pretty great," she said almost too casually. Annalisa had hoped for jumping jacks. "So I do need help right now," Patty went on, "and you're more than qualified. All the winter clothes are coming in, and with Christmas around the corner, it's super busy. I can't guarantee you a full-time job, though, which means you might not have a job at all if I poach you from Ted Miller right now. You know how he can be, I'm sure."

"Yes, I do, but I'm willing to take the risk." The opportunity to finally make decent money was too tempting. Besides, she was exploding with excitement inside.

Rising to her heels, Patty said, "I don't want to promise anything until I've spoken with him, so don't get your hopes up quite yet, but let me see what I can do. He simply takes some finessing, a skill you and I both seem to have a handle on."

Annalisa smiled broadly, feeling like she'd just been knighted a city girl by one of Portland's finest. "Thank you so much," she said, almost breathless. "I won't let you down."

Patty seemed pleased. "You'd better not."

Feeling like she'd finally gotten a break, Annalisa prayed that Ted Miller wouldn't get in the way. She went for a walk along Congress Street but was back in time for her 9:00 a.m. shift. Just before her lunch break, Ted Miller found her adding blue stickers to a bunch of older items that needed to be moved out.

"Got a minute?" he asked.

Annalisa backed away from the rack, thinking this could go very well, or very badly. Mr. Miller was not the kind of man who liked being undermined.

"We've decided to move you up to Advertising."

"Really? Thank you, Mr. Miller." Annalisa almost broke into a dance.

He straightened his bow tie. "Just remember who looks out for you. I had to go out of my way to make this happen."

Annalisa knew it had nothing to do with him, but she let him take the credit. "You've been a great boss. I'm really going to miss you." This might have been the biggest exaggeration of her entire life.

"Let's just hope you're not getting in over your head, little girl. Now head up to Personnel, and they'll get you switched over."

Annalisa immediately stopped what she was doing and rode the escalator toward the next level of her life, thinking she couldn't wait to call Nonna.

And to write Thomas.

Chapter 23

Finally, Her Voice

A confidence Annalisa had never known came to visit that October of 1970. She was given a giant pay increase, earning twice what they'd paid her in the Bargain Bin. She was the youngest employee in the Advertising Department and had her own slanted desk that looked out over the city. Along with finally achieving financial freedom, she found great joy in breathing life into the winter outfits with pen and ink.

After a long few years of hardship, things were working out, as if she were becoming one of the women she drew. More important, she took these lessons home to her studio. Armed with even more knowledge of the latest fashions, she painted these wonderfully fierce women strutting through life with determination. She painted so quickly, too, as if her confidence was her creativity's caffeine.

In fact, she couldn't keep up with the demand in Walt's shop and had raised the price to ten dollars a painting. To her complete disbelief, she was now paying her rent with her art. For the first time in her life she allowed herself to indulge. She began to dress like her women on the canvas. *That's right, canvas.* With her increased income, she was working on canvas more, which only made sense, because she'd found her voice, and it was time to take her art—every single piece—more seriously.

With her increase in income, she allowed herself more than a few indulgences. She first spent time down in the Bargain Bin, finally taking advantage of her discount, but she even spent money at the makeup and perfume counters and on the racks of new arrivals on the first floor. The next thing she knew, she was replacing pieces of furniture in the apartment and even treating Nino or Aunt Julia or Nonna to dinner when they'd come to town. This was how it all happened, she learned. Hard work eventually paid off.

She saved her favorite paintings, though, waiting for the day when she would burst into Sharon's warehouse to blow her mind. Annalisa could already see her female subjects looking back at her from the walls of the warehouse in April. It wasn't yet time, though. Having only just realized her potential, she wanted to make sure her new portfolio proved to Sharon that she'd finally learned how to connect and that she was more than one of her teacher's talented students. How could Sharon disagree, for Heaven's sake? Annalisa was her own embodiment of these paintings.

In her last lesson, Sharon had shared one of her favorite quotes, something Amedeo Modigliani had said. "'When I know your soul, I will paint your eyes.'"

Annalisa had replied back, "Exactly! I know. I get it now. You just wait and see what I have coming your way."

She went home for Thanksgiving and felt like a successful woman as she regaled her family with all the stories of her first five months in Portland. The most exciting news was that Patty had just offered her a full-time position as a fashion illustrator, giving her a generous salary with benefits. Nonna and everyone else was so proud of her, that she'd finally made it on her own. She knew even her mother was looking down at her with applause.

After such a long hard road, Annalisa had found her voice and was making good money, and life was beautiful and uncomplicated, and nothing could get in her way and then . . . Thomas called.

"I'm in New Orleans," he said, "flying into Boston tomorrow. Coming home."

It was December 12, and Annalisa was swamped with work at Pride's and trying to get together her portfolio for Sharon.

Talk about having the wind knocked out of her. As much as she'd enjoyed their letters, the last thing she needed was to have an actual interaction with him in person. Forget about guarding her art; what about her heart? In the silence after his words, she forced herself to remember how their relationship had screwed up so many things.

"I guess you need your car, don't you?" she asked, not meaning to be so harsh to him. "Sorry, I didn't mean it like that. I am *slammed* with work—finally landed a full-time position—and you caught me off guard. Wow, you're coming home." She hated it when she rambled, but he'd just dropped one heck of a bomb on her.

"Yeah, I've got three weeks of leave before I ship out. I'd love to see you if possible. And you're right; I'd like to borrow my car, if you don't mind."

Ship out, she thought. He was really going to war. "Yeah, of course," she said, not giving a damn about the car. All that she could think about was that she was the reason he was going to war. "It's parked in my lot downstairs."

Thoughts of losing him all over again pricked her eyes. As much as she wanted to see him, though, she couldn't. The war didn't change the fact that they were better off apart, so she tried to think of the best way to exchange keys without putting herself in a vulnerable position. "What time do you arrive?"

"My bus gets in at around one."

She took a thankful breath. "Gotcha. I'm gonna be at work."

"I figured." She could hear his disappointment, and she couldn't blame him. She was disappointed in herself. Why, after half a year, was he still so present in her heart?

"It's Christmas season," she said, feeling a need to explain herself. "We're already working on the spring line, and I'm still trying to put together a portfolio for Sharon Maxwell. I know you remember her, the—"

"Anna," he said, stopping her, "it's no sweat. I just thought I'd try." With a more chipper tone, he asked, "How are you, anyway? I'm jazzed to hear you're busy."

"Thanks," she said. "Yeah, busy just the way I like it. When do you actually leave? Maybe we could connect after Christmas?" She didn't just say that, did she?

"I leave from McGuire on the sixth."

She wasn't ready for any of this—his call, his voice. His going to Vietnam. The man she loved was coming home for a little while to very well say goodbye to his friends and family. A goodbye that might be his last. And here she was fumbling around with a way to avoid seeing him.

Kicking herself for being so . . . so . . . selfish, she said, "Yeah, let's get together after Christmas. Maybe we can meet in the Mills for lunch or something."

"Yeah, if you can find the time." She could tell he was let down, and it reinforced her decision to avoid the meeting. She had to hold strong—for both of their sakes. She couldn't just assume that he wouldn't make it back. And when he did, they'd still have the same issues as they'd had originally. Or worse. The last time, Emma had ended up in the hospital, and he'd ended up with a draft notice. Their misfortune quite possibly had no limit.

No, they'd gotten through the first six months. Why cut open old wounds? Even as she thought that, though, she knew her own wounds hadn't healed at all.

"You know what I can do?" she said, needing to get off the phone before she had a mental breakdown. "If it's okay, I'll leave the keys at the watch shop. Walt can give them to you. You can walk from the bus station." She hoped he wouldn't ask to come see her at work.

"Yeah, that's great, Anna." He didn't sound angry at all but more bummed out. She wouldn't dare tell him that it was her fault, not his, that she couldn't allow herself to see him.

219

"And you don't have to bring the car back," she said. "I'm so appreciative, but I'll be buying one soon." Even the notion of buying a car with her own money was empowering and reminded her to stay strong.

"Save your money," he said. "I'll drop it back off on my way out. We don't have to see each other."

As much as she wanted to say, "I do want to see you; it's just busy around here," she didn't dare. He knew exactly what she was doing, and she wasn't about to deny it.

Regarding the car, she said, "If you really want to leave the car, then thanks." She set the receiver down for a moment to collect herself. Then, "It's good to hear your voice, Thomas." It truly was, but no good would come of the two of them seeing each other in Portland. It was her city now, not theirs.

The transaction went down swimmingly, meaning Thomas had come the next day, met Walt and retrieved the keys, then headed home to Davenport without once seeing Annalisa. She certainly felt bad, especially since he'd been so kind to her by leaving her the car, but it was true: she had to focus on her career.

As much confidence as Annalisa did have in her new paintings, which were night and day from what she'd been doing before meeting Sharon, she was beyond terrified to show her teacher her progress. Thomas's return was such a distraction that she'd gotten nothing of consequence done since their phone call. He might as well have been standing behind her easel, waving his hands and making bird sounds.

She laid out each of her top choices on the same big table in Sharon's studio where she'd first introduced Sharon to her work and wondered if Walt's father had felt like this when he'd slap a piece of meat in front of a customer. There was certainly a loss of magic as she began to make money with her art, an extra layer of pressure getting in the way of her creativity.

As often was the case, the Grateful Dead played from the record player. The same woody incense filled the air. Sharon studied each piece, and Annalisa waited as if her entire life was in the balance. It truly was. For Annalisa's entire life to blossom, all Sharon needed to do was say, "You've done it. I don't know how, but in six months, you have risen to the artist you're supposed to be." It would be a confirmation more than anything else, as Annalisa knew she'd done it.

"This isn't you," Sharon said, kicking the leg of the metaphorical stool upon which Annalisa stood.

The balloon of confidence that had been inflating since mid-October popped like Sharon had stuck a pin in it. Annalisa grew angry, as if Sharon had slapped her out of the blue, the red mark on her cheek the same as a failing grade stamped on a test. "What do you mean, it's not me? Of course it's me. This is me connecting with my subjects. These are the women I understand. This is my voice."

Sharon looked at Annalisa, up and down, up and down, making her feel uncomfortable in her fancy outfit she'd bought the other day at Pride's.

"I don't think it's you."

"How would you know?" Sharon was wrong, as simple as that. Or she was jealous.

Her teacher went to the record player and lifted the needle off the record. The Grateful Dead gave way to a silence Annalisa wasn't ready for. When Sharon turned back, she said, "I don't think you can figure out all the answers in half a year."

"I'm not saying I have all the answers," Annalisa agreed, "but I know that you and Jackie have told me to find myself as a painter. Well, this is me. This is what I love, and apparently Portland likes them, because I can't keep them on the walls."

Sharon approached her and stopped when they were face-to-face. "What do you want me to tell you? That you're ready for the big time? That you should be on the next bus down to Manhattan? Or that I'd like you to be part of my show? I don't think you're ready, and you're not alone. None of the students in these classes *or* in my classes at the college are ready. It takes years, sometimes a lifetime, to realize our inner artist."

Annalisa's head felt dizzy with anger, disappointment, and frustration. She'd been painting her whole life!

"Only you can know what you're meant to paint," Sharon said, "but I told you in the beginning of our classes that I would give you everything I have. In this case, it's the very difficult position of honesty."

She pointed back at the women on the paper making up Annalisa's portfolio. "I don't think that those women are you, and I sense a great feeling of emptiness that hurts me inside. I don't think this is where Annalisa Mancuso stops getting better. These are great, don't get me wrong, and I'm not surprised you're selling them. I'm telling you, though, as a teacher and as someone who greatly admires your talent, you can do better."

Annalisa's anger rose into her cheeks, and she felt her jaws bite hard against one another. This whole thing with Thomas had left her on edge, and she'd definitely found her inner tiger. "You know what it is, Sharon. You're just going to push me no matter what. Because the minute you tell me I'm great, you're worried I'll drop out of your stupid classes." Annalisa couldn't believe she'd just said that, but . . . if Sharon was going to be honest, so would she.

Sharon dipped her chin. "I don't think you mean that."

"I appreciate what you've done for me," Annalisa said, looking around the room at Sharon's work, "and I do think that I've learned a lot, but I'm done here. You don't get me. Jackie doesn't get me either. And that's fine. I can do it on my own."

Her teacher crossed her arms and frowned. "Suit yourself."

Annalisa collected her art and stuffed them into her tote. No doubt she would continue to get better. She wasn't stupid, expecting to be a master at eighteen years old. But she was starting to think that Sharon might not be the right teacher. Maybe Sharon and her hippie ways and her damn art show weren't the pathway Annalisa needed. She was doing fine just the way things were.

Feeling Sharon watching her, Annalisa marched out of the studio and started the long walk from the empty warehouses of the Old Port back home. The thing was she was a grown-up now, and she needed to trust her instincts. She had definitely reached a new level in her painting, no matter what Sharon said, and her instincts were now telling her that it was time to move on.

Chapter 24

TREMBLING LIPS AND A HEART ON A WINDOW

Annalisa worked long days at Pride's and was at the same time attempting to break through the veil of doubt Sharon had draped over her eyes. All of it, she knew, was a distraction from Thomas, though. The busier she kept herself, the less she thought about him being back in Davenport, saying his goodbyes. He most likely was putting all his focus on his sister, trying to comfort her before his departure. Was he also being driven mad to know Annalisa was so close?

The problem was that she had become a terror to work with at Pride's, snapping at anyone who dared to challenge her, just as she'd done to Sharon, and with regard to her art, she felt like she'd lost her groove. Sure, Sharon had knocked her down pretty harshly, but even more so, Thomas was still waving his darn arms and making bird sounds behind her easel.

Leaving him out of it for a moment—as if she could—how could she not be onto something with her new style? Customers specifically sought out her work at Walt's shop. Bottom line, Sharon had broken the pact of a great teacher by shattering Annalisa's excitement. Maybe Annalisa could do better, and she was trying, but why couldn't Sharon offer just a bit of praise for once? Annalisa knew it wasn't Sharon's jealousy or her need for Annalisa's weekly payment, as she'd so rudely suggested before marching out.

She couldn't exactly say why Sharon was so opposed to her new pieces, and maybe that was why it hurt so badly. If, in fact, she hadn't found her voice, then she was worse off than she had been even before moving. Perhaps out of shame more than anything else, she chose to drop out of Sharon's classes.

Though it never seemed to get easier, Annalisa was no stranger to fighting through emotional turmoil in order to break through the plateaus of her creative journey, and that was what she worked toward, finding a place of confidence again, despite Sharon and Thomas.

On Tuesday, January 5, 1971, Thomas called, and she'd never needed to hear his voice more. In fact, she'd stared at her phone more than once, waiting for his call. Her world was unraveling, and he was the only one who could understand. In fairness to him, though, she had no right to lean on him anymore, having hidden from him for three weeks. She wondered if he could feel all this turmoil through the phone line as they spoke.

"Anyway," he said, moving on from a klutzy chat about each other's Christmas, "I was hoping we could have lunch on my way through town to drop off the Beetle." Then he gave her a lifeline. "No pressure, though; I know you're busy."

With the demands of Pride's and this uphill battle against her creative demons, the entire thing with Thomas being in town was absolutely killing her. No matter how much she was working *or* how bad an idea it was to see each other, she needed to make time for him. What kind of person couldn't find an hour for lunch to spend with someone she cared about before he went off to war?

In a moment of weakness, as her mind debated his proposal, she knew that she was simply justifying her much-deeper need to see him. Between her emotional and artistic rut, she felt like he might be the escape she needed. It wasn't that she could allow their relationship to go back to what it had once been, but maybe a little time with him could quell this heartache, which was more obstinate than Annalisa or even Nonna.

"Let's do it," she said, thinking: *What did you just get yourself into?* They agreed to noon, and she asked him to buzz her apartment upon arrival. She would pop down to meet him. As she'd said as much, though, she froze. Surely, he would want to come up and see her life as she'd described it in her letters. It was one thing to have lunch, entirely another to let him into her new life.

Having dropped out of Sharon's classes, she finally had Tuesday nights free. In the case that she did let him up, she decided to clean for a while. She wasn't exactly messy, but her crazy workload definitely didn't leave much time for house chores. Staying busy seemed to be her only medicine, and every Tuesday night wrought fresh pain as she imagined the rest of her class hard at work under Sharon's tutelage.

In the morning, she put a little extra time into her attire. She wore a double-breasted shearling coat that fell almost exactly to the length of her black wool miniskirt—a cut of which Nonna would not have approved. To complement her outfit, she first tried her black leather knee-high boots with turquoise jewels she'd attached to the buckles, but questioning her motives, she'd changed into a pair of Tony Lama boots that she'd found in a vintage store.

First thing she did when she walked into work was ask Patty if she could take a little longer lunch to spend time with her ex-boyfriend before he shipped off.

"Take a couple of hours. By the way, you look extra good today," Patty said, eyeing her outfit. "Are we still claiming not to like him?"

Annalisa glanced down at her jacket and skirt. "We're just friends. Doesn't mean I can't look good, though."

"Well, you give him a reason to come home, okay?"

After an eye roll, Annalisa replied, "He'll need a reason other than me, or he'll be one disappointed soldier when he steps off the plane." Even Annalisa didn't believe what she was saying. In truth, she had no idea what she was doing allowing herself to see him. She was damned either way.

Wearing a smock to protect her outfit, she spent the morning on her stool, attempting to draw an imaginary woman wearing a light-weight green coat over blue denim that hung on a metal rack a few feet past her slanted drawing desk.

After months of illustrating these dresses, she was still having fun being in the industry and enjoying first peeks at the newest fashions, but the actual work of drawing the ads with pen and ink had become easy, essentially a rote experience. Not today, though. Nothing was coming easy. She didn't feel connected at all to the women she was trying to draw to life.

On cloudy days like today, they opened the drapes on the windows overlooking Congress Street, so she spent more time than usual with her pen resting next to the inkwell and her eyes looking out over the city she now called home. Seeing Thomas was wreaking all sorts of havoc in her heart, like she'd downed a second and third cup of coffee. She was nervous to see him for so many reasons, the strongest being that today might be the last day she *ever* saw him. The idea was a knife to the gut. She hated to think that way, to give any light to the idea, but the war was far from over, and the news seemed to get only uglier.

A few minutes before noon, she went out into the dreary and cold day. The recent snow had partially melted, leaving the sidewalks slippery with hidden patches of ice. Rounding the corner to her apartment, she saw that he was early, the yellow Beetle parked in the small lot by the stairs. He stepped out to greet her, and she gasped.

The army had transformed and even consumed him. His head was shaved, and he had the steel-rod posture of a soldier. She'd thought he might have been in uniform, but she also knew that soldiers preferred not to draw attention these days due to the ever-growing antiwar senti-ment. He was dressed simply in jeans and a sweater.

He stopped five feet from her. They stared at each other for a moment, and she could hear her heart thump. What if the men in green had cut all his kindness out of him? He smiled warmly, though, calming her worry, and she sensed that he hadn't changed *that* much. More to the point, she realized that she loved him more than ever. Seven months it had been. Wasn't time supposed to heal all? If anything, time had thrown gas on the flames of her longing for him.

One of the many lessons that Walt had taught Annalisa about time was that not all seconds were equal. Some lasted longer than others. The following seconds inched by as if they were waiting on a seed to sprout. What in the hell was she doing here? Everything—both of their lives—was on the line.

"Wow," he whispered with a grin that showed her how much he'd truly missed her. "You look good."

She thanked him with a smile, then, trying to lighten the energy, said, "You've thickened up, haven't you?"

He glanced down at his arms. "They put me to work; that's for sure."

Agonizing seconds ticked by. She was so thrilled and excited and terrified to see him. No other man could ever make her feel this way, and she wondered if she'd done it all wrong by leaving him.

"I missed you," he said, his words blowing up her skirt.

"Oh, hush," she said with a light smirk, determined not to show how weak he made her. She couldn't do that to either one of them. "Didn't they toughen you up down there? It's only been what, six months?"

He chuckled quietly, and she wondered if they might hug. She hoped they would. In the following silence, she saw a deep craving in his eyes that grew in intensity until she had to look away. He stepped forward, though, catching her from falling into awkwardness.

Pulling her into a hug, he held her tightly. She squeezed back, missing him so badly her eyes watered. Feeling his heartbeat against hers made him so much more real and made her question every decision she'd made since the day she'd left him.

When he let go, he held her shoulders. "Hey," he said, his breath clouding up in front of him, "what's this all about?" He wiped a tear from her cheek.

Though she almost turned away, she didn't. "I hate this war more than anything in the world, and I can't believe you're going to that awful place."

He stood strong in his army posture and looked deeply into her eyes. "Don't worry about me, Anna. I'll be fine."

She wanted to tell him that he could never assure her of such a thing. Instead, she wiped her eyes and shook off the sadness.

"How's Emma?" Annalisa asked, knowing she couldn't dwell in this intimate moment any longer without having a complete breakdown. "I've tried to call her a few times but . . . you know . . ." Talking about Emma wasn't much easier, though, as Annalisa still felt like she'd failed her.

"She's okay," he admitted. "Still not eating much. Or smiling much, but she seems to have found a few friends, so that's a big deal. She's a junior now; can you imagine? She's like you, can't wait to get out of Davenport. She might move down here and go to UMPG."

Annalisa recalled how Emma had wanted to follow him to New York. Knowing her, she'd probably follow her brother to Vietnam if they would have let her. "If she does, maybe we can see each other. I really hope we can get past what happened. Did you tell her we were having lunch?"

He shook his head. "Nah, I didn't think it would help anything. She's still so fragile . . . but she'll come around. Trust me. She still loves you; she's just so vulnerable. That's all. How about your family? How's Nonna? I wish we could let her run the mess hall."

"She'd be good at it, wouldn't she? Nonna's Nonna, you know. We see each other about once a month. I have to drag her down here kicking and screaming. According to her, I'm lucky the deviants haven't robbed me yet. Nino comes down every once in a while too. He finally dumped the beater and bought a Mustang with his money from working at the mill. The Mancusos are just busy being the Mancusos."

He smiled. "Tell them all hello for me. Or goodbye, in this case. So you got a place in mind for lunch?" he asked. "Let's get you out of this cold."

Already, Annalisa could sense them falling back into step with one another, finding that ease and comfort that she missed so badly.

She led him to a new hot spot that had just opened up near Pride's, the kind of place she *never* could have afforded when she'd first moved here. Well-dressed and chatty men and women on their lunch breaks filled the twenty tables of this French bistro.

"So did Tigerland turn you into a tiger?" she asked, as he pushed her chair in. He seemed to be the same gentleman he'd always been, maybe even more so.

He settled into his seat and pulled a napkin into his lap. "You would never believe it. Shall I show you my new skills?" He started to stand, as if he were going to perform some sort of silly kung fu move.

"Please don't," she pleaded, looking around.

They shared a wonderful smile, these two tigers still circling each other as if destiny would never allow otherwise.

"We had some good times, didn't we?" she said, thinking that they'd been the best of times.

As they dined on haddock with mashed potatoes and haricot verts, they laughed like they hadn't missed a beat in the more than six months since they'd seen each other. He wanted to know everything about her life, and she happily shared, feeling so joyful to show him that she'd achieved her dream. He was still the same good listener and might not have talked about himself at all had she not prodded him with questions.

His life was the army life now, and he told her everything about his training as a soldier, learning to march and to fire M16s and shoot mortar rounds. Half his speak was so foreign to her, but she understood enough to know that this man that she . . . loved was turning into a soldier just as his best friend, Mitch, had done. He told her that he'd heard Mitch was fighting somewhere near the Laotian border.

Annalisa held back her political opinions. She thought about all the protesters spitting on soldiers and calling them baby killers, and despite her hate for the war, she had no hate for the soldiers. How could anyone? Guys like Thomas were doing their duty for their country, and as he spoke in his army acronyms and talked about his flight out of McGuire Air Force Base the next day and what he expected in the months to come, she knew that the man she loved was a man of great honor.

What would it be like when he returned from the war? If she still felt the way she did now, how could she keep denying them a chance? He was right here in front of her, the reason for her being, proof that love existed—a bushel of apples dropping on her head—and yet she had to remember the consequences. As much as it hurt, as if *hurt* was a worthy word for what she felt inside her heart, she couldn't allow them to be any more than this: ex-lovers bathing in the delights of the past.

Several times, as their conversation weaved from the seriousness of the war to the silliness of being human, she wondered what it would have been like if she hadn't ended their relationship and if he hadn't been drafted. Would they still be together? Would she still be painting? Would he still be on track to go to dental school? Would he have been cut off by his father? Would Emma still be alive, or would she have attempted suicide again—this time, potentially succeeding?

Ultimately, considering she hadn't painted anything groundbreaking lately, she wondered if it was all for nothing. Had she given up a chance at love only to go on and become nothing more than a hobby artist like the other women in the Mills?

Elvis's "Suspicious Minds" played in her head, the push and pull that seemed to define the connection between them.

"Why are you here?" a voice inside asked her. "What are you doing dragging this man along?"

While still carrying on a conversation with Thomas, she screamed to the voice in her head, "I don't fucking know!"

~

"So this is it," she said, pushing open the door to her apartment. How could she not have let him in? He'd been a part of this dream for so long—he'd been the first one to truly support it. Her head was a freaking mess, and she wanted to run out to the balcony and leap to peace. What kind of God would force her to make a decision between the man she loved and her art? What kind of God would let her fall so deeply for a man whose life could be ruined by that same love?

"You've been busy," he said, looking at the paintings hanging on every wall of the living room. "I'm no expert, but I think you're ready for museums."

"Wouldn't that be nice," she said, trying to stomp on her emotions as if they were a fire spreading over a yard of leaves. If only Sharon Maxwell agreed with him.

Forcing herself to stay in the moment, she gave him a tour of her work, showing her progression from last summer to now. He took a long time, looking at each piece, and his interest meant the world to her.

"I thought I was getting somewhere, but Sharon definitely planted a seed of doubt." Annalisa told him what her teacher had said, and how Annalisa had probably ruined any chance of ever showing her work at Sharon's show or any reputable gallery in town. She'd not told anyone about her eruption at the studio, not even Nonna, as she was too ashamed.

As she had expected, telling him made her feel so much better.

"You are getting somewhere, Annalisa. I see it."

"I don't know," she said. "Some people can work their whole lives and not achieve greatness. There has to be a natural talent, stuff that can't be taught." She couldn't believe she was admitting this out loud to someone. "What if I don't have that kind of talent? Anyway, just the struggles of an artist. I haven't done much since Christmas. Who knew there was such a thing as painter's block?"

What she didn't say mattered most of all, but she couldn't dare cross that line. The question she wondered more than any other was: What if she'd given up their love for nothing?

"Don't even go down that road," he said. "Not only are you the most dedicated person I've ever met, but you do have talent. Everyone knows it." He spun around the room. "Look at all these. Don't question yourself now. You've come too far." His unflagging support was a bucket of love dumped over her head, and she didn't know what to do with it.

Thomas pointed out the window to the balcony and beyond. "There it is, the Leaning Tower of Treeza."

"That's it," Annalisa said, sliding open the door and feeling the cold air whipping in, cooling off the fire inside her core.

He took a long look at the chimes she'd made from the pieces in Walt's shop and then cast his eyes over the view she'd drawn for him in the letter she'd sent last summer. "I would sit in my bunk before lights out and look at your drawing, imagining you and this view. Makes me so happy to actually see it."

If he only knew that she'd sat out here and thought of him, too, ached for him, really. And here he was, and she was so damn confused.

He rested his hands on the railing as Annalisa buttoned up her jacket. "Wherever I end up going," he said, "I'll be thinking of you standing out here, maybe thinking about me sometimes."

"Of course I'll be thinking of you, silly," she said, almost too quickly. *Because I love you,* she thought.

Attempting to keep her emotions at bay, she pointed southwest. "That would be Louisiana, somewhere out there." She moved her finger to the right and noticed its shake. "Then Vietnam."

Thomas grabbed her finger and brought her arm down. "Don't be afraid."

For a moment, she thought he might kiss her, and she had no idea what she would have done. Or perhaps she did know. She'd welcome it, bathe in it, but then one kiss would lead to another, and then they'd be right back to last year, back to that night in the waiting room of the hospital where he'd slugged it out with his father while Emma crept back from nearly dying down the hall. If only they lived in a world without consequences.

Despite all the terrible that would come, she would have risked it all just to connect with him so intimately, to taste his lips and to finally even tell him how much she cared. How nice it would be to let it all go for a minute, to eschew responsibility and give in to her desire.

Instead of kissing her, he let her hand go and frowned. "I need to get going so I can catch that two o'clock bus."

In an instant, the wind seemed to die, and the chimes stopped singing. Even her heart stopped fluttering. Though he was respecting the boundaries she'd drawn, she'd hoped he would break them. That was not who he was, though, and his chivalrous act made her want him all the more.

The moment was gone, and her mind returned to his destination. By the time she was having dinner the next night, he'd be breathing Vietnamese air.

Fighting off tears that would have frozen on her cheeks, she put a hand on his strong arm. "You be a warrior, okay? Be strong and don't let your guard down. That's how you come home." She wished she could tell him that she'd be waiting on him, but she couldn't.

"I'll be okay over there; don't worry."

What an impossible notion, to not worry.

They hugged hard, and she whispered a prayer up through those hazy clouds to God, asking that Thomas come home safe and sound. No matter what might become of them, she desperately wanted to lay eyes on him after the war and know that he'd made it back home safely. Letting go of all rationality, she wondered if maybe they could give each other a chance after the war.

They returned to casual conversation as they left the apartment, and she gave him a ride to the bus station. Navigating the icy parking lot, she followed him to buy a ticket and then to his waiting bus. They'd made it just in time. Part of her wished they could talk more, that maybe he'd take a later bus, but today wasn't about her. It was about Thomas boarding a plane en route to one of the most dangerous places on earth.

After another hug, he climbed the steps with his duffel bag slung over his shoulder. He stopped at the top and turned. "Do big things, Anna."

She didn't know what kind of words of encouragement to offer in reply. Her big things didn't feel so big anymore, considering his destination. Finally, she said, "You come home now."

"I will," he promised. His tightened cheeks attempted to hide his feelings.

The bus driver came from inside the station, straightening his navy blue cap. "All right, lovebirds, time to go."

"Keep writing me," he said. "Promise?"

"I promise." Emptiness swelled inside her.

"And pick up your brush."

"Yeah." She wondered if those might be his last words to her . . . *pick up your brush*. The thought traveled like a snake's venom through her body.

Tremendous emotion and thousands of words silently passed between them in their last look. She almost told him she loved him, but she couldn't muster the courage to say it.

Instead, she replied, "Goodbye, Thomas Barnes. I'll see you when you get back."

He pressed his lips together and gave a nod. "Goodbye, my incredibly talented and beyond extraordinary friend, Annalisa Mancuso. You keep being one of a kind, and I'll see you in a year."

Her heart felt dusty and barren.

He turned like a soldier pivoting to a command, and the door folded closed. Black smoke belched from the back of the bus as it began to pull away.

Thomas appeared in the back window, waving at her. She returned the wave, and then he drew a heart on the window, framing himself. She choked up as she stared through the heart into his brave eyes until the bus was gone.

She should have kissed him. She should have told him she loved him. What if she never saw him again and this had been her chance? Sharon Maxwell's words about finding connection stung her as the image of Thomas waving at her drifted away, like a smoke ring disappearing in the air.

Chapter 25

WHO IS WE?

That Thursday, after a visit with the girls in the Bargain Bin, Annalisa rode back up the escalator and went into the small kitchen to pour herself a cup of coffee. She was debating whether or not to even attend Sharon Maxwell's art show in three months, as Annalisa had not once spoken to her since walking out of her studio. She wasn't even sure if she was welcome and knew an apology was long overdue.

Annalisa was painting, though. Armed with a newfound resolve—no doubt spurred by Thomas's visit—she was back at it with an almost vitriolic assertiveness. If she couldn't have him, she better damn well keep chasing her voice.

As she passed through the hall of offices leading to the Advertising Department, coffee in hand, Ted Miller appeared.

She still avoided him at all costs and was mid-pivot in an attempt to escape when he said, "Ah, there she is. We haven't seen you in a while."

Annalisa's first thought was, *Who is we?* She couldn't stand it when people did that.

Stalling her retreat, she flattened the disgust on her face and let out a happy, "How are you, Mr. Miller?"

"I'm very fine," he said. His shirt was moist with sweat near his underarms, and she sipped tiny breaths so as not to smell his body odor.

"What are you working on today?" As he asked the question, he unabashedly ran his eyes up and down, inspecting her.

Swallowing her disgust, she said, "We're trying to wrap up all the Demi Flores stuff now." Flores was whom everyone in fashion was into right now. She sidestepped and started toward her destination. A group of managers was huddled in a circle, chatting farther down the hall.

"Now hold on," he said. "Why are you in such a hurry?"

"Lots of work to be done, Mr. Miller."

"I'd like to ask you something."

She stopped, closed her eyes, took a long breath, and then turned back to him.

"My nephew just moved to town from Boston—a smart kid—and he needs someone to show him around. I thought a good-looking broad like yourself would do the trick. Care to meet him?"

Annalisa shook her head. "Sorry, I don't have time for anyone right now. I've got so much going on here and outside of work." Not that he cared, but if he only knew how heavy Thomas was on her mind, he wouldn't be wasting his time.

Mr. Miller dipped his chin and looked at her hand. "Still no ring, though, huh? Shame a girl like you hasn't found anybody yet." Oh, she had, and that was the problem.

Annalisa couldn't take another moment of conversation. As she bade him a good day and turned to rush away, he said, "Let me know if you change your mind about my nephew. Who knows what could happen with your soldier boy?" With that, he smacked her on the bottom.

Annalisa spun so quickly she nearly broke the heels off her shoes. Not today. She had no tolerance whatsoever. Here she was having given up love to establish herself, and he had no right to touch her, to get in the way.

A part of her tried to suppress the rage. She knew as well as anyone in this building that this was a man's world, and anything she did other than let this go would be detrimental to her career.

That thought was so far down the tunnel, though, that it didn't stop her from raising her right hand. "Don't you ever touch me again," she spat through gritted teeth. Her hand was ready to swat him. She could feel hot coffee spilling out of the cup in her left hand.

"Whoa, little lady," he said, lifting up his hands in retreat, as if he'd done nothing wrong. "Let's settle down here."

Annalisa looked in his dirty little eyes and felt rage boiling up inside. There was no amount of rationality strong enough to stop her. Instead of hitting him, she slung the coffee toward his shoes, spilling half of it on his pant legs below the knees.

The steam rose as he reached for the burn, rubbing his legs like they were on fire. The huddled managers all turned, and Annalisa could feel her job—the one she'd fought so hard to earn—slipping away.

The fire inside burned too hot, though. "Don't you ever touch me again!" she snapped. "Or any other woman in this building. *A fanabla!*" Go to hell.

He glared at her. Annalisa thought he might hit her, but at the last second, he glanced at their coworkers gawking at the spectacle.

Breathing like a bull through his nose, he said, "I hope that was worth it." Lowering his voice, he continued, "You just ruined your whole life. You'll never find another job in this whole fucking town."

Tapping into the deepest part of her core as a woman, she asked, "Do you think you're the first man to get in my way?"

Then, as she stared into his beady eyes twinkling with victory, the reality of what she'd done hit her. She'd just let him win. She wasn't the first in Pride's to get a smack on the bottom. Maybe this week. A woman had to tolerate this sort of thing if she wanted to work and not sit at home all day, and she knew that. Even Patty, who was as strong as any woman Annalisa had ever known, let men get away with unacceptable comments. Otherwise, you were waging a war that you might not win. Whether Annalisa liked it or not, she'd just risked her job to stand up for all the women at Pride's and everywhere else who were fed up with such injustice.

Without engaging further, she marched down the hall past the others. As she disappeared into the Advertising Department, she heard Mr. Miller ranting about how she'd just made the biggest mistake of her life.

It was quiet as she entered, a sleepy feeling, especially compared to the commotion she'd just escaped. Her coworkers thankfully hadn't heard. Trying to breathe through her feelings—the fury, the determination, the regret—she walked past the cubicles filled with copy editors to her desk by the window. She said hello to her neighbors and perched on her stool, knowing it was only a matter of time before she'd be fighting for her job.

Sure enough, she heard Patty's high heels crossing the floor ten minutes later. Annalisa had been sitting there, staring at her empty illustration board, thinking that what he'd done should be a crime. But she knew reporting him would do nothing. In fact, her slinging coffee on him was the more serious offense. No one would care that he'd touched her. No one would care that she'd stood up for her fellow women.

Annalisa closed her eyes, feeling Fate wrapping her fingers around her neck. Patty asked her to follow her to her office. Once she'd closed the door, she said, "I don't like him any more than you do."

Annalisa paced back and forth, explaining to Patty that she had no choice but to defend herself.

Patty sat back in her chair. "I admire what you did, but you can't. You just can't."

"What was I supposed to do? He smacked my butt."

Patty shook her head. "You're preaching to the choir. If it was up to me, he would be pushed out the window."

Annalisa stopped pacing and put a panicky hand on her chest. "Patty, I need this job. I've worked so hard to get here." Had she really just lost everything she'd worked for?

"There's no doubting your work either," Patty said. "You're my favorite employee, but this is out of my hands. I fought for you, but I only have so much pull. You attacked Ted, honey. I want to pin a medal on you, but you and I are alone in this one. Men run Pride's, and we're just lucky to have a role. I hate to say that, but it's true. You know I'll help you find another job, but your time here is done."

With the only strength she had left, she thanked Patty for the opportunity, stood up, and exited the building through the revolving doors.

Ted Miller had won, and Annalisa had failed Patty and all the other women who would have killed to have her job. She'd failed herself and even her family back home, who'd been cheering for her. She'd been making so much money that she sent monthly checks back to Nonna. What would Nonna say? Annalisa had enough savings and was making enough from selling her pieces at Walt's shop to not have to retreat back home yet, but still, what would she do now?

She couldn't make a living selling pieces out of a silly clock shop. What she needed was a gallery to finally take her in, but who would? Annalisa couldn't bear the idea of showing her latest portfolio to Jackie after walking out on Sharon. Surely the two had spoken about it.

"Yeah, Jackie," Sharon probably said, "that Annalisa didn't stick around." Jackie might have replied, "Oh, what a shame. She was good."

"I know, but I'm not sure she had what it takes."

Annalisa felt like a child, telling Sharon Maxwell of all people that Portland loved her paintings as evidenced by her selling out of them at the clock shop, as though that was proof of her greatness. Maybe she needed to go somewhere else, maybe Boston or even farther—anywhere to get away from this madness. But would running really help? She gave up love to be an artist, and that was what she had to do. Or both her and Thomas's heartache would be for naught.

Pushing into Walt's shop, she called out his name. "You wouldn't believe what just happened. I'm now out of a job because . . ."

He was having a coughing fit at his desk in the back, and she rushed his way in a panic. This was a much more serious cough than she was used to. "You okay, Walt?"

As she reached the counter with the cash register, where she'd had countless conversations with him, she saw that the handkerchief he was coughing into was covered in blood.

—

"What in the world is COPD?" Annalisa asked Walt, taking a seat on a neighboring chair. It had been twenty minutes, and he'd finally stopped coughing and gone to the restroom to clean himself up.

Back at his work desk, he said, "A symptom of getting old is what it is. Chronic something or other . . ."

"No, seriously, Walt." She had come to care so much about him and couldn't fathom losing him.

"Chronic obstructive pulmonary disease," he said. "I should have quit smoking long before Gertrude made me."

"When was that?"

He sat back and crossed his legs, then cleared his throat. "Which time?"

She gave a chuckle. He was such a sweet man.

"Gertrude died in sixty-one, so the last time I quit must have been nineteen fifty-seven or so. She'd been after me about it since the day we met."

"Why didn't you tell me about being sick, Walt? Why aren't you taking better care of yourself? What's the doctor say? I keep telling you that it's too dusty in here, and now you tell me you have some sort of lung disease. I'm not going to let you work in here one more day without cleaning it up."

"My goodness, young lady, don't get all worked up. I've been on medicine for a while now, and this is just the way it is, part of getting old."

She felt so frustrated with him and grilled him about the details. She finally said, "I'm going to spend the rest of the day cleaning this place up, and if it takes me all week, then fine." This man needed help right now, and Annalisa wondered if sometimes things did happen for a reason. Maybe she'd lost her job just in time. The poor guy had no one—except her, of course. Walt had come to feel like the father her real father never could be.

"Don't you have work today?" he asked.

"Yeah, about that. I was fired for dumping coffee on the shoes of an ass . . . er, I mean, chauvinist pig. So I happen to have a lot of time on my hands." Annalisa caught him up.

"My goodness," he said. "You're right. It's the world we live in. You know what, though? To me it means you're meant for bigger and better things."

She tossed up her hands like she was throwing confetti. "Like what? I'm doing my best to paint, but it's not coming out easily, which means I'm in trouble. It's either I wait tables or crawl back to Payton Mills with my tail between my legs."

"I'd hire you," he said. "I mean full-time."

"That would be a wise move," she joked. "I'll take over all the clocks. I'll take your little tool set and twist the thingies until they start working again. Your shop will sing around the clock."

"I'd be happy to teach you horology, but I could also use more help around the shop." He cleared his throat. "As you can see, I'm slowing down. If you're willing to help me get this place cleaned up—as you yourself suggested—then I don't see why you couldn't do a few other things too. You could help me advertise, run the books, keep things clean, and keep selling your paintings—maybe raise the prices. I'm sure you can sell them better than I."

She stood on the other side of the counter and was blown away by the kindness of his offer. "Don't think I'm not appreciative, but I don't want to be your charity case."

"As much as I'd like to disagree, I can't do this by myself anymore, and I'd be lucky to have you. That's the bottom line. Your paintings are already bringing me new business. Let's get you in here to breathe new life into the place, just like you do with your illustrations. You can take over every wall if you like. This is not about charity. I would have offered earlier, had you not had a job."

"If you're not careful," she said, losing herself to the idea as the clocks ticked around her, "I'll take you up on it."

"I hope you do. Believe it or not, I think adding more of your art to my shop might bring new visitors in and make me more money. It's starting to feel like a museum in here. Just the other day, someone mistook me for taxidermy."

Feeling a hint of excitement, she popped out of her chair. "I'd put everything I have into it, Walt." It wasn't an art gig, but she'd be helping him, and he'd mentioned giving her more wall space. If she could tap back into her muse, she could keep selling pieces until a better option came around.

He uncrossed his legs and sat up. "*That* is one thing I've no doubt. Your commitment to everything you do is a wonderful virtue."

She opened her arms. "I want a hug."

He waved her off. "C'mon, now. Don't embarrass me."

She didn't back down and lifted him up into a big hug, feeling in his weary and weak body a surrender of sorts, like he didn't have much fight left. How had she not even noticed?

She felt like such a terrible neighbor and person for not seeing that he was in trouble. Yes, she saw that he was hurting over the loss of his wife, and she'd been listening to him cough, but how had she not offered more assistance? Why hadn't she offered to cook him dinner or to help him clean his shop?

She'd been so darn involved with her own grief at losing her parents and Thomas, and she'd been so focused on a career, that she hadn't done anything for this kind and lonely man. It felt very much like her life back in the Mills. She'd let her grief prevent her from loving Nonna the way her grandmother deserved to be loved. Well, that wasn't going to happen again. As Annalisa let go of Walt, she decided that not only was she going to breathe life back into his shop, but she was going to attempt to breathe life back into him.

Chapter 26

A Side Trip for Love

Accepting a much more meager salary than her pay at Pride's, Annalisa started working for Walt that very day. The commute (all the way down the stairs and around the corner) was about as good as it gets, and she found plenty to do.

For a week straight, she cleaned every square inch of the shop, filling a dumpster with useless parts and ridding the place of dust. She still hadn't created any new pieces but had plenty to sell, so she cleared more space for art and set up a nice leather couch facing the main wall.

Though she didn't have much experience with finance, he taught her in the following weeks how to run the books. He was a patient and good teacher, and when she'd get frustrated, he'd urge her to keep pushing through. As she got better, she discovered he'd missed collections from multiple customers, and she started tracking down payments via phone.

She used what she'd learned at Pride's to start an advertising campaign in the *Portland Press Herald*, urging people interested in the finer things of life such as art and timepieces to come visit. The ads worked, and even in the dead of winter, Walt enjoyed more foot traffic than he'd seen in years. The excitement seemed to be just what he'd needed, and he started to come alive. In truth, they both did, and Annalisa found her muse again.

Whereas getting in front of the easel had been such a labor since Sharon had let her down, the act of painting began to tug at her again, as if there was nothing she'd rather do. Was this newfound creative surge a result of what she was doing for Walt? If so, she wanted more. The idea reminded her of those times when she'd tried to convince Nonna that she couldn't truly paint unless she got out into the world. Well, maybe it wasn't just about living, but about loving too.

After a lot of convincing, she dragged him to the Bargain Bin to replace his dreadful sweaters, and she had tremendous fun cleaning him up. She'd even talked him into letting her clean his apartment, which was a shocking experience, seeing the life he'd been living only one story below her.

When Annalisa entered his place the first week of February, her heart broke. She pondered what he'd said about love and how losing his wife must have been a death sentence. That was what the apartment felt like, a place for him to wait until he could join her. She thought she'd recognized a spark of youth in Walt after she'd helped him with his appearance and the shop, but that spark had not burned bright enough to lead toward a clean apartment.

A musty odor struck her nose. His furniture was as tattered as the one sweater he used to wear. The walls were mostly bare, save one painting she'd given him recently. Making herself at home, she opened up the fridge to find exactly six items: a jar of peanut butter, a gallon of milk, a plate of leftovers, two apples, and a stick of butter.

"Walt Burzinski, do you even eat?"

"Yes, I eat," he replied from behind her.

She turned to him, wagging a finger. "You can't live like this."

Walt stood with his fists on his waist. "I've made it quite some time without any assistance at all."

She matched his stance. "No more. I'm not having it. You're too good a man not to take care of yourself."

He let his hands fall to his sides. "You'll see when you get older, young lady."

"Then I hope someone is there to snap me out of it like I am to you."

Several minutes later, as she gawked at an old mattress that rested on the floor in his bedroom—no frame at all—thinking this man needed and deserved love more than anyone in the world, she said, "Would you like to have dinner with Nonna and me Friday night? She's coming down for the weekend."

He brushed the idea off. "Oh, no, that's too much."

"No, really. Please. You'll be doing me a favor. She's much better behaved when we have company." She pulled open the window blinds to let the light come in, and as the sun shot across the floors, she felt that same light filling her heart.

꒰꒱

"I haven't eaten this well in a long time," Walt admitted, sitting around the wobbly table that served to separate the living area from the kitchen with Annalisa and Nonna. Bowls of Annalisa's Italian wedding soup steamed up in front of them. A baguette and a large chunk of Parmigiano-Reggiano rested on a cutting board next to an open bottle of Chianti.

This might have been only the third or fourth time Walt and Nonna had shared conversation since Annalisa had moved to Portland, and Annalisa thought the two would make an adorable pair if they both weren't so grumpy and stubborn.

"Elena," Walt said, having taken to Nonna's real name, "when did you come over from Italy? Was it straight to Payton Mills?"

Nonna looked offended by the question. Annalisa could see she was fiddling with her hands under the table. With her bottom lip jutting out, Nonna said, "I was about Annalisa's age. Came over with my father from Naples."

Walt straightened his glasses. "I see."

Nonna paused, and the air filled with tension. Annalisa was about to say something when Nonna let out, "My mother was dead."

That's how you reel him in, Annalisa thought to herself, taking a long sip of her red wine.

Walt made a brief humming noise, as if that was his way of saying he was sorry for intruding on her personal space.

Annalisa wanted to tell Walt he needed to up his game, and she wanted to tell Nonna that if she ever wanted to find love again, she'd better warm up a little.

Finally, Walt leaned toward Nonna. "I'm sure you weren't even born yet when I came over in nineteen oh four from Białystok."

Annalisa grinned to herself. Maybe Walt did have a few cards to play.

Nonna read right through it. "No, no. I won't tell you my age."

"Sorry," Walt said, throwing up his hand. "I'm not asking your age. I'm simply wondering when you came and if you came through New York like me."

Nonna nodded with an ever-so-slight look his way. "Yes."

"Yes, what, Nonna?" Annalisa said, nudging her grandmother with a foot under the table.

Nonna glared at her granddaughter like she was about to launch across the table. As she answered Walt with a quick, "Yes, New York," she kicked Annalisa right back, much harder than a nudge.

Annalisa's mouth sprang open in shock, feeling a bruise coming on from the therapeutic-shoe attack.

The two had one of their stare downs, which Annalisa had missed. But only slightly.

Poor Walt sat there quietly, and Annalisa thought he had a long way to go in understanding Italians.

Annalisa won the contest as Nonna crossed her arms and slid her eyes left. The place where Nonna had kicked her throbbed.

Walt stepped in to save the dinner from all-out war. He said to Nonna, "Can you believe what your granddaughter has done with the shop?" Annalisa had given the tour upon arrival that afternoon.

"I'm very impressed," Nonna admitted, almost like she was confessing to a crime.

"If she's not careful," he said, "we might have to rename the place. Maybe the Clock Shop Gallery. I've never seen someone work so hard."

Annalisa thanked him. She couldn't have been more proud or thrilled of how she'd helped Walt with his shop, and maybe his life some too. He looked sharp tonight, a far cry from the man she'd found coughing blood a month earlier. Helping him in the last month had put wonderful smiles on her face and had somehow returned her love of painting to her. She wasn't stopping, and that short commute allowed her to even grab a few minutes during lunch.

She pointed at Nonna, who still stared off to her left with her arms crossed. "I guess I have a little bit of Nonna's Roman gladiator, fight-to-the-death blood in me."

Nonna spun toward Annalisa. "How dare you."

"Relax." Annalisa broke into a laugh, and Walt followed closely behind, though his was more conservative and careful, like he was a firefighter touching a doorknob.

"I'm very happy to be here," he said, clearing his throat, "and to know you all. You're both very charming."

"If you say so," Annalisa said, thinking that, judging by the rare smile on his face, maybe he did understand Italians.

Nonna finally spoke up in a surprisingly warm way. "We're both very grateful for what you've done for Annalisa, Walt."

"I don't know exactly what I've done for her," he said. "She's the one who bravely stuck her hand down and pulled me out of my hole."

After a rough start, the rest of the dinner went wonderfully, and Annalisa was so happy to see both Nonna and Walt lightening up so.

Between bites of a tiramisu that she'd made, Annalisa thought of a way to gently nudge their relationship forward. Asking forgiveness for the deceit she was about to enact, she asked, "Walt, when are you going to take us for a drive in your Plymouth? I think Nonna would have a blast."

"Anytime you'd like," he replied, looking like she'd asked a dog to play fetch. An old dog but a happy one nonetheless.

"How about tomorrow before we open?" Annalisa asked.

Walt looked perfectly delighted. "You're on."

Minutes before eight the next morning, Annalisa and Nonna descended the stairs to find Walt polishing the hood of his Plymouth Belvedere, the one Annalisa had backed into last June. The air hovered around freezing, the sky mostly clear of clouds.

"Look at this beauty," Annalisa said, seeing that the front bumper was as good as new.

"Good morning," Walt said, hitting one last spot on the hood. He folded the rag. "What a day for a drive."

Knowing she was about to get in all kinds of trouble, Annalisa jumped into her lie. "You won't believe this, but I just got a call from a friend of mine. Her boyfriend's broken up with her, and she's crying, and . . . anyway. She really needs me."

She looked at both Nonna and Walt, who showed you-can't-fool-me looks on their faces. "Maybe just the two of you could go?" Annalisa felt bad for lying, but not bad enough. Even when Nonna fired missiles with her eyes, she shrugged it off. "I was going to be stuck in the back seat anyway."

Walt took a confident step toward Elena. "I'd love to still take you, if you're interested."

Annalisa's heart swooned.

Until Nonna looked at her, as if she either needed permission or a way out. She couldn't be sure, but Annalisa thought she saw in her grandmother's face the fear of risking her heart again after losing Nonno.

"Are you kidding me?" Annalisa said, deciding to answer for her grandmother. "She'd love to go." Walt was a gift that Nonna was being given, and she couldn't dare turn it away.

"Maybe we can do it another time," Walt conceded, clearly reading Nonna's skeptical face. "I think we all know what's going on here." Walt was just as afraid as Nonna.

To everyone's surprise, Nonna made the leap. "I suppose I still have time for a drive."

"Really?" he asked.

Nonna's face warmed. "It would be nice."

Annalisa would never forget the change in both of them, their bodies, their faces, their energy, as if their decision to let the light in on their lives had snuffed the pain they'd been suffering for so long in missing the ones they used to love.

Walt opened up the passenger-side door, took Nonna's hand, and guided her in. Annalisa wondered when either one of them had touched the hand of the opposite sex. It was very much the cutest thing she had ever seen, and she couldn't help but feel like she'd done something that actually mattered for once.

He scurried over to his side and cracked open his own door. Looking back at Annalisa, he said, "Don't worry; I'll take good care of her."

"I know you will," Annalisa said with a sly wink.

He let out a subtle smirk that said it all. Walt Burzinski was smitten with her grandmother.

Annalisa ducked down to say goodbye to Nonna one more time. She waved through the closed window.

Nonna shooed her away.

—

"I can't believe you," Nonna spat as Annalisa pushed into the apartment after work that day. "I don't want you meddling with my life." She stood at the stove, making *soffritto*, the holy trinity of celery, carrots, and onions. Funny how Nonna could take over any kitchen she was in.

Thomas had written his first letter from Vietnam, and Annalisa felt hesitant to read it. Was she making the right decision by corresponding with him, leading him on? They couldn't keep playing this game for long. With them, it felt like they needed to fully love each other or shut each other out.

"What can't you believe?" Annalisa asked, looking at his handwriting on the envelope. Not only was this proof of life, but it was proof that she was still on his mind. As dangerous as that idea was, it was also utterly delightful.

Nonna waved her knife at Annalisa. "That was very embarrassing, the game you played today. Don't meddle with my life. You worry about yourself."

Annalisa crossed over the black and white tiles of the kitchen and invaded Nonna's space. "It worked, didn't it? How was the drive? Don't tell me you didn't have fun. Walt says he had a blast and that you're a very interesting woman."

The volume of Nonna's knife hitting the chopping board increased. She pretended to ignore Annalisa breathing down her neck.

"Nonna, how was it?" She put a hand on Nonna's shoulder. "You had fun, didn't you? Walt's adorable."

Nonna slid her pile of celery to the side with her knife and then reached for a peeled carrot from a ceramic bowl. "Back away or I'll stick you."

Annalisa gave her a little space. "He likes you, you know?"

Nonna chopped the carrot like nothing else in the world mattered.

"And you like him," Annalisa said. "Don't you? Why won't you admit it?"

"We had a nice morning," Nonna said, as if she had confessed to Father Laduca back in the Mills.

Annalisa looked back at Thomas's letter, and it tugged at her. She might be hesitant to read it, knowing it would be like opening Pandora's box, but that wasn't going to stop her. No way.

"I'd say you had a nice time," she said. "Walt was late to his shop for the first time in . . . who knows? Just admit that you had fun."

Nonna set down the knife with great gusto. "It was cold."

"Yeah? And? What did you talk about?"

Nonna twisted her head to Annalisa. "Enough of this. I have dinner to cook."

Annalisa stared at her for a long time, craning her neck dramatically, until Nonna broke into a Nonna smile with her signature discretion. She buried it as quickly as possible.

Annalisa touched her own nose, a gesture of love between them. "That's what I thought." She held up the letter. "Thomas wrote. I'm going to go read it in my room."

"You and your Thomas," she heard Nonna say as she raced to the bedroom. Tearing it open, she read each word as if it were a kiss.

You know what I miss? French fries. And I miss Nonna's meatballs. More than anything, though, I miss your smile.

She missed his too. She missed everything about him.

I'm safe and sound, by the way. Not that this is a walk in the park, but it could be worse. I am marking the days on a calendar I keep in my pocket. Though I won't know my DEROS for a while, I'll be home before the end of the year. Please tell me you're painting again; I can't bear the thought of you giving up.

Annalisa sketched Thomas a giant plate of pasta with meatballs, and she accompanied it with a long letter about what she'd been doing, helping Walt and painting prolifically.

She told him all about Walt and the shop and how she'd attempted to set Walt and Nonna up. As she relayed the story to him, she felt so much joy inside, and to her great surprise, she ended her note with: *Maybe Sharon was right, that I need to do better at connecting with people. You might have told me something like that too one time.*

After signing her name, she lifted the paper toward her face, but she stopped an inch away from sealing her letter with a kiss of plum lipstick. Connecting with Walt was one thing; committing to Thomas was quite another—and that was what such a gesture would mean. She couldn't send him mixed signals, and she still had to choose her art over him if she was ever to master her craft. In fact, she wasn't even sure if she should read any more of his letters as she reminded herself what was at stake. So much worse than losing him would be resenting him for destroying her dreams.

Chapter 27

Pasta and Sauce

Walt was right about Annalisa being better than him at selling her paintings. She was clearing out a year's worth of work, selling a piece a day at a time, even at higher prices. As word spread, other artists—some from her circles, others out of the blue—asked if she'd sell their paintings, too, for a commission, of course, and she thought it was a great idea.

Annalisa felt like a mini–Jackie Burton as Walt's clock shop attracted customers strictly interested in the art on the walls. And between collecting old debts, selling art, and the increase in watch and clock sales due to foot traffic, March would be the most profitable month for the store in six years. She'd finally recovered from being fired and had proved she didn't have to go back to Payton Mills, that she could continue the pursuit of her voice.

On March 19, she received Thomas's second letter, and she found herself debating whether to even read it. Most important, the letter was verification that he was alive. Not a day had passed since she'd watched him drive away on that bus when she didn't feel her worry for him. Maybe that was all she needed from this letter. Every rational part of her knew that he had crept back into her life like a burglar and that he was dangerous, and reading his words would only prolong the heartache.

She set the letter on the table and went into her room to paint. Proving her point, she felt distracted by the darn thing, as if it were taunting her, and she couldn't tap into her muse on any level. Having taken a break from painting her strong women, she'd been working on a series of portraits from her imagination—modern-day men and women searching for belonging in the world. With his words waiting in the next room, she couldn't focus at all.

Giving in, she dropped her brush into a cup of water and retrieved the envelope. Getting comfy on the couch, she dived into his words.

You know what I miss? he wrote this time. *You.*

Annalisa stopped and read the first line again. He seemed to have the ability to strike like a dart to the bull's-eye of her heart.

> *I know we're friends, and if that's all we'll ever be, then fine. I refuse to keep pretending like I don't love you though. You are what is keeping me alive over here, and you're the reason I want to come home.*

She paused, knowing he'd reached the point of no return. She was either leading him with her correspondence, or she was officially pulling him.

> *I wanted to ask you something. I'll understand if you can't or don't want to, but I'd like you to come see me. I have a week of leave in Hawaii starting May 24, and I'm getting a hotel room on Waikiki Beach. Come stay with me. Even if only as a friend, it would be so nice to spend some time together. By the way, I'm not mentioning it to my family, so let's keep it between us.*

She finished his letter, which included an address in DC that would get her response back to him faster if she chose to come. Setting the letter down, Annalisa sat back and closed her eyes, letting his request marinate. How nice it would be to set eyes on him, to touch him, to tell him that maybe she could make room for both him and her art. And . . . it *was* Hawaii. She saw them strolling the beach at sunset, hand in hand, laughing once again.

Reality hit her. Never once had she flown in her life, and she had no idea how much a ticket to Hawaii would cost. Money aside, could Walt handle things for a week if she did leave? Wait, was she really considering the idea? Getting on that plane would be another leap toward love, and the last time she'd done that, it hadn't worked out so well. Who was to say this time couldn't be different, though?

She had no idea what to do. Not until a little bit later that night. The highlight of Annalisa's year—maybe even her life—had been that her efforts in matchmaking Walt and Nonna had paid off. As much as they'd tried to hide it, Walt had admitted that they spoke on the phone regularly and had seen each other a couple of times.

It just so happened that Nonna was in town when Annalisa received the letter from Thomas, and while Annalisa debated his invitation, Nonna was out with Walt having dinner. Thinking a walk might clear her head, she pulled on a jacket and scarf and went out into the early evening. She walked all over town, thinking the cold was good for her, distracting in a way. She dipped into a dive burger joint for dinner on her way home.

Meandering back along Congress Street, lost in her internal dilemmas, she noticed Walt and Nonna strolling ahead, hand in hand. Unable to resist, Annalisa watched them with a full heart.

The couple stopped under the curtain of Walt's shop and stood very close, laughing with each other. To see both of those grumps laughing would have been enough to satisfy Annalisa, but then Walt planted a kiss on Nonna's lips.

Annalisa squealed so loudly that both Walt and Nonna turned, but Annalisa was able to duck behind the corner of a building before they could see her.

It was a quick glimpse she had of the two, their happy faces and lonely lips meeting one another under the warm and filtered yellow of the streetlight above them, but it was long enough for the image to imprint like fingers in warm wax into Annalisa's memory.

As she watched Walt escort Nonna to the steps, Annalisa felt like a veil had been pulled from her eyes. What kind of fool was she to think that her love for Thomas was getting in the way? He wasn't her father, and she wasn't like her mother. He'd done nothing but support her, and she knew he always would. All she had to do was have faith in him. And in herself. No one would ever pry the brush from her hands.

With this newfound clarity, she realized that she didn't even own a bathing suit, and she was going to need one. Because she was getting on that damn plane to go see Thomas, no matter the cost or consequences. Enough of letting fear win. A life without love was not worth living.

Almost equally as powerful as her pull to Thomas was her urge to get in front of her easel to capture what she'd just seen. She could so clearly see the faces of these two people who had buried their first loves now finding love again, and she realized how important love truly was—no matter the risks.

No, she couldn't bury her love for Thomas for one more minute.

Modigliani's words rang in her ears: "When I know your soul, I will paint your eyes." She felt a deep, visceral connection to both Walt's and Nonna's souls, and now she could paint their eyes. How could she ever forget seeing Nonna standing on her toes in her orthopedic shoes, reaching up for the lips on Walt's wrinkled and dazzled face, his loving eyes?

Not wanting to interrupt their moment, Annalisa circled the block before ascending the stairs to her apartment. She found yet another smile when she saw that Nonna wasn't home. Was she spending the night with Walt?

Deciding to write Thomas back in the morning, Annalisa went straight to the studio in her bedroom and went to work on the image of Walt and Nonna, knowing beyond all doubt that it would be the finest piece of her entire life. She worked through the night, taking nary a break until after the sun had risen and only when she heard her front door open and shut.

She chose not to pick on Nonna for wearing the same clothes as the night before and instead tugged her grandmother into the bedroom to show her the piece Annalisa had spent all night working on. This one she'd done on canvas, and it captured the entire scene, from the top of the awning that read WALT BURZINSKI'S WATCH AND CLOCK REPAIR all the way down to Nonna's feet up on their toes. Right smack in the middle were their lips touching in quite possibly the most beautiful vision Annalisa had ever experienced.

She thought Nonna might snap at her for spying, but she did no such thing. Instead, her lower lip pushed out, and she turned to Annalisa. "It's . . . it's wonderful, *nipotina*."

Annalisa's heart soared, and she knew that she'd found her voice by looking through the lens of love, and she knew she could never stop painting—even if she never made another dime. She also knew that not only could love and art coexist, but that art—at least her art—required love just as pasta required a sauce and just as she required Thomas in her life.

She crossed her arms. "I have to tell you something, Nonna."

Nonna slapped her own forehead. "Jesus, Mary, and Joseph . . . what is it now?"

"Thomas wrote me and has asked that I come visit him in Hawaii while he's on leave. In May."

Annalisa didn't know what kind of reaction to expect, but she was pleased that Nonna didn't instantly scold her. After a brief moment of thought, her grandmother said, "And are you going?"

As if someone had asked her if she would be interested in having wine and cheese with Michelangelo, she nodded the strongest yes of her life. "Seeing you with Walt last night . . . it woke me up. I've been so freaked out that I'd end up like my mother, but I've never really let myself consider that I could get lucky and end up like you. I know losing Nonno almost killed you, but I know it was worth the pain to have him in your life. And now you have Walt, and it's . . . it's so beautiful."

Annalisa breathed in her rich feelings for Thomas, and she burned with an urge to race to Vietnam and track him down and tell him that she'd finally figured it out, that not only could love and art live in parallel but she could only realize her true potential with him in her life.

"I love Thomas, Nonna. Like you loved Nonno and maybe how you feel about Walt. And as much as I've tried to be smart about it, and carry on without him, it's not working. I don't want a life without him in it. He's my everything."

Nonna crossed her arms, and Annalisa feared the worst. But her grandmother once again surprised her. "Then you'd better go find him and tell him how you feel."

Annalisa's eyes widened, and her mouth popped open. "Really?"

Nonna gave a mild chuckle. "If it's been this long and you still can't shake him, then maybe it's time to let yourself love him instead."

The hairs on her arms rose, and her spine tingled. Though she was going to Hawaii no matter what the outcome of this conversation, Nonna's support validated both her feelings *and* her decision. Stepping toward her grandmother, she wrapped her arms around her and squeezed her tight.

—

After leaving a travel agent to discuss a ticket to Hawaii, Annalisa found Sharon Maxwell at her warehouse space. She had red hair now and was deep into working on a piece on a massive canvas. Annalisa felt bad disturbing her, but she couldn't go another minute without sharing her latest breakthrough—and, of course, apologizing.

She knocked on the door, and Sharon put down her brush to answer. Annalisa glanced down at her tote, wondering if Sharon would even want to see what she'd done. Or if she even wanted to see Annalisa.

"I was wondering if I'd ever see you again," Sharon said, her smock covered in wet splotches of reds and purples. A large sparkly beaded necklace hung from her neck.

Annalisa realized how much she'd missed her teacher. Perhaps the biggest of those lessons Sharon had taught her was right at the end, when she'd said that Annalisa's women were empty.

"I'm sorry, Sharon. I don't even know what to say. I was a brat and a know-it-all."

Sharon opened the door wider, almost as if she'd been waiting on Annalisa. "Do you think I've never walked out of a lesson before? It's the artists who don't lose their temper that sadden me, because they are the ones who don't care."

"I care so much," Annalisa confessed, feeling like she was about to go to her knees. "All I want is to be great. Not for anyone else but for me. I want to know that I've done something with my life and the little bit of talent I've been given."

"You already have, Annalisa. No doubt in my mind. At the same time, you're just getting started, right? I'm hoping you've come to say you'll join my classes again."

With desperation flushing her face, Annalisa said, "I absolutely want to join your classes again."

Sharon clapped her hands together, her bracelets jiggling. "You've made my entire week." Inviting Annalisa in, she caught her up on who had left and who the new students were.

Then she pointed at the tote. "What do you have?"

Annalisa smiled, and that same fear she'd had in the past rose back up. It wasn't quite as bad, though, and she was able to swallow it. In fact, even if Sharon hated what she'd done, it didn't matter. Because Annalisa knew what did matter—what she'd put on the canvas in the last few hours and what she'd done these past months in her own life *mattered*. Love wasn't a potion you drank to distract yourself from reality. Love was the key to living a life that mattered.

They went into the studio, and Annalisa unclasped the button and pulled out the stretched canvas of Nonna and Walt. Setting it on Sharon's desk, Annalisa backed away, once again admiring what she'd done. It might not be a Picasso or a Mary Cassatt, but by God it was an Annalisa Mancuso. It was her subject's eyes, the windows into their souls, and in their movement, the way Nonna was reaching up to Walt, leaping into his heart. And Walt, his lifting her up, telling her to trust him, that he'd love her with everything he had for as long as he could.

Sharon looked at it for a long time, and when she turned, Annalisa steadied herself for whatever was coming.

"It's about time," Sharon said. "I don't know what you've been doing and where you found it, but you did. You found you, honey."

Annalisa felt her shoulders shake as she broke into a cry. She opened up her arms to Sharon, and the two embraced. Annalisa cried tears of joy for finally doing something with her life—and not just with this painting. She cried for all the hard work she'd put in and for her mother, who'd never gotten a real chance.

As she wiped her eyes after the hardest cry that she could remember, Sharon lifted up the painting and handed it back. "Now go do this again. And again. And again."

Chapter 28

ALOHA, MAINERS

The last week of May, Walt drove Annalisa to Logan Airport in Boston. She hugged him goodbye and reminded him to take his medicine. Nonna was helping out at the shop while she was gone.

After checking in, Annalisa boarded the first airplane of her life. She'd first tried to read a book but was too excited and kept her eyes out the window for most of the journey. When the wheels touched down in Honolulu, she had absolutely no idea what to expect. The only communication she'd received was that he'd be waiting for her, as she'd sent her flight details.

She joined the other passengers exiting the gate and lost her breath when she saw him. Private Thomas Barnes stood in his uniform at the gate when she deplaned. She'd never seen him so handsome. For a funny moment she thought she was one of the girls in Elvis's *Blue Hawaii*, and he her own private Elvis.

"Aloha," she said, noticing as she came closer a scratch along his cheek. What had he seen and done in the few months he'd been in Vietnam? She couldn't—and didn't want to—imagine.

"Look at you." He smiled, making her feel to her core how much he'd missed her. He lifted up a lei of lilac and white orchids and hung it around her neck. He stepped back as if he had no idea what to do—hug her? Kiss her? As if he was letting her make the choice.

She hadn't come all the way to Hawaii to be friends, and he hadn't just fought through half of his tour to shake hands. Letting herself go just as Sharon had taught her, Annalisa pressed her lips to his. The passengers around them clapped, as if this were any normal reunion.

As they pulled apart, she said, "What's new, soldier boy? That's a heck of a tan."

He laughed. "Damn, I missed you."

"You're not going to get all mushy on me, are you?" But her own heart felt pretty soft.

"So what if I am?"

Annalisa thought his eyes looked different, like he'd lost some of his youth. "I missed you too."

They retrieved her bag and called a taxi that took them to a simple hotel called the Moloka'i on Waikiki Beach. They entered their first-floor waterfront room, and she rushed to the patio only steps from the sand. Annalisa's first glimpse of the beach and ocean felt like a mother seeing her child for the first time. The creamy sand was a stick of butter melting into the water, and she couldn't imagine that all those shades of blue even existed. For a Mainer who'd barely crossed borders, this was proof enough that God had His hands all over the world, mixing in colors even the great masters could never emulate.

To the far left, past the long line of hotels, stood some sort of beautiful mountain, but it was nothing like the mountains of Maine. This one was surely volcanic, and it was treeless and jagged, almost otherworldly. She looked out toward the horizon, wondering what else was out there waiting for her.

Thomas joined her, putting his hand on her waist and kissing her neck. "I'm so glad you came."

His breath gave her goose bumps. "Me too," she whispered, feeling the exhilaration of a free fall into love. Would they make love while they were here, she wondered, or would she get scared and pull the cord?

She couldn't bear losing him to the war, couldn't even bear the idea of it, so she was afraid that she was setting herself up for the greatest loss of her life.

But she couldn't bear not loving him, either, so she had to have made this leap and taken the risk. No longer could she let her fears guide her. She knew what was right in her heart.

They breathed in the view, watching the sun worshippers lie motionless on their chairs, and the lovers strolling along the dazzling waterline, and then out in the ocean, a cluster of longboarders sharing a seemingly never-ending line of perfect curls. Other soldiers were there, too, some with girlfriends or wives, and some clustered together with other fighters on leave from their nightmare.

There was a powerful dichotomy at play between those men and their current surroundings, and Annalisa could feel Thomas's energy—all their energy—in this brief respite from their violent situation. She could only imagine what they were going through, but she'd watched and read enough news to know that they'd experienced things that would make even the most hardened warriors tremble.

The intimacy of the room made her wonder what was to come. This was the first time they'd ever had their privacy as a couple. She thought he might have ripped her clothes off, but he stretched out on the bed and watched her with a smile as she unpacked, peppering her with questions about life back home.

As she talked, she knew he was listening, or trying to, but she could tell he was somewhere else, too—almost reminding Annalisa of Emma's behavior. That was okay. She knew it had nothing to do with her being there. By the end of the day, she hoped to quiet his demons. She couldn't even begin to imagine what he'd seen in the five months he'd been in Vietnam, and more than a little slack was warranted.

When she told him about losing her job at Pride's and what Mr. Miller had done to her, he popped up and cut angry eyes at her. "You fucking kidding me?"

"It's not a big deal," she said, feeling like she'd poked the bear. What a potty mouth he'd developed since he'd been away.

"They fired you?" he asked, setting his feet on the carpet. "I assumed you quit."

She hung a new sundress in the closet. "I didn't want you to worry, so I left that part out."

Thomas shook his head, and she could see that he was doing everything he could to hold back. Ted Miller was lucky he was thousands of miles away.

Annalisa plopped down next to him and put a hand on his arm. "Ted Miller is long gone, and I like my life better now." She filled him in on what she hadn't told him in the letters, the night she'd seen Nonna and Walt kiss. "That was the night I realized that I wanted to go to Hawaii, that I had to see you." She looked up into his eyes, so eager to tell him what she'd discovered. "Life's just too short, isn't it? Forget all the things that could go wrong. I'd rather get them all wrong with you than all right without you."

Mr. Sunshine suddenly came alive. If he'd been checked out earlier, her words brought him right back to the present, and she could see that he'd been waiting to hear her say these things for a long time. "This is what I've been saying all along."

She ran her fingers along the stubble on his face. "I know you have, and I'm sorry it's taken me so long to come around."

He lovingly put his hand on her back. "I would have waited a lifetime. You know that."

"I do." She kissed him and then told him about the painting she'd made of Walt and Nonna, because she wanted to finish her point. "Sharon was really impressed. Not like, 'Oh, good job, little student.' She saw what I already knew, that I've finally figured out my voice. It's like I'm opening my eyes for the first time, and I see . . . I see love everywhere, and I'm finally not afraid to connect. And I feel love." She put her hand on his heart, feeling it thumping back at her. "I finally feel connected."

He placed his hand on top of hers, already looking younger than when she'd first seen him. "I feel it too. I love you, Anna. That will never change."

Knowing it was her turn to show him how she felt, she pushed him down onto the bed and leaned over him, kissing him a thousand times and pressing her body into him. "I love you, too, and I'll never stop."

She expected his hands to run wild, even wanted them to, but he seemed content with kissing. Considering he'd never been content with just kissing, she calmed her own libido and asked, "You okay?"

He sighed. "Sorry, Anna. I'm worn down."

Undeterred, she rolled over to his side and put her hand on his chest. "Don't worry about it. We have an entire wonderful week together, sitting under the sun, drinking mai tais, dancing, letting it *all* go."

"I need that."

She focused on his chest rising and falling. "Is it that bad over there?"

He made a face like she'd asked him if it snowed in Maine. "It's no cakewalk, especially . . ." He shrugged. "I like the guys in my platoon. That's what matters."

"Hey, I can take it. Tell me . . ." But could she take it? She didn't want to think about losing him anymore, and she could only imagine what kind of nightmarish stories he could tell.

His chest rose high as he drank in a big breath. "I think the best thing to do this week is not talk about RVN."

She glided her fingers across his cheek. "I'm here for you, either way." Her heart hurt for him, and the war sank into her chest, the unimaginable things he'd seen seeping into her. "You're halfway done, Thomas. We're there. Keep doing what you're doing, and it'll be over—and we can start the rest of our lives."

~

Over the course of that first day, she fought hard to be Thomas's cheer-leader, digging him out of the gloom. Even when the topic of Emma came up, Annalisa assured him that his sister would come around and turn out okay. Then she'd steered the conversation toward calmer waters. He told her about some of the silliness and pranks he'd been a part of in Vietnam (boys will be boys . . .), and they laughed about the day they'd met and how hard he'd pursued her.

By that night, he was smiling again. With wet bathing suits under their clothes, they sat at the bar, drinking rum punches and laughing at one drunk soldier who attempted to dance to a Stones song on the radio. The bartender was back and forth between the blender and the beer keg, moving as fast as he could to help his patrons numb the pain.

Annalisa felt so far away from what those men had experienced. Some of them were drafted and some of them had enlisted, and now they were in it together, fighting a war that Annalisa was sure no one would ever win. They looked like pawns to her, Nixon's play toys. Sure, she didn't understand it, and she knew there were politics at play that she'd never be privy to, but this war had to end.

Thomas told her a few bits and pieces about his experience. She felt like he was dulling it down some, but even so, it was heartbreaking to hear him speak of VC soldiers waiting in ambush and losing guys he'd come to love in an instant from a sniper bullet. She let him talk as long as he needed to, no matter how hard it was for her. She found it so hard to imagine the boy she'd first met at the museum dropping grenades into a tunnel full of NVA.

As they continued to talk, he seemed to drift away, as he'd done several times that day. He kept looking to his right, toward the beach, as if someone was watching them, and she wondered if this was how every soldier felt back in the real world.

Clearly ready to leave RVN behind, he said, "So tell me more about your paintings. What have you done since the one with Walt and Nonna?" She could also see that he was trying to engage, despite his distractions, and that meant the world to her.

"Well," she said, excited to share, "I was walking back from Sharon's, after I showed her the piece, and I saw this young boy stumble and hit the sidewalk, busting up his knees. His father was right behind him, racing to lift him up. It was like lightning striking down on me. I couldn't wait to get home and paint, and when I did, it was . . . it was like I was finally capable of feeling them. The subtlest change in the world to the eye, but I was in their skin as I filled in the details. Oh, Thomas, it might sound silly, but—"

"It's not silly at all," he said.

Feeling the rush of that experience, Annalisa sipped her rum drink and continued. "I could feel both the dad's love for his son and the son's reliance on his father like they were my own feelings." She paused. "You never quite master art—not many people do—but I know that I've finally found my voice. It's always been about people, but I've finally figured out how to truly bring them to life." She lowered her voice, looking into the eyes of the man she'd never stopped loving. "It's about opening yourself up in the real world. An artist can't hide in her studio and make magic. She has to get out there and love. My voice is all about and because of love. Because of my love for Nonna, for Walt . . . for you."

His cheeks filled with joy.

She put her hand on his thigh. "It doesn't have to mean that all my paintings have to be lovey-dovey, not at all. That was the me that was all giddy about you back in high school, painting those silly red hearts." No, the paintings she'd done since Nonna and Walt's kiss had come from the soul of her being, and they were real and honest, nothing mushy about them.

He pretended to be upset. "You're not all giddy about me now?"

"Giddy is only the start of it now," she admitted. "I'm just saying . . . the painting I did of Nonna and Walt and the ones I've done since have come from deep within, a very real and honest place. I guess that's what my voice is. People loving people."

He smiled proudly. "That's my girl," he said. "That's my girl."

She shrugged. "Forever and always."

Running with that idea, he asked, "So what happens when I get back home? Between you and me. Is it forever and always?"

Though she'd thought about it, she had no idea. "You still want to go to New York for dental school, right?"

He kissed her with pineapple breath. "After this whole mess, I just want to get back and be with you. I want to be among people loving people. I can take or leave dental school. I can go wherever you need to be for your career."

She smiled at the thought of how lucky she was to have found him. In fact, she allowed herself to imagine, for the first time, a rich life with Thomas Barnes. Had she changed so much in a few months? Was the grief that had plagued her going away? Yes. Yes, it was . . .

He seemed to grow lighter with every passing minute, and soon he was inching closer to her, kissing her and touching her. She was loving every minute of it, his touch, his love, the setting, and when the Guess Who came on the radio singing, "No Sugar Tonight," she smiled at the lyrics she heard in her head.

As the band sang the chorus, Annalisa sang to Thomas, "No sugar tonight for poor Thomas, no sugar tonight for my T."

It was Thomas who laughed first, and then they were folded over, making the others at the bar turn to see what in the world was going on.

With an irresistible grin, he said, "So what do you say we move this party to the minibar?"

After polishing off their drinks, he reached for her hand and interlaced his fingers with hers. They laughed all the way back to the room, but once they realized what lay behind the hotel door, their playfulness shifted. Keeping her gaze, he let go of her hand to jiggle the key into the lock, and when he pushed the door open, Annalisa felt her entire body swell with desire.

With ease, he picked her up and pushed open the door with his side. She wrapped her arms around his neck and breathed in the intoxicating scent of suntan lotion and the sea.

With her still in his arms, he carried her to the bed and then gently placed her down. His eyes penetrated her with such intense desire that she thought her white gauze cover-up might lift itself off her body.

"I'm so happy, Anna."

"Oh yeah?" she said as she pulled him on top of her. "Why's that?"

He kissed her softly. "Because you're here and because we're back together and because I'm . . . I'm so tired of being without you."

Her lips pulsed as she tasted the remnants of salt lingering from their day at the beach. "I'm tired of being without you too. I love you, Thomas. Don't ever think differently."

"I've never doubted it." A smile played at one corner of his mouth. "We just had to wait for you to come around."

She lifted her hips to pull off her cover-up, revealing the bottoms of her flower-patterned bikini. She raised her hands as Thomas helped her out of it and tossed it aside. Looking up at him with a smirk, she nodded her consent.

He lowered himself on top of her, and her pelvis arched toward him, wanting to feel hard evidence of her effect on him. Needing more of his skin, she unbuttoned his shirt and traced the scars and scratches of his time in the jungle with her fingers. He followed her lead with gentle hands as he reached behind her and unhooked the clasp of her top. They continued to undress each other until the two beings became one.

As she was swept away by this man, she understood exactly what it meant to make love, and she knew that she was absolutely ready. He was gentle but wild, a man attempting to tame a tiger, and they pressed into each other with such passion that the walls of her heart shook, and a blast of colors splashed onto the canvas of her soul.

⁓

The week took on wings, and they rarely left each other's side, barely letting their eyes or hands or lips stray from each other. They took long walks on the beach after breakfast and spent their days sitting under an umbrella, or building sandcastles, or swimming, never running out of conversation. She never strayed far from her sketch pad and found endless inspiration there by the sea with the man she loved. They'd laugh to tears during dinner and then dance to the local bands until their inner urges led them back to the room.

On the last night, they meandered down the beach to a spot the concierge had recommended, where they tried sushi for the first time in their lives. Thomas was back to his old self and couldn't stop talking.

Sitting across from Annalisa at a small table by the window, he picked up his chopsticks and attempted to pinch one of the pieces of tuna rolled in rice and seaweed. "What's the point here? Why not just a fork?"

She broke into laughter, watching him fumble for it. "I'd forgotten how graceful you were."

Following another few failed attempts, he shrugged and exchanged the chopsticks for a fork. After finally enjoying a bite, he said, "Who knew? Raw fish and seaweed. This is really good."

She stabbed a piece with a fork, dipped it into soy sauce and wasabi, and enjoyed her first bite. "That is good."

He sipped his cold beer from a chilled glass. "We should go back and open up a sushi spot in Portland."

"Something tells me," Annalisa said, swallowing, "that sushi might not catch on back on the mainland for a while, but it is good."

"Are you kidding me?" He went for another piece. "Nonna would dig raw tuna."

"Oh, would she?" Nonna didn't stray far from Italian food.

He grinned. "Sure, just put it on top of a heaping pile of pasta instead of her meatballs."

The night was like that, full of silliness and back to the way things had been, two people finding happiness in the midst of the crazy world around them. Life without this man didn't exist, not the way it was supposed to, and she couldn't be the artist she wanted to be without loving him at the same time.

While they were finishing off their beers after dinner, Thomas reached across the table for her hand. "I want to ask you something." She felt a tremble in his fingers.

Concerned, she said, "What is it?"

He was lost in her eyes, as if he were hypnotized by them.

"What?" she asked again.

Letting go of her hand, he slid his seat back and stood. Then he reached into the pocket of his khakis, drawing out a small box. Annalisa's heart leaped. Was that what she thought it was? Rounding the table, he nervously and adorably lowered to one knee and gazed up at her. He opened the box and held it out, showing a gold band.

With those slivers of stardust looking up at her, he asked, "Annalisa Mancuso, will you marry me?"

She lost her breath, couldn't believe this was happening—hadn't even considered the possibility. The truth of her feelings came out as her lips curled up. Her entire body tingled as she said, "Yes. Yes. Yes! And yes! And even more yeses!"

He lit up. "Here I was thinking I'd have to convince you."

As she looked at the man offering his life to her, though, she thought there could be no other way. She knew now more than ever that she did believe in love. Because they *were* love. She hadn't believed in such a feeling growing up because she never could have believed in it until she met him.

"Yes," she said, pulling him up and pressing her lips into his.

He slipped the band onto her finger. "I owe you a diamond when I get back."

"I don't care about a diamond," she assured him, looking at this symbol of their life together. "You just come home in one piece, okay?"

Standing now, he touched her cheek. "Not even the entire North Vietnamese Army could keep me from coming home to you now."

The reality of his coming home made Annalisa realize what they'd committed to. She thought of Nonna and what her family would think. Then, with a chill, she thought of his family, who didn't even know she was here.

"So . . . ," she started. "Do your parents have any idea?"

He returned to his seat. "I thought we could wait until I got home to deal with them. What do you think?"

She thought about it. Hiding their engagement from Mr. Barnes was one thing, but keeping it from Mrs. Barnes and Emma felt wrong. "I don't know. Maybe we should tell your mom and your sister, at least. Maybe *I* should tell them."

"I thought about writing them, but my dad gets the mail most of the time. I really don't want you to have to deal with him while I'm there."

She completely agreed, remembering how awful his father had been at the country club. "What if I just called the house and broke the news, asked your mom and sister to keep it a secret? They might appreciate it, you know? The last thing I want to do is give your sister another reason to dislike me."

He tapped the table. "Yeah, maybe so. You know women better than I. But don't feel like you have to. We can tell them together."

"I think it could be a nice gesture," she said.

After a pensive beat, he said, "Yeah, I think you're right."

As the two newly engaged lovers strolled along the sand, Annalisa accepted that they might never have a smooth ride. There would always be things like Vietnam and his family, but so be it. The alternative of not having him was worse. No matter what got in the way, nothing could stop the two of them from living out their lives together. All they had to do was have faith, because some things were as sure as the stars.

Chapter 29

An Artist Comes Alive

"So . . . I got engaged," Annalisa casually mentioned from her seat in the back of Walt's Plymouth Belvedere. She wondered who would turn around first, Walt or Nonna.

"What's that, young lady?" Walt asked, turning down the bouncy jazz on the radio. They were fighting Boston traffic on their way back from Logan Airport.

Annalisa leaned in between the two seats, hoping that Nonna wouldn't lash out at her. She could smell the polisher Walt used on the shiny dashboard. "I'm getting married," she said, the thrill of the news tickling her insides.

Nonna's head twisted as quickly as a triggered mousetrap snaps down on its prey. "You what?"

Annalisa held up the gold band that she'd been hiding since meeting them at the gate. "Thomas proposed to me. We're engaged." No matter Nonna's response, Annalisa loved feeling the words as they left her tongue.

"Congratulations, young lady," Walt said, gifting her a smile as he turned down the music even more. "Isn't that something, Elena?"

Walt glanced over to his girl with, most likely, the same curiosity with which Annalisa was looking at Nonna. She could easily go either way.

Nonna held a hard and straight face as Annalisa's heart pounded. The car went so quiet that Annalisa could hear Walt's dusty lungs working overtime. Even his regular breathing had taken on a sound like an old air-conditioning unit. Her grandmother crossed her arms and looked away, boring a hole in the dashboard.

It was all for show, though, because she then turned back with a loving, toothless smile. "I couldn't be more happy for you, *nipotina*."

Annalisa nearly let loose a floodgate of tears, and with a full heart she reached up and touched Nonna's shoulder. "Thank you, Nonna. I've been terrified to tell you."

Nonna raised her left hand. "I guess the times are changing, aren't they? What do I know? Besides, who else will ever hold your heart like him?"

"Only you, Nonna."

Nonna jokingly side-eyed her.

Annalisa sat back in the seat. "We haven't made any plans yet, but he'll be back from Asia sometime in December; then we'll have another six months somewhere in the States. So maybe a wedding in August or so next year."

With one hand on the wheel, Walt reached for Nonna's hand. "That is one occasion I wouldn't miss for the world."

"I hope you'll have the wedding in the Mills," Nonna said, talking over her shoulder.

Annalisa had expected such a request. She scooted to her left so she could see Nonna's face. "I'm thinking so, but we didn't make any decisions. His parents don't even know yet."

Nonna glanced back at her. "He hasn't told them?"

As much as she wanted to keep a lid on their engagement until Thomas returned, she knew she couldn't do that. "We're not going to tell his father until he gets back, but I'm going to call Mrs. Barnes and Emma today. They don't even know that I went to see him."

"I think telling them is the right thing," Nonna offered, confirming Annalisa's decision.

She looked at her ring. Though his parents' reaction wouldn't change how much she loved Thomas, it would be nice to have their support. "I'm sure they'll want to do something at the club. Can you imagine the Mancusos taking over Davenport?"

A few minutes later, she said, "Hey, Walt, I've been thinking. How would you feel about hiring someone else to help with the shop? I'm getting back on track and taking lessons from Sharon again, and I really need to make some more time to paint. I've never been so motivated."

Walt considered the idea as he putted along in the right lane. "Do you have anyone in mind? I think it's a wonderful idea. Matter of fact, we sold half our inventory while you were gone, so it is time you get back to work. Turns out your grandmother is quite the saleslady."

"Where do you think I got it from?" Annalisa asked, nudging her grandmother's arm.

～

As Walt flipped the sign on the door of the shop, Annalisa told him she'd be down shortly and ascended upstairs with Nonna to make the call to Davenport. She needed to get it over with as quickly as possible.

After sitting through judgments of her life's work by both Jackie Burton and Sharon Maxwell, she would have thought she had unshakable nerves, but she could barely breathe as the phone rang, thinking that her secret trip to Hawaii could detonate any potential familial relations.

"Mrs. Barnes? Hi, it's Annalisa." As much as she didn't want to make this call, it was her love for Thomas giving her the strength.

"Oh my goodness," she replied in her typical jovial voice, which could either be sincere or far from it. "What a blast from the past."

"I know." *Here we go,* she thought, *the moment of truth.* "I was . . . I'm calling to share some big news. How's Emma, by the way?"

"She's good, wrapping up school for the year. I think one more exam to go. So to what do I owe the pleasure?"

No use stalling any longer. Annalisa looked at Nonna, who was searching the fridge for dinner ideas. "I have a secret I'd like to share with you, but I was hoping we could keep it from your husband." She was sure Mr. Barnes was at work, which was why she'd chosen to call in the early afternoon.

A long pause. "Is this about Thomas?"

Annalisa sat up. "I just went to visit him in Hawaii. He was on leave." She realized how many secrets she'd been keeping. It wasn't just one! "We've been writing, as you know, and we both realized that we still love each other so much." Annalisa hated the silence on the other end and wondered what Mrs. Barnes might be thinking.

She forged ahead. "He asked in a letter that I come see him. While I was there, he proposed to me. And I accepted, of course."

More silence, this time a black hole of it, swallowing Annalisa's excitement. At least the cat was out of the bag, though.

"I knew you two were writing," Mrs. Barnes admitted, "but I had no idea what was bubbling up between you." She didn't sound upset, only surprised. That was a start.

"I love your son with all that I am, and I'm sorry I didn't tell you that I was going to Hawaii, but . . . we haven't spoken in so long, and . . . he needed me."

"I understand. How is he?"

Annalisa was feeling better by the minute and was so happy that they'd agreed to share the news. "He's excited to get back home, and in the meantime he's handling it well. You'd be very proud of him."

"And you're getting married . . . ," Mrs. Barnes said, processing this life-altering news. Annalisa could only imagine what it would be like to stand in the woman's shoes right now.

She switched the phone to her other ear. "We wanted to tell you and Emma but thought it might be best to let Thomas break the news to his father when he gets back. Don't you agree?"

"Yes," Mrs. Barnes said quickly, any other option seemingly absurd. "It'll be our secret. I'm sorry. I'm still getting over the shock. I'm very happy for you all. Oh my goodness. Did he have a ring?"

Thrilled that Mrs. Barnes seemed interested, Annalisa filled in the details of their week and the proposal. As Mrs. Barnes ran out of questions, Annalisa said, "I was hoping I could tell Emma. Is she back from school?"

Mrs. Barnes had apparently been thinking about Emma's reaction. "Actually, I'd like to tell her myself, if you don't mind. This is going to be big for her. I'm sure she'll be thrilled, but it's probably best I pick the right time."

Annalisa was let down. "Oh, okay. I'm sure you know what's best."

"I'm so glad you called, Annalisa. Let me wrap my head around the news, and let's talk again in a day or two. I want to talk weddings and grandbabies and all those things."

How incredibly gratifying to hear Mrs. Barnes's chipper tone. "Please let me know when I can talk to Emma. I'd still love for her to come down for a weekend at some point. We'd have a lot of fun."

"I think it's a wonderful idea," Mrs. Barnes said, more jovial than ever. "Talk to you later."

After they'd hung up, Annalisa looked toward the kitchen. Nonna was slipping her apron on. "That went better than expected, actually," Annalisa said to her, flushed with optimism. "At least one person in his family is on board."

Nonna tied the apron around her waist. "That Emma. She's a real handful, isn't she?"

Annalisa walked into the kitchen and stole a sprig of parsley from the bunch on the cutting board. "Makes me realize how difficult I must have been when I moved in."

Nonna smacked her hand. "Raising kids is never easy. You'll see."

"Ha! First things first," Annalisa said, smacking Nonna's hand back in a gentle tease. "Don't get ahead of yourself, old woman." She bit into the parsley with a crunchy smile.

⌐

Not even her jet lag could slow her down. After a more formal chat about hiring someone with Walt, Annalisa ran back up the stairs, kissed Nonna on the cheek, then went out to the balcony to get to work. There were so many images she'd brought back from her trip that she couldn't wait to get onto the page, but one had burned into her memory like no other.

It was the morning Thomas had escorted her to the airport, walking her all the way to the gate. Just before she'd disappeared through the door leading toward the plane, she'd turned back to him. He stood there in his green uniform, her fiancé, with a look of such incredible power: longing and strength at the same time. She could feel him not wanting to let her go, and at the same time his duty pulling at him from behind. In essence, she felt Thomas more than ever before, and she could sense how badly he wanted to get through the rest of the year so that they could start their life together. Never had Annalisa felt so loved than in that moment.

Even as she sat to sketch him, she knew that she would call the piece *The Last Goodbye*, as that would be the last time they ever told each other goodbye. She painted all the way to dinner and then raced back out for another session afterward, capturing him with her paints for the first time. Working through the night, she put the finishing touches on his army-green eyes around five in the morning. Standing back to admire the piece, she found herself more mesmerized by the man she loved than by her own technique in bringing him to life.

Annalisa hired one of her fellow artists in Sharon's classes to work at the clock shop so that she could put more time into her painting. In the weeks that followed, as the warmer temperatures crept higher toward estival perfection, she became incredibly prolific. Setting up her easel all over town, she felt like she'd taken the world by its tail. Everywhere she turned, she saw opportunity, new subjects to bring into her artistic world. The more she painted, the easier connecting with them became.

The moment of truth came when she decided to bring some of her latest works in to show Sharon and her fellow classmates. It was the last Tuesday in June, one year after first attending these classes. A month earlier, Sharon had asked one student per week to bring in their portfolio to share. Tonight was Annalisa's turn, and she was both eager and apprehensive as she carried her orange tote to the front of the class. She felt naked standing there, like the model whom they'd painted a year earlier.

These were artists that she'd come to know well—her circle when she did agree to the occasional social function. They surely wouldn't boo her off the stage, but would they see something extraordinary in her? More important, would Sharon? Annalisa had certainly found her own satisfaction in what she was doing, and she might be able to accept that as enough, but she did want to be seen as extraordinary, no doubt about it. She wanted to know that her voice mattered.

Unclasping the orange tote, Annalisa drew out the first of five paintings she'd chosen to share with the class. To set the stage, she showed them the painting that had set her on the correct course. She told them how much this image of Nonna reaching up to kiss Walt had impacted her, and she described exactly what her breakthrough had taught her. She even opened up about Thomas and Hawaii. She couldn't dare leave out how it was her external life that had elevated her art, all thanks to Sharon's urging.

After answering a few questions on her technique, they gave her a round of applause that filled Annalisa's cheeks with pride. She worked her way through the others, talking technique and inspiration, but focusing mainly on the stories of her subjects.

As the class ended, Sharon waved goodbye to everyone and asked, "Annalisa, would you mind hanging around for a few minutes?"

"Sure." She was terrified that Sharon was going to hit her heart with another sledgehammer of brutal honesty.

When the last of the students had disappeared out the exit on the other side of the warehouse, Annalisa, tote in hand, approached Sharon.

Her teacher put on a smile so warm that Annalisa lost her breath. "I love where you're going," her teacher told her. "Especially the one of Thomas. It's my favorite yet."

Annalisa beamed. "I'm really trying."

"No," Sharon said. "You're not trying. You're doing. You bring in another ten pieces like this before the end of the year—your absolute best ones—and you've got a spot on these walls in April."

Her words knocked Annalisa sideways. "What?"

"You heard me," Sharon said, still wielding her smile like a magic wand. "You are one of the most talented and hardworking artists that I've ever known. Don't get me wrong; you're still young and have your work cut out for you, but what I see in your pieces is an experience and wisdom well beyond your years. I'm not telling you that you'll be someone one day. You are someone, and I'd be honored to let you join my show. In fact, it wouldn't be the same without you. What do you think?"

Annalisa barely heard her tote drop to the floor. She couldn't believe it. The realization of her dream and all the hard work she'd put into it hit her like a tidal wave. She was no longer trying to be an artist. She'd just been shown the door to her destiny. Sharon Maxwell, one of the finest painters on the East Coast, had told her that Annalisa Mancuso had a seat at the table.

"I'd love it more than anything in the world," Annalisa finally spit out, racing to throw her arms around Sharon. "Thank you."

"No," Sharon said, squeezing her, "thank you."

"I'll start as soon as I get home," Annalisa promised her when she let go.

"Just don't forget what got you here. Keep living and loving. Don't forget to mix in your soul with your colors on that palette, okay?"

Annalisa nodded, finally knowing exactly what her teacher meant.

Chapter 30

CINNAMON BUNS IN THE OVEN

Under a July sky streaked with white wisps of cirrus clouds sliding by its puffier sisters higher up, Annalisa found Walt polishing his Plymouth. It was the kind of day that begged for you to be outside and get out into it. Even for Annalisa, she knew she needed to step away from her easel and experience life.

Admiring the state of Walt's car, she said, "If you'd dote on Nonna the way you do on that Belvedere, she'd probably move in with you."

Walt didn't take the bait but offered her a charitable smirk.

Annalisa and Walt had made it a Saturday summer morning tradition to take a cruise through town or toward the sea and then stop by the market on the way home. Annalisa took Sharon's wise words about "living and loving" to heart. Sure, painting as much as possible was the key to getting better, but *living* as much as possible was the secret to making true art.

What better way to live and love than to spend these cherished mornings with Walt, whose declining health showed her how valuable each moment truly was?

On their drive through Cape Elizabeth, Annalisa talked about her latest endeavors. Outside of working for Walt—growing the gallery and training their new hire—all Annalisa did was paint. "It's the one thing that takes me away from thinking about him," she admitted, sticking her hand out the window into the warm air. "Or worrying about him, to be more accurate."

Her worry was very real. Thomas hadn't responded yet to her last letter, which wasn't like him. Though Nixon was slowly pulling out troops, two hundred thousand American men were still in Vietnam, so the war was a long way from over.

As evidenced by the splatters of paint on her jeans and shoes today, she typically painted with her coffee all the way until she stepped out the door, and then after work, she'd paint late into the night. No way was she going to return to Sharon with a portfolio of anything other than the best work she'd ever done, and that required working her way through more than a few mediocre pieces to get there. Even Michelangelo had his duds that he burned.

Thomas would be home in December, spending the last few months of his commitment back on American soil. Then April would come and Sharon's show. What a dream to think that Thomas would be home safely—God willing—and he'd be there for her, supporting her, as she joined the ranks of the best and most innovative artists in New England.

By the time they reached the market, she had left her other worries behind and had become laser focused on one single item waiting for her in the near future: a cinnamon bun. Amid the farmers and the artists and other vendors was a baker named Eli, who made the most incredible pastries in the world. She always looked forward to indulging, but today she was particularly needy for one of his magical creations, as if she hadn't eaten in days.

The vendors were lined up along the sidewalk on the Lincoln Park side of Federal, and they stood behind tables toppling over with boxes of fresh produce and flowers. Their trucks were backed up behind them, many with large scales dangling from their camper tops. The open tailgates revealed even more produce waiting for their eager clients.

When Annalisa and Walt came upon Eli's table halfway down the line, the baker said, "My favorite artist, Annalisa Mancuso. Did you finally bring me a painting? I told you I'd trade you free cinnamon buns for life!" Eli drove a VW bus that was backed up behind him, and folk music played from the radio, a banjo and guitar dueling with each other.

"That's *exactly* what I need," Annalisa said. As the sweet smell of those cinnamon buns hit her, she decided she could have eaten every single one in the case, on the table, and in the van. Upon looking at the man who was most likely somewhere in his forties, one wouldn't know that he was a pastry chef. Unless he ran daily marathons, he did not consume his own inventory.

"You know, Eli, my fiancé is going to come home and not even recognize me if I keep coming back here." She loved how the word *fiancé* leaped off her tongue, each time giving her a shot of love. "The only way I know to solve the problem is if you stop making these things," she said. "I have zero discipline."

Using tongs, Eli lifted a cinnamon bun up in front of him. "Something tells me he'll be just fine. What's life without guilty pleasures? And hello, Walt. Good to see you too. Shall I cut it in half for you all?"

Leaving Eli, Walt and Annalisa strolled farther into the park and sat on one of the benches facing the Parisian fountain in the center. Sitting here had also become a tradition that Annalisa cherished. What was the point in painting if an artist couldn't take time to breathe in moments like this?

Walt had told her that the elm trees that had once shaded the park had succumbed to disease a few years earlier, so the sun sprayed down past the leafless branches. However, there was a beauty to this park and a great presence, and this particular spot became where Walt told her about the history of Portland. Her heart had broken when he'd told her weeks earlier about how there had once been a thriving Little Italy, but that the Italians had spread apart and some had fled.

Today, between bouts of coughing, Walt expressed his fear of what the Maine Mall was doing to their city. They had already seen a decline in foot traffic in the city and in their store.

"I wonder if Pride's will go out of business," she said, wiping beads of sweat off her brow. She almost complained about the heat but then thought of Thomas trudging through the humid and sweltering mess of Vietnam.

Walt coughed for a little while and then spat out, "Life used to be so much simpler."

"I bet." She thought about how even the world wars were simpler, with clear motivations to fight. Every day blurred the already-lost point of Americans losing their lives in Vietnam. After taking her last bite and losing herself in the deliciousness, she said with her mouth full, "But we still have these. Can't get any simpler than that." The sweet flavor coated her tongue with pleasure.

"Quite true," Walt agreed. "There might not be a Little Italy, and we might just lose our downtown to the Maine Mall, but there will always be a park bench."

At the same time, they both said, "And there will always be cinnamon buns." They shared a smile, and Annalisa thought that, finally, life made sense.

Then, a cloudy sensation came over her, and she reached for the arm rail of the bench. The heat was getting to her quickly. Her head swam as she slipped away from consciousness. *So hot out,* she thought. Everything happened in slow motion as she fell into Walt's lap.

~

While they waited for tests to be run at the Maine Medical Center, Annalisa fell in and out of sleep. She was beyond weary, thinking that maybe they'd given her something. She felt them sticking her with needles and moving her body around. She was afraid, worrying that something might be very wrong.

It was in this haze that Annalisa peeled open her eyes at the touch of someone by her side.

"Nonna," she said with squinted eyes, "what are you doing here?" How long had she been out?

Nonna patted her hand. "Oh, Annalisa," she said with great concern. She put her hand on Annalisa's cheek, as she'd been doing all Annalisa's life. "You work too hard."

Annalisa heard the chirp of the heart monitor, the steady metronome of life. "It was hot out today; that's all. Who brought you down? What time is it?"

"Hey, cuz," Nino called out, looking up from a sports magazine.

She was very grateful to see them. "You guys really didn't have to come." She reached for the paper cup of water by the bed, and Nonna helped her take a sip.

Walt was there, too, and the four of them talked for a few minutes, mostly about what might have led to Annalisa's fainting. When the doctor walked in, everyone parted. He wore a thick gray mustache and was only an inch or two taller than Nonna.

"How are you feeling?" he asked in a nasally voice.

"Better, I think," Annalisa said, though that wasn't really true. She felt dazed but didn't want to worry everyone. Mainers had trouble in the heat; no surprise there.

She'd already forgotten his name, but the doctor turned to everyone else in the room. "Could you please give Annalisa and me a moment?"

Once the door was closed behind Walt and Nino and Nonna, he approached her bed. "Ms. Mancuso," he started, "you're pregnant."

She burst into laughter. "Did Nino pay you to say that?" Even as she joked, though, realization dawned: she knew it was true. Her body had been dragging lately, changing. Oh God, what was happening?

She was pregnant? But . . . the birth control. She thought she'd just overworked herself.

"I'm quite serious," he said. "Congratulations."

Come to think of it, she had been late. How had she not put it together?

He kept blabbing on, but she wasn't processing any of it. She was way too young to have a baby, too young to be a mom. Her throat constricted at the severity of her mistake, trusting her pills. What had she done?

Oh God, what had they done?

Interrupting whatever he was saying, she asked, "Are you positive?"

He raked his mustache with his fingers. "You are undoubtedly pregnant, Ms. Mancuso."

A surge of anger ran through her. This was *not* how she'd planned things to occur. They were supposed to get married, and she was going to establish herself in the art world, and then—only then—was she going to become a mother, helping Thomas realize his dream of becoming a father.

"Please stop calling me Ms. Mancuso," she snapped, wanting to jump out of her bed and run away. "I'm not even twenty yet. With all due respect."

Shouldn't she be happier? Why wasn't this news landing in a better way? Women dream their whole lives for this moment. Pregnant? She wasn't ready to be pregnant. That was the business of a woman closer to thirty.

The short doctor adjusted his stethoscope. "I figured you'd want to tell your family yourself, as opposed to me intruding."

"Thanks," she said, still breathing in the peripheral edges of the news. It was a kind gesture, she thought.

But a baby inside her? Thomas's baby. What would *he* think? God, what would she do until he returned? How would her body react? Would she be able to still tap into her creative side? What about the paintings she owed Sharon? How could she possibly keep doing what she was doing at the shop? What about waiting until the right moment? And what would Nonna say?

A few seconds after the doctor excused himself, her three visitors reentered the room. Annalisa considered holding back the news, only until she could wrap her own mind around it, but her tongue betrayed her.

"Turns out it's a little more than dehydration," she confessed.

Her trifecta, Nonna, Walt, and Nino, stood by her bed like three people in a painting, frozen there waiting on more. She really couldn't take Nonna lashing out on her right now and was terrified that she'd be judged.

Nino, towering over the other two, said, "Well, out with it. What is it?"

Unable to look at Nonna, she found comfort in Nino's bright eyes, up there hovering near the ceiling like lights in a pair of lighthouses. "You're going to be an uncle." Only then did she slide her eyes down toward Nonna, inching them really, ever so slowly, almost like she had dipped her toes into the Atlantic, testing the temperature.

"You're pregnant?" Nonna asked. She slapped a hand onto her forehead and then crossed herself. "Ay yai yai." No one could say *I told you so* without a word like Nonna could.

Already feeling exhausted, she seared Nonna with her eyes. "Thanks for the support. I knew I could count on you to knock the last of the wind out of my sails."

Nino and Walt seemed to slip into the background as Nonna stepped closer.

Where she struggled to find words, Annalisa did not. "Don't judge me. I'm sure God is doing enough of that. He probably can't wait to get me into the confessional at Saint Peter's." Come to think of it, she hadn't been since before Hawaii. At least she'd made it a few times this year.

"Why couldn't you resist the temptation?" Nonna finally said. "Why couldn't you wait a little longer until you're married. Until you're ready."

Annalisa felt like she was being kicked while she was down. She didn't want to be pregnant any more than Nonna wanted her to be.

"It's not the nineteen fifties anymore," she said. "We're at war. My fiancé is in the middle of it. The rules don't apply like they did in your little bubble growing up in Naples." Annalisa didn't care that her cousin and Walt were back there somewhere. When she and Nonna needed to express themselves, an audience did little to temper their roars.

"You think this is the first war I've ever been through?" Nonna asked. "There's never an excuse to go against His word."

How could Annalisa argue? Still, couldn't Nonna lighten up some?

"I'm not going to sit here and let you lecture me," Annalisa said, keeping her temper at bay. "I'm not going to do it. We had sex, okay?" Annalisa felt a rush of frustrated emotions punch her in the chest. Unless someone had a time machine in the room, all this nagging her wasn't helping.

Saying what was really bothering her, she let out, "I don't even know if he'll make it home to meet this baby, so don't go on about how I've disappointed you." The fearful thought lunged at her once it had left her mouth. No way she could raise their baby alone.

If only her mother were still alive. She would have understood and never attacked Annalisa, especially while she was lying in a hospital bed, wrestling with the news herself.

Nonna shook her hand in the air. "You haven't disappointed me, Annalisa. I hurt for you. I know this isn't what you wanted."

Annalisa raised a fist back. "No, it isn't! Not at all."

The first tears came on like a hard rain, and Nonna went to her, putting a hand on her. Annalisa couldn't take it. This wasn't what she wanted at all. She was too young to have a baby, to *raise* a baby. She was still a child herself. She didn't know enough about the world to teach someone else. She still had her own life to live.

Nonna said into Annalisa's sobbing, "I want you to come home."

Annalisa felt like she'd been slapped. "What? You have to be kidding. I'm not coming home."

Nonna patted Annalisa's side but was firm about her suggestion. "How are you going to raise a child in the city by yourself?"

Annalisa glanced at Walt, wishing he might do something, but he'd taken a seat and was staring at the floor. "Thomas will only have five more months overseas," she said. "I'll be fine."

Nonna leaned in. "You can come back in the meantime."

"I can't come back," Annalisa said. "I know you like your life there, but it's not for me. I like the city. Besides, I'm not leaving Walt's store. He needs me."

Walt was still silent, sitting next to Nino but far from the conversation. He'd learned to stay out of their way when the two Italians fell into disagreement.

Nonna said, "He managed to do just fine before he met you. Don't think you're that special. It's time to come home."

Annalisa didn't say that he was older now, and she wasn't so sure he could run it without her help. The assistant they'd hired wasn't capable of filling Annalisa's role. "I'm not leaving everything I've worked for. Sharon is waiting on my pieces for the show. I can't give that up."

"It's not about you," Nonna said. "You're going to be a mother soon. You need to let go of all these dreams now and focus on the baby."

Annalisa wanted out of that bed. "I know you're trying to help, Nonna, and I really appreciate that . . . but Thomas will be home soon. He'll finish his commitment only a few months after the baby is born. Why don't you move down to Portland? I would love for you to be more involved with our lives. And you'd be with Walt."

Nonna tutted, as if a move to Portland was an impossibility. "I'm too old to move anywhere."

"Suit yourself," Annalisa said, "but know that we'd love to have you. Truly, Nonna. I can't imagine you not being involved with our baby. I won't stop trying to convince you."

Nonna wagged her finger at her. "Try all you want." Then she added, "I won't be far; you know me and babies."

~

Sitting at the dining-room table that evening, as she tried to find the excitement she should be feeling, Annalisa wrote a long letter to Thomas. Actually, she wrote several but tore them up halfway through. He didn't need to take on her worries of how she'd manage without him until he came home. Or how they could give their baby the best life. Or how she could possibly continue to paint. Annalisa could worry about all this on her own for now. The only thing he needed to know was that she was pregnant and happy, and soon they'd be a family of three.

When she finished the letter, the other five attempts crumpled up on the table, she didn't hesitate in kissing her signature, leaving rose-red lipstick marks before folding it closed. She was out of stamps, so she decided she'd swing by the post office during lunch the next day.

She sat there for a long while, staring at the unstamped letter and then into the negative space between her paintings that covered the walls and then out through the porch to the dark of the city. Was sending this letter the best idea? She thought back to Hawaii, back to Thomas's reaction to her getting fired, back to those conversations when he'd said he hated being so far away from her. Sure, the news of a baby would be a strong new reason to come home, but didn't he have enough reason anyway? As much as it might help, it might hurt too. He might be worried about Annalisa and how she had taken the news and not keep his mind fully where it needed to be for his survival.

She closed her eyes and prayed, asking for a clear vision. Her prayer turned to more fear as she realized Thomas wouldn't want her working and pregnant, and he'd worry that she would go crazy trying to go it alone. He'd want to be here helping, paying the bills.

He knew her so well that he'd know how the baby might hurt her career. How could she keep painting as her energy levels declined? He'd consider all these things, and he'd kick himself all over again for letting his grades slip. He could have avoided all this by holding on to his deferment. He might even consider dropping out of college so that he could be a better father. He might drive himself crazy figuring all this out while working through the nightmare that was the Vietnam War.

What about his family? How would they react? Bill Barnes would find a way to be even more furious, whereas Elizabeth Barnes might be thrilled. During both of the phone conversations they'd shared this summer, she'd mentioned how excited she was to prance her little grandbabies around town and how much she'd love it if Thomas and Annalisa would move to Davenport. Annalisa had simply shrugged the idea off, assuring her she and Thomas would make such decisions together upon his return. Annalisa wondered what kind of grandmother Mrs. Barnes would be. Aloof with a side of fortitude? Distant with a side of engagement?

And then Emma. As much as Annalisa would hope that she'd be thrilled by the news, knowing that she'd be an aunt, she might instead be knocked back into her shell. Annalisa wanted nothing more than to share with Emma, a way to reconnect with her, but she couldn't take the risk. Despite the fact that they were going to be sisters, Emma still hadn't shown any interest in having a relationship with Annalisa, who had attempted to speak with her two times by phone and had even extended an invitation for a weekend in Portland. So the chances of Emma being anything other than hurt and angry were infinitesimal.

By the time the bells of midnight chimed, she'd decided to wait on telling Thomas and his family. She even thought it might be fun to surprise him in person as he set foot back on the safe ground of American soil in December. The idea was absurd, though. She pictured Thomas stepping off the bus.

In a jolly holiday voice, she said out loud, "Hi, Thomas, welcome back from the war. This? That's your giant baby inside of me—your little Hawaiian gift coming to a theater near you in February. No, I can't imagine Waikiki Beach is good for population control. By the way, turns out pills are not one hundred percent effective!"

Chapter 31

Knocked Down Like Bowling Pins

Thomas finally wrote in September, and Annalisa let herself breathe again. Her belly had swollen, and the Mancusos all knew of the pregnancy, each of them trying desperately to lure her back home. She appreciated very much that she was still welcomed with such open arms, despite her sins.

> *I'm coming home to you December 3, can you believe it?*
> *It hasn't been easy, but I've made it and I'm coming home.*

She read the date again: *December 3.*

A tear dropped on the *3*, spreading out and soaking into the paper. As excited as she was, it was a terrifying notion, a few more months. Surely, he'd be super vigilant and not try to be a hero. She thought of Michael, who was just shipping out to Vietnam for his tour after extensive training as a medic.

> *Sorry I haven't written. I barely have time to even write this*
> *note now. But know that I'm healthy and ready to make a*
> *life with you. I've written my family to let them know that*
> *I'll be moving to Portland and attending UMPG as soon*
> *as I'm done with my commitment next summer.*

Annalisa could only imagine how his family was taking the news about going to Portland—especially Emma and Mrs. Barnes, who knew of the engagement. If they knew she was pregnant, it would be even worse.

As his DEROS approached, Annalisa kept her own head down, working as much as her body would allow. She was coming to grips with her new reality, knowing that even if she could get back to painting like before, the next year or two would certainly hamper her career. And yet, not only was she becoming comfortable with the being inside of her, but she'd started feeling excited about what was to come.

She'd climb in bed and talk to her baby and tell him all about the world and how his daddy was coming home soon. She didn't know the baby would be a boy, but that was what she wanted. As much as men drove her mad, she couldn't imagine putting a girl out there to fight the same battles she had; it was tough for a woman.

She played him Elvis, Aretha, the Jackson 5, and all the records she'd bought from Recordland since moving here. She told him that their new life would begin on December third, when his dad came home from the war. She told her son that she'd never loved anyone more than she loved Thomas, but she promised her baby that she'd love him just as much.

At Nino's urging, Annalisa drove up for the Spartans–Eagles game on the second Friday in September. She was now into her sixteenth week but wasn't showing much at all. A light jacket covered the very tiny bump. Knowing the clock to being a mother was ticking, she wanted to feel young again for just a little while.

After the game, Annalisa walked with Nino back to the parking lot where he had parked his red Ford Mustang, a far cry from the beater of the old days. While she had started her new life in Portland, Nino had taken a job at the mill and was making decent money, considering he was still living with his parents. He had his arm around her and was telling her about his latest ex-girlfriend when Annalisa noticed Emma with a few friends. She was thrilled to see her away from the grips of her parents.

Annalisa broke away from Nino and caught up with her. "Emma! I'm so happy to see you! I hoped you'd visit me this summer."

"Yeah, sorry," Emma said, breaking away from her friends. "Been busy."

"Well, you have to come to Portland soon," she said, before thinking that soon her belly would be showing. She added, "Before it gets too cold."

"I'll see what I can do." Emma couldn't have been much more rude.

"Listen," she said, reaching out to touch the girl's arm. "I want to find a way for us to work things out. We're going to be family soon, and I care about you. We're going to be sisters. I miss you."

Emma tilted her head and looked down at Annalisa's hand on her arm. "I have no interest in a relationship with you. Will you just stop?"

Annalisa's heart hit the ground as she pulled her hand back. "Why would you do this? C'mon, Emma. We had so much fun. Let's work through this. I want to be friends. Sisters." She wanted to say that her son would need an aunt, his only one.

For a flash, Annalisa thought Emma might come around, but no, she didn't. "Please stop bothering me."

Annalisa sighed, feeling like she'd lost Emma forever. But she said, "I hope one day we can get past it; I'm not going to stop loving you. Take care, Emma."

She returned to Nino with her head down. "Sorry, that was Thomas's sister. I don't know what else to do with her."

He put his arm around her shoulders. "You know, I told you to find someone rich, but damn, cuz . . ."

She glanced back and saw Emma watching her. "I know; believe me. But you can't pick who you love, can you?"

"Shoot," he said, "I love 'em all."

—

Fall was here. October 15. With the watermelon now in her belly, Annalisa had moved her entire summer wardrobe into boxes. Not that she could have worn any of it anyway with the extra weight. She'd done her best to stay fashionable as her body changed, but there were the occasional days like today when she'd shaken her head angrily at the mirror, thrown on one of her larger dresses, and gone to work.

Thomas had written only once more, and it had been a brief and unsatisfying letter. She wished she knew more of what he was going through. Was he safe? As excited as she was about his return, she was worried too. The explosion and misfiring of hormones weren't helping at all. Annalisa's letters to him were brief, too, so she totally understood. It was all lies anyway, her not telling him about the baby, him not speaking of the war. Maybe she should have told him but felt like it was too late now. Surely, he wouldn't be that upset. She had her reasons, namely that she didn't want to throw anything more on the plate of a soldier who was trying to survive the last months of his tour.

It was all good, she kept telling herself. She was doing what she had to do—painting as best and as much as she could while taking care of their baby and her body—and he was doing what he had to do, which was make it out alive. Only two more months and she could surprise him with the news that he was getting what he wanted after all, not only her but a child as well.

"How many days until he comes home?" Walt asked from his desk as Annalisa said goodbye for the day.

She didn't need to look at the calendar to answer. "Forty-eight."

"Forty-eight days," Walt echoed. "That'll go by in a flash."

"I hope so. Can I do anything else before I go put my feet up?" Her brain was fried from looking at numbers all day with their new employee. The business of pregnancy was not for the faint of heart.

Though she was still dragging herself to art classes, focusing on the lessons was increasingly more difficult.

"No, no," he said. "Go take care of yourself."

"I'm bringing you dinner down later, okay?"

He removed his glasses. "You don't have to do that."

"I think I do," she insisted. "You keep coming in here skinnier and skinnier. You'll vanish if I don't look out for you." With a particularly decisive shrug, she said firmly, "I'm not asking. Listen for a knock around seven. I'm making sausage and peppers."

"Thank you." He slipped his glasses back onto his wrinkled nose. "Sounds delicious."

On the way up, Annalisa found a letter from Mrs. Barnes, which was rather shocking. It was the first time the woman had written her in their entire relationship. She couldn't even imagine what its purpose would be. Talk of a wedding? Or was it something worse? Had Mr. Barnes found out about their engagement? Maybe it was good news—perhaps Emma was ready to visit.

Upstairs and out of breath, Annalisa sat at the table, or more like plopped down, as was the case these days, and she carefully opened the envelope.

A photograph spilled out, and her heart froze. It depicted Thomas in his jungle fatigues kissing a Vietnamese woman on the lips. They were sitting next to each other in white plastic chairs and leaning toward one another. He looked happy, a smile pulling away from where their lips met.

Everything she'd let herself believe about love shattered all at once. To think she'd given him a chance, finally letting him in. She instantly saw him on his knees at the sushi restaurant, offering the gold band that now wrapped around her finger. The ring felt like a serpent strangling her, and she pulled it off as quickly as she could.

Annalisa's fists tightened, and she would have punched him had he been standing there. She stared at the picture for a long time, feeling love crumbling to dust in her hands. There was a letter in the envelope, too, but she wasn't sure she wanted to read it. Truthfully, she didn't have to. The look on Thomas's face said it all.

Annalisa wasn't stupid. She'd heard the stories of soldiers finding lovers in Vietnam. Some women were okay with it and had accepted their men back. Bile crept up Annalisa's throat at the idea of Thomas cheating on her with this woman. Even before she read the letter, Annalisa felt herself falling back to the person she used to be, the girl who didn't believe in love.

This was exactly why. The hollowness she felt inside as her eyes glazed over was numbing, like everything that she'd worked toward had been a waste. As she came to grips with what might happen now, especially with her baby, Annalisa began to hate him. Before she even read the letter, she hated him.

As a chilly numbness spread over her, she finally unfolded the letter and flattened it on the table.

> *Dear Annalisa,*
> *I know I've been hard to deal with lately, and I'm sorry for that. Thomas being gone has not been easy. We all should have done better to be kind to you. But the past is the past. Thomas has fallen in love with a young woman from Vietnam. Her name is Linh, and he's bringing her home. I figured you should see this photo he sent recently. Anyway, good luck to you. You're a pretty girl. I'm sure you'll find someone soon.*
> *Kind regards,*
> *Elizabeth Barnes*

As numb as she was, she could still think. Now it made sense why he hadn't contacted her as often. And even why Emma was still avoiding her and had reacted in such a way at the game.

Moments passed and she felt so empty. The numbness passed, too, and she felt her heart aching in ways she'd never known, as if it might give out on her. A terrible sadness rushed over her, and as she considered her baby, their baby, she hated that this precious being had to endure life on earth.

It made her retch to think about how she'd given Thomas her virginity while he was already very possibly sleeping with this woman. Once again, Nonna had been right all along. *Screw him,* she thought, for tricking her into loving him and for destroying her dreams and for painting a big stroke of black across her whole life.

Utterly devastated and mad as hell, she flung the letter, the photograph, and the envelope onto the floor and dropped her head onto the table and cried. How dare she believe in love. Hadn't she learned anything from her parents' relationship? What a fool she was . . .

It made no sense. They'd connected so deeply in Hawaii, and he'd been so incredibly in love . . . or at least he'd acted superbly well. Was she nothing more than another girl? Nothing more than this fling he was having between battles? Annalisa didn't want to believe it.

Wanting a better explanation, she decided to call Mrs. Barnes. Sitting on the edge of the couch, she dialed their number, and the line was answered after one ring.

"Hello?" It was Emma.

"Hey, Emma, it's Anna." Her voice shook over the syllables. She didn't know what Emma might know about the letter. "How are you?"

"I'm fine. And you?"

"I'm . . ." She swallowed past a thick throat. "I'm looking for your mom. Is she around?"

"Yeah, but . . . are you okay?"

Emma's kind question touched Annalisa's heart, but how was she to answer it? "I'm miserable, to be honest."

Emma took a breath. "Yeah, I bet. I guess you got my mom's letter?"

So she did know. Annalisa could barely get out, "Yes, just a minute ago."

"I'm sorry," Emma said compassionately. "I can't imagine what you're going through." Then her tone changed. "My mom thought you might call and told me to tell you that it's best you don't reach out anymore."

"What?" Annalisa started to cry.

"Look, I'm really sorry. Apparently, he's very much in love and bringing her home and all that." With a hint of kindness, she added, "And I'm sorry that I haven't been nice to you. Or thanked you for what you did."

Annalisa shook her head, still so incredibly baffled that this was happening, that her soul mate had fallen in love with another. How could he have found anything like what the two of them had?

Annalisa pinched the bridge of her nose. "Thanks for saying that, but I don't understand. How long has this been going on?" She couldn't stop herself from crying.

Emma sounded equally upset as she said, "I'm going to hang up now. Please don't call here anymore. Goodbye." Then a click.

Annalisa dialed back but no one answered. She tried three more times before realizing that she'd been cut out of the family like a cancerous tumor.

Chapter 32

The Days (Daze) After

Leveled to the core, Annalisa collected the letter and the photograph, crumpled them up, and tossed them into the garbage. Nothing would ever be the same again in her life.

Half of her wished him here so that she could ask and understand why he'd done it, why he'd worked so hard to earn her trust and love—only to squash it in such horrid fashion. As the minutes ticked by, her anger turned so red inside that all she wanted to do was move on. She couldn't sit with these feelings any longer. No, she wanted them all to go away, to cut them out just like the Barneses had just cut her out.

She wanted Thomas to go away.

Their baby kicked, reminding her of the one connection between them that could never be severed. How could he have done that to their child? Then she remembered he didn't know about the baby. As angry as she was, she didn't want to tell him. Ever.

Thinking about her baby's future, she moved to the couch and curled up, holding her knees, searching for answers in the swell of fear. A need to protect her baby came over her. Ugly yet possible scenarios played out in her mind. She imagined the Barnes family with all their money somehow trying to take the baby. Mrs. Barnes had mentioned grandchildren enough. She imagined Linh raising Annalisa's child. Or at the very worst, she imagined a life where she had to share her baby with Thomas and his family, shuffling the child back and forth every other week or weekend. Annalisa couldn't bear that. She couldn't take that risk.

There on the couch, still raw from the opening of that fateful envelope, she decided that she had to protect her baby from the agony of love and loss. She had to protect her baby from a man who was ultimately untrustworthy. And therefore she had to keep the baby a secret from the Barneses—all of them. All the anger that had replaced her sadness gave her strength. This was her baby, not his, and she couldn't bring him into the world with a terrible father and an unloving family. No, Annalisa had been there. She couldn't let her son live the same fate.

Not wanting to drag Walt into her plan, the first decision she made was to call Nino and enlist his help. She needed to return Thomas's car and the ring he'd put on her finger. Her cousin had just gotten off work. Filling him in on what had happened, she asked, "Would you follow me to Davenport? I want to do it at night so I don't have to speak to his family."

"I told you he wasn't good enough for you, cuz. Of course I'll help."

Annalisa thanked him and hung up. Her mind raced as she searched for Thomas's car keys.

Love to fury in an instant. Thomas's service in that god-awful war held her back from hating him. How could she blame him for losing his way in a world where such evil crimes were committed? She hated the circumstances and she hated the war, but maybe she didn't hate Thomas.

But she couldn't forgive him.

All she wanted to do was remove him from her life.

—

On the long drive to Payton Mills, she rode a wave peaking in fits of steering-wheel-hitting rage and bottoming out in miserable, gut-wrenching sobs.

Why had she been so dumb? Now everything was ruined. She'd come to not only accept but get excited about the pregnancy. It was part of their dream. *Their* dream. Now that he was gone, did it matter? She was back on her own, and how in the world could she make it? Her own stupidity and hope for love had put her back on a one-way track to being barefoot and pregnant in the Mills. How could she possibly raise a child alone in Portland? She had her hands full enough taking care of herself and Walt. She could have made it until Thomas's return, but now she would be alone forever.

She met Nino at his house and gave him a quick hug. He tried to comfort her, but she wanted to focus only on the task at hand. When they reached the Barneses' neighborhood, they exchanged vehicles. Once she had figured out how to operate his Mustang, Annalisa led him into the Barneses' driveway. Only a few lights shined from the windows of the big white house. It was 9:00 p.m., and a strong salty wind rushed up from the cove.

Following her instructions, Nino pulled up behind Mr. Barnes's Cadillac and left the yellow Beetle there. An envelope carrying the ring and a short note waited to be discovered on the passenger seat.

It's over, Thomas. If you ever cared for me, please do not contact me again.

What else could she say? An explanation would have been nice, but not at the risk of losing her baby. She remembered how he'd respected her wish that he let them go when she'd first broken up with him as they walked through her neighborhood. Hopefully, he'd show the same decency after reading this note. The last thing she wanted was to hear his excuses. The proof was in the photograph.

Nino rushed back to the car, and she began to back away. In the rearview mirror, she saw Mr. Barnes coming out the front door.

Annalisa knew he'd be pleased to see they'd finally gotten rid of the poor Italian girl.

It was the end, she thought, as the big white house disappeared from view. The end of her era with Thomas, with the VW, with Davenport. She'd never come back here again, and she couldn't ever forgive him. And he would never know that his child would enter the world in February of 1972.

They pulled over, and Nino reclaimed the wheel. Driving back to the Mills, Nino showed his concern with questions that she wished she could answer, but ultimately, she was dead inside and didn't have an answer for anything anymore.

"Wanna go get some beers?" he asked. "Are you staying the night?"

"No," she said quickly. "I'm tired. I just want to get to my bed and never get out."

He glanced at her. "I get it. So when you do get out, what will you do? You have to come back to the Mills. Let the family get involved."

Annalisa had been thinking about it endlessly. It would be so easy to go back home, to surround herself by family, but that would make her a failure. Another woman with grand dreams knocked down by reality.

"I don't know," she admitted. "Everything was so perfect, and now this . . . the end. Thomas was supposed to be with me to raise our child. Together. A family. How can I do this alone? What kind of life could I give a child?"

"Knowing you, you'll figure it out," he said, trying to become her cheerleader.

She stared out the window at the trees whizzing by. "I'm right back where I was. Maybe I'm not meant to be a mother. That's the truth of it. What if I screw it all up? I've screwed up so much already."

"Don't think that way," Nino said. "You'll be a great mom. Look at all our crazy aunts, running all over the place. If they can do it, you definitely can."

"I'm not so sure. Walt is not feeling well these days, so I'm working like a dog. I don't have enough savings to afford childcare. Girls like me can't raise a child without a family, but the idea of going back to the Mills makes me . . ." She breathed in. "It makes me feel like a failure."

"That's the last thing you are, Annalisa. Why would you ever say that?" He was a terrible driver, swerving like he was drunk and much more focused on their conversation than their safety.

She glanced at him. "That's exactly what I feel like, and everything around me is burning too. I just . . . it sounds awful to say, but maybe adoption would be best. For me and the baby." Saying the word felt like a betrayal to the little one inside her. It made her sick, and she could already sense God and Nonna judging her. The decision was hers, though, and at that moment, it seemed like the only answer. She could give this baby to a family who could support and raise him or her the right way, giving it the life Annalisa had originally hoped to offer.

The deep woods of Maine seemed to offer no consolation, no answers. Was this place even her home anymore? She didn't feel like a Mainer. She felt like an outsider. When the smokestacks of the mill came into view, she felt her father's ghost fill the car.

~

"It's your body and your decision," Walt said on a frigid mid-December day, "but if you want to keep the baby, I'll help you." The city was lit up with Christmas lights, but for the first time in her life, Annalisa was far from festive.

She hated being a charity case, but he was insistent. "I'm not your problem, Walt. Lord knows you have plenty to look after with your health."

Walt shot a serious look at her. "You're anything but my problem. All I can say is that you should follow your heart. I'm not going to get in between you and your grandmother, as I'm sure she has her own opinions. Mine hardly matter."

Nonna had taken the news of Thomas's infidelity without any shade of surprise rising on her face. It was as if she'd seen so many bad things in her life that nothing shocked her anymore. That day when Annalisa had first told her, she'd clapped her hands and said, "Then you move back home, and we raise this baby together."

Though she was endlessly grateful to Nonna for the offer, Annalisa had replied the same as always. "And give up?"

Walt coughed into a napkin. "You have options. That's what matters. I suppose the right answer is waiting; you just need to find it."

"Where in the world do I find the right answer?"

"You're heartbroken, Anna. When you're heartbroken, making decisions about the rest of your life feels impossible. Maybe you need to face your feelings of losing Thomas before you can decide what to do with your baby."

It was all too much. She felt like everything was raining down on her. Walt and his COPD, Nonna getting older, a baby on the way. Thomas coming home.

As her problems poured over her, her being alone made the fight lose its worth. How would she ever paint again? Enough of the awful roller coasters involved with being an artist. It was time to consider hanging it up.

～

When the world entered 1972, all Annalisa could do was think of Thomas, wondering about his location and plans, wondering about this foreign girl with whom he'd fallen in love. Had he truly brought her home? Was she that much better than her? What had been his reaction when he'd returned to Davenport to find his car, the ring, and her note?

Did he even care? Would he care that she was carrying his baby? The questions were a rusty anchor shackled to her ankle, pulling her down.

Her hurting was so bad that she dreamed about him, conjuring up scenes of what could have been. She could see him by her side, playing with their little boy. She saw the three of them sitting at the table, eating and laughing. She saw Thomas putting skis and skates on their son for the first time. Even when she wasn't dreaming, she heard and saw things that weren't there. Sometimes she'd hear the phone ring and know that it was him, but then it wouldn't ring again. Sometimes she'd open her mailbox and see a letter with his handwriting, only to reach for it and realize it had been a mirage.

These thoughts—these feelings of still loving him despite his breach of trust—were driving her mad. He'd completely destroyed her life and hadn't even had the decency to come find her and apologize. Moving on must have been easy for him. If only he knew what he'd done to her.

Always the good cousin, Nino had been spending a lot of time with her in Portland. Like Walt, he helped without asking anything in return, and those two men kept her from taking a stance against all the men in the world.

It was the fourth day of January and one of those rare winter nights when the temperature outside hovered around freezing and, for Mainers, was warm enough to sit outside with a blanket on their laps. For Annalisa, the cold served to numb the pain she couldn't seem to shake.

Enjoying only one glass herself, she had opened a second bottle for Nino. He was hilarious when he drank, and their laughter spilled down onto the street. They'd pulled their chairs up next to each other so that they could share the blanket. The scent of charcoal and sizzling steaks came up from another building, a neighbor grilling out on their balcony.

"You wouldn't have to live with Nonna," he said. "You and I can get a place."

"You want to live with me and a baby?" Annalisa asked. "What's that going to do for your game?"

He shrugged. "Fair point. So when are you going back on the market? Don't tell me you're gonna retreat into your shell like the old days. The kid will need a dad."

She wasn't sure any kid needed a dad, though Nino's father was a good man.

"I will never go back on the market," she said. "You kidding me?"

"Oh, you're just worried no one would want you, all ripe and plump like you are."

Annalisa burst into a laugh and grabbed his shirt collar and raised a fist in jest. "I can't believe you just called a pregnant woman ripe and plump."

"Be careful; you're going to make me spill my wine." When she let go, he said, "Do you want me to lie? Then you wouldn't believe me if I told you you're still hot. Once you push that baby out of you, you'll shrink right back to what you were."

He was ridiculous. "I just hope I can start painting again. I thought I'd found my voice, but that turned out to be another false turn." As if on cue, the wind chimes caught the breeze and rang. She thought that might be her mother telling her to quit feeling sorry for herself.

"You're still sad. Give it time. You'll pick it back up soon."

"I'm open to it, but I can't stand the thought of touching a brush. What would I paint? A big black canvas? I have nothing to say creatively."

In an extraordinary act of kindness, Nino reached for her hand. "I think you need a hug." He set the blanket on the back of the chair and pulled her up. She didn't know how badly she needed a hug until he squeezed her tightly and she broke into tears. They held each other for a long time, and for a few moments, she didn't feel lonely.

As the chimes continued to ring, though, she had this strange feeling that someone else was on the balcony with them, watching them. She let go of Nino, feeling almost afraid.

"You'll get over it," Nino said, sitting back down. "You've been up and down all your . . ."

Annalisa wasn't listening anymore because she'd glanced down toward the street and swore that she'd seen Thomas. Only for a moment, and by the time she'd leaned toward the railing to get a better look, he was gone.

Or maybe it was just the glass of wine and heartache.

"You're not even listening to me," Nino said.

She took her eyes away from the street, sat back down, and pulled the blanket back over her.

"My point is," he said, "move back home and start painting again. Forget about him."

She shivered. "In case you've forgotten, his baby is inside of me."

"Find another rich guy and move on. And if he turns out to be a jerk, divorce him and take his money."

Nino really had it all figured out, she thought. "Why in the world do I need to find anyone? I'm happier alone. The last thing I want is to feel like this again. You focus on you. Why aren't you married?"

"I'm trying; believe me." He reached for the bottle of Chianti and refilled his glass.

"You'd be a good dad," she told him.

"You'll be a good mom."

"I don't know," Annalisa said, feeling her mind slip back to the possibility of adoption. It wasn't too late to give her child a better footing in life. Talk about failure, though. How could she ever paint again if she knew she'd sent a child out there to fight the world alone?

"You're going to keep it, right?" Nino asked, sensing her thoughts.

"I still don't know." Annalisa pulled off the blanket and stood. She leaned against the railing and tickled the chimes with her hands. Looking down, she saw that a man had exited the phone booth and was attempting to hail a cab. The Leaning Tower of Treeza had shed all its leaves and was dressed in a dusting of snow. She could hear the sad sound of a sax coming from a club a block down, and for some reason the brassy sound made her feel so old. Just last year, she was in love and free and not pregnant, and the world was full of opportunity. She was alone and pregnant and lost.

Part III

FEBRUARY 1972 TO MAY 1979

Chapter 33

CELIA

Annalisa was a complete wreck by the time her daughter was born on February 3, 1972. Not believing that she had what it took to be a great mother, so much of her wanted to give her baby up for adoption, but she'd decided against it. The decision had nothing to do with Nonna's insistence or Annalisa's fear of God. Her decision to keep the baby came down to the fact that, when she really sat to consider the idea of letting another person raise her baby, she couldn't bear it. She couldn't stand the thought of going on and living a life, knowing that her child was out there.

Her contractions started around four in the morning, and she knew her baby was ready to enter the world. Because Annalisa's due date approached, Nonna had been staying with Walt for a week, helping Annalisa every way she could. Waddling her way to the living room, she dialed Walt's number. In moments, she was lying down in the back seat of his Plymouth as he raced the three of them to the Maine Medical Center. During her attempts to quell the pain by following the breathing technique she'd learned, she realized how terribly afraid she was to take on such tremendous responsibility.

"It's a girl," the doctor said as he handed Annalisa her child in the delivery room. She'd endured seven hours of labor and was covered in sweat, deathly tired, but she couldn't help but laugh at the gender.

During all those times she'd referred to "him," God must have been snickering at her.

When Annalisa held her baby girl for the first time, she felt love and confusion at the same time. Even in that most precious moment, Annalisa questioned whether she could be a good enough mother to raise her daughter without a father. She named her daughter Celia after her mother, but that hefty name gave even more weight to the heft of raising a human being.

Annalisa stared into the bluish-green eyes of this dark-haired child and even then could see Thomas in her. She kissed Celia on the cheek and pulled her into her chest, thinking that nineteen was entirely too young an age to take on such enormous responsibility, especially alone.

When she looked into the eyes of her daughter again, she turned her lips up into a smile. Perhaps there was no better comfort that Annalisa could offer than a mouth showing happiness, even if the curvature of her lips was a serious deceit. But even then, barely human, Celia could surely read through it. Annalisa felt like an impostor, stretching her mouth into a lie. She wasn't happy at all.

Holding this tiny beautiful being in her arms filled her heart with the magic of life, but she couldn't pretend to tell her baby that life would be a waltz of love and joy. This poor baby would have to figure out her way through the world, attempting to slay the never-ending demons, and like Annalisa, Celia wouldn't have a loving father by her side.

Nonna was in the room for the birth, and she'd gone out to retrieve Walt. The two came in and gushed over Celia. Nonna took the baby from Annalisa's hands, desperate to introduce herself to her sixth great-grandchild. Annalisa could hear the Mancuso clan outside the door, all waiting to get a peek.

Welcomed by Walt and a host of Mancusos packed into her apartment bearing hand-me-downs and baby gear, Annalisa carried Celia into her apartment for the first time. Though she knew it should be a happy moment, she was terrified. Since deciding against giving Celia up for adoption, she had tried to make sense of staying, but it was feeling more impossible by the minute.

She hated herself for not being more thrilled and tried to remind herself of all the women who dreamed of this day. It wasn't that she resented the baby; it was just scary. In fact, it had nothing to do with Celia at all. It was Annalisa thinking she couldn't do it, that she would be inadequate. Despite all her worries, having her family gathered around her was reassuring and comforting.

Annalisa gave Nonna the baby and excused herself to her bedroom. She opened up a window to the city and then crashed onto her bed. With the sounds of her loved ones in the living room and the city she'd once dived into with youthful vigor taunting her from the open window, she buried her face into a pillow so that no one would hear her cry.

If she didn't follow her family back to the Mills, she'd be alone. That was why she was crying most. Loved ones waited in the next room, and she had a baby . . . but she was alone.

As the hollowness of that realization hit her, she decided she couldn't fight off moving home any longer. She'd tried to ignore it, but there was no rational way for her to stay.

It was time to go back home to the Mills.

Time to give up all her dreams and retreat back to reality. She might never get out of Payton Mills, but that didn't matter anymore. Nonna was right. She couldn't be selfish and chase silly dreams. It was time to focus on being a good parent.

When she returned from her bedroom, having washed away her red face, she told Nonna her decision. "I guess it comes down to the fact that I just don't have any fight left."

Never had she felt more defeated.

~

In the morning, Annalisa pushed into Walt's shop with Celia in her arms. He stood with a customer in a fedora showing off a grandfather clock he'd brought in. "Look at you out and about," Walt said. "How are you feeling?"

"To be expected, I guess. A little lighter on my feet."

Walt must have seen the sadness in her eyes and asked the customer to excuse him. He led Annalisa to the back of the store, where he reached for Celia. "May I?"

"Of course."

Walt cradled Celia in his arms. It was strange to see him take her child in such a loving way. "How's this new world treating you?" he asked sweetly. "You have so much ahead of you."

Annalisa thought that was an understatement. So much ahead and so much of it awful. "Walt, I have to go back home."

He took Celia's little hand, and she grabbed on to his thumb. Without looking at Annalisa, he said, "That may be best."

"I apologize. I've let you down, and I hate that. You've given me every opportunity and allowed me a chance at my dream, but this little one has changed things. I just can't do it on my own."

With Celia still holding his finger, he looked at Annalisa. "You haven't let me down in any way, young lady. Every decision you make needs to be about you and this wonderful girl. I've lived my life."

A tear dripped down her cheek. "I can't thank you enough for what you've done for me, Walt. Seriously. No one has ever done so much. I can't bear to think of what you're taking on with your shop now."

"Annalisa," he said gently, his eyes on Celia, "I've managed to run a watch shop for forty years—and most of it without you. I can figure it out. Look what you've done here. You've breathed new life into this place . . . and brought me new customers." He touched his chest and coughed some. "You've breathed new life into *me* despite these damn lungs."

Annalisa felt so lonely for him. "Why don't you come back with me? Find a little place in Payton Mills. I feel like we're family. Nonna would just die if you picked up and moved."

He handed Celia back. "This is my home, dear, but it's not that far away. Surely you'll both come see me."

Feeling slightly optimistic, Annalisa said, "Yes, you know I will. Whenever I can get a ride. What can I do for you before we go? I can help find a new tenant."

"Just take care of the two of you. Whatever that requires. Don't look back. You've done more for me than you'll ever know. You've become like a daughter to me."

"And you, like a father to me," she cried, thinking she couldn't endure the pain of any more goodbyes.

He pulled out his handkerchief and coughed into it, reminding her that he wouldn't be around forever. When he'd stopped, she said, "If you moved to the Mills, I could take care of you. I'd love nothing more."

"That's very sweet of you," he said, leaving it at that.

"Nino is coming to get us tomorrow. I'll get packed and then clean the apartment. It'll be ready to show by the time I leave."

He reached for Celia's foot, her little white slipper. "Don't feel defeated. Life throws curveballs." He shook the foot. "This is one beautiful curveball."

Another tear came. Celia was beautiful, but Annalisa felt so incredibly depleted inside. "I just hope I can be a good mother. Right now, it doesn't feel possible."

"I have no doubt that you'll be a wonderful mother, but I suppose parenting is no different than anything else. It takes a little practice. Try it on for a while and see what happens."

Annalisa brought Celia up to her chest. She hoped he was right. Because right now, she felt like the little human in her arms was not where she belonged.

—~

Annalisa thought she'd hit her lowest low when she'd finally admitted to Walt that she was leaving Portland, but walking head down into Nonna's house with Nino was the ultimate moment of defeat. She'd been the determined one who would find her own place in the world, no matter the cost. She'd left Payton Mills, knowing there was something bigger for her out there. After she'd graduated high school, they had watched her go and had wished her luck, and she'd felt so proud driving away in Thomas's VW that day.

Only to come back home. Her clothes, sewing machine, a few of her paintings, and her wind chimes were packed in Nino's car.

Her feelings of defeat made no sense, because the entire Mancuso clan waited for her, and they didn't treat her like a failure. Some of them had been there for the birth, and now they were here for her return. She could barely get Celia through the door before they stole her away.

Feeling another cry coming on, she excused herself to her bedroom and fell onto the bed. She was right back where she'd started. For almost three years she'd planned her escape, and she'd failed.

Nonna knocked and came in, taking a seat beside her. "This is all normal," she said.

"I don't know about that. This doesn't feel right. None of it. I feel like I'm living someone else's life. I'm a terrible mother. Sometimes I look at her and feel so angry. She's the most beautiful girl in the world, and all I can see is Thomas and what he did to me and the life she's taken from me." Annalisa couldn't believe the words coming out of her mouth, but they were true.

Nonna sighed and paused. "You have a lot of life to live. You can't figure it all out within two years of graduating from high school. This is nothing more than a setback."

"A setback? This is more than a setback. I don't feel like I'm starting over again. I feel like I'm crawling into my own grave and giving up."

"That's up to you, no?" Nonna asked. "I know you have what it takes to be a good mother, but you've been a free spirit. It may take some time to connect with that person."

Annalisa sat up on the bed, her feet on the rug. "I keep wondering if I need to put her up for adoption, and now it's too late. What would everyone think of me? Now that they've met her. Now that she has a name? It's too late, and I failed her."

Nonna let out a subtle smile. "You young ones think it's all supposed to be sorted out, that there are answers out there. I'm not sure there are. Quit trying to decide what the rest of your life will look like. Embrace these moments. You have plenty of time to learn how to be a good mother."

Annalisa shook her head. "I wouldn't even know how to start."

"You can start by getting out of bed," Nonna said, repeating her advice from one of the days after Emma's overdose. "When it comes to being a mother, that's your first victory."

"I just want out, Nonna."

Nonna patted Annalisa's hand. "That's the one thing you can't have."

There was no doubt that Annalisa had every opportunity to learn how to be a good mother. She watched Nonna taking care of Celia in awe. Nonna could somehow make three incredible meals a day, keep the house clean, and keep Celia laughing all the way to bedtime. Annalisa thought it funny that she'd been painting those women walking in and out of Pride's, thinking they embodied strength. Now, Annalisa knew no one embodied strength more than Nonna.

It seemed impossible for Annalisa. For the next few weeks, Annalisa could barely get out of bed, which meant she couldn't even enjoy that tiny victory.

Sometimes she'd listen to Celia crying in the crib next to the bed and do nothing about it. She couldn't bring herself to get up and try to comfort the girl. What was she to say? Pretend that the world was okay? Annalisa thought that the less she poisoned Celia with her bad energy, the better. Then Nonna would come bursting into the room, any time of the night, and sweep up Celia into her arms and rock her back to sleep.

Annalisa was not capable of this kind of mothering. She was still caught up in thoughts of Thomas stomping on her dream, thinking that only thirty minutes away, he might be back in school at Weston. Or maybe he was in Portland. Either way, he was surely with Linh.

Linh. The name stung every time.

They'd been destined to fail since the beginning. It was awful to think that the warning Thomas's father had issued at the country club that night they all dined together was spot-on. Annalisa and Thomas were too dumb to see that their limited understanding of the world wasn't enough to guide them through the hard times. Their relationship was destined to get in the way.

Reminding herself that she had to suck it up and be the mother she needed to be, Annalisa kept stretching her lips, attempting to find the smile she once had. No matter how hard she tried, though, she couldn't feel the smile, couldn't feel the joy she needed to show her baby that life was full of opportunity and joy.

Each day took her further away from herself, and her bed became both her sanctuary and her prison. Celia's cry became a reminder of everything she could have been and everything she wasn't. If she wasn't careful, she would never paint again. She felt further from it each day, especially as Sharon Maxwell's annual show in April came and went.

Chapter 34

An Unexpected Encounter

Annalisa's struggles did not dissipate in the passing months leading into summer, and despite her family's constant reassurance, she was not growing into being a mother. She tried when she could, but the hurt she felt inside crushed her, and at times she wondered if her pregnancy had triggered some illness that the doctors couldn't find.

Getting out of bed in the morning often felt like an impossible undertaking, but sometimes the guilt of her failure as a mother was enough to force her to wake and nurse Celia. Still, as soon as Nonna or another family member took over, she'd climb back into the bed and lie there in her miserable thoughts. She barely ate, barely smiled. When she looked in the mirror, she couldn't even see who she used to be. Her eyes were hollow, and her ribs showed. The lines on her face were that of someone a decade older.

For so many years, she could see the beauty in even the simplest sights. Not now. Nearly all her life, she'd been bursting with the urge to paint. No more. As far as she was concerned, she was now done forever. The world didn't need more artists, she decided. It was the selfish dream of a girl who didn't quite understand the big picture.

She couldn't stop thinking about the mothers around her, girls she'd grown up with in the Mills. They seemed to be so comfortable holding their babies, pushing strollers down the street, going to meet their husbands for playtime in the park. As evidenced by their smiles, they were happy to spend their Saturdays cooking for their husbands toiling away in the yard. These same mothers appeared to enjoy nursing. For Annalisa, it couldn't have felt more unnatural, and she hated how her nipples cracked and bled. No matter how painful, though, Nonna wouldn't allow her to stop. Truthfully, Annalisa wanted to continue—despite the pain—as she knew it was best for her baby.

Without a car, Annalisa and Nonna counted on other family members to take them around town to run errands. Nino, who had proved to be a wonderful uncle figure, would often pick up Annalisa and Celia, and they'd go on an adventure. As unhappy as Annalisa felt, she faked it as best she could. Though Nino could see right through her attempts, she hoped her baby could not.

On a warm day in early June, they went on such an adventure. When Nino asked what they should do, Annalisa said, "Can we go by Harry's and get some ice cream? I want to see if I can get my old job back."

"Yeah, sure." He paused. "But are you sure?"

She was not at all sure. "What else am I going to do?"

"I don't know. I'm sure you could get a job at the mill."

Annalisa didn't tell him that she'd rather kill herself. That was where her father had worked. "I don't think that's for me."

"Why don't you open a little gallery? Something like you had in Portland. The tourists would go crazy for your work."

"With what money, Nino? Even if I did, we only get traffic in Payton Mills in the summer when all the tourists drive through. How would I make money the rest of the year? What would I sell? I haven't as much as picked up a pencil since Celia was born. Before that even. I don't even see color anymore."

Nino turned back to look at Celia in the baby seat Walt had gifted them. "Just get over yourself and marry a rich man. Use your looks to your advantage."

"My looks? Those are long gone."

"You're such a pain, cousin. Seriously, get out there and start dating again. Every guy in this town has his eye on you. All you have to do is smile a little."

"You're a broken record," she said, growing irritated. "I don't want to marry someone just to have some security. I may have lost who I am, but I still have a little dignity."

They pulled onto Main Street, and Nino looked for parking. "I think you're confusing dignity with Mancuso hardheadedness. If you'd say yes to one of the guys who asks you out at church, you'd see. Not everyone cares."

"I don't want to talk about it anymore." It made her stomach hurt thinking of anything to do with love. Everyone told her that heartache goes away. Hers hadn't waned in the slightest. If anything, it was getting worse.

"I can't have Nonna support us any longer, and I need to save for a car. I definitely can't ask you to keep carting us around for the rest of our lives."

Nino slowed the car. "Yes, you can. That's what family is for."

Moments like this lifted her up. She might not believe or have any interest in romantic love, but familial love was a certainty.

"Celia is my responsibility." She turned back to her daughter, wishing she could be stronger.

They parked in a slanted spot outside of Harry's, and Annalisa felt herself being sucked back in by Payton Mills. If she wasn't careful, she would end up marrying someone she didn't love just so that she could quit taking from her family. She hated that feeling of being a burden almost as much as being a failure.

Now that she'd tasted what it was like to love, how could she possibly fake her way through a marriage to someone she didn't care about? After knowing the pain of heartache, how could she possibly set herself up to feel that again? Would it be worth it just to find a father for Celia?

The smell of vanilla always hit her when she pulled back the glass door to Harry's and the bell rang, and it was an apropos scent, as that was what her life felt like, and that was exactly what her life would be if she settled for some guy just to make her life easier.

Annalisa pushed the stroller as she looked around the shop. A young girl with curls spilling off her head was restocking the candy jars. That used to be Annalisa. This girl would one day be in the same spot as her, being urged to settle for one of the boys from the Mills who had no interest in ever leaving.

"Can I help you?" the girl asked.

"I used to work here," Annalisa said, thinking of the days when Thomas used to come see her, and when he'd strut in, and the bell would ring, Annalisa's own bell would ring too.

"Oh, that's neat. You must be Annalisa, right? Harry's told me about you."

"That's me. Is he around?"

"He's in the back. Let me grab him. I know he'll be excited to see you."

While Nino eyed the tubs of ice cream through the glass, Annalisa picked up Celia and said to her swaddled baby, "This was my old life. Your mommy used to work here."

Celia was adorable and had started to develop a more distinct look, so clearly divided between Thomas and Annalisa. Celia's curious and loving smile looked like it had been sculpted from Thomas's face, but the little girl had Annalisa's occasional suspicious glare. Like Annalisa, she also had a full head of dark-brown hair. Sometimes, when she looked at her daughter, she felt her heart hurt. Not today, though. Today, looking upon her daughter made her happy. Maybe that could be considered a victory.

"Look who's come home," Harry said from behind the counter. When he noticed Celia, his voice rose an octave. "And look at this little one." He rounded the counter and opened up his arms.

"Meet Celia," she said.

Unlike Eli at the farmers' market with his gooey cinnamon buns that he never touched, Harry was a result of a man living amid candy and ice cream for most of his life. He was unhealthy, but as sweet as the jelly worms, and he'd been a great boss. He spoke to Celia for a little while and eventually handed her back to Annalisa.

"She's really beautiful. I wondered when you'd bring her by."

Annalisa had been avoiding this place. In fact, she'd been avoiding Main Street as best she could because she was tired of running into people who always said something like, "Once you get out there into the rest of the world, you realize the Mills isn't so bad. Right?"

Right.

"What brings you back to town?" Harry asked. "I thought I'd never see you again." He added a hello to Nino.

Being the small town that Payton Mills was, Annalisa was sure he knew most of the story, so she figured he was making small talk. "Oh, you know Nonna wouldn't let that happen. Actually, I've moved back for a while." She didn't know why she added that last part. *For a while.* Where else was she going? She wouldn't be leaving here for the rest of her life.

"Aren't we lucky then?"

Annalisa glanced at the girl now stocking gummy peaches, then whispered, "I hoped you might have some work for me. Even something part-time?"

He looked at the girl, too, and slowly nodded. "I could give you some part-time work. We're busy now, but I'm not sure after season."

Annalisa had a feeling that would be his answer. "I'd take anything you have to offer, Harry." Anything to keep her from working at the mill or marrying a man she didn't love.

"I'd be happy to bring you back." He set eyes on Celia. "Has she had her first taste of ice cream yet?"

Annalisa shook her head. "Never. She's too young."

"Oh, nonsense," he said lovingly. "Let her have a little taste. Trust me."

"C'mon," Nino told her. "Live a little."

"Fine." Why pretend to be responsible now?

Harry bounced his eyes across the colorful flavors. "We have to pick the perfect flavor for her first ice cream. How about vanilla? A tried-and-true classic."

"No way," Annalisa said, thinking she didn't want her daughter to know anything vanilla in her life.

"I know," Harry said, rounding the counter and reaching for the scoop. "Butter pecan is what dreams are made of."

"No!" Annalisa snapped, so loudly that the girl stocking the candy, Nino, *and* Celia, who rested against her chest, all turned their heads. "Sorry. It's a big decision."

"Okay," he said. "Not butter pecan. Not vanilla. How about we let you pick?"

Annalisa set Celia down in the stroller and looked through the glass at the flavors, wondering how many scoops she'd scooped here over the years. She'd had a few favorites. At one time, it had been strawberry and then lemon sorbet. During the last few months before she'd left, she had a love affair with mint chocolate. "How about mint chocolate?"

"Bold choice," Harry said.

"For a baby?" Nino asked. "Babies don't like mint. Give her that bubblegum-looking stuff."

"A mother knows best, Nino." Harry took a sample and handed it to Annalisa. "Why don't you do the honors?"

With everyone in the store watching, Annalisa said, "Okay, honey, let's see what you think of ice cream." She held the tiny spoon close to Celia's mouth.

Celia's nose wrinkled as she smelled it. She moved closer, hesitantly. Then her little tongue poked out and licked the green deliciousness.

For Annalisa, watching Celia's eyes bulge and her cheeks inflate was like seeing blue sky after a month of rain.

"Isn't that wonderful?" Harry asked. He even started clapping.

Annalisa was too busy processing her own emotions. As Celia tasted her first ice cream, it felt like Annalisa was experiencing her first true taste of being a mother. Before that moment, it had been all about the pains of no sleep and nursing and giving up her dreams, but for those seconds in Harry's General Store on that June day in 1972, she tasted the beauty of being a mother. She saw a little girl, curious and eager. She saw a being completely in love with her mother, despite her mother's emotional absence.

She'd gotten so used to forcing her face muscles into a smile that she was caught off guard when her lips turned on their own. Even more shocking was the elation that followed the smile.

Saying goodbye to Harry, Annalisa pushed Celia out of the store with a much-happier spirit. She carried a cone of mint chocolate in her hand. Nino was still inside chatting with Harry and had said he would catch up in a minute.

Annalisa was still on a high, thinking she'd never forget the look on her daughter's face. As she pushed the stroller past the fried-fish restaurant where Thomas, Emma, and she had watched the draft, the smell of frying food pulling at her, she decided she would race home to draw the image before it escaped her memory.

Then she saw Emma Barnes, and a shot of adrenaline and alarm surged through her body.

At first, she hoped it was just another mirage. She'd been seeing things ever since that day she'd opened up the envelope from Elizabeth. Out of instinct, she pushed the stroller faster, trying to disappear. She risked another look farther down the block.

From outside a little tourist trinket store that sold items like Maine T-shirts and lobster key chains, Emma stared at her. Unless Harry had slipped something in her ice cream, Annalisa was not imagining this sight.

Emma stood frozen on the other side of the street. She wore brown washed-denim bell-bottoms and a formfitting cream top that showed that she'd become a young woman since Annalisa had last seen her. It looked like a couple of Emma's friends were a few steps ahead of her. Despite everything telling Annalisa to run, to push that stroller as fast as she could, she stopped.

Emma looked down at the stroller and then back up at Annalisa. Fresh pain rose within as Annalisa was reminded of the strong camaraderie they'd found in their shared pasts, and she would have loved to continue to be in her life, to help her break out of the darkness.

She considered a dash across the street to say something. Perhaps she should beg her not to tell her brother. Emma certainly knew of Annalisa's trip to Hawaii. Maybe Emma had surmised in those few seconds that Annalisa had moved on and married someone in the Mills and had a baby.

If Emma did tell Thomas, would he even care? The more time swallowed the past, the more it seemed like a silly high school affair. Annalisa knew different, though, and she realized as she looked through the eyes of his family member that Annalisa still loved Thomas with everything she had. And she loved Emma too.

As if Emma could sense Annalisa's thoughts, she frowned, and a flash of pain glimmered in her eyes. Annalisa was a second away from calling out to her when Emma turned and walked away.

As if someone had handed her a sip of oxygen while trapped underwater, Annalisa breathed in desperately. She looked down at a yawning Celia and then back across the street.

Just like that, Emma was gone.

"What's *your* problem?" Nino asked, coming up from behind.

With her hands on the stroller and questioning if she should have chased after Emma, Annalisa turned.

"Holy moly," Nino said, "you look like you've seen Elvis."

"I wish." She searched down the opposite sidewalk, wondering if she'd made it all up. Maybe she'd lost her mind.

"Can you take us home?" Annalisa asked. "I'm not feeling well."

"Yeah, sure. Did something happen?"

"I . . . I . . . I saw Thomas's sister."

His lower jaw jutted forward.

～

"I'm almost positive it was her," she told Nonna back home. Annalisa had just put Celia down for a nap and was helping Nonna put away the clean dishes.

"Don't worry about it. You have enough going on."

Annalisa set a casserole dish into the cabinet with a bit too much force. "How can I not worry about it? If she tells Thomas, who knows what could happen?"

Nonna turned off the sink and wiped her hands. "Forget about it. This was all a long time ago now."

"I don't know if I can stay here. You don't know Thomas's father. If they realize I've been keeping a baby from them, it could be bad."

"Where would you go?" Nonna asked. "No one is taking my great-granddaughter away. Don't worry about it. She might not even have seen you."

"We stared at each other!" Annalisa screamed, wondering why Emma had looked so bothered by their encounter. She sipped a relaxing breath. "Sorry."

"Thomas might be curious, but that's it," Nonna said. "I'm sorry to tell you, but it sounds to me like he's moved on."

Annalisa couldn't even bear to hear his name. "Or he might be curious enough to come find me. Anyone who looks at Celia will see the resemblance, especially him. I can't live here any longer. I can't raise his daughter forty minutes away from him."

Nonna began to dry the utensils with her dish towel. "It's time you pull it together and quit thinking about him. Whether Emma saw you or not, it doesn't matter. Jesus, Mary, and Joseph, you're still hoping Thomas will come walking through the door. My *bambina*, he's gone." She lowered her voice. "It's time you let him go."

"I'm not holding on to him," Annalisa insisted, reaching for a mixing bowl and trying not to have a full breakdown. "I don't want him to walk in the door. I hate him. I gave him everything, and he cheated on me. He lied and told me he loved me. And he put a baby inside of me that I'm not fit to mother."

With those words, Annalisa marched out of the kitchen.

"Basta!" Nonna yelled. "You can't keep running away!"

"I'm not running away!" she yelled back into the kitchen. Annalisa didn't care that she might wake the baby.

Annalisa stomped into her room and started throwing things. How dared Nonna say she still wasn't over Thomas? It was none of Nonna's business.

Chapter 35

Home School

Some women become mothers on the day they find out they're pregnant. Some become mothers on the day they give birth. For Annalisa, she didn't fully become a mother until midway through August, six months after Celia was born.

The summer dragged her along as if a rope were tied to her bound wrists, and those beautiful days of July and August meant nothing to her but more hours of failing. She felt like an impostor, a woman wearing the wrong clothes, the wrong jewelry, living the wrong life—an art forger copying someone else's work.

Though nothing had yet come of her encounter with Emma, a day didn't go by when she wasn't worried that Thomas would appear to take Celia away. Then again, maybe that would be better. Annalisa certainly wasn't up for the challenge.

As usual, Nonna was right. Annalisa was still heartbroken. Despite the taste of pure love she'd felt when Celia tasted her first bite of ice cream, with every day, the child looked more like her father, and Annalisa couldn't be in the same room as Celia without thinking of him. How could her love for him have been so wrong?

Wallowing in this heady malaise, she still wasn't eating, and she questioned her faith and purpose. She was trying; it wasn't that. She hadn't given up, but the puzzle pieces weren't fitting together. The true smile she'd felt for a moment at Harry's was a distant memory now, a flavor she couldn't even taste in her mind anymore. That idea she'd had of painting Celia tasting her ice cream . . . she hadn't even pulled her art supplies from the closet.

By mid-August, she wondered if she'd ever be able to move on. Not that she was interested in dating again. She was just trying to figure out if she'd ever be able to smile again. Or would she keep darkening Nonna's house with her depression?

The answer would come on a Sunday morning.

Nonna had taken Celia to church, a place Annalisa hadn't gone in a month. She didn't like the feeling of being stared at by people who knew everything about her. If the Mills succeeded in one thing, especially within the Italian community, it was gossip. Annalisa couldn't handle having her mistakes twist and turn through the ears of the congregation. She didn't like the attempts by men wooing her after mass either.

While her grandmother and daughter went to church, Annalisa lay in bed drifting in and out of sleep. Even when she was awake, she felt better in bed, far away from all the misery around her. She heard Nonna and Celia enter the house, so it must have been close to noon. Within a few minutes, the entire family would be over for brunch, and if she didn't get out of bed, Nino or one of the other family members would run into her room and drag her out, calling her *ragazza pigra*. Lazy girl. Could there have been a worse insult?

A few minutes later, she could hear more voices. They were collecting. Her time was running out. Pressing herself up, Annalisa dressed and stumbled down the hall. She said hello to everyone without offering eye contact and then turned to find Nonna on the floor in the living room, sitting with Celia. Aunt Julia was telling Annalisa about a popular boy at church who was single again, but Annalisa wasn't paying attention. She saw only one thing.

Celia had sat up for the first time with a grin as wondrous as the stars.

Even years later, Annalisa would say she'd never seen a sight more beautiful, and it was in that moment that Annalisa fell in love with her daughter. It was then that she truly became a mother, and her face stretched in a way she'd never known, save perhaps her times with her mother and with Thomas.

Nonna looked up from her position on the floor. "She just sat up."

"I can see that." She'd almost stayed in bed and missed a milestone. Enough was enough, Annalisa said to herself, rushing to her daughter, falling to her knees, and opening up her arms. It was a silly comparison, but she felt like she'd been seeing black and white her whole life and then woke up today to see color.

"You're such a big girl now." She pulled Celia in, and the infant collapsed into her lap, giggling.

Annalisa's smile stretched wider, and something told her she wouldn't forget this feeling now; she wouldn't lose the sensation. The transformation felt everlasting, not a brief taste but a movement into a new world. "I love you, Celia. So much."

"I'm such an idiot," Annalisa said to Nonna, an apology for all of it, the hard times she'd given Nonna when she was younger, the handful she'd become since moving, but most important, for not living up to the woman Nonna and Annalisa's mother had set out to raise.

"I'm sorry," Annalisa said, whispering in her daughter's ear. "I'm sorry for the way I've been." She picked her up and promised her, "I'm here, my love. I'm right here, and I'm always going to be here. From now on."

Annalisa turned and saw that her family looked at her with prideful, happy, and wet eyes. She drew in a long breath of air as they all went to her, surrounding her in a swarm of love.

Walt came up the next day to spend the afternoon with Annalisa and Nonna, and shortly after he'd arrived, they congregated on the front porch while Celia slept. The flowers Nonna had planted in pots earlier in the year were in full bloom, stretching toward the sun. Annalisa had hung the wind chimes she'd made next to her mother's, and they trickled out a pretty song.

Annalisa told them, "I don't know how to explain it, and I wouldn't say this out loud ever again, but I'm not sure I loved her until now. Is that just terrible? I mean I loved her, but not the way I see mothers love their children. Certainly not the way my mom loved me. Or you loved me. Something's different now. It was like I . . . I don't know. Like I didn't even see her. Like I blamed her for something she had nothing to do with. I can't believe I've been like that."

Nonna rocked slowly in her favorite chair. "You think you're the only one who has taken a little while to figure out becoming a mother? Or a father? No. This is not easy, what we parents do. It takes time to learn."

"She's right," Walt said. "Don't beat yourself up. Though we lost our child during birth, I can only imagine that you must shed a bit of who you are before you can wear parenthood well."

"I'm so sorry, Walt," Annalisa said, realizing she'd never known. How awful that she'd cried on his shoulder about the difficulties of pregnancy and becoming a mother, when it was exactly what he and Gertrude had always wanted.

"Please don't," he said. "That's not why I'm telling you."

Annalisa sighed. "I'm ready to be Celia's mom. I guess I had to come back here to the Mills to figure it out. That's why you wanted me back, Nonna. Wasn't it?"

Nonna inclined her shoulders.

Annalisa looked around at the tiny houses of the neighborhood. "I get it. I see why you like living here. I'm starting to see the beauty of small-town life, and I love being surrounded by family. It's just that . . . I need more right now, or different."

Nonna leaned toward her. "If you want more than what you're living, take it. Show your daughter what's possible. If I know anything, it's that you're the toughest girl I know. If you want a life in Portland—or Rome, for that matter—then you go take it, Annalisa. Celia will be happy to join the ride."

Annalisa couldn't believe she was even considering the idea. She couldn't believe Nonna was the one urging her on.

"Your apartment just so happens to still be available," Walt interrupted.

She couldn't believe it. "You didn't rent it out?"

He smiled. "I've been holding it for you."

"What?"

"Something told me you wouldn't last long before coming back. Nonna's right. You have dreams, and they're strong. Show Celia that nothing can stop you."

"What about the shop? Do you still . . . ?"

"Let's be honest," he said, patting his thigh. "It was a lot brighter with you there. It's not the most normal life, but let Celia hang around while we work. Who knows? She might grow up to become a horologist. Or even an artist." He gave a sly grin. "Wouldn't that be scary?"

The flicker of hope that twinkled deep within her brightened, and she imagined her return to Portland. For those few seconds, she forgot about Thomas and what he'd done to her, the life he lived with another woman not far away, and Annalisa realized that she couldn't let anything stop her. They were right. Annalisa needed to show Celia what she was made of, and that a woman doesn't have to give up and die just because she dared to love.

Annalisa looked back and forth between Nonna and Walt. "I guess I'm moving back to Portland."

Over the fall and winter of 1972, Annalisa often caught herself wondering in awe at what love had done to her. How could she not believe in the power of it after what she'd seen it do? It had buckled her and knocked her down and broken her. Love had also lifted her up, though, and saved her from the heartache.

The love she felt for her daughter now was a love supreme. Was it more powerful than how she'd felt for Thomas? She wasn't sure, but were they even comparable? That was when Annalisa began to understand the vastness of love, the complexity of it. Yes, she thought this much about love lately, which was odd for a person who hadn't believed in it. She'd loved her mother and Nonna and her grandfather and her other family members, but those were the only loves she'd understood growing up.

Love could hold you under the water with its grip clutching your neck, your body convulsing into lifelessness, or it could sweep you up and away into an explosion of joy. Love could be a ravenous and passionate need for another human, like she'd felt for Thomas, or it could be equally powerful in that unwavering way that she felt for Celia.

No matter what the category, love put her back in front of the easel, and it didn't take her long to get back in front of Sharon Maxwell, who told her that she could be a part of her show the following April.

That was all Annalisa needed to hear. She painted with a vibrancy and spirit she'd not yet known. Even when it seemed impossible to find the time as a single parent working at Walt's shop, she made the time. So what if she was tired? Nothing could stop her from gathering back up her chops and expressing herself with all these new and exciting feelings of being a mother. Why had she ever thought that being a mom was different from being a woman or that chasing a dream was something mothers couldn't do?

Her typical day started around 5:00 a.m., and she'd get in an hour or more of painting before Celia even rose for the day. After getting her daughter squared away, she'd head down to the shop, where she kept a second crib. By the time Walt would come in at nine, she'd organized Walt's work orders, polished the countertops, and prepped her gallery for showing. Once the rush of the morning subsided, she'd head back upstairs to put Celia down and to get another painting session in. If *bring it on* was her motto, *naps are opportunities* was her slogan. She took care of Walt, too, and found time to run his errands and cook him the occasional meal.

When winter came, Celia became increasingly more mobile, which made things even crazier. On a busy day during the Christmas rush, Celia crawled out of the shop. By the time Annalisa realized her daughter had escaped the pen, Celia had worked her way to Congress Street in the snow. Despite a few similar episodes, Annalisa found her groove and settled into the urgency of her life.

The only thing that would trip her up was when she saw Thomas in her daughter's face. Had there been a better way? No matter how angry she'd been, was hiding Celia from him the right answer? There was the possibility that Emma might have told him about the baby. If so, was he curious at all? Or did he fear that the baby might be his? If so, was he relieved that she hadn't told him?

She hadn't seen Thomas in a year and a half. Was he back in school in Davenport? Or had he moved to Portland? Surely she would have seen him if so. Or maybe he wasn't in school at all. Maybe the woman he'd brought home had pushed new plans upon him. Were they married yet? Had he married her in the same spot behind the club where his mother had suggested he marry Annalisa? How did the Barneses feel about him bringing home a Vietnamese woman? Was Linh pregnant? Had Emma told Thomas about the baby she'd seen with Annalisa?

Though she was in a much-stronger place and these questions didn't bog her down, Annalisa had to wonder: Did he ever think of her? How had he not come to find her and explain himself? She might have been able to move on more easily if he'd just said that the war had messed him up and offered some sort of an apology.

Despite her better days and the strength she'd found, she did still miss him. As she came back to life and found confidence again, men had started asking her out, but she always declined. She was more certain than ever that love existed, but she was equally sure that she had enough in her life.

She hated that she still loved him, but that was the way it was, and she'd come to accept that her feelings for him would never go away. She'd have to learn how to live with those feelings just as so many women who had lost their men in the war were doing, still loving him despite the impossibility of their reunion.

Chapter 36

TURNING BACK TIME

In February of 1973, Walt told Annalisa that it was time for him to retire and that he had found a nursing home. The old Annalisa might have thought of herself first, of how she had just lost her place to live and work. But she didn't.

She was rearranging several paintings, making room for a few more she'd done during a recent prolific burst, most likely brought on by her excitement about Nixon signing the Paris Peace Accords the month prior, when Walt stunned her with this admission.

"What are you talking about?" She set down the canvas in her hands and leaned it against the wall.

"It's too much." He sat on the leather couch that faced the west wall. She'd painted it white, which she thought was a wonderful contradiction to Walt's blacks and browns on the other side. He coughed hard into his handkerchief. "It's time I hang up my career and take my next steps. I've found a good place that'll be just fine."

Each cough broke her heart. As much as she did see the youth in his eyes, his body had gone downhill, and not only his lungs. He'd slowed down and couldn't stand for very long without starting to wobble. His hands shook constantly.

"That's such a big change. Are you sure? This shop has been your life."

"And life moves on." The ticking clocks seemed to verify that fact.

The implications of his statement made her frown, but knowing she would never convince him otherwise, she said, "You know I need to approve. You deserve the best place in the area."

"It'll do. A little place in Scarborough."

Annalisa waved a finger. "No, no, no. Give me time to do some research."

A sigh. "If you insist."

"It goes without saying." She sat next to him. "Have you told Nonna?"

Walt nodded solemnly, taking a labored breath. How heartbreaking it must be for her grandmother, Annalisa thought.

Putting an arm over his shoulders, she said, "Maybe we'll move her into the room next door. Or get you two a private villa with a Jacuzzi. Even a view of the water."

He glanced over before setting his eyes on one of the paintings. "As much as I'd like that, your grandmother will outlive me by forty years."

"Even the grim reaper is afraid of her."

He chuckled. "Even him, yes."

"This must be very hard, Walt." She pulled him in and leaned her head against his forehead, wishing their time together in the shop didn't have to end. What would she do without seeing him bent over his desk, peering through his spectacles at a watch, tossing out grumpy comments?

He wrapped his arm around her, patting her back. "I'm working my way through it." She could smell his age in his breath. After a pause, he said, "I'm not going to sell the building, Anna. Don't worry. You'll have a place to live, and I've thought about the shop. If you'd like to continue, I'd love that. There are plenty of watches and clocks to sell, which could keep you busy for a while until you convert the whole place into your gallery."

They let go of each other, and she stood to face him. "You don't have to worry about me," she said, caught up on the idea of not seeing him every day.

"I'm not worried about you. No one needs to worry about you, but I do want to help. That's why I'm going to leave you and Nonna the building when I pass."

Her mouth fell open. "What?"

"You heard me."

"You can't leave us the building." A wave of tremendous love came over her as his enormous gesture registered.

"As a point of fact, I can. It's mine. I won't have any use of it where I'm going."

"Oh, don't go talking about dying." Annalisa couldn't stand thinking such terrible thoughts. She'd had enough death poison her life. As strong as she felt lately, losing him shook her foundation.

He breathed in and coughed into his napkin again. "Nothing would make me happier than knowing you three are set up after I go. You can keep running the shop, and you'll have a free place to stay, and the rent from the other tenants should help too. If you don't want to keep the shop, fine. Rent it out. If you don't want to keep the building, sell it. I'm not leaving it as a burden. I'm leaving it to you, because it's what I want to do. It makes me happy."

Annalisa wiped the tears of appreciation dripping down her cheeks. "I don't know what to say."

He scoffed. "You mean for once I've knocked all the words out of you?"

"I don't want you to leave." Feeling the burn in her cheeks, she whispered, "I don't want you to go."

Annalisa had already known too much death in her life, and she couldn't imagine saying goodbye to Walt, but as he sat there, coughing and talking of his plans, she felt grateful for the time they'd shared already, and she committed to focusing on their time together going forward.

"There's one more thing," he said. "I'd like to give you my Plymouth."

"Oh, stop, Walt. You can still drive."

He shook his head. "Unless you want me to give it to Mrs. Eleby, it's yours."

Another long tear escaped, sneaking down her neck and settling under her blouse. She felt his pain and also Nonna's, thinking that her grandmother would have to say goodbye to the second love of her life. How awful.

They were interrupted by a new customer, and the two of them went back to work. It was a woman who'd seen one of Annalisa's pieces at a friend's house and just had to get something for herself.

She left a while later with two paintings, and Annalisa thought that watching a customer walk out the door happy was as satisfying as dipping her bristles into paint.

When the bell above the door chimed again, Annalisa pulled herself away from the thoughts of losing Walt and readied herself for another sale.

"May I help—" she started and stopped.

Jackie Burton stepped into the shop. Her blackberry hair was pulled into a ponytail, and she wore a black sweater and a red wool skirt. "I thought I'd better come see who was stealing my customers."

Annalisa smiled and approached the curator, who'd in many ways started her journey. "I'm so happy you're here." Then she dipped her chin. "It's only just a few customers."

Jackie looked around, and Annalisa proudly admired what she and Walt had created. The right side of the shop was still covered in timepieces. On the walls behind the displays full of world-class watches hung the wall clocks and cuckoo clocks. Walt sat at his bench in the far back behind the cash register, tinkering. The center of the room still featured the grandmother and grandfather clocks, each of them exquisite and rare. And then there was Annalisa's gallery, which was slowly taking over.

Jackie walked that way, crossing onto the Oriental rug that served to establish the gallery as its own room. "I never could have imagined. Everyone keeps telling me about the gallery in the clock shop." She took her time inspecting—and perhaps admiring—each piece on the wall.

Annalisa told her about each artist, like the incredibly talented Jenan McClain from Burlington, who finger painted landscapes that made Annalisa want to jump into them, and the slightly loopy Mark Salvarino, who had developed an amazingly strong voice as an abstract expressionist under Sharon Maxwell's tutelage.

Then Jackie set her eyes on Annalisa's pieces, all variations on the theme of love. People loving people. She stopped on a painting Annalisa had just finished that morning. In fact, the paint was still drying. It featured a line of women and children standing on the tarmac at an airport, holding a giant WELCOME HOME banner.

The news had been covering the return home of soldiers from Vietnam as part of Operation Homecoming, and she'd been enthralled by this sight several days earlier. And, of course, she'd been leveled by all these images, as she had once wished that she would be welcoming her soldier back from the war. It wasn't hard to slide into the skin of those holding the banner, the minutes ticking toward a reunion; the act of painting them was one of the many steps she still took on the long journey to healing her heart.

Resting her elbow in the opposite palm, Jackie pinched her chin and studied the painting. Annalisa stepped away, letting the curator do her thing.

When Jackie turned, she said, "Annalisa Mancuso. You've done it, haven't you?"

"I'm working at it."

"You always will be, but you have, no doubt, found your voice. I'm simply stunned."

A wave of contentment settled over Annalisa as she remembered her seventeen-year-old self walking into this woman's gallery with her orange tote.

"And I must say," Jackie added, "your eye as a curator is impressive. A clock shop and gallery. Who would have thought?"

Annalisa beamed. "That means the world to me, Jackie."

"I know you're doing well, but if you ever did want me to represent you, I'd be more than honored. Your work would be stunning on my walls."

What a long hard road she'd traveled to get here, Annalisa thought, allowing herself a pat on her own back. "Thank you. If you only knew how much your offer means to me, but . . . I think, for now at least, I'm going to stay here and see what happens. I'm having so much fun."

Jackie gave a knowing grin as she took another peek at the wall. "It is fun, isn't it? Well, the offer stands if you ever change your mind. Sharon told me you'll be showing in April. I couldn't be more proud." She started back toward the door.

Annalisa followed her, saying, "You had something to do with that, you know? I'll never forget meeting with you at your gallery when I was seventeen. Even though you told me no, you gave me what I needed to press on."

Jackie glanced back at her. "You always had what you needed to press on. I'm just bearing witness to a wonderful artist coming into her own."

At that moment, the clocks and watches struck noon.

⌒

"I knew you couldn't retire," Annalisa said, seeing the box of watches Walt had fixed. It was now the first week of April, and the United States had finally withdrawn all troops from Vietnam. Walt had been living in a nursing home she'd found for him in Freeport, which was much closer to Nonna anyway. To her delight, Annalisa had learned that Nonna visited Walt even more than Annalisa and Celia did.

Annalisa tried to come up at least twice a week, and she'd always bring him a box of watches to fix. Every visit, she'd retrieve the repaired ones and leave a new batch.

"It gives me something to do up here," Walt said, resting in his bed. Annalisa had done her best to brighten up the room with flowers and paintings from some of her other artist friends. A framed picture of Nonna rested on the bedside table. On the wall by the door hung the painting Annalisa had done of the two of them kissing under his awning.

He'd become so weak that he spent most of his days horizontally, aside from his morning adventure with a walker out to the back patio. He'd lost twenty pounds, which he could ill afford, and his skin sagged on his face and arms. Still, his mind was sharp.

"Hey, you," Walt told Celia, who was now walking and talking, "get up and give me a hug."

"You hear Wawa?" Annalisa said to Celia, lifting her up.

"Wawa," Celia said, landing on the bed with a smile and reaching for him.

Walt wrapped his arms around her. "You're sprouting, aren't you, little one? What a joy this is."

Celia reached for an ear and tugged at it.

"They're big, aren't they?" he asked.

Annalisa snickered, thinking that Celia was a ball of light, brightening up the world around her.

Walt sat up and put Celia on his lap, and they conversed for a while—or as best as they could with her limited vocabulary. He was great at making her laugh, and Annalisa found herself so grateful that her daughter had gotten a chance to get to know him.

After putting her in the chair, facing *Sesame Street* on the television, Annalisa lifted up a white bag.

"Are you getting tired of these yet?" She had brought him a cinnamon bun from the farmers' market every week since the market had opened in April.

Walt opened the bag and the sweet scent filled the room. "I doubt they make them this good in heaven." He took a bite with his eyes closed, relishing the flavors.

"You should see the shop," she said. He hadn't been down there in weeks.

"I would love to."

"You'd be very happy." She still hadn't changed the name of the shop, but other than the few watches Walt was fixing, Annalisa had let go of the repair side of the business. At his urging, she'd made room for even more art, and along with her own, she was now selling art for seven different artists, along with a steady rotation of watches and clocks.

"Maybe we can go by after your show?" he asked.

"You really don't have to come down for it," she said, thinking that he surely didn't want to deal with the hassle.

"You must be joking. I wouldn't miss it for the world. After what you've done to get there."

She patted his hand. "Would you ride with Nino and Nonna?"

"What a pleasure it would be." He'd lost so much of his grumpiness lately, and she thought he might have found his nirvana in the last year.

Walt pointed to his jacket on a coatrack. "Do me a favor and hand me my pocket watch."

Once she'd retrieved the Waltham for him, he looked at it and then up at her. "I want you to have this."

She gasped, once again in awe of his love. "Don't do that. You've given me enough."

"Who else would I give it to?" He took her hand and put the pocket watch in her palm, closing it. "There was a time after Gertrude died,

350

before you walked into my shop, when I thought my time was up. It's funny. You fix timepieces all your life, and you become one with them, one tick after another. Your whole life abides by the hands swinging around. But then *you* showed up and everything changed. I don't know if I'm making any sense, but you gave the horologist more time. You gave me a reason to live. When you hold this watch from now on, remember that you have the ability to turn back time. Not many are able to do that."

Annalisa sniffled. "I'll cherish it." This was a goodbye she couldn't handle, and she wished that he could keep fighting for a few more years.

"If I might offer a little advice," he said. "You give so much to those around you. Don't forget to take care of yourself. I do hope that one day you'll give love a second chance."

Annalisa tittered. "Don't do this."

Walt lowered his glasses down his nose and peered over them. "Thomas made a big mistake. The biggest in his life, and he'll pay for it. One day he'll know it and come begging. Don't go taking him back."

"No, Walt, I won't." She held up the watch, seeing Thomas's face in the reflection of the silver. "But I don't hate or hold any grudges." In fact, as much as it hurt to admit, she still loved him. She didn't say that, though.

"The war changes people," she continued, "and I think he must have lost his way. Who knows? Maybe I'll tell him about Celia one day, but no, I won't ever take him back. After what I've been through, I'm not sure I have enough in me to give a relationship like that another shot."

Walt lowered his voice. "Anna, one day a man is going to come along, and you'll forget all about Thomas."

She looked back at Celia, who was lost in the world of Big Bird and Kermit. "Between you and Celia and my family, I have all the love I need."

He stumbled into a cough. "Humor an old man and say yes the next time a guy asks you out. Will you do that?"

"That's not fair."

"It's my dying wish."

"Oh, c'mon. First of all, you still have some fight left in you. Second, don't 'dying wish' me. That's something Nonna would do. Don't let her rub off on you."

"It's true, young lady. There's nothing I want more for you than to find love again. Promise me you'll say yes when the time is right."

Annalisa glared at him, knowing damn well that *if* and when a man did ask her out again, she'd have to say yes.

For Walt.

And the idea terrified her.

Chapter 37

FLYING WITH WINGS

"Which one is your favorite?" someone from the group of people circling Annalisa asked.

"That's easy," she said, pointing at one of the eleven paintings hanging on the brick wall of Sharon Maxwell's studio. It was packed with buyers and journalists and enthusiasts from all over New England.

Annalisa turned to the man, who was scribbling on a notepad. "I call this *My Celias*." She was still blown away at the pricing Sharon had chosen. One sale could buy her a car. "That's my mother and my daughter, and this is the . . ." A rich set of emotions hit her, feeling her mother's presence as if the wind chimes were singing from above.

She stopped and collected herself. "This is the only time they ever met, on the canvas here."

The piece was set on their side porch in Bangor under the wind chimes, and it captured her mother sitting in front of her easel, with Celia resting on her knee. Her mother was giving her granddaughter her first painting lesson.

All her paintings had meant so much to her, but during the process of this one, she'd finally found peace with her mother—and maybe her father a little bit too. She'd decided that nothing about life was easy, and sometimes it gets the best of us. No matter what, it wasn't worth holding on to anger. Maybe one day she'd even paint her father.

Someone asked if she used a palette knife at all, but Annalisa's attention had gone across the warehouse to the entrance. Thirty-plus Mancusos poured through the door. Jubilant tears pricked her eyes when she saw Nino pushing Walt in his wheelchair, with Nonna walking by his side. Aunt Julia pushed Celia in the stroller next, and then came her uncles and aunts and cousins.

"Excuse me for a moment," she said, breaking through the circle of people. As her clan approached her, she was once again reminded how lucky she was to be a Mancuso, and she saw very clearly that the family and the small town that had rescued her from her loss in Bangor were the exact essence of life. As they came her way, cheering so loudly that every person in the entire warehouse turned, she decided her next painting would be with every last one of them. They, the Mancusos and Walt Burzinski, were the reason she was standing here today, finally, after all these years, realizing her dream.

Annalisa turned to her left and saw Sharon Maxwell watching the scene with her silver eyes. Without a word spoken, her teacher threw up her arms into stars and let out a brilliant smile. Feeling a fullness in her heart that she thought she might never know, Annalisa raised her own arms and spread them as wide as she possibly could.

This was life, she thought, staring up through the ceiling to heaven. This was what it was about, and she felt the power of her mother rush through her.

Walt Burzinski was issued his wings two days later, with Annalisa and Nonna by his side. They held his hands and watched him go, a whisper drifting off into the clouds as the chirp of the monitor flatlined. Annalisa could almost see the life run from his body, and she raised her head up, saying a prayer and thanking God for putting him in their life.

It was a bout with pneumonia that finally got him, and she was thankful he went peacefully. Seeing Nonna saying goodbye was the toughest part. The two of them had come to love each other, and Annalisa was reminded how painful love could be. She had already watched Nonna say goodbye to her husband, and before that, her son—Annalisa's father. The more people you loved, the more goodbyes you had to endure.

And yet Annalisa realized in the hours after losing Walt that all the pain that came with loving was absolutely worth it. What was the point of living if you spent it in fear? What was the point of life without love? She thought about her promise to say yes the next time someone asked her out.

For the first time since seeing the photograph of Thomas and Linh, Annalisa considered the possibility of finding love again. She thought of Walt and how he'd found renewed life through love. She thought of Nonna and Walt's relationship, and how they'd both decided it was never too late to love. Maybe their coupling was a message to Annalisa. Thomas might not have worked out, but why should she let him sour the chance of her finding true love?

Several days later, Walt's lawyer called her. He asked that she and Nonna come see him the next day. When the lawyer detailed what Walt had bequeathed them, Nonna and Annalisa nearly fell to the floor. The building, the shop, his Plymouth, and his money. It turned out that his wife had come from a wealthy family. Annalisa suspected he must have lived such a modest life because he would have felt guilty living off his late wife's money. And maybe he was too consumed by pain to enjoy it anyway.

The final surprise was that he'd left them a house on the ocean in Bar Harbor.

"Say that again," Annalisa said, glancing at Nonna and wondering if her mommy brain was confusing her.

Sitting up in his leather chair, the big cheery lawyer with sideburns chuckled. "You heard me right. Walt owned a house in Bar Harbor they call Graystone. It's yours now."

"Graystone," Annalisa whispered, remembering the name written on the back of the photograph she'd found in Walt's closet.

She turned to Nonna, sitting in the chair next to her. "He had a house in Bar Harbor? Did you know?"

"He may have mentioned something about it."

Annalisa reached for her hand. Walt's death had been so hard on them, but Nonna especially. "Do we really have a house in Bar Harbor?"

"Overlooking the Atlantic," the lawyer added. "Right on the water."

Chapter 38

GRAYSTONE

Poor Italians from Bangor and Payton Mills don't have second houses in Bar Harbor. In fact, they don't have second homes. Many of them have never even gone to Bar Harbor, only knowing it as a haven for the rich and famous that might as well be a thousand miles away.

Annalisa and her parents used to visit Acadia National Park for a picnic and hike, and then they'd pass through the town for a late lunch before returning home. She remembered it feeling so untouchable, so far away, even when she was standing on Main Street.

So for Annalisa, Celia, and Elena Mancuso, to drive their Plymouth Belvedere up the coast of Maine to their house on the water in Bar Harbor was a surreal experience. Annalisa didn't feel worthy of such a gift, and she definitely hadn't earned it, but she'd once told Walt that one must be just as good at receiving gifts as they were at giving them. Leaving Nonna and Annalisa his full inheritance had brought Walt tremendous joy, and Annalisa was determined not only to accept his gift with open arms, but to live each day with a vitality that would have made him proud.

That was why she'd rolled down her window and worn a smile that rose from the core of her soul as they rode north through the late spring air that had dried up the mud, making way for the reward of summer.

Weeks after first hearing that she and her grandmother owned a place with a name, she still couldn't get over it. Other than the picture of Walt and Gertrude on the shore there, she hadn't even seen pictures, but she'd heard through the managing real estate agency that Graystone was one of the true gems of the Mount Desert coastline.

More than once on the drive, Annalisa faked holding a phone to her ear and said in a high-society Boston accent, "Sorry, we can't make Paris this year. We'll be summering at Graystone again." Every time she said "Graystone," the word turned into fireworks as it left her mouth.

Nonna was still heartbroken over losing Walt, too, but let out a subtle smile whenever Annalisa attempted such silliness. Turning to the little one in the car seat behind her, Nonna said, *"Tua mamma é pazza."*

Having been in the city for so long, Annalisa found it incredible to drive through the mountains, surrounded by tall trees. They exited Route 1 and dropped south to cross over the Trenton Bridge into Bar Harbor. As she drove through town, following the light traffic downhill toward the water, she had a strange sense that she was entering a new era in her life.

They parked on the pier and watched sailboats with crisp white sails full of the ocean wind race past each other in the harbor. Annalisa and Celia swung on the swings in Agamont Park, and then the three of them meandered up Main Street. With Nonna inching behind, using her cane, Annalisa pushed Celia up the hill in her stroller, finding herself in awe of this slice of heaven. Nature had never played a strong part in her work, and in this moment she wondered why. It felt like the great outdoors was missing now, as if she had to get up here and immerse herself in it, just as this town was so immersed in it.

They passed men and women in global fashions, dipping into the shops and galleries to find a rare book or to have their shoes polished or to buy a new purse or piece of art. She couldn't get over how fancy the town felt, while at the same time being so quaint and away from it all.

She saw a lot of families, too, generations together, laughing and horsing around. It made Annalisa chuckle to herself, thinking that she sure had come a long way from the disgruntled teenager who hated the Mills, because she had a sudden craving for small-town life again. The city could be exhausting, that urgency serving as one cup of coffee too many, almost out of balance, whereas this place felt even-keeled yet full of energy. Bar Harbor was exactly what she'd never wanted until now.

"What do you think, baby? Wanna grow up here? I have a good feeling." Annalisa wished she'd brought her paints and brushes. What was she thinking? At least she always carried her sketch pad.

Celia stumbled through an incoherent sentence as ice cream dripped down her chin, and Annalisa was pretty sure that her daughter would be happy anywhere.

Annalisa jumped back into her silly accent, impersonating her daughter in the future. "Oh, I grew up at Graystone on the shore. Married a banker from Manhattan and sailed with the Vanderbilts." Celia didn't understand a word, but that was okay.

When Nonna caught up, Annalisa turned. "Isn't this the most beautiful place in the world, Nonna? What if we moved here?"

Nonna rolled her eyes, the knob of her cane striking the sidewalk like a hand of a clock ticking toward their destiny. "Here we go again."

"I'm serious," Annalisa insisted, her creativity simmering from within. "I feel so inspired here. Don't you? Everyone in the Mills could come see us all the time. I wouldn't want to do it without you. Celia needs her great-grandmother now."

After all these years of trying to get Nonna out of the Mills, Annalisa found a glimmer of hope in her eyes. "We'll see."

"Really?" Annalisa imagined being with Nonna again, having Nonna's presence around Celia. Nothing could be better. "I'm sure there's a good Catholic church. I could open up a gallery. Lord knows there's potential to make money here, at least in the summer."

"We haven't even seen the house," Nonna said, keeping along well. "One thing at a time."

Following a map, Annalisa led them up the hill to find the real estate office, which was in a converted old house with a roof that needed repairs. A green awning read: STEWART REALTY.

After a brief wait, a striking man with slightly disheveled brown hair appeared. He was dressed like he'd just hopped off a yacht and had this slightly rebellious look to him, as if he'd been up to no good in a far-off port.

"Welcome to Bar Harbor," he said. She heard *Bah-hah-bah* and thought this was truly another world up here. "My name's Glen Stewart." After a reverent pause, he said, "I'm sad to hear about Walt."

The ladies thanked him, and then he directed his attention to Celia in the stroller. "Who is this little one? Let me guess. A year and a half?"

"Close," Annalisa said, thinking he had a refined charm. "Fifteen months."

"Well, look at that. She must be eating her spinach."

Glen was tall—not as tall as Nino—but tall enough to make Nonna look half his size. Annalisa guessed he was a year or two older than her.

"You're as beautiful as your mother and your aunt," he said to Celia, offering a sweet smile.

Nonna caught his meaning quickly and shook her head. She never liked to be wooed. Or did she? Was that a smile hiding in there?

Annalisa corrected him. "This is my grandmother Elena."

He feigned great shock at his mistake and leaned down to make her acquaintance. "We're so happy to have you all here. I'm excited to show you the place. Walt and Gertrude were longtime family friends, though we hadn't seen Walt in years. He stopped coming up after she died. I was pretty young, but I remember him well. Have you driven by yet?"

Celia looked restless, so Annalisa picked her up and rested her on her shoulder. "No, this is our first time up here, to Bar Harbor."

"It's just starting to wake up, as you can see. We do weekly rentals for the main house, which typically pick up in May. A writer rents the apartment above the garage for a few months every summer."

Annalisa shifted Celia to her other hip while nodding to Glen. Walt's lawyer had shared these details.

"We can continue to help manage the property, or you can take it over," he said. "Do you know what you're thinking yet? Will you come up during season? I hope you're not planning on selling." He blushed. "We could help you sell; there'd be plenty of takers, it's just . . . I'd like to see more of you up here." An inviting smile eased out of him.

Annalisa almost rolled her eyes at his not-so-subtle advance but spared him the embarrassment. Who knew? Maybe she was ready to take the leap again.

"I don't know what we're thinking," she said, swaying to keep Celia settled. "I don't even know what we're getting into."

Glen adjusted his early sixties Oysterdate Rolex, glancing at the time. Annalisa had learned a lot about watches over the years and liked his taste. She didn't tell him as much.

"Let me grab the keys," he said, pivoting and disappearing down the hall.

She watched him walk away and then turned to Nonna, who chuckled silently.

"Is this funny to you?" Annalisa whispered, thinking of Walt's last request.

When Glen returned, Annalisa let out, "You'll have to come over for dinner while we're here." She wondered if Walt had heard her from up in heaven.

⁓

Annalisa followed Glen to Sols Cliff Road. As they left town, the Maine wilderness came alive. The house was two miles south of town, down a secluded gravel driveway that cut through a thick forest. Though the lawyer had told her it was on the water, she didn't believe it until she pulled in and saw the one-hundred-and-eighty-degree views of the Atlantic.

Graystone was a New England paradise, a cedar-shingle-style house with stone accents perched over a rock shelf that dropped down into the sea. Two tall stone chimneys rose from the sharply angled roof. A small balcony protruded out on the second floor on the street-facing side, a vantage point that surely offered a glorious inland view of the forest. A rooster weathervane on the roof indicated an easterly wind. Off to the right, down a short drive, separated from the main house by a patch of wild shrubs and sea oats, there was a detached garage with the apartment Glen had mentioned.

The Annalisa of her youth would never have imagined she would be here. Her entire family might never believe her until they put eyes on it themselves, which was all she could think about. She wanted every Mancuso in Maine to come visit. This wasn't only her and Nonna's place, Annalisa thought. This was the Mancusos' Graystone, the Little Italy of Bar Harbor.

"I want to see the water," she told Glen, rushing past him with Celia in her arms. Nonna leaned on her cane, taking in the house, possibly thinking about the life Walt lived before she'd met him. Annalisa wondered if it was hard for her to imagine Walt loving Gertrude so much that he'd been unable to visit this place again—or even talk about it—after she'd died.

The yard was well kept. A patch of grass wrapped around the house. As she rounded the side, the vast Atlantic came into view, disappearing into the horizon like blue sky into the atmosphere. Past the grass was the rock shelf that cascaded down into the water. Like tiny islands, a few rocks protruded from the water farther out, causing little stirs of white foam. The wind blew cold, and Annalisa held Celia tight. She saw a set of steps carved into the rocks that led down to a little beach to the left. Without another look at the house, she felt pulled to the ocean.

"Can you believe this, Celia? This is ours. I don't even . . ." She didn't know whether to cry or shout. Who needed a Catholic church with such close proximity to God right here in their backyard?

Down the steps, she reached the patch of gray sand where tiny waves rolled in, gently shuffling the shells, a piece of calm amid the otherwise fierce shoreline.

She strolled along the sand to the water and looked east. Blue for as far as she could see, pure calm today, an oil slick all the way to the edge. A flock of seagulls chased a school of fish fifty yards out.

This was where the photo of Walt and Gertrude had been taken, she realized. Breathing the image in with the salty air, she choked up, feeling them both and wishing he could be there, wishing she could have met Gertrude. She squeezed Celia, knowing they were both probably not too far away.

She turned back and looked up past the granite shelf to the house. Taking in this surreal moment, she crossed herself.

Nonna had worked her way to the backyard and was gazing out. If Annalisa wasn't mistaken, she was smiling.

"Not bad, right?" Glen asked, coming down the last step.

"I could get used to this." She set down Celia and let her play on the sand.

"It's my favorite house on the island," Glen admitted. "All of them have their charm, but there's something about this place."

"Where do you live?" she asked, watching Celia's curiosity lead her toward the water.

"I'm back in town. A little house on West Street near the water, but I've lived all over Bar Harbor."

The wind had knocked her hair into her eyes, so she pulled it back. "You never left?"

They both turned when they heard Celia's giggle as she raced away from the water inching toward her after a tiny wave. "I left for four years to go to Harvard, but came right back up." He took a long breath. "Boston was nice, but I missed being up here."

Annalisa locked eyes with him. "I can imagine."

"Then you might stay?" Hope showed all over his face.

For a fleeting few moments, she saw all kinds of possibilities in his eyes—her own possibilities. Maybe there was life on the other side of Thomas. Maybe all she needed was to get out of Portland.

"I think I'm ready for a change," she finally said. "That's for sure."

He grinned, as if he knew her future was here. "Let's go see the house."

⌇

"What's it like in the off-season?" Annalisa asked during the house tour. "The locals must love it."

Glen switched on a lamp. "Oh, we do, but it's not as quiet as you might think. Cold, but plenty to do."

The living room was the center and soul of the home, and Annalisa wondered if that was where she might set up her easel. Several beautiful windows, perfectly polished, looked out at the sea. He told them Gertrude used to play the Baldwin piano in the corner. A fireplace with a neat stack of logs waited for fall. The furniture was colorful and elegant, and Annalisa was quite sure that it had been Walt's wife who'd been in charge of decorating.

"And the kitchen, oh my God," Annalisa said. "What do you think, Nonna. Could you manage? How about that dining-room table? The Mancusos couldn't even fill it on a Saturday night."

Nonna nodded, and Annalisa could sense her grandmother's wheels spinning. Maybe she would leave the Mills if Annalisa pushed hard enough.

Annalisa could only imagine how much inspiration she'd find here.

The master bedroom took Annalisa's breath away. There was a four-poster bed, a beautiful antique dresser, and a matching vanity. The bathroom featured a claw-foot tub that Annalisa could soak in while looking out the windows to the water—that was, unless Nonna wanted this room, in which case Annalisa would happily go down the hall.

"How are the schools?" she asked, peeking inside of a giant closet full of empty hangers.

He unrolled a hand. "Great schools and great teachers. Celia can ride the bus. It's all very safe."

This life seemed too perfect, Annalisa thought, when a loud whistle filled the air. "What in the world is that?" she asked, glancing at Celia and Nonna, whose ears had perked up too.

"Ah, it must be lunchtime," Glen replied, glancing at his Rolex. "That's the fire station whistle. It goes off every noon and nine p.m."

"You're kidding?" Annalisa thought about Walt's shop and those noon and midnight bells.

"That's how you know the tourists from the locals," Glen said. "The tourists are the ones who jump at noon."

Tears filled Annalisa's eyes, and she said to Nonna, "What are the odds . . . ?" Was this Walt saying hello from his spot in heaven? Was this why he'd fallen in love with Bar Harbor in the first place, Graystone being as connected to time as his shop in Portland?

Annalisa felt the hairs rise on her arms, and she went and put an arm around Nonna. "We're moving here, all three of us. I'm not taking no for an answer."

Chapter 39

The Farmers' Market

Three months after they moved to Graystone, Celia had grown into a little handful, a mini-Annalisa always looking for trouble. She would throw temper tantrums that rivaled any that Nonna or Annalisa had ever thrown, and Annalisa was sure that God was paying her back for her devilish behavior as a teenager.

Now that the US was out of the war, the country was working its way toward a better place—even with the whole Watergate thing going on. If only Elvis was in a better place as well. To Annalisa's great dismay, her favorite singer wasn't taking care of himself and was going downhill quickly, gaining weight and losing his musical direction. She wished she could speak to him and tell him about her own journey and how there could always be light found ahead.

Annalisa, Celia, and Nonna had moved into Graystone in late May, only two weeks after first setting eyes on the place. Glen had chased after Annalisa most of the summer, until she'd finally convinced him that they'd be better as friends. It wasn't that she was still avoiding love; it was just that he wasn't the one. Now that she'd had the real thing, she couldn't settle for less. But maybe one day . . . meanwhile, Annalisa was painting more than ever and had opened a gallery downtown that was already becoming the talk of the art community.

She'd proved herself as a curator just as she had as an artist and had found her niche by carrying works by artists who nearly dripped with passion. Though she had no set rules, the artists she worked with didn't paint lighthouses or lobsters. Be it the abstract expressionist or the pop artist or the portraitist whose work hung in her gallery, they all worked with tremendous heart, so much so that a serious buyer couldn't walk out of Annalisa's gallery without wet eyes.

In constant search of new artists, Annalisa traveled all over New England, chasing leads from the gossip in the art community. When she found artists she wanted to represent, they looked at her like Annalisa had once looked at Jackie Burton, and those eyes of admiration and respect were what kept Annalisa going.

These trips over the summer were her chance to get a break from being a mommy, and there was no place she liked visiting more than Portland, which always reminded her of her journey. After a particularly fruitful two days in August—the Plymouth overloaded with new acquisitions—Annalisa stopped by the farmers' market on the way home to peruse the new artist booths and to visit Eli and buy a cinnamon bun.

Annalisa was in a particularly saucy mood, and she'd been thinking about dating even more lately. Being back in Portland reminded her of that brave woman who had left the Mills to start a new life. The one thing she'd been missing was romantic love, and it had required quite the journey for her to admit that fact.

Now, she felt full of all types of love, from her relationships with her artists and buyers and friends to her daughter and Nonna and her family back in the Mills. She'd come to love the Mancusos so much that she often wished she could move them all up to Bar Harbor. They liked the Mills, though, and she couldn't blame them. As much as she'd wanted to run from it, the truth was that she'd only been wanting to run from herself. The Mills had nothing to do with it. In fact, she was living the small-town life she'd run from, and she wouldn't trade it for the world.

It was in these musings that life decided to disrupt her plans once again. Carrying a bag full of a variety of cherry tomatoes and a beeswax candle, she was working her way toward Eli's booth when she stopped to check the time. She'd promised Celia she wouldn't come home late.

She drew out Walt's Waltham pocket watch from her purse. Three minutes past ten. She could be home before two if she hurried. She snapped closed the front of the watch just as someone called her name.

She turned to find Mitch Gaskins—Thomas's best friend—looking at her. He sat on the hood of a parked car, holding an ear of corn. Several kernels were caught in his beard. The past gripped her like a strong hand grabbing her ankle while she was sleeping, and she remembered meeting him for the first time at the football game, while he was home after basic training.

"Damn, it's good to see you, Annalisa." He laid his corn down on a plate, slid off the hood, and reached for the cane leaning against the car. Had he been hurt during the war? Balancing himself, he came to a standing position and looked at her with an astonished grin. "Never thought I'd see you again."

Annalisa smiled back and dropped Walt's watch into her purse. "I can't believe it. Mitch Gaskins. Is that really you?"

"In the flesh," he answered. "Most of me, at least."

They hugged, and Annalisa felt the murky waters of the past tugging her harder. She was happy to see him, but this was a reunion for which she was not prepared.

"Where are you now?" he asked, resting against his cane. "I figured I'd run into you if you were still here."

"No, I left last year," she said, glancing around, suddenly terrified that Thomas might be with him. "I'm up in Bar Harbor. I'm actually on my way back—just had to stop for a few goodies."

"Bar Harbor? I never would have guessed."

"You and me both," she agreed. "And you? You live here?"

"Yeah. Ever since I came home." He looked to his leg. "I took a bullet to the knee, so my tour ended early. My dad and I opened up a couple of auto shops, one near the mall and the other in South Portland. Thomas is here, too, you know?"

"What? He lives in Portland?" Hearing his name was a bucket of ice over her head. Her attempts to pretend like his name wasn't all over her brain during their chat fell short.

"No," Mitch said, rubbing his beard. "He's still living up in Davenport, one more year to go at Weston. But he's here at the farmers' market. Did you see him?"

Annalisa's heart kicked hard, throwing her mind into a scramble. "No. I . . . I . . ." She felt an urgent need to rush out of there.

He raked his beard. "Yeah, that was the one thing that shocked me when I got home, that you two weren't together. You were the only sure bet I would have made back then."

"Things change, don't they?" She looked around, thinking she really didn't want to see Thomas right now. She was keeping a baby from him, for God's sake. And as her body was clearly showing her, she still had strong feelings for him that she couldn't bear letting him see.

"Some things change, I guess," Mitch said.

Don't do this, she thought. She'd been thinking of how she'd finally moved on, and now Thomas was reeling her right back in, destroying her progress.

Annalisa had to ask, "Is he still married and all that? I know he met that girl over there." The moment the question left her lips, she wished she hadn't asked. It was better to keep it all buried and get out of there.

"What girl?" Mitch asked, his forehead wrinkled in confusion. "After you, Thomas didn't . . . ." He shook his head. "Thomas will never love someone else. He's got the Annalisa blues."

A strange feeling that something terrible had happened began to scratch at her insides. "But I saw the picture. That girl. Mrs. Barnes said he was going to marry her."

"The girl he's with now?" Mitch looked around to make sure this person wasn't within earshot. His deep voice escalating in pitch, he asked, "Robin?"

"I thought her name was Linh?"

"I don't know a Linh," Mitch said. "He's kind of dating Robin, but they're not serious. I'm telling you. You broke his heart, Annalisa." Mitch looked down at her hand. "You're not married?"

She had never been more confused in her life. Part of her still wanted to escape before she learned more and before she saw him, but her curiosity won.

Ignoring Mitch's question, she said, "Mrs. Barnes said he'd fallen in love with someone in Vietnam. That's why I left him."

"What? This is news to me. I feel like I'd know."

She could still see the photo that had changed everything. Maybe Thomas hadn't brought her home. Still, why was Mitch covering for Thomas after all these years?

"You didn't hear anything about another . . ."

A voice came from behind. "Oh my God."

She knew Thomas's voice better than any sound in the world, save perhaps her daughter's giggle. Correction: their daughter's giggle.

"Is that you?" he asked as she attempted to steady herself.

Annalisa sipped some air and turned. Thomas Barnes stood there, more than three years older than she'd last seen him but barely changed at all. His hair had grown out some, and he was well dressed in a light-blue shirt tucked into khakis with loafers.

Her throat went dry. Searching for something to say felt like painting with a dry brush. There was nothing there.

Thomas held hands with a redheaded girl, but Annalisa watched his hand slightly loosen around hers. "It *is* you."

"Hi," she said, doing everything she could to hide the emotions exploding inside. The anger and attraction. Had time not softened how much she hated what he'd done to her?

In the uncomfortable silence, as the two searched each other's eyes, the redhead stepped forward and stuck out her hand. "I'm Robin. You must be Annalisa."

Annalisa broke eye contact with Thomas. "How'd you know?"

The redhead shrugged. "Just a hunch."

"It's nice to meet you." Annalisa glanced back at Thomas, who smiled with his lips pressed together. She instantly felt the guilt of lying to Thomas about Celia. He had no idea he was a father. At least she didn't think so. Surely, he would have asked about her. Celia looked so much like him that if he ever did see her, he'd know. Oh God, so much rushing through her. She'd considered tracking him down but always shied away. Now she wondered if she'd made the wrong decision.

"How are you?" he asked. "What are you up to?"

Annalisa barely got out, "I'm good, thanks. Just ran in to get something on my way home."

She saw joy collect in his cheeks and eyes, and she knew she was indeed still on his mind. As if they were the only two in the universe, he focused on her and asked, "Where do you live now?"

The redhead sidestepped and started a conversation with Mitch.

"Bar Harbor," Annalisa said, and she could hear the shakiness in her voice. Standing there alone with him was too much. The tension in the air grew thick like the fog that coated the mornings at Graystone, and she felt like her face betrayed her as she fought to keep from going dizzy.

She hated that Thomas saw her this way, her face a billboard advertising how much he still affected her after all these years, and she desperately needed to get out of there. Apparently, Mitch wasn't privy to all the facts; she'd seen the photo.

"Anyway," she said, "I've gotta run, but good to see you. I'm glad things are going okay." She hoped he couldn't hear the weakness in her voice.

Thomas glanced over at the redhead, as if he wanted to explain himself, as if he had so much more to say. "Yeah, you too."

She seriously had to leave. With his smile and easy look, he was digging open old wounds with a knife and pouring salt into them, causing her some sort of anxiety attack.

"I've got to go," she blurted out too obviously, the idea of escaping making her feel better.

Starting with his shoulders, his entire body frowned. "I understand. Well, it's good to see you." He seemed perplexed by her rush to get out of there.

She couldn't help it, though. Offering a wave and a goodbye to Mitch and the redhead, Annalisa rushed away. She didn't have to turn around to feel him staring at her. There were so many questions she wanted to ask, but she couldn't.

Why hadn't he come to find her upon his return? That made no sense, especially if he hadn't brought a girl home. Not that she would have given a cheating boyfriend a second chance. No matter what had come of their relationship, he'd definitely kissed her. And where there was kissing, there was certainly something else. The war was not an excuse for stepping on their love with a breach of trust.

It wasn't that Annalisa wanted him back—despite how much she still loved him. At least she didn't think so, but seeing him was so painful.

Climbing into the Plymouth on Congress Street, she collapsed into the seat. She gasped for air, gasped for how she'd felt before he'd just rocked her world. Looking through the windshield at the car ahead of her and then the busy street, she clutched her chest and focused on her breathing. How would she react if he knocked on the window now? She might have a heart attack. She turned and scanned the area back toward the market. Lots of people were coming and going. Thankfully he wasn't one of them, and her breathing started to normalize.

How could he have such a strong effect on her after all these years?

This was exactly what love was, she thought, a feeling you have for people who didn't always deserve it. She remembered that same feeling with her father, hating him for everything he'd done to her mom and her, but at the same time, she'd never failed to hug him with forgiveness over and over. This was one of the faces of love: painful and unavoidable.

Afraid he might come find her and see her this way, Annalisa pulled away. She hadn't gone by Walt's place in a long time, but something drew her there. She found a nearby parking spot and stepped out of the car. A wealth of memories flooded in: Walt, the noon and midnight bells, the day Jackie Burton walked through the door and offered Annalisa a spot on her walls. She and Nonna had sold the building, and a clothing boutique now occupied the shop.

Looking up to her old balcony, she saw very clearly Thomas and her during his one visit to her apartment. She remembered pointing a shaky finger at Vietnam, so incredibly unsure of what lay ahead. If only she hadn't gone to Hawaii. Her thoughts led her gaze left to the Leaning Tower of Treeza and the phone booth across the street, the scene she'd drawn him while he was in training.

Dipping back into the car, she found some change and then slipped into the booth, sliding the door closed behind her. She'd stared down at this booth for years as a watcher, imagining the lives of the men and women inside, but she'd never been inside herself. Until now.

When Nonna answered, Annalisa said, "I just called to check on you guys. Everything going okay?"

"All's well. Glen is about to pick up Celia and take her down to the Village Green. She's cleaned up from a bath and dressed in her finest." Glen had become a good friend to all of them, the uncle Celia would never have.

The image was like a dose of calm. "Can I talk to her?"

A moment later, she heard, "Momma."

Her voice was exactly what Annalisa needed to hear. "I just wanted to say I love you, Celia."

Her daughter replied with something that made no sense but was rich with love, a love that uprooted even more guilt. Annalisa's crime wasn't as simple as having kept her daughter from her cheating boyfriend. She'd also been lying to Celia, and that was so much worse.

"I'll see you in a few hours," Annalisa whispered and then ended the call.

She left the booth and stared back up at the balcony one last time. Had she protected Celia or hurt her with this deception? And what if Thomas found out now? What would happen? As much as she had justified hiding Celia from him, she never could absolve herself of the guilt of her crimes. Celia was getting older, starting to understand things. She would be asking about her father soon. Annalisa wasn't sure what she would say.

Climbing back in the car, she gathered her wits and made the long drive back to Bar Harbor.

Chapter 40

Run, Rabbit, Run

Annalisa unloaded her new pieces at the gallery and arrived home just in time to catch Glen returning Celia from their day downtown. She'd been gone only two nights, but it always felt like an eternity, her time without her daughter. She heard a car door shut and dashed outside. Setting eyes on Celia was still like seeing a shooting star, and her mouth stretched into a smile.

"Hi, *bambina!*"

With a windup musical clown in her hand, Celia stumbled toward her, almost falling but then opening her arms. Her daughter wasn't afraid of anything and had busted her knees up almost daily during her ambulatory pursuits.

As she lifted Celia up into her arms, she saw an intruder on the property that stopped her heart. There through the tall trees, at the start of the driveway, was a VW Beetle. Not just any VW Beetle. Thomas's banana-yellow Beetle. The one he'd lent her, the one that had led her to freedom in Portland, the car that had swept her away on her first adventure, which would define the rest of her life.

The Beetle that she'd left in a driveway in Davenport with a note and a ring.

In the driver's seat sat Thomas. He'd stopped the car fifty feet away.

She shook her head to make sure she wasn't seeing things. How many times had her loony mind made up this scene? She wasn't completely caught off guard, as she'd seen him earlier at the market *and* he'd invaded her mind every minute since, but still . . . was this truly happening?

That drive back home had been one long journey through the past, thinking of every day of their relationship, starting with that night at Fairhaven and then running into him at the game, then him winning over her family, the draft, the time she'd seen him before he left for Asia, and then that last time in Hawaii.

Never could she have imagined more love and pain all in one life—even as young as she was. Not that she was special, but what they had was certainly one of a kind. In the end, just like every other time she'd found herself flipping through the pages of their story, she wondered how it had all gone wrong. How something so beautiful could have been destroyed. Men cheated and relationships ended, but she'd thought their connection was different. She couldn't believe that the rest of the world, the rest of the couples out there, had loved each other the way she and Thomas had.

"You okay?" Glen asked, approaching her. "Who is that?"

Annalisa was scared to death. Were she and Thomas really going to do this after all these years? Have a real conversation? Why had he driven up here? How had he found her?

She looked at Glen, who'd once tried and failed to replace Thomas. "I need you to take Celia down to the beach."

He obviously heard the urgency in her voice and looked at her with concern. "What's going on?"

"It's Thomas." That was all she had to say. Once they'd settled into friends, she'd told him about the roller coaster that was her time with him.

Glen looked at the VW. "Oh."

He reached for Celia, who clung to Mommy's neck. "Hey, C, let's head down to the water, see if we can find any crabs."

The Beetle started their way as Annalisa handed her over. Without another word, Glen rushed her toward the beach.

Thomas's face came into view through the windshield, and her heart thumped like a gong struck in a tribal dance.

When he stepped out of the car, she said, "If you say you were in the neighborhood, I'll throw something at you."

He smiled, and she thought he seemed very happy, sincerely satisfied and in a good emotional place, which only served to make this day so much more difficult to experience.

"You wouldn't believe it," he said. "I was asking around town and heard wind chimes. Turns out you own a gallery downtown, and a set of wind chimes hangs in the entryway. I charmed the girl in there into telling me where you lived."

"Oh, you charmed her, did you?" Annalisa said, falling into easy conversation, just like the old days despite the secrets she kept. She almost told him that she had made those wind chimes with their daughter but didn't think that was the best way to break the news, or if she wanted to tell him at all.

"Actually, I told her I was your cousin." Tapping into his inner Marlon Brando, he spun his hand in the air and said in his best Sicilian, "My name is Vito Mancuso. I've lost my cousin Annalisa's address. Can you please help me? We haven't seen each other in years, and I'm late to meet her."

With more of his charming smile coming at her, Annalisa dipped her chin. "Vito, huh? I guess I need to beef up my security."

After sharing a brief grin with her, Thomas glanced at Glen and Celia, who were headed toward the steps to the water and seemed to surrender to a rush of nerves. "Anyway, I'm sorry to show up like this. I . . ." Suddenly, he was as speechless as she.

Annalisa didn't know why he was here or what the hell she was going to tell him. The years once again filled the air, and her love for him swelled.

Thomas looked around, fidgeting with his hands as if he didn't know what to do with them. "I can't go another minute without talking to you," he finally said, jabbing his hands into the pockets of his khakis. "Shit, Anna, I miss you. I don't know what happened. Mitch said something about another girl? You thought I met someone?"

Annalisa stared into eyes that were sometimes blue but today were green, still not knowing where to start. This supposed misunderstanding? Their child? The feelings they both so clearly still had? She could barely breathe as the idea that she might have messed up cast doubt on everything she'd done since finding that photo.

"Why don't you come in?" she said with a trembly voice as she started to the front steps, gesturing for him to follow.

He looked relieved, like he was worried she might tell him to go. If he only knew . . .

As they reached the entrance, he asked, "Are you sure? I don't want to—"

"Come in, Thomas," she said, holding the door open for him. "We've got some catching up to do."

The pope, John F. Kennedy, and Frank Sinatra greeted them from their positions above the holy water font on the wall in the foyer. He looked into the dining room and up the fancy staircase, and Annalisa knew he had to be wondering what had led her here.

Graystone definitely looked like the Italians had moved in. Shrines of the Virgin Mary graced almost every room. There were washed and starched doilies and crucifixes absolutely everywhere. They'd kept the furniture, but the walls were now covered in art that Annalisa had collected or painted.

"Smells good in there," he said, poking his head into the kitchen, clearly delaying the intent of his visit. He referred to the smells of the *sugo di pomodoro* simmering in two giant pots on the stove. Bulbs of garlic, bunches of basil, and baskets of homegrown tomatoes rested on the counter next to the pots.

"It's sauce day in the Mancuso house," she said, leading him that way. "Nonna is still at it."

Brazenly making himself at home, Thomas buried his nose into one of the pots and took a good sniff. "God, I miss your family's food. I used to lie there at night in the jungle and dream of eating dinner at Nonna's house."

That was his fault.

Or was it? Had she vastly overreacted? Something wasn't adding up, and the foundation of her secrets seemed to be crumbling. "You didn't have pasta night over there?"

He pulled himself away from the smell. "The navy might have, but no, not in the army. We pride ourselves in removing all enjoyment from eating. Never will I touch ham or lima beans again. So you're still painting all the time? I loved what I saw at the gallery."

She didn't want to talk about painting right now, but she answered him anyway, putting off the inevitable for a few more minutes. "Yeah, I'm still having fun, staying busy."

As what happened between them filled the room, she said, "So what are you doing now? Did you finish school?" How often had she wanted answers to these questions?

"Working on it." He stayed safely on the other side of the counter. "I'm back at Weston and in hot pursuit of a career in academia. Emma's a year behind me, studying psychology, of all things. We're living together in a house near campus."

"I'm happy to hear you and Emma are together," she said, wondering if his sister had told him about the baby. "And that she's in school. Good for her."

He locked eyes with her. "Yeah, she's definitely coming around."

She and Thomas could have had such a rich life together, she thought, reminded of how much he'd fought for her and how well he'd treated her. Until he'd kissed another girl.

Finally looking away, she waved him toward the living room. "I think Nonna's in here. Come say hi."

"Yeah," he said, finally leaving his spot by the stove. "I'd love that."

Nonna sat at the sewing machine repairing a torn pillow and humming along with a Mario Lanza record spinning nearby. If she wasn't in the kitchen or in her recliner, this was where she'd be. Her little sewing table was pushed up under one of the windows overlooking the sea, and she could sit there for hours without getting bored.

"Look what the cat dragged in," Annalisa said, thinking that maybe she should have warned Nonna before leading him in.

"Hi, Nonna," Thomas said, stepping into the room to face her. "It's been a long time."

Nonna switched off the machine and turned. Her eyes bulged like balloons as she crossed herself. "Jesus, Mary, and Joseph. Yes, it has."

Then her wide eyes met Annalisa's with question marks in her pupils. She probably thought the same thing, that Thomas was about to find out the truth. No way could she let him leave without telling him about Celia. Her guilt over hiding his daughter tore at her like a shark on flesh. He would have said something by now if Emma had clued him in.

Thomas and Nonna embraced and caught up for about five seconds before Annalisa interrupted. "Would you mind giving us a chance to chat? Glen took Celia down to the water. Maybe you could see what they're up to?"

Her grandmother was clearly still in shock, but she jumped at the opportunity to get out of there.

She used her cane to stand, and Annalisa and Thomas watched her walk out the back door to the patio into the cloudy August afternoon.

Annalisa's mind was a wild storm, lifting up her thoughts and slinging them around like a hurricane snatches up and tosses cars. Why was he here?

"She hasn't changed a bit," he finally said, approaching one of the windows to enjoy the view. He turned back. "Is she okay to get down there by herself?"

Annalisa's eyebrows shot up. "You think a few steps can slow her down? Good thing she didn't hear you say that." Annalisa dragged a finger across her throat.

He cracked up, which acted like a rope and bucket pulling up all their memories from down the well. "I can't believe you have a daughter. Gosh, I feel awful barging in."

We made her together, Annalisa thought and then decided they'd both better find a seat before the revelations came. Yes, he had cheated on her, but she had hidden his daughter from him. Her sin was more unforgivable. Today was her day of reckoning.

She opened the back door, feeling sick about what was to come. "Let's go out here."

The sun sprayed welcome warm rays as they walked out onto the deck, where a line of wooden chairs faced over the water. A breeze rose up from the ocean, making the two sets of wind chimes sing. The only other sound was the waves slapping the rocky shore below.

Approaching the railing, they took in the view, blue and more blue, for what seemed like forever. "This is heaven," he said. "What a perfect day too."

"We suffer all winter for days like these, don't we?" she said, looking left down to the beach, where Nonna was joining Glen and Celia after negotiating the steps with her cane. Annalisa gathered her hair into a ponytail to get it out of her eyes. "How is your family?"

He glanced over, his shaggy hair dancing in the wind. "My dad died. I don't know if you heard that."

"No. I'm sorry." She wasn't a fan of Bill Barnes, but she was saddened for Thomas's sake.

"Pancreatic cancer," he said. "It got him quickly. He died while I was finishing off my commitment at Fort Dix early last year."

"That was the same month Celia was born. And your mom?" She wondered if he was doing the math, figuring out that she'd been in Hawaii nine months before then.

"My mom's pretty good; she's dating someone. He's not half-bad, though the bar was not high. So how long have you lived here? You've done well for yourself."

"We moved here in May." How long could they talk of trivial things? She supposed she could go on forever, because her truth would have to follow.

"Nonna too?" He seemed mesmerized by the view, his head twisting left and right.

"Yeah, can you believe it? We got her out of the Mills, finally." She drew in the familiar smell of kelp and salt as she gripped the wood of the railing. Every second made her feel more and more guilty about hiding Celia from him for all these years, especially in the confusion Mitch had brought to light.

"What's your husband's story?" he asked. "I can't imagine he's happy with me being here."

"I'm not married," she said so quickly her words could have been a guillotine. "He's not my husband. I was never married."

Thomas looked like the Bruins had just won the cup again. "Get out of here."

She shook her head and couldn't help but let a smile take her over. *Stop it,* she wanted to tell her face, but she had no control.

"Are you single?"

Annalisa nodded with a sigh, a yes with a caveat. He was getting ahead of himself.

Interpreting her silence correctly, he said, "Look, I think there's been some miscommunication."

There it was, the point of no return. "Why don't we sit down?" she asked, backing up into one of the chairs, knowing she might collapse otherwise.

He sat in the seat next to hers and twisted her way. "I didn't meet anyone in Vietnam. Is that why you left me?"

What? Was he lying? She'd spent so many years distrusting him that she wasn't sure what to think. With more pain than she intended to reveal, she said, "I saw her, Thomas, the two of you. I saw the picture. Don't lie to me."

His brow furrowed like that of the wrongly accused. "What picture? I'm not lying. I don't understand."

"Your mom sent me the picture of you and Linh."

"Linh?" He looked honestly perplexed. "Who is Linh? What are you talking about?"

"The girl you were kissing in the picture," Annalisa said, anger stirring in her words. "I understand you were at war and that things were ugly, but don't lie to me. Not now. We're long over."

Thomas shifted his chair to face her and leaned forward. "I have no idea what you're talking about. I swear to God. There was no girl in Vietnam. There must be some mistake." He was taking this accusation with great seriousness, chipping away at her wall of distrust but rebuilding another with bricks of her frustration.

"Your mom wrote that you were bringing the girl home. I really don't see any point in not telling the truth."

The strings of his neck tightened with anger. "My mom sent you a picture? Do you have it?" She could see he was racing in his mind for an explanation. "There was never a girl."

Oh God, what had she done? Something wasn't right; he wasn't coming off as guilty. "No, I don't have it. I threw it away."

He looked up toward the sky, where five seagulls soared by. "Hold on . . ." It was a sincere search for an explanation.

Long after the birds were gone, he seemed to figure it out. Taking fistfuls of his shaggy hair, his elbows splayed out like wings, he said, "You're talking about Thien."

"Ah, his memory comes back," she replied with dark sarcasm. For a second, she'd thought he might have actually been innocent, as if someone had doctored the photo, and she'd actually let herself taste what it was like to love him again. But only for a moment, and now she was close to asking him to leave. Then again, she couldn't wait to hear his excuse—or his lie. He was more like his father than she had ever thought. Might as well satisfy her curiosity before they said goodbye forever.

He inched to the edge of his seat. "That kiss—"

"That's the one." She'd been so worried that she'd done something wrong, but at that moment she felt more than justified in keeping his daughter from him. He'd wronged Annalisa, and unforgivably so.

With his eyes boring into her, he said, "It's not what you think. I swear to God."

Her jaws tightened as she looked for any evidence of further lies on his face. She noticed the faint scratch under his eye that he'd had in Hawaii, and she remembered how much he'd loved her then. What did he mean, it wasn't what she thought? A kiss was a kiss. Wasn't it?

He clasped his hands together and met her eyes. "There was a journalist named Jimmy that followed our platoon for a while, and he had a crush on this girl named Thien, who worked at a restaurant at Long Binh Post, the base where I was stationed for a while. He'd talked her into sitting down with us, and he was taking pictures of her. She was next to me. To make him jealous, she turned and kissed me. It wasn't even a thing, I swear to God."

She couldn't let him off the hook so easily. These were the same lies her father had told, and her mother had gobbled them up. "What a convenient story, Thomas." She was amazed at how angry she still could get after this long. "So you sent your family the picture and told them, 'Hey, guys, this is some random girl and me kissing? Hold on to it for me.'"

He shook his head so hard it might fall off. "No, Jimmy offered to send a bunch of us his shots, from, you know, three weeks of running with us. I gave him our address back in Davenport."

Though she wasn't sure what she believed, he seemed to have an answer for everything. Had he been prepping this lie for years? Or on the drive up? Or had she made some sort of mistake? He'd earned her trust and love like no one else on earth. He'd never lied to her. As questions pounded down on her, she started to come around to the possibility that he was being completely honest and that *she* was the one who'd messed up.

He kept moving toward her, like he might fall off the chair. "Look, Anna, this is all wrong. Is this why you left me? This picture?"

She repeated herself with frustration. "Your mom said you were bringing her home, that you'd fallen in love." It was already clear, though, that he hadn't done that; she was just rambling, drowning in quicksand.

He shook his head, as confused as she was. "I don't believe my mom would have done that. I've never mentioned Thien to my mother, or anyone. She wasn't anything, a girl who used to bring us Cokes. I barely remember that day. Or her."

Annalisa threw her hands up and then dropped them on her lap. "I saw the picture. I read the letter, signed by your mom. She said Linh, not Thien. I'd rather you leave now than continue lying to me." But he wasn't lying, was he? He'd never given her any reason to think he was lying about anything.

Leaving the chair, he moved to his knees and took her hand. "On all that I am, I swear to you, Anna. That kiss was nothing I wanted. She caught me completely off guard, and there was nothing between us. Jimmy was the one that was into her." He paused and stared up to her with pleading eyes. "I proposed to you. You were my everything."

His words came out dense with truth. All these years. He was out of her life for all these years, and for what reason? Nothing made sense, but she was starting to think that this was all her fault, them not being together. Celia not having her father.

Trying to hold it together, she asked, "So your mom lied to me?"

"I don't know what's going on."

Annalisa looked down to the beach.

At their daughter.

What was happening?

She couldn't have felt any worse inside. It was her own weakness and distrust in people that had done this, and here he was, the man she loved, holding her hand and looking at her innocently. Was it possible they could have been together all along, she waiting for him when he landed like one of the women holding the WELCOME HOME banner in her painting? It didn't matter now, either way. She'd destroyed any chance they had for redemption when she'd chosen to hide Celia from him. He would never forgive her for that.

Thomas finally let go of her hand, and she feared he might never touch her again. "I've been a wreck for years. Are you kidding me? I never would have cheated on you. You're the reason I made it home from 'Nam. My heart was broken when my parents told me you'd moved on." His eyes watered as he looked at her with more love than she could handle. "I'm still broken."

The first tears escaped her eyes, sliding down her cheeks. He was still on his knees, and she wanted to grab him and pull him up, to let him know that he'd done nothing wrong, but she felt unworthy of him now. She was a dead woman walking, a prisoner about to pay dearly for the crimes she'd committed, and she had no right to act otherwise. She'd hidden a child from this poor man, this guy who'd done nothing but love her from the moment they'd met.

As though an idea had come to him, he pressed up to a stand. "I'd like to call my mom, Anna, and get to the bottom of this. Why don't you come inside with me? We can call her together? I need you to know I'm not lying."

She didn't want to lose him now, and every second raced toward the end. She'd been wrong to think he'd cheated, and if she hadn't kept Celia from him—if she had only given him the trust that he'd earned, then they would have a chance to reclaim lost time. Helping Walt turn back time might have been possible, but she couldn't turn it back for herself.

On the verge of collapse, she struggled to say, "Go call her. I just need a few minutes to sit with all this, okay?" She told him the location of the phone. Anything to get him away for a second so that she could figure out how to respond, how to tell him the truth.

He nodded with an optimism that she would soon crush. "Let's figure out what's going on. Maybe this can all be worked out. Just let me get to the truth." With that, he started back inside.

The truth, she thought. *The truth will destroy us all over again.*

She almost stopped him, saying that he didn't need to call her, that she believed him, that the truth stood next to her like an executioner with a raised ax.

But he'd already gone.

Chapter 41

What Could Have Been Could Never Be

While he called his mother, Annalisa stood and went down the ten steps of the deck to the edge of the green grass. The wind blew hard against her as she looked left to the beach below. Celia was seated on the sand, playing with a piece of driftwood. Nonna leaned on her cane, talking with Glen.

"What have I done?" she whispered up into the heavens. "I don't understand."

Had his mother told the lie to break them apart? Had his whole family been behind it? *Eighteen months,* she thought. That was how long Celia had lived without her father. And Thomas had been kept in the dark for longer than that. She wallowed in purgatory, wishing to God that she'd done things differently.

The door shut behind her, bringing her back. He crossed the deck and then down the steps, meeting her in the grass. "My mom didn't send that letter."

Annalisa threw up her hands. What the hell was going on?

His eyes searched all over the place for answers. "She's not lying. I don't know what's going on, but . . . she's not lying. And I'm not lying."

"I know that," she whispered, taking a step toward him, wanting to wrap her arms around him.

He pressed his eyes closed, clearly in as much pain as she was. "All she said is that Emma had mentioned something about you having a boyfriend, and then a few days later you left the ring and the note back at the house."

A light flickered in Annalisa's mind. "A boyfriend? I didn't have a boyfriend. What was Emma talking about? When did you find out? While you were away?"

He was even more optimistic now, as if she was a moment away from cracking the case. "Yeah, Emma wrote me. I was still in-country."

"And that's why you never wrote me again . . . ," she said, making sense of it all. The light turned brighter and then it hit her. "Did Emma do this?" she asked, almost to herself, a pain making itself known in the pit of her stomach.

Annalisa locked eyes with Thomas, both of them putting the idea together at the same time.

He said, "Do you think she . . . ?"

"Wrote the letter?" Annalisa asked. "Yes," she said. "Yes, I do." She searched her memory, finding the letter and rereading it in her mind. She remembered Emma hanging up on her. She'd never actually spoken to his mother.

"I wouldn't put it past her," Thomas said, stepping closer to Annalisa. "She told me that she saw you with a guy at the Spartans–Eagles game, and that not too long after you'd left that note."

"What guy at the game? You mean Nino?"

He shrugged. "You tell me."

"I was with Nino," Annalisa said again, thinking this couldn't have been happening. "Did she never meet him?" She tried to remember.

His eyes danced as he thought back. "I don't think so."

"All Emma ever wanted was to get me out of the way," Annalisa said, feeling more sure with every second. "Would she have faked a let-ter? Forged your mom's signature? Then written you about it? All to get you to let me go so that you'd return to Davenport? So that she could have you to herself?" *Yes,* she thought, answering her own question.

What an incredible betrayal this was. Were people that messed up in the world? Was Emma really that insane?

His eyes looked like hollow sockets. "I can't imagine she would have done that."

"She got what she wanted, didn't she? You're both going to Weston, probably both going to New York." Slogging past the idea, she asked, "Why didn't you come find me anyway? You came home and just gave up?" Had they really lost out on all these years because of a stupid letter Emma wrote? Because of a photograph a journalist in Vietnam had taken?

"I did come find you," he insisted. "Despite your note asking me not to *and* Emma telling me about this other guy. A couple days after I got back to Davenport, I drove to Portland. You were on the balcony with some guy. It was dark, so I couldn't really see, but you were up there with someone. I heard you joking with him and saw you hug him, and . . . and I . . . I didn't want to screw things up for you."

"What are you talking about?" Annalisa tried to remember being on the balcony with a guy. "You mean Walt?" That didn't make sense, though.

"No," Thomas said, as eager for answers as her. "I assumed it was the guy Emma mentioned, and I just wanted you to be happy. Lord knows I wasn't in the shiniest of places after my tour. I guess I figured you might be better off."

"There was no boyfriend," she insisted with a fist through the air. "I never even saw Emma except . . ." She was back into searching her memory. "The last time I ran into her was at the Spartans–Eagles game. I was . . . I was with Nino." Annalisa remembered having her arm around him. Had Emma thought he was a boyfriend?

Then it hit her like a truck running a red light. "That was Nino with me on the balcony. Seeing me with my cousin is why you gave up?"

Thomas's face melted. "I didn't know. He didn't look like Nino, but it was dark." He dropped his head and pinched the bridge of his nose. "The war, Anna. When I read your letter, I was in a bad place. I go over there to fight for my country, and I come home to get spit on. Tons of guys over there were getting broken up with all the time, girls writing to say they were moving on. Everybody back home was against what we were doing. And against us. I just thought you'd had enough. And I couldn't have blamed you. I'll never be the same after what I saw."

"But you should have trusted me." She wiped her eyes.

He looked at her like she was crazy. "It's not that I didn't trust you. I just felt like we were back to the same damn thing, like the last time you'd broken up with me."

Annalisa knew he had a point. *She* was the one who'd not trusted him, and *she'd* gone on to hide his baby.

"When I drove to Portland," he said, "I didn't even know what I was going to say. I think I just wanted to see you. But then I saw you two together, and I was just too exhausted. Even if a guy hadn't been up there, I might not have gone through with it. I felt like a beggar, being there after reading your note. By the time I got back to Davenport, I was so damn angry. I never wanted to see you again. Never wanted to hear your name again. As if that would have helped me get over you."

He'd been two hours away the whole time, still loving her. Oh, how that hurt. "It was *Nino* up there, for God's sake. I just don't get it. All you had to do was ring the bell. Or call me."

"I didn't want to mess up your life. You asked me not to anyway." He spun around and interlocked his fingers behind his head, looking out over the water. "What a damn idiot I am. My sister, my damn sister, kept us away from each other?"

There was no other way around it. And they'd fallen for it? In her weakness, Annalisa had fallen for it.

Another silence scorched the air. She looked back down to the beach, to their daughter. Right then, she knew she had to tell him the rest. The one thing he didn't know. And she knew the space where they were now, looking at a second chance, was about to end.

"Were you ever married?" he asked, his question a rope tossed down into the quicksand in which she was sinking deeper. "Or is Glen her father?"

Annalisa shook her head, not ready for truth to come out but knowing it had to. "No."

"Is her dad still in the picture?" More optimism poured out of him, and she wished to God there was a way she could save them. To stop the inevitable.

She looked at him and through him, speechless and bewildered. His never-ending love for her was about to die.

Leaving his question behind, he replaced it with another, all of them dripping with his frustration. "Why didn't *you* come find me? How could you have given up on us by looking at a picture?"

She latched on to the last question, her last grip before she fell into the depths of her lonely hell. "It wasn't just the picture. It was the note your mom wrote. Emma had just hung up on me, telling me it was best to never call there again."

They both had strong points, but that didn't solve the problem. "How could you not have come to me?" he asked again, this time a quiet plea to recover the past.

She shook her head. "I was furious. How was I to know your sister had lied? I saw the picture."

"You should have found me and let me explain. You owed me that. You know me better than that. You were my everything. I never would have done that to you." His voice cracked, and his cheeks quivered. "You're still my everything."

His words crushed her, and her face flushed with sadness, feeling all the more responsible. She loved him, too, and in this tiny space before she told him the truth, she tasted a second chance. But her decision to hide Celia would soon destroy it, and the time was now.

The time was now.

"There was another reason," she said, wondering how this possibly could have happened, how their whole lives had been ruined.

"What?"

She pointed down to the beach. "Because of her."

He was on the edge of exploding, his hands in the air, his head shaking. "What does that mean, because of her? Because you cheated on me?"

"No, Thomas," Annalisa whispered. "Because she's our daughter."

Time stopped. Even the waves seemed to subside.

"What are you talking about?" The words barely left his mouth.

"She's yours, Thomas," she finally let loose. "I got pregnant in Hawaii, and she's yours."

Her confession was like lighting the fuse on a bomb, and she waited for the terrible explosion to come. He stared at her for a long time, his mouth open, his eyebrows curled.

As she started to apologize, he turned away from her and walked to the end of the grass to where the boulders lowered to the sea, looking at Celia for the first time, knowing that he was her father. She watched him, feeling pure misery for having kept his daughter a secret. Her crime was no lesser than Emma's.

When he finally looked back at Annalisa, she couldn't read what he was thinking. Sure, he was shocked, but was he angry too? He looked more deflated than anything, like a marathon runner who'd fallen short of the finish line, his feet bleeding through his shoes, his lungs running on empty.

"What's her name?" he finally asked, misty eyed.

"Celia." She said she was sorry with her eyes, knowing she'd screwed up everything, lied to the two people who mattered most to her in the world, and destroyed the best thing she'd ever had.

He repeated the name in bewilderment. "Why didn't you tell me?"

She almost reacted defensively but knew that wasn't a fair response. "Because at first I didn't want you to worry about us while you were gone. And then after the letter, from your . . . your sister, I was worried you and your family would take her from me."

He winced, like he'd been shot in the shoulder. "Take her from you?"

"I was worried that you'd come home with your new girlfriend and start a new life and then try to take my baby. Or that your father would."

"I'm not my father. I wouldn't have let that happen."

She knew that. She'd always known that inside. "I was a poor girl from the Mills, Thomas. I figured you or your parents could have found a way to drag me into court. I don't know."

She wiped the tears from her cheeks. "Besides, I thought you had moved on. Thousands of relationships were destroyed by that war. I thought we were destroyed too. You were different in Hawaii. It made sense."

"Of course I was different." His sadness carved deep lines in his face. "If you had seen what I saw, you'd be different too. Three days before I landed in Honolulu, I stuffed my friend's intestines back into his body, watched his . . ." He stopped, sparing her the details.

She never could have imagined that he'd seen such terrible things, and she couldn't handle the pain she saw in his eyes right now. He'd done nothing but love her and fight for his country, and she'd had such little faith in him that she'd left him and taken away his child.

He wept hard, each of his tears draining her of life. "Jesus Christ, Anna, tell me this isn't happening."

Those lines on his face grew deeper, and she braced herself for what was coming, worried he might turn into a shaking lid atop a pot of boiling water. She deserved it, though, and wouldn't have blamed him. Everything was her fault. At worst, all he'd done was let a girl kiss him.

He surprised her, though.

Instead of anger came a smile that, starting with his eyes, covered his whole face. There was no boiling water to begin with. Returning his eyes to Celia, he said, "She's really my daughter?"

"Our daughter," Annalisa corrected him. "She's eighteen months, born February 3, 1972."

He blew out a giant blast of air, like he was letting go of anything else. "She's so beautiful. So damn beautiful."

"I'm so sorry," she whispered, a tiny cup of water on a wildfire. "So, so sorry."

"Stop," he said, walking up to her with a kind, understanding look, the creases on his face flattening. "My sister did this. Not you."

Annalisa loved him for not hating her at that moment, even though she deserved that much and more. "Why aren't you angry with me?" she asked.

With extraordinary compassion, he reached for her hand and said, "What good is that going to do? I'm here. Right now. With you. I woke up this morning not thinking I'd ever see you again, and now we're standing here, and I feel . . . hopeful."

Where her own hope was gone, a seed was planted. Did they still have a chance? Could he actually find a way to forgive her for what she'd done? Because she knew that she wanted one. She might not deserve one, but she wanted him back, and she never wanted to lose him again.

He took her other hand, only a small space between their bodies. "I'm not angry, Anna. Not at you, anyway. This was my sister's doing. And as much as I'm fucking destroyed, I'm also hoping that you and I can . . ." He paused.

"Yes?" she said, hoping he'd take the leap and give her one last chance.

"That you and I can find what we lost."

Had she not been looking into the depths of his soul, through his eyes that were now the color of jade, she might not have believed him.

But she knew he meant it. That was how much he loved her, and that was how much he'd always loved her.

A river of tears poured out of her as she said, "Yes, that's what I want too. I want you back, Thomas." Forget her guilt. Forget her crimes. It wasn't about what she'd done. It was about this moment and this man, who deserved so much more than her, but for some crazy damn reason wanted only her.

He pulled her closer, their bodies touching, their fingers interlaced. "You're single?"

"Yes. And you? What about the girl at the market?"

"No. Well, we were dating for a little while, but she and I were over the minute I saw you. I have never loved anyone else. Never in my life. All I've ever wanted is us."

Annalisa put her forehead to his chest and then looked up at him. "I'm all yours, Thomas. Everything that I am is yours. For always."

She thought he might kiss her, but he let go of her hands and pulled her in with his strong arms, hugging her like never before. As if there were no further to fall, she fell in love with him all over again. No woman on earth had ever been so lucky or been so loved.

When he let go, he said, "I don't even know how, but can we pick up where we left off? I can't go another day without you or our daughter."

She wiped her eyes and nodded over and over. He put his hands on her waist, and they inched toward each other just like that time at the drive-in when they'd first kissed. The hole that had been cavernous in her heart filled with each second. It was all too much, but it was everything she wanted, and when their lips met, it was the missing piece to her world, an explosion of colors that she'd never seen.

She wrapped her hand around his neck and pulled him in, their passionate kiss swallowing up the time since Hawaii that they'd lost to lies, fanning an ember that had never really burned out.

He touched his lips where hers had been, the happiness on his face enough for a lifetime. "If you only knew . . ."

"I do know," she said, immeasurably happy herself. She knew how badly he'd missed her, missed kissing her, missed being with her, because she felt the exact same way . . .

After a long embrace, they separated and he said, "I don't know what to do about my sister."

A part of Annalisa didn't want to blame Emma. "She was young and didn't want to lose you. And she was . . ." Annalisa saw Emma back when they'd first met. "She was troubled, Thomas. More than I ever was."

"Well, she's happier now, and why wouldn't she be?" He'd come out of his fog and sounded stronger. "She got what she wanted, and I refuse to look past it. She nearly ruined our lives; she did, actually. She took me away from the love of my life and our daughter."

"She didn't know I was pregnant." Even as Annalisa said that, she thought it might not be true. Even if Emma had seen the stroller, though, she couldn't have known it was Thomas's baby.

"You being pregnant has nothing to do with it," he insisted. "She's looked me in the eyes a thousand times. She could have made this right."

Annalisa didn't want him to lose sight of the good in today, and she didn't want to allow herself—or Thomas—to turn against Emma. Had she not been smothered in love herself, Annalisa might have turned out the same way. "Maybe there's an explanation, like you said."

"No," he disagreed, clearly coming to his own conclusion. "I know my sister. This is a strategy game that she thought out many moves in advance. All to push you out of the way so she could keep me in town. She got lucky, really. To make it this long without being found out. Did she really think I'd never run into you again?"

"I was starting to think that."

"I guess I was too," he admitted. "But you know what? Nothing can get in the way of you and me. We've proved that time and time again. The only thing that matters is that I've found you." He looked back down to the beach. Celia was dragging her stick in the sand, drawing a picture. "And that I've found her. My daughter."

His knowing the truth now was an everlasting peace. Annalisa might have screwed up, and she'd have to forgive herself for that, but for now, he'd forgiven her. And more important, he and Celia would soon reunite.

She slipped her hands onto his waist. "You're going to be such a good father. The best there ever was."

He glided his fingers across her cheek and the side of her head, petting her lovingly. "Does she know about me?"

A shake of the head, trying to throw off the guilt of keeping Celia from her father. "She's too young to understand. I told her you went away; that's all."

"But now I'm here."

"Yes, you are." She hoped in that moment that there would be no more obstacles, that now they could truly be together. "So what do we do now?"

Thomas put his finger to her chin, lifting her lips to his. "Whatever it is, we do it together . . . if you two will have me."

Shivers rose up and down her body, the kind most girls would surely never know. With an iron will, she said, "Together, yes. Absolutely."

Then she couldn't help but say with a watery smile, "If we get married, though, I'm not changing my name. An Annalisa Barnes signature just isn't going to cut it on my canvases. It would feel like I was burning the Italian flag."

Thomas wiped his face on his shirt again and said laughingly, "Fine, then. Maybe I'll even take your name."

"I'll consider allowing it. And I might even let you put up a blue picket fence out front."

He grinned as their faces dried to pure joy. "Wouldn't that be something?"

Annalisa stuck out her hand. "Would you like to meet her?"

"More than anything in the world."

They walked together toward the steps. "While we're getting everything out," she said, "there's one more thing I have been keeping from you; it's kind of serious."

He sighed and mumbled something to himself. "Hasn't there been enough for one day? I'm not sure how much more I can handle."

She held a straight face, winding up the tension.

He stopped at the top of the steps. "What is it?"

She couldn't hold back anymore. "The day I drove into Portland for the first time to meet Walt . . ."

"Yeah?"

She flashed her teeth. "I backed into Walt's Belvedere with your Beetle."

He smiled and then broke into a laugh. "If that's the last of your secrets, then I think we're going to be just fine." He shook his head, still laughing. "Now I'm gonna go talk to my daughter."

Annalisa followed him down the steps, watching him with a full heart. He took two at a time. When he hit the sand, he slowed some, showing a twinge of fear. Nonna and Glen stepped out of the way and let him take in his daughter for the first time. He crept up to her and dropped his knees into the sand.

Glen started back up the steps, knowing he didn't need to be a part of this moment. Annalisa put her arm around Nonna.

"Hi," Thomas said. "I'm Thomas."

She babbled a long string of mostly incoherence.

Annalisa let go of Nonna and knelt down next to Thomas, putting her hand on his back. "Celia, this is your father. Say 'Hi, Thomas.'"

Celia hit the sand with the driftwood and made a mark. Then she looked at her father. "Hi, Thomas."

With his knees in the sand, Thomas crawled to her and drew a heart with his finger at her feet. "You're an artist just like your mother, aren't you? I'm not much of one, but I know a few shapes."

Celia, who didn't understand a word, looked at him and let out a smirk. Annalisa, on the other hand, burst into tears. Yes, they'd missed some time together, but there was so much more to be had.

Chapter 42

PEOPLE LOVING PEOPLE

May 1979
Davenport, Maine

Annalisa and Thomas had visited his mother in Davenport at least three times a year since they were married, but pulling up to the big white house on the water was different this time, as Thomas wasn't in the car with her. Emma was back from the West Coast after being gone for years. Not having spoken to his sister since confronting her about the lies, Thomas had decided to stay home.

Annalisa didn't blame him. Though she'd mostly forgiven Emma and had exchanged letters over the years, it had taken her almost six years to find the strength to actually face her in person. It was one thing to forgive and love from afar, but to actually set eyes on the person who took so much from them had required even stronger intervention.

In the end, it had taken the insistence of her now seven-year-old daughter to make her come around. Celia was desperate to meet her only aunt and kept prying. Each request pushed Annalisa further toward finding the strength in her heart to let a woman who'd done so much damage back into her life.

Then one day it happened. Annalisa woke with a clear vision, knowing that, for her sake—and her daughter's—it was time to take the final step toward repairing her relationship with Emma. If she couldn't teach her daughter about complete forgiveness and compassion, then what was she teaching her at all?

Emma had written dozens of letters from different places out west, begging for forgiveness, and though Thomas had refused to answer, Annalisa had always taken the time. Remembering that she'd once been in a similar plight, she knew that Emma needed to know that she was still loved. In fact, it was love that had turned the light on Annalisa's darkness, sparing her from Emma's fate.

When Annalisa looked at her happy and healthy daughter, so incredibly loved by Annalisa and Thomas and Nonna, and a host of family and friends, she was reminded that Emma had never been given such a chance. So maybe Annalisa wasn't ready to face Emma or spend time with her or introduce her to Celia, but she'd decided responding to the letters—keeping Emma up to speed with Celia's life, if nothing else—was a gift that she was happy to give.

In the past weeks, though, after Emma wrote to say she was coming home for a few weeks before moving to Morocco with the Peace Corps, Annalisa knew she had to do more. Especially considering her creative voice—her entire artistic raison d'être—was based on love and the idea of people loving people. That notion could not and would not exist only on the canvas.

As she'd come to this revelation, she'd tried to convince Thomas to come with her, telling him that they had to move on, for Celia's sake, if no one else's. But Thomas had no intentions of overcoming his anger with his sister, and he had no intentions of ever speaking with her again.

Even after all that time, Thomas could still get swept away by anger when Emma's name came up. Maybe he could have forgiven her for the letter she'd forged and sent along with the photograph, but when Emma had admitted to knowing about the baby, seeing the stroller and counting the months since Annalisa's visit to Hawaii, and knowing it had to be Thomas's, he'd drawn a line impossible to cross.

His choice did not affect her love for him, though, because he'd found the courage to face so many of his war demons, and he'd loved Annalisa and Celia with all that he was, and he'd certainly shown his ability to forgive when she had confessed to hiding Celia from him. It was just that he saw a very clear line between Annalisa's and Emma's crimes, and in his eyes, his sister deserved no absolution.

She and Thomas shared their journey, but when he'd rejected the idea, she'd decided it was a personal path and that she had to go at it alone.

Annalisa looked at the huge wooden door. Emma was on the other side. Her throat went dry thinking about it. With a burst of love surging through her, she stepped out of her truck and removed a gift-wrapped box from the back seat. Praying for courage, she made the long walk across the gravel drive to the front of the house.

As she ascended the stairs, the front door cracked open, and Annalisa thought she might have a heart attack. Was it too late to change her mind?

Mrs. Barnes appeared and came out onto the porch. With sincere appreciation, she said, "Thank you for coming."

"I'm really happy to be here and to have a chance to catch her before she leaves."

She touched the bottoms of her shoulder-length gray hair. "How is my granddaughter?"

Annalisa came to a stop a few feet from the woman and sighed. "Celia's very mad at her mommy for not letting her come."

A loving smile stretched across her face. "I bet she is."

"I told her we'd come back this weekend. I just . . ." Wings flapped in her stomach. "I thought I should come by myself first."

Mrs. Barnes smiled understandingly.

The two women looked at each other, knowing today was a very important day—for both of them. Emma's lie had hurt Mrs. Barnes, too, who was kept away from Celia for the first part of her life. Perhaps even more painful to Mrs. Barnes was the fact that her only two children hadn't spoken to each other in so long.

Mrs. Barnes touched her heart and said with incredible sincerity, "The fact that you're here . . . it means more than you'll ever know." With that, she invited Annalisa inside and led her to the living room.

Annalisa answered her mother-in-law's casual questions while wrestling with her anxious emotions. No matter how many letters they'd exchanged, seeing Emma in person could dredge up all sorts of emotions that she'd thought had been dealt with, the remnants of sadness, anger, or even worse.

When she finally crossed through the open doorframe that led into the living room, Annalisa could feel her pulse throbbing in her wrists, so much so her arms felt heavy. There, on the couch, underneath the painting Annalisa had never liked, Emma waited for her. As the young woman stood, Annalisa's eyes widened. She'd half expected the little girl she knew from years ago. Though she'd seen a more blossomed Emma in Payton Mills that time, Emma was still a child to Annalisa.

Not now.

Emma's straight brown hair was even longer now, almost to her waist. She was barefoot and wore a long sundress and looked very pretty, the years having done her well. But her nerves showed on her face and in the way she stood almost defensively. It was in this timidity that Annalisa realized how much love she herself had in her heart, because she felt none of the feelings that she'd feared might be excavated during their reunion. No, instead, an overwhelming rush of compassion rose within her, and she smiled with everything she had, hoping her love would show and could wash all over Emma and let her know that everything was okay—even if Thomas wasn't there.

"I'm so happy to see you," Annalisa said warmly, meaning it deeply. She was also glad to see Emma had put on some weight and looked much happier. "I don't know what I was expecting, but wow. You're a woman now, a beautiful woman. Twenty-four now, right?"

Emma blossomed with relief before Annalisa's eyes. "And still kicking . . ."

Annalisa chuckled as she set the gift down on a nearby chair and then went to her, wrapping her arms around her, showering her as best she could with all that love she had in her heart. Emma felt much warmer, her skin and the way she hugged, and Annalisa could sense that this hug was the remedy Emma had still needed, the letters only the first part of the prescription.

Letting go, the women faced each other, and much of the awkwardness had been snuffed out by their embrace.

"Celia's been asking about you," Annalisa said, excited for her daughter to finally meet her aunt.

A light shined from Emma's face. "Yeah? She's growing up so fast. If you only knew how happy it makes me when you send me pictures and share stories. I feel like I really know her."

"And I think it's time you do." Now that this was out of the way—and actually much less of a thing that Annalisa had made up in her head—she couldn't wait to bring Celia down. "I thought we'd come back this weekend for a couple of nights." Thomas hadn't balked when Annalisa had suggested that if things went well with this reunion, that she bring their daughter down to Davenport. As long as he didn't have to deal with his sister, he was fine.

Emma pressed her eyes closed for a moment. "I would love that more than anything in the world." She looked like she might start bawling.

To save her, Annalisa said, "So the Peace Corps. You're such an inspiration. I can't imagine doing what you're doing."

Emma perked up even more, the layers falling off. "Yeah, I'd toyed with the idea during school, but then . . . you know, things changed."

"Did you find out what you'd be doing yet?"

"They just informed me yesterday. I'll be helping out at a boys' home in Marrakech, at least at first. I'll be over there two years, so it might change."

"How incredible," Annalisa said. "To be honest, I'm kind of jealous, you going out and helping in such a way."

Emma almost laughed at the statement. "You're doing your part; trust me. There's something I didn't tell you in the letters. *You're* the reason I'm going." She looked away, grabbing a quick breath. "Your letters over the years are what helped me find my way."

Annalisa beamed, so happy in her heart to hear that, and so glad that she was here now.

"Seriously," Emma said. "I wouldn't have blamed you if you hated me—still hated me—and I know writing me back wasn't easy. But you did it anyway, and I'd say those letters were the second time you saved my life."

As Annalisa listened to Emma and was reminded of how much they were alike, she knew that love had won out in every way, and not in any piece of her, not even in the far-off galaxies of her soul, did she hold any resentment for Emma, and she couldn't wait to see Celia rush into Emma's arms, giving her aunt a dose of love of which only a child was capable.

"That means a lot," she told Emma. "And I'm sorry it's taken us this long to see each other, but I'm glad it's happening." Annalisa remembered the gift on the chair. "Oh, I brought you something." She picked up the box, wrapped with cream-colored paper and purple silk ribbon, and handed it to Emma.

"As if you haven't done enough," Emma said.

"It's just a little thing." But it wasn't. It was a big thing, one of Annalisa's most prized possessions. "Please open it."

Emma set the box on the long chestnut coffee table and started unwrapping. When she pulled open the box, pulled off the tissue paper, and reached inside, Annalisa hoped this gift would mean a lot to her. It hadn't been easy for Annalisa to let it go, but she knew they had magic in them, and that was what Emma needed.

Emma's gasp as she lifted the wind chimes out of the box answered Annalisa's question. The keys and cylinders pinged against the gold pendulum bob, at once evoking memories of her mother and of life in Payton Mills and then in Portland—those dense years of growing up.

"I don't know if you remember when we were painting on my porch. You said one day you wanted a forest of singing trees, and—"

"Of course I remember," Emma said, glancing over at Annalisa with wet eyes. "They're beautiful."

"I thought maybe they could start your collection," Annalisa said. "I made them the summer I moved to Portland, when I lived above the clock shop." She'd written Emma about her life over the years.

"Yes. The owner's name was Walt, right?"

"That's right," Annalisa said. "Most of these pieces are from old clocks that I found in his shop, and I . . ." Annalisa choked up, remembering the day Walt had given her his pocket watch, telling her she had the ability to turn back time. That watch rested in Thomas's plaid blazer, the one he wore almost every day to the high school where he'd been teaching, but these chimes belonged with Emma.

She found her words and continued, "It might sound kind of silly, but Walt told me that I had the ability to turn back time. If that's true, then this is me winding back the clock."

"You can't give me these," Emma insisted, a tear rushing from her eye.

"They're mine," Annalisa said. "And I want you to have them."

Emma held them up high to appreciate them. "But . . ."

"This is my way of saying I love you, Emma. They've brought me so much peace and creative energy over the years, and I want to extend that peace to you. When you hear them ring, I want you to remember that we all make mistakes and that it's never too late."

Emma began to cry as she lowered the chimes into the box. When she let go of the wire, she found Annalisa's eyes. "I'm . . . I . . . I'm sorry," she finally said. "I'm so, so sorry. It's been all this time, and I'm still thinking about it."

"Let it go, Emma," Annalisa said, not wanting her to relive it any longer.

Emma pressed her lips together as her eyes glistened with tears. "It's unforgivable what I did, and I hate myself for it. For what I did to you and to Thomas. To Celia."

Annalisa felt so much pity toward her. "It's *not* unforgivable, Emma. You were young. We all do stupid things when we're young."

Emma put her hands on her own cheeks and stared down at the floor, as if she was revisiting the moment that she'd made the decision to tell her lies. "It was more than a stupid thing."

Annalisa wasn't going to disagree on that point. "What happened can't . . . it can't define the rest of our lives. You've suffered enough." She stepped forward and embraced her sister-in-law, squeezing her hard, showing her how much she loved her. As Emma cried into her shoulder, Annalisa felt true peace wash over her. It was one thing to respond to letters, but making this effort had been what they both needed.

As the seconds passed, Emma's crying came harder, and Annalisa could feel all her years of pain. She wanted to tell Emma that Thomas had forgiven her, too, but the truth was that the war had changed him, and he'd come home a different man. Yes, he was a great father and husband and person, but he couldn't get past the eighteen months that Emma had stolen from him.

When the two finally broke away from each other, Annalisa wiped Emma's cheeks, wishing she could drag Thomas in here and wipe away the rest of Emma's pain. Life wasn't always that easy to put a bow around, though, and that was okay.

All Annalisa could do was offer her own love, and she brought Emma in for another hug and said, "We are sisters, okay? Always and forever, I am here for you."

As Emma wept harder, both of their joyful tears washing over each other, Annalisa thought that this was exactly what life was about: people loving people.

Epilogue

December 2019
Portland, Maine

Three days after retrieving the wind chimes from the tree for Emma, Annalisa pushed through the crowd of Mancusos in the lobby of Casco Hospice to get her hands on her two grandchildren: two boys—three years apart—who were growing up entirely too fast. Patrick was graduating from high school in a few months and would be setting out to make his mark on the world just as Annalisa had done in 1970 when she'd left the Mills for Portland.

"Nonna!" the younger one, Adam, said, catching a glimpse of Annalisa. Was there a better designation in the world? He went to her.

Annalisa's heart filled as he hugged her waist. "Look at you, *nipote*. All grown up now, aren't you?"

Patrick in his John Lennon glasses appeared, and she pulled him into the hug too. "What's it been? Two weeks? I can't go this long without seeing you. Any news on colleges?" She held them for a long time, taking in the love she felt for these two.

"Hi, Mom," a voice interrupted.

Annalisa patted the boys' heads and let them go, then turned to Celia and her husband, Jakub. "I'm so glad you made it," Annalisa said, kissing their cheeks and pulling them both in.

Jakub was a hotelier in Manhattan and had, funnily enough, approached Celia at the Whitney Museum of American Art while she worked as a research conservator there. Whereas Annalisa had rejected Thomas, Celia must have learned from her mother's mistakes, as she had accepted his invitation to dinner, and they'd been married six months later. That was twenty years ago.

They still lived in New York, where Celia had finally landed the job of her dreams as a conservator for the Guggenheim. Unable to stay away for long, Annalisa and Thomas had bought an apartment near Central Park so that they could spend as much time as possible with Celia and her boys. Maybe one day Annalisa could convince them to move up to Bar Harbor, but she knew a little something about wanting to live in the city.

A sweet, dashing man who'd turned out to be a great father, Jakub asked quietly, "How is she?" He was referring to Emma.

Annalisa felt her bottom lip droop. Other than to feed Emma's cats the past few days, she had barely left Emma's side. "Dr. Gorky says today might be her last."

Celia, who had taken on her father's hazel eyes but held fast to her Italian genes, put her hand on Annalisa's shoulder. "I'm glad we made it then. How are you holding up? Have you spoken to Dad?"

"I spoke with him this morning briefly," Annalisa replied, and then, without much to add, she shook her head. No, he wasn't coming. She'd read him Emma's last letter shortly after helping her write it three days ago, but he'd quickly moved on to another subject, as if he couldn't breathe when Emma was on his mind.

Annalisa turned toward the crowd in the lobby. "Emma knows she's loved, and that's what matters."

Celia and Jakub and their two boys turned with her and looked at the leaves of the Mancuso and Barnes family trees. Though Thomas had not found a way to forgive her, the rest of Emma's family had, and they'd been visiting her steadily—two or three at a time—yesterday and this morning. Her clients, too—veterans from the Vietnam War and forward had popped by to say their goodbyes.

Annalisa took her grandchildren's hands. "Why don't we go back and see her?"

Even the boys had come to know their great-aunt over the years. When Emma returned from her stint in the Peace Corps and moved to Portland to get certified as a counselor, she'd become exactly the aunt that Celia had asked about for so long. Though she wasn't welcome at Graystone because of Thomas, she spoke with Celia often on the phone and very often invited her down for weekend visits.

Emma had started her practice and bought her house in Cape Elizabeth around the same time Celia got her driver's license. By then, the two had become very dear to each other. In fact, it was Celia who'd helped Emma hang the wind chimes from Walt's shop in the backyard, becoming the first of so many in Emma's collection.

Sadly, due to Emma and Thomas's separation, she wasn't able to be there for the birth of Celia's boys, but she'd jumped into their lives as quickly as she could, as if she were still making up for what she'd done.

"She's a little tired from all the visitors," Annalisa warned them, approaching the door, "but she's desperate to see you." As she knocked, Annalisa fell back in time, thinking of the moment she'd knocked and pushed open the door of Emma's room in Davenport and found her with her mother's pill bottle. What a long way her friend had come since then.

Annalisa led Celia and her family into the room. Sitting up in her tilted bed, Emma cracked a faint smile. "You came . . ."

"Of course we came," Celia said, approaching her aunt, leaning down and kissing her cheek. Annalisa sat in the chair by the window as Jakub and the two boys joined Celia by the bed, and Emma listened with a weak yet full heart as they shared the latest from their life in New York.

Outside, the snow fell in clumps, like God was shearing his sheep up above. Thomas had always said Emma came alive in the winter, so it made sense that she would meet her maker in the winter, too, coming alive in heaven for the first time.

Ten minutes later, the boys left Annalisa and Celia to spend some time with Emma alone. They pulled up two chairs to the bed, and Emma asked about her work at the Guggenheim.

"Oh, you know," Celia responded, smoothing her hands together. "It's a mad race, but I love it. I'm getting my hands on a Picasso tomorrow, so that's kind of exciting."

Emma slid her pleased eyes to Annalisa and muttered, "She's just like you, isn't she?"

"Like me on steroids," Annalisa admitted. Celia had pursued a master's degree and career in art preservation just as diligently as Annalisa had and still continued to chase excellence with her brushes.

Emma commented on how quickly the boys were growing, and Celia lit up, speaking about their plans after graduating high school. Annalisa found herself profoundly pleased that she'd made peace with Emma, and it had been wonderful to see how much Celia and Emma had connected over the years. It was a seven-year-old Celia, after all, who'd urged Annalisa on, refusing to cease asking about her aunt, whom she'd never met.

Emma seemed to be turning paler and weaker by the minute. As if they were on the same page without even planning it, Celia and Annalisa did their best to be animated and cheery. Celia had a filterless sense of humor—much like her mother—and no one else could make Annalisa laugh to tears like her own daughter. And every time they succeeded in drawing a smile out of Emma, it felt like a great success, like they were buying her a few more moments of life.

The only topic they tended to avoid was Thomas.

Emma had stopped asking about him.

Sadly, even Emma's best smile would be short a full curve, as she had wanted only one thing her entire life, and that was her brother's love.

Annalisa didn't claim to understand Thomas, and he was still as unpredictable as when they'd first met, but the one fact she knew beyond all else was that Thomas would let Emma die without seeing her. He never replied to her letters. He never called. And he certainly would never forgive her, no matter how much Celia and Annalisa urged him. Though she would never judge her husband for his decision, it certainly saddened her.

Annalisa and Thomas had lived a good life—even great. He was a wonderful teacher who found tremendous pride in steering the youth of tomorrow. There had always been the tension of the past, though. He'd changed in a lot of ways during the war. He wasn't the Mr. Sunshine that she'd first met in the museum. It was like he was 99 percent happy, and their lives were 99 percent perfect, but the shadow of the past was never too far from Thomas, and Annalisa had come to accept that this was the way things would always be.

Celia helped Emma to a glass of water that ended up dribbling down her chin. After wiping her clean, Celia said, "We're gonna try to get into Eventide tonight," referring to her favorite restaurant in Portland.

Emma was the one who'd first taken her there. "Oh, what I'd do for one last lobster roll."

"We'll bring you one," Celia promised.

Emma looked like she might say something like, "You better hurry," but instead, she reached for Celia's and Annalisa's hands. The three of them looked at each other, and Annalisa had a terribly sad feeling that this was it. The end. She was saying goodbye. Oh, thank God she'd let Emma back into their lives.

"I love you girls," Emma said, dashing her eyes back and forth between the two.

Annalisa felt a tear roll down her cheek. She and Celia leaned in, saying, "I love you too," and they hugged Emma as best they could, her frail body nearly disappearing in their hands.

Then there was someone at the door, and they all turned. Annalisa said, "Give us just a—"

Thomas Barnes, seventy years old but still clinging to his younger years, stepped into the room, his hat and coat in his arm. Annalisa nearly lost her balance. He smiled at his wife and daughter and then looked past them to the woman on the bed.

"Emma?" He approached and took his wife and daughter into a hug. Then they stepped aside so that he could get to his sister in time.

As he took her frail hand, Annalisa and Celia held each other and wept. This was her hero, Annalisa thought, the man she loved more than any other. And this was one of the many thousands of reasons why she loved him.

"Can you hear me?" he asked Emma, whose eyes had glazed over.

For a second, Annalisa worried that she'd passed before speaking with him.

Turning back to Annalisa, Thomas asked, "Can she hear me?"

"I can hear you," Emma uttered, filling Annalisa's heart with joy. He'd driven down from Bar Harbor just in time.

Thomas turned back to his sister with relief. "There you are." He leaned down to kiss Emma's cheek, and she let loose a smile that said it all.

"You took your sweet time, didn't you?" Emma said as the two stared happily into each other's eyes.

Then Annalisa watched Thomas's shoulders bounce as he succumbed to a cry like she'd never seen, and the two siblings fell into a hug that lasted a long time. Holding her daughter, Annalisa felt so much love in that room that she thought the snow outside might melt and give way to an early spring, all in a few seconds. People loving people. Was there anything better?

Unraveling his arms from his sister, Thomas stayed very close to her, holding one of her hands with both of his. The two whispered back and forth, and at one point Emma even laughed, albeit weakly. Then she closed her eyes. No heart monitor was needed to know that she was departing.

Annalisa came up behind her husband and put her hand on his back, red paint still on her fingers from painting that morning. Never had she been prouder of him, and perhaps never had she loved him more. Celia approached from the other side of the bed, leaned down, and kissed Emma's forehead, and then the three of them met eyes, now knowing for sure that theirs was a bond of love that nothing could break.

What Annalisa would never forget—what no one in that room would ever forget for the rest of their lives—was that seconds later, as they felt the life of Emma Barnes rise up out of her body, the wind chimes began to sing.

She turned and looked up. Sure enough, as if they still hung among Emma's choir of singing trees, without a draft, without a breeze, the chimes she'd made of Walt's old timepieces had gently come alive. Annalisa had always been a religious woman, but she'd never witnessed proof of God until that moment.

They didn't sing a loud song, and one had to listen closely to hear them, but the chimes were certainly moving and pinging against one another, evoking a wondrous melody. And Annalisa knew, deep within, that the unseen breeze stirring in that room was Emma's spirit singing a song of happiness, her unseen spirit singing a song of love.

Acknowledgments

John Burroughs wrote "leap and the net will appear." Never has this quote been more applicable in my life than with this novel. I leaped, and the net that appeared was woven tightly of a team of talented and brilliant people who helped me realize the story I was after. I am eternally grateful to all of you.

Chris Werner at Lake Union Publishing has a mesmerizing understanding of story, and I don't know how I pulled off writing my novels before we started working together. Thank you for taking the wheel and setting me on the right course in the early drafts.

Thanks to the entire Lake Union team. A writer couldn't be luckier than to be under your roof, and I've felt your amazing support from day one.

My developmental editor, Tiffany Yates Martin, is a dream come true. There were moments when I thought this project was slipping through my fingers, and she jumped with me into the trenches offering abundant and brilliant guidance. From helping me find the exact purpose and direction of the story to your incredibly wise and subtle suggestions that served like last-minute brushstrokes to bring a painting to life, this book is far better because of you. Thank you, my friend.

My agent, Andrea Hurst, is incredibly multitalented. Aside from my wife, she's the only one who can talk me off the ledge. In addition to her exceptional work as an agent, she is nothing short of a literary wizard wielding a wand of astounding editing prowess. Andrea is a master at finding the cracks in the foundation of a story, and even better, she knows how to fix them. Thank you, Andrea, for being you *and* for telling me the one thing that got me here, to the end of this book. You said, "Boo, there's a reason you couldn't let this story go; you're meant to write it." Those words never left my side during this project. While I'm at it, there was something else you told me. "Replace the word *writing* with *painting*. That's how you can feel her passion." Bull's-eye.

Patty Bonner, I hope I made you proud. Much of this was your journey, and it was exhilarating to live it for a while. You are unequivocally the best mother-in-law in the multiverse.

Liz Thurston, with your wind chimes you gave me the soul of this story. We've never even met, and I feel a deep bond. The world needs more people like you.

To my beta readers, I couldn't do it without you, truly. Thanks for always making me look more talented than I really am. Big hugs.

Jenan McClain, how dare I even start this novel without talking to you. Enormous thanks for helping me understand the painter's journey. Technique is only the beginning, isn't it? The true magic of art lies in the artist tapping into the depths of their soul, a fact you prove time and time again with your pieces.

Jean Johnson, my dear friend for so long, thanks for offering up your love of fashion to help me dress Annalisa. I hope you enjoy what we did together.

Three Facebook groups were tremendously helpful during my research. I suppose I should apologize first, as I'm sure I got a million things wrong, but hopefully I got a few things right. Thank you, "Portland Maine Encyclopedia of the 1960s, 70s, & 80s," "Growing Up in Bar Harbor," and "VietnamWarHistoryOrg." It was wonderful getting to know you and your worlds, and I hope you don't mind if I continue to linger.

Though I wouldn't dare pretend to understand being a soldier, my research led me deep into the Vietnam War, and I've come away with even greater respect for you warriors who fought and continue to fight for our country. Thank you to the vets who spent time answering my questions, including Dr. Chris Christenson, Steve Kearns, Ross Tarver, and Mario Ortega. Y'all are inspirations to me. Thanks to all the heroes of the Vietnam War; I am in awe of your courage.

You, my readers, are who make this all worth it. I am so appreciative for your continued support and steady flow of encouragement. I vow to keep entertaining you until they dig my grave. And maybe even afterward, if I can manage it.

My wife, Mikella Walker, you are the reason I get out of bed in the morning. You are my everything. Thank you for your brilliance, your kind heart, your support, your love, and your editing and writing skills. When I look at the cover of my books, I always see your name next to mine, especially when I think of the intimate scenes that I first mangled and you had to rescue. I love you, Mikey.

And to our son, Riggs, thank you for constantly reminding me what matters and giving me endless writing fuel. If we're being honest, you're the reason I get out of bed in the morning . . . because you're jumping on my head. Don't ever stop.

About the Author

Photo © 2018 Brandi Morris

Boo Walker is the author of *An Unfinished Story* and the Red Mountain Chronicles. Boo initially tapped his creative muse as a songwriter and banjoist in Nashville before working his way west to Washington State, where he bought a gentleman's farm on the Yakima River. It was there among the grapevines that he fell in love with telling stories. A wanderer at heart, Boo currently lives in Valencia, Spain, with his wife and son. He also writes thrillers under the pen name Benjamin Blackmore. You can find him at www.boowalker.com and www.benjaminblackmore.com.